FEAST OF THE UNCLEAN

JONATHAN DANIEL

AUTHOR'S NOTE

Hi! Jonathan here. I wanted to take a quick second to thank you for buying Feast of the Unclean. Seriously, I know you have a lot of choices when it comes to horror fiction, and the fact that you made the decision to spend your money on my book means the world to me.

I had a lot of fun writing this. I genuinely hope you have a lot of fun reading it. Stick around at the end of the book, I've added a couple of pages of "behind the scenes" information for you where I talk about how I came up with the idea and how this book came into being. I hope you enjoy that little peek behind the curtain.

If you find yourself liking the book (and even if you don't) I would love it (and I'm using 'love' in the strongest way possible...like bordering on creepy) if you took a moment to leave a review on whatever platform you purchased Feast of the Unclean. As an indie author, I live and die by reviews. Seriously, it's that important.

Now, let's visit Jericho Springs.

Do you feel that?

Something in the woods is watching you...

Where the host was taken, no birds sang. The ground soured.

— THE GOSPEL OF ASH 6:6

Take this body, take this wine,
Feed it to the ones in line.
Call it holy, call it just,
The feast was made for dust to dust.

— THE BLACK HYMNAL, DIRGE XVII

And the breath of the Lord passed over them, and it smelled of rot.

— THE GOSPEL OF ASH 11:4

1

Caspar Green shouldn't have been in the woods, and he knew it. Dinah had begged him not to go, not to take the job. With a raised eyebrow and seductive smile, she'd promised to put Joshua to bed early. The smile had been forced, Caspar knew. But that was how badly she'd wanted him to stay home.

Now, as he hurried down the hill to where Moses stood chopping a small oak tree into smaller pieces, Caspar wished he had not lied to his wife. But all the extra shifts at the pulpwood mill in Patton Mills had gone to white boys, and the money offered for cutting firewood for the bootleggers was too enticing to ignore. And Caspar and Dinah needed that money. Their son Joshua needed his medicine.

"You done already?" Moses asked as Caspar jogged the last few yards. Moses threw another log onto his already large pile. Caspar was a big man, his body muscular and toned from years of hard work, but Moses was a behemoth. He towered over Caspar and was at least half again as wide. With such size came ridicule, especially from the whites, but Caspar had never known Moses to lose his temper or show any signs of anger. He was a devout man and always said that anger was the wedge the Devil needed to pry you away from the Lord.

Caspar looked back up the hill. "Salter and that peckerwood Blackwell got dynamite."

Moses stopped in the act of positioning a new piece of wood for cutting. His eyes were hard. "Dynamite?"

"They's gonna blow that hill open. Says there's a stream, a natural spring in there they need for the still." Caspar glanced around the woods. The trees were still, no breeze stirred their boughs. Not even a single squirrel flitted about the branches. "You don't think the Klan can hear it, us being all this way?"

Moses continued to stare up the hill, but slowly shook his head. "We're deep enough. Mr. Cleary's been sending crews deeper and deeper to avoid those boys. I'm more concerned that we're going to be blamed for the deaths of two crackers." After a moment he added, "We should move a bit farther." The two men retreated another thirty yards. They positioned themselves behind a pair of hickory trees and waited.

A sharp whistle was the only warning they had before an earsplitting *boom* rocked the forest. Beneath Caspar's hands, the tree trembled as the shock wave crashed past them. He flinched, ducking his head as small branches and hickory nuts rained down. Several feet away, Moses lifted his own head and gave a wide-eyed look at Caspar.

"How many sticks they use?"

"Four." Before Moses could say anything more, another shrill whistle echoed through the trees, followed by Salter's voice calling for them to come up.

Freddie Salter and Jimmy Blackwell stood at the base of the hill among a field of rocks and torn earth, their hands on their hips as they stared at the opening they'd created. The trickle of water had grown into a small stream.

"Y'all get on in there and clear them rocks away," Salter said, pointing at the hill. "They's blocking the flow. Once you get them out, we may have to hit it again." Moses and Caspar began the tiresome work of pulling the larger stones away.

The last of the rocks was removed, revealing a ragged hole in the hillside. Through it, the water poured more freely. Caspar knew it wouldn't be enough.

"Goddamnit," Salter grumbled and spat on the ground. He sighed. "Something must've broken loose and is blocking the water. We're gonna have to get in there and clear it out." He pointed at Caspar. "Get your ass in there. You,"—he pointed at Moses—"get back to cutting wood."

Caspar wedged himself through the hole, ignoring the pain of the rough rocks across his arms and back. The stream was ice-cold against his palms as he pulled his legs in. Crouching in the light that filled the blasted hole, Caspar gaped at his surroundings. The hill was hollow. Several feet overhead, roots like rotting fingers hung from the ceiling. Slowly he stood. The chamber was about ten feet across. But to his surprise, it stretched into the distance, vanishing into darkness. His sweat-covered skin prickled as the cooler air pressed against him. The floor of the cave was a mix of loose rock and packed dirt. In the faint light from the opening, Caspar couldn't see the stream of water but could hear it trickling.

"What are you waiting for?" Salter called, his face framed by the opening. "Find the blockage and get to work."

Caspar thrust his hand through the hole. "I need a flashlight." There was some discussion but after a moment, Salter slapped the heavy cylinder into Caspar's palm. "Don't fucking lose it, boy."

Caspar clicked the light on and trained the beam along the floor. The trail of water glistened in the light and Caspar shifted the beam, following it to a pile of rocks through which it seeped. He ducked and reported what he'd found and was already moving toward the obstruction when Blackwell ordered him to hurry up and clear the rocks so the water would flow.

Caspar quickly set to removing the obstacle, tossing the stones to one side of the cave. By the time he moved the last of the rocks, the water had increased from a trickle to a steady flow. From outside the cave came the triumphant cries of Salter and Blackwell. Caspar dipped one hand into the thickening stream and palmed some of the icy water into his mouth. He rinsed, spat, and repeated the process.

The water was so cold it hurt his teeth. He wiped his hand on his pants and trained the flashlight on the rest of the cave. The ceiling angled to the ground, ending the chamber about thirty feet away. The stream of water disappeared into the darkness of the rocks, probably to the deeper spring that Salter had mentioned. A smell of wet, rotting vegetation mingled with a sharper mineral scent left a sour film on Caspar's tongue.

Time to go, he thought. But as he turned, something at the edge of the light, to the right of the stream, caught his attention. He pointed the beam and sucked in a fearful breath as the spot fell on the black hollow eyes of a human skull and several scattered bones. Intertwined with the rest of the skeleton were heavy loops of iron chain. It wove through two dirt-streaked ribs, around the hands, and through the lower jaw.

"What in God's name?" Caspar breathed. Despite the trembling in his guts, he stepped carefully over the stream and knelt by the scattered remains. With numb fingers, he reached out and touched the links of the chain. It was thick and rough and proved heavier than he would have expected. Caspar turned the section of iron chain over, following its path into the confusion of half-buried bones.

Pain flared in his palm and he hissed, letting the chain drop to the ground. Caspar tightened his hand into a fist, the pain pulsing beneath his clenched fingers. After a moment, he relaxed his grip and studied the cut. It was small, barely a quarter of an inch long. Still, a trickle of blood welled up and ran along his palm to his wrist. There it bent and dripped from his joint to the ground, where instead of landing against the soft black earth, it pattered against the cracked lines of the skull.

And soaked into the bone.

Dumbfounded, Caspar watched as the blood continued to drip onto the skull and immediately vanish as if the bone were a rag or sponge, soaking up the liquid. A tugging sensation tickled his palm, gentle at first but quickly growing heavier.

More insistent.

Caspar turned his hand over. The blood flow increased from a thin line to a trickle to a stream. The sensation of something pulling out of him hummed up his arm. The runnel of blood cascaded over the skull.

Caspar tried to look back at the entrance to the cave, felt the cry for help rising to his tongue, but was unable to shift his head even an inch. The words died in the back of his throat. Panic flared in his chest, a hot explosion that sent waves through his body.

I can't move! Dear sweet Jesus, why can't I move?

But that wasn't true, he saw. Caspar watched as he gently placed the flashlight on the ground before reaching for the bones. He felt none of the movements; it was as if he were watching someone else pluck a fragment of bone about the size of his thumb out of the loam. His fingers held the lump before his face for only a moment before bringing it to rest against the cut in his palm.

Slowly, rocking the shard back and forth, he worked it inside the wound, pressing it into the flesh.

The pain came then, but his scream trickled out as a high-pitched, weak wheeze.

The bone slipped the rest of the way into his palm with a wet squelch and lay there beneath his skin like a fat tumor, bulging grotesquely. Amid the whirling panic and terror that screamed through his mind, Caspar fought to regain control over his fingers, to pull the bone back out. Instead, his free hand retrieved another splinter from the pile, brought it to his forearm and with a sharp jerk, used it to slice open the skin and stuff the bone inside.

In his mind, Caspar screamed as the process repeated. Cuts were formed all over his body and pieces of bones packed into the bleeding wounds. In the cave, the only sounds were the soft gurgling of the stream and the muffled voices of the men outside.

A new sensation came over him. A feeling of connection, of being tethered to something by invisible ropes. Only these ropes didn't feel like they stretched out into the darkness of the cave. Rather, they extended inward, passing through his own flesh and blood, through his own soul. Something heavy and eager tugged at the unseen ends of those ropes, pulling its way hungrily from some darker void.

As Caspar slid a section of finger bone into his cheek, the thing at the other end of those ropes groped out of the swirling darkness in his mind. Hands of blackened and burned flesh reached out. Hooked fingers ending in hideous claws grasped and pulled.

Caspar found his voice. It smashed through the paralysis like a sledgehammer through a wall and came tearing out of his throat like a tormented animal. His scream crashed around the cave, reverberating and amplifying in the tight space. He continued to scream, kneeling in the dirt, his body torn and bleeding, as Salter and Blackwell shouted through the cave's opening. When they received no answer beyond Caspar's tormented shrieks, they forced Moses to wedge himself inside.

The large man scrambled over the loose rocks of the cave. Caspar turned his broken, bleeding face to Moses. The smaller man's eyes bulged with terror, his mouth stretched, locked open, emitting only soft, pained gurgles. Moses whispered a call to God and staggered back. He shouted something to the others that Caspar couldn't understand. The presence within his soul, the thing that groped and pulled itself out of the darkness, chuckled in hungry anticipation as the two white men climbed into the cave and gathered around.

Behind Salter and Blackwell, Moses stood with his hands dangling uselessly by his sides. His face was ashen and his lips quivered with whispered prayers. Overhead, the roots and vines that hung from the ceiling writhed like worms searching for fresh earth. Caspar saw all of this even though his eyes weren't turned toward it.

He saw it because the thing inside him saw it.

Willed it.

Rejoiced in it.

Moses said something, the words thick and muffled as if filtered through a brick wall. The ground shuddered like a sleeping giant stirring from a centuries-old nap. Rocks and dirt clattered against the ground. Through his terrible second sight, Caspar watched as a black, shifting blanket of liquid rushed out of the darkness and slithered up Moses's legs. The big man shouted as the blanket reached his waist, one of his large hands clawing at the dirt. His fingers left deep furrows in the ground as the black tide pulled him into itself.

The blanket spread wide, moving off the Black man, and Caspar screamed inside himself against the truth of it. It wasn't liquid. It was a surging mass of black insects, spiny legs, black carapaces, and twitching antennae amid the writhing mass.

The insects had pulled Moses into their throng. Only the man's terrified face and one arm remained visible. Caspar's brain shrieked for him to help, but the presence within him only smiled wetly as Moses vanished into the tide. As soon as he was enveloped, the surging blanket of bugs withdrew into the inky blackness of the cave.

A few feet away, Blackwell was screaming. The skinny man stood straddling the flowing water, his arms out wide as large gray ropes wrapped around his limbs, holding him in place. Once more, without seeing, Caspar knew what was happening. *The roots came down and got him.*

More roots extended from the ceiling, slithering through the air like snakes through lake water. They reached Blackwell's horror-stricken face and with no hesitation at all, pushed into him. Two forced their way into his open mouth, stunting his screams. Weak, wet, gagging sounds filled the cave as the white man's throat bulged. The skin rippled as the vines pushed their way deeper into his neck. Blackwell convulsed as two more roots pushed into his eyes, sending blood cascading down his cheeks. More roots found the man's ears and wormed their way inside, pausing only briefly as they met light resistance before continuing.

Vines encircled his chest and limbs like belts. They wrapped, constricting tighter and tighter. The sound of Blackwell's chest collapsing was like a gunshot, filling the cave and battering Caspar's ears.

On all fours, Salter pawed at the ground in his desperation to get free of the cave. He made it only four feet before rising from the ground as if lifted by invisible hands. He hung, limp, several feet over the dirt floor. His body twisted and jerked, each movement coming with the gunshot-like *crack* of bones breaking. Bulges formed in his pant legs at horrible angles as bones broke through the skin to stab at the material. Salter twisted in the air until he hung upside down. His destroyed arms dangled over his head, the twisted remains of his hands brushing the ground.

The sensation of fingers, like hard pliers against his skull, forced Caspar's head around. The muscles in his neck strained as he twisted to see the broken man dangling in midair. Caspar's eyes met Salter's. *He's awake. He's still alive.* Salter stared at Caspar with a childlike pleading. His mouth opened, trembling lips struggling to form words. His jaw snapped to one side and away with a *pop* that reminded Caspar of snapping a leg off a roasted chicken. Blood streamed down Salter's face. A final, single *crack* echoed off the rocks as his entire chest imploded. Salter hung suspended by nothing for a heartbeat, then collapsed onto the floor of the cave.

In the ensuing silence, Caspar's mind filled with flashing images of blood-soaked flesh, exposed entrails covered with writhing maggots, and screaming entwined with a voice whispering rhythmically in a language he'd never heard. The words crossed his consciousness like slugs crawling across his brain in search of the depths of his soul.

Caspar followed them down into the blackness.

When he opened his eyes again, he saw the confusion of tree branches backlit by the soft purple of an early morning sky. Caspar lay where he was, his thoughts thick and sluggish, and tried to understand what had happened. Had it all been a dream? Or was he dead, a victim of Salter's mishandling of the dynamite?

A breeze fluttered across his skin, warm and sweet as he inhaled. This was no dream. He sat up, wincing at the aches and dull pains that covered his body. Hesitantly, Caspar turned his hand over and opened his fingers, exposing his palm.

The bulge was gone, the cut no more than a faint scar against the skin. He checked the other wounds, the places where he remembered the bones had been inserted, and found all the gashes completely healed.

He twisted around, saw the craggy mouth of the cave amid the moss and vines covering the hill. Salter's wooden crate sat nearby, the straw inside it spilling over the edge like stuffing pulled from a child's toy. Caspar's eyes drifted to the blackness beyond the hole in the ground. It stared back with cold indifference, like the single eye of a demon observing its plaything before dragging the pitiful soul screaming back into the depths of the Pit.

A flash of memory, the sounds of the other men screaming as their bodies were ruined, sent Caspar up, his feet scrabbling to find traction. He ran stumbling through the woods, arms waving wildly as he careened off trees in his panicked haste to get home. He ran, oblivious to fresh cuts and scratches he suffered as he scraped against rough tree bark or as low branches or thorny vines snagged at him.

He ran with singular purpose, driven as much by his fear as his need to see Dinah and hold her, to feel her strong arms around him. He needed to feel her, to smell her, and to pull Joshua close and reassure himself of their truth, their realness. He wouldn't tell her what had happened, not at first. Maybe not even in ten or twenty years' time.

Instead, he would ask her to draw him a bath, maybe make some of her stew. They still had a little bit of the chicken left, he hoped. That would be enough. His stomach grumbled painfully at the thought of food as his legs propelled him through the forest.

By the time his small house appeared in the distance, the hunger pangs had settled into a constant, acidic knot, sending his guts twisting in agonizing spasms. A dizzying numbness had started to creep its way into the fringes of his thoughts, growing into a louder buzzing the closer he got to the small house. Caspar stumbled on, one hand pressed tightly against his stomach. The sun had started to peek over the horizon, painting the small dirt path and the scattered homes along it in a gauzy, golden hue.

Somewhere in the yard of one of his distant neighbors, a dog barked. Caspar pressed on, ignoring the chickens that roamed freely in the yards, his focus only on the small three-room shack that housed his family.

Dinah was singing softly to herself in the kitchen when he

lurched inside. The home smelled of coffee and bacon, of Dinah's sweat and perfume undercut by the sharp tang of Joshua's sickness.

As he pushed the door closed, Dinah came quickly into the living room, hands twisting around a towel. Her eyes were wide with concern, growing wider as she saw the state of her husband.

"What's happened?" she asked, hurrying to him. Her small but strong hands guided him to a nearby chair. Caspar took a shuddering breath and told her the story he'd concocted, that the law had come and he had to run. Halfway through, Dinah interrupted him, "Baby? Can you hear me? Honey, say something." Caspar's brow furrowed in confusion. He started again, but once more his wife cut in with pleadings for him to speak.

"Mommy?" Joshua asked from the doorway to the rear room of the house. Dinah shifted to put herself between Caspar and his son.

"Go get dressed, baby," she said without looking away. "We have to go down the street to visit Mrs. Dean." Joshua began to protest but his mother snapped his name and he retreated. Focusing on Caspar, Dinah placed her hand along his cheek. "I'm going to leave him with Mrs. Dean and fetch Elias Garner. He'll take a look at you." She stood and hurried into the rear of the house, calling out for Joshua to hurry up.

Caspar sat, staring at the dark doorway through which his wife and family had gone. His vision dimmed, a hazy darkness furring the outer edges. The sour pain in his gut shifted into a burning coal that pulsed, growing brighter and hotter, searing away the soft tissue around it.

A swelling within him blossomed, expanding so violently that it stole Caspar's breath. Only, the swelling was deeper. Something filled him, pushing apart his very soul as it seeped in and expanded, taking its place within. The thing that had been at the end of the ropes that stretched through him returned, stepping fully out of the darkness.

The pressure within Caspar's body swelled. The force of it pressed against every single inch of him. Small flashes of pain erupted across his arms, his leg, his cheeks, and neck; brilliant flares of agony followed by an oozing, trickling warmth. With great effort,

Caspar turned his eyes to see that the cuts on his palm and arms had reopened. He stared in paralyzed horror as the skin continued to tear, the wounds widening in short, violent jerks.

A long, bony finger, its flesh the color of burned charcoal, emerged from the cut in his palm like a nightmare worm erupting from a corrupted apple.

"Okay, baby," Dinah said from the doorway. She entered the living room, her threadbare shawl draped over one forearm. Her other hand rested on Joshua's shoulder, holding the boy next to her. Joshua turned his fear-widened eyes to his father. "Caspar? Baby?" Dinah asked.

Caspar tried to answer, but a sudden, terrible lump in his throat choked off all speech. He trembled, eyes locked on his family as the cuts across his body widened with the wet sound of flesh tearing.

The last things Caspar heard were the screams of his family and hideous, mocking laughter from a voice thick with death and rot.

2

It left the dwelling, stepping out of the intoxicating scent of blood, meat, and the fading ecstatic sensations of fear and sorrow. Pausing on the grass, it considered the darkened landscape and hissed. The calmness, the soft wind, the quiet clouds drifting overhead . . . everything hurt. The peacefulness of the land crawled on its skin like a liquid fire, slithering and searing, burrowing in to consume its soul. The teeming life it perceived all around threw fuel on the fire. Its hatred was an impossibly black ball deep within.

It remembered the pain, the weakness.

It remembered the bindings.

They would regret those sins.

Pushing through the torment, it concentrated, finding the thread, feeling the gentle pull. The bloodletting within the house, the symbols etched into screaming, writhing flesh in the moments before death pulled the soul into the tormenting void, had created the connection, tenuous as it was.

It entered the forest, following the thread, heeding the call. The others were there, somewhere. It would find them. Had to find them.

And the blackness would consume everything.

The land would scream.

The world would be drowned in blood.

2 MONTHS LATER

3

Jack Carmelo stood in the cramped, hot basement room and regarded the mutilated remains that, less than an hour ago, had been five men. He was amazed at how bright blood was after it left a body. Even in low light, as it was now, blood was so much brighter than one would expect. Also, there was the matter of how much a body contained. After all these years, he was still surprised at the sheer volume of it. And when the vessel was ruptured, it went everywhere. The walls and ceiling were crisscrossed with lines of arterial spray. Thick maroon drops dripped lazily from the pipes like condensation.

It would take a lot of work to clean this up.

May have to burn this whole building, he thought as he returned his attention to the scene. Atop a filing cabinet in the corner, a gray metal fan rattled as it oscillated back and forth, sending a wave of hot, foul air pushing across Jack's face.

The smell was another thing. The salty, metallic stench was cloying. You could wash the blood off your skin, could get it out of your clothes most of the time, but you could never get rid of the smell. That smell seeped into you, wormed its way into your brain and made a home there. The best you could hope to do was learn to live with it, make peace with it, and pray that you wouldn't throw up in front of the other guys.

But this . . .

Jack cleared his throat and spat. The wad of phlegm landed with a moist *slap* above the right eye of Patrick McCarthy. Immediately below that, the rest of Patrick's head was missing, sheared away, leaving only a pale lip of flesh beneath which the small sliver of bone could be seen.

Fucking Micks.

Absentmindedly, he spun the handle of the axe in his right hand, the head of it scraping gently across the concrete floor. With his other hand, he reached into his front pocket and touched the small coin that rested inside. The feel of its patterned face brought other images, memories of Bobby, to the surface of his mind. Bobby lying twisted and broken, dozens of bleeding holes across his chest and side from the shotgun blast. The laughing faces of the men gathered around. Patrick McCarthy's grim face as he held the smoking gun pointed at Bobby's corpse. Patrick leveling the barrel at Bobby's nose, his finger tightening on the trigger.

Jack's mother on the dirty floor of their small apartment kitchen, her skirt pooled around her knees as she screamed and cried. Jack trying to hold her, to comfort her, but receiving only angry slaps as his mother cursed the business that Bobby had gotten into. It had almost killed her that the funeral for her oldest son had been a closed casket.

Jack spun the axe again and let his eyes play over the carnage spread around him. Miraculously, despite all the violence that had occurred within such a tiny space, the poker table in the center of the room remained upright. A few crumpled dollars were in the center, flanked by a pair of cards—three of hearts—held in place by a splash of blood.

Jack didn't move when the sound of footsteps and Tony Detti's slightly labored breathing came from behind as the large man descended the stairs. "Jack, you all right? You been gone for—" Tony's statement died in his mouth. His feet scuffled on the floor as he drew up, seeing the carnage in the room.

Tony Detti was a big guy, having gained sixty pounds in the last two years. His thin mop of black hair, messily brushed across his head and held in place with a near constant slick of sweat, reflected the soft overhead lighting. Above cheeks pockmarked with old acne scars, his dark eyes stared at the confusion of flesh. "Jesus, Mary, and Joseph. What did you do?" he breathed. Carmelo stared at his old friend and said nothing, waiting for the large man to collect himself. Tony's mouth worked for a moment, making him look like a grouper just pulled onto the dock. Finally, he managed to ask, "The fuck you thinking? Look at this. Who— Oh, for Chrissakes. The fucking McCarthy boys? Jesus on a crutch. You know what's going to happen when O'Banion finds out about this?" Tony regarded him the way an adult looks at a child who's spilled his milk all over his father's briefcase.

"There were two others," Jack said. His voice was soft, calm, and sounded distant to his own ears. He pointed, a general wave of his finger in the direction of limbs, hands, and ravaged torsos. "Not sure who, though."

Tony's eyes focused, widened. "Holy shit, that's Jacob Turski."

"Who?"

"Adrian Turski's nephew."

"You sure?"

Tony poked the air with a thick finger. "See that weird stain over his left eye? What's fucking left of it anyway. Birthmark. That's Jacob, all right. I don't know the other guy." Jack looked at the teapot-shaped mark on the dead man's face. Tony cleared his throat. "Is this all of them?"

"Yeah. Considering I was able to pop Eamon Flynn and Cormac O'Shea a few years back."

"Do you feel better?"

Jack shook his head. "I want to kill them again. I want to send something of theirs back to O'Banion. Hand, foot, head. Doesn't matter, as long as he gets the message."

"He had nothing to do with what they did to Bobby," Tony said. His voice was stronger, the shock of the moment having passed. "Sending a message to O'Banion wouldn't do shit except cause trouble for the boss. Not that there's anything big enough to send. For Chrissakes, Jack, you told me you had a quick errand in here. I thought you were picking up something."

"Would it have mattered?"

"Of course it would have. I'd have come with you, made sure things didn't get out of hand. Not like that, don't look at me like that. I meant, made sure you weren't outgunned."

Jack's fingers turned the coin in his pocket over and over. The trolley token had been Bobby's. He'd carried it everywhere, claiming it was his lucky charm. It was the only thing of his brother's that Jack had, having fished it out of Bobby's pockets after the McCarthys and their pals had left the scene. He tightened his fist around it, the smooth rounded edges biting into his palm.

Rest now, Bobby.

"I'm hungry," he said and placed the axe against the wall.

"That's going to have to wait," Tony said. "You know what this is going to do? The shit that's going to blow back on the boss?"

"This had nothing to do with him."

Tony's jowls shook as he nodded. "Exactly. This wasn't sanctioned. I'm not saying it was wrong, believe me. This was a long time coming, and you were due. But you didn't get permission for this. Those mooks a few years back, nobody cared about. They weren't important and, you know, you made it look like it wasn't intentional. But this . . . The McCarthys were big enough that O'Banion won't be happy. But that ain't the real problem. It's Turski we gotta worry about."

"We could burn the building."

"No good, though I like the way you're thinking. The businesses on either side, you know? Can't risk the fire getting out of hand. And a building this old? It'll get out of hand fast. Come on, we gotta get you cleaned up and I have to tell the boss about this. He needs to be prepared for what's going to come. And that Polish son of a bitch is going to come heavy and hard."

Tony put a hand on Jack's shoulder and gave a gentle but unyielding tug. Jack allowed himself to be guided out of the room, his shoes squelching in the thick, cooling blood. Tony led him up the stairs and through the empty warehouse above. Bright afternoon sunlight streamed in through windows high in the warehouse walls, angled beams where motes of dust floated lazily. As they wove through the racks of boxes and supplies, Jack caught sight of a few flies buzzing about. *It never took them long to find a body*, he mused, as Tony took a moment to peer out the door. Ducking back inside, he said, "Okay, it's clear. Go straight to the car."

Jack held out his hands. "I think I'm going to get it a little messy."

Tony ran his eyes along Jack's bloodstained clothes. "Fuck. Okay. One second." He left the warehouse, slipping inside moments later with a thick wool blanket. "Wrap up in this. Get in the backseat and lay down."

"The boss at the club?" Jack asked.

"Hotel. You think I'd take you to the club looking like that? The bathroom ain't big enough for you to clean up in. No, you're going to make yourself presentable in one of the rooms while I talk to the boss."

"And then?"

"Then you're going to hope he doesn't want to crush your nuts with his boot. Come on."

The drive to Cicero and the Hawthorne took about twenty minutes, during which, Jack lay in the small back seat of Tony's car and watched the tops of buildings slide past. The sun was bright in the clear, cloudless sky and considering it was in the low fifties, he was glad for the blanket. Now that they had moved beyond the warehouse and its grim basement, Tony found his second wind and spent the majority of the drive scolding Jack, who interrupted him only once to ask for a cigarette. Tony grunted irritably but passed a pack over the front seat. Lighting it, Jack considered the cigarette. It was a pretty good blend. Normally he was a Camel man, but Lucky Strikes weren't too bad.

The car jerked to a halt. Beyond the window near his feet were the dark red bricks of the Hawthorne Inn. Each window of the building had the shades drawn despite the nicety of the day. A few cars sputtered past, the sounds of their engines fading as Jack lay back, finishing his cigarette while waiting on Tony to waddle around the back end of the car to open the rear passenger door. When he did, he made a hurried "Come on" gesture. Jack slid out, keeping the blanket around his shoulders, and moved quickly into the lobby without glancing at the suited man standing beneath the awning to one side of the door.

The lobby of the hotel was small. A set of dark stairs curled up and out of sight to the left of the door. Standing around the lobby were four more hard-faced men wearing suits. The air was foggy with tobacco smoke, and the men silently watched Jack as he and Tony entered. Across from the entrance was a single, heavy, unmarked door where another man stood, hands clasped in front. He gave Tony and Jack a nod in greeting. Tony bumped Jack with the back of his hand and pointed at the steps.

The climb to the third floor was slow, Tony heaving and wheezing the whole way, but ultimately Jack stepped into a hallway that was as silent as a tomb. Thick maroon carpet led to a single door at the far end of the corridor. There were other doors leading up to it, but Jack knew they were unoccupied rooms. The boss had made sure of that. Standing at the door to the penthouse was a tall, thick man wearing a dark suit. His hat rested on the seat of a cushioned chair behind him.

Jack followed Tony down the hall until he stopped at a door to one of the unoccupied rooms. He held it open for Jack. "There's a change of clothes in the closet. They're Paul's, so they may be a little tight on you. You get cleaned up while I talk to the boss." Without waiting for Jack to respond, Tony shut the door, putting a little more power into it than necessary. His footsteps faded as he continued toward the far room. Jack let out a long sigh and turned to get ready.

When he was showered and dressed—Tony had been right, the

jacket was tight in the shoulders and loose in the waist—he opened the door to find Detti leaning against the opposite wall, smoking. Without speaking, he tilted his head and led Jack to the end of the hall. The thick man remained at his post next to the hotel room door, his hat still on the chair.

"Jack," the guard said.

"Angelo. How's your mom?"

The big man shrugged, a wagging of his shoulders. "She has her days. You know."

Jack patted the man on the arm. "Give her my best, will you?"

For a small, three-story hotel, the penthouse was considerably big, consisting of a bedroom, a small kitchen, and a living space. Tony pointed to a chair in the sitting room. "I'll let him know you're here."

Jack didn't sit. Instead, he drifted to one of the windows on the far wall and peered through the curtain. The vista was of the alley and a solid, windowless brick wall of another building.

"Jack Carmelo," a voice boomed behind him. "You mind telling me what the fuck you were doing with an axe and the McCarthy brothers?"

Swallowing hard, Jack turned and faced the man who stepped in from the kitchen, smoke blowing behind him from a thick Cuban cigar wedged into the corner of his mouth. "Just handling business."

Al Capone stopped a few feet away and glared up at Jack, his eyes squinting slightly in the smoke. He gestured toward the closest chair. "Sit. You and me need to talk."

Capone took his time before speaking. He stared at Jack through the haze of smoke, rolling the cigar slowly from one side of his mouth to the other. Jack sat still, returning the look, knowing that this was just Al's way. The boss plucked the cigar from his lips and pointed it at Jack. "So they're the ones who killed your brother." It wasn't a question, but Jack nodded anyway. Al chuckled. "That's a long time to wait to get even. Nine fucking years."

"I didn't want them to expect it."

Al's eyebrows went up. "They sure as fuck didn't expect you to bust into the middle of their afternoon poker game swinging a goddamn fire axe, I can tell you that much." He pulled the cigar from his mouth again and pointed at Jack. "I remember your brother."

A strange fluttering stirred in Jack's chest. "Really?"

"Not personally. But I remember seeing him around. Running errands, doing pickups, that kind of thing. Nice kid. Bright." Al's eyes twinkled through the gray smoke. "I seem to remember seeing you a time or two also. Always tagging along. Thought you was keeping out of sight."

Jack smiled at the memory.

"But that doesn't give you the fucking permission to go and bump off five fucking members of the North Side Gang!" Al screamed, shattering the moment. His cheeks were flushed and spittle arced from his lips. Jack said nothing. He remained still and kept his eyes on the boss. "Did you ever once consider how O'Banion or Turski were going to take this? How it would affect *my* fucking business?"

"I didn't know Turski—"

"Of course you fucking didn't! How the hell did you even know they were there?"

"I've been watching them for a few years. The poker game is new, only within the last five months. It's a personal game. Not one designed to draw in marks."

Al sighed, blowing smoke toward the ceiling. "I know why you did it, Christ knows I get how you feel about the Irish, but still. O'Banion isn't going to just take this. I don't care how far back their transgressions go. The McCarthys were on their way up in his group. Because of this, because of your impetuousness, we're going to see an increase in attacks on our shipments. For Christ's sake, you turned them into hamburger! There's going to be fucking repercussions!"

Jack took a deep breath. "I'm sorry about that, I really am. But—"

"Oh, fuck your sorry," Capone snapped. "They're going to demand your head. This is going to have a ripple effect. There's no way they don't think this wasn't a hit."

"I'll work with Tony and get the guys ready for a retaliation."

"You think they're going to hit us straight on?" Capone chuckled. "That's not O'Banion's style. That fucking Polack, sure, he'll come at us, try to carve you to pieces. But O'Banion will use that as a distraction to step up attacks on our shipments. The Irish prick is already hitting us regularly, but this is going to give him an excuse to really start trying to move in. Not to mention, the cops on his payroll will be like flies on shit. They can't ignore a crime like that."

"We got cops too."

"That ain't the point!" Capone yelled. He stared at Jack, eyes narrowed, chest heaving with rage. Jack watched as the emotion drained away, a tide receding, leaving a smooth patch of sand. "While I understand why you did it, and can't argue about getting your payback for what they did to Bobby, they're going to demand your head." Al continued, his voice calm. "Other than you being an impulsive fuck, you're one of my best guys. You know that, right?" Jack didn't answer. "You're going to have to get out of town for a while. Let things cool down. But I'm not sending you on a fucking vacation. I have something for you to actually do."

Jack remained quiet while Capone crossed the room to a decanter and glassware set atop a small credenza. He poured two whiskeys and handed one of the cut crystal glasses to Jack. The golden brown liquid smelled fantastic and Jack took a small sip, licking his lips as it burned down his throat.

"Where do you need me to go? New York, Seattle, LA?" A gentle swelling of hopefulness rose in him at the prospect that he'd be asked to go to Seattle or LA. The West Coast was supposed to be beautiful.

Capone grinned over his own glass and asked, "What do you know about moonshine?"

"You talking about the swill that people make in their bathrooms with those cookers the Genna brothers were selling? What about it?"

Capone shook his head, his smile growing wider on his plump face. "I don't mean that shit they're making over in Little Italy. The Gennas have that corner and I don't care about it. I mean down south. Moonshine. The stuff the hillbillies make out in the woods."

Jack thought for a moment. "Nothing. I've heard rumors that they have some pretty big stills down there, that they run them deep in the woods where Prohis or the ASL rarely would go. From what I understand, the quality is shit. But what can you expect from a bunch of inbred hillbillies?"

"Do you like your drink?"

Jack started to answer, then understood what was being asked. "Are you serious? This is from—"

"Some shitkicker down in Alabama. I received a case a few months ago and I'll be damned if it's not quality stuff. Yeah, it's made by a bunch of ignorant rednecks. But . . ." He shrugged, finished his drink, and turned to pour another.

Jack sipped again and marveled at the taste. There was a sweetness to it that he'd not noticed before. "It's different from what we're getting from Canada."

"It's better," Capone said. "And it's cheaper. I sent Carlo Morelli down a while back and he met with the head of one of the operations down there. Man named Cleary. He agreed to produce for us. He's got several stills spread out all over down there. Has a whole network. Kind of like us, only not quite as organized or smart. But they should be able to send us around thirty-five thousand gallons a month. I'll save you the math, just know that's a pretty good bit of cash once the bottles get to our warehouses."

The last of the whiskey slid out of Carmelo's glass and down his throat. He waved off a refill. "So what's this have to do with me? You want me to go down there and supervise?"

Al lit another cigar. "Something like that," he said as he flicked his lighter closed. "First of all, I've not heard from Morelli in three weeks. You know him?"

"Yeah."

"Then you'll know how that ain't like him."

"You think he got pinched? Or offed by a Prohi?"

Al's shoulders went up and down. "That's for you to find out. If he did get himself offed, then I'll need you to make that right." He gave a knowing look that not only conveyed that Jack was to understand the subtext, but that Al was referencing Jack's business only a few hours ago.

"I can do that," Jack said. "That all? It may not take long to find him. Big Italian like Morelli must stick out like a sore thumb among all those dirty hillbillies."

"There's more," Al said. "The ink is barely dry on the agreement we made with Cleary, but I need you to convince him that he has to increase that amount from thirty-five thousand to fifty a month. That will make up for what we're going to lose thanks to your little fiasco. On top of that, he's not been producing what we initially agreed to, so you'll need to find out why and remedy that. I'll let you decide how best to steer him back to the path of correctness. We set the current agreement at fifty cents on the gallon. You can offer him up to seventy-five. No more."

Images of stomping through the woods of Alabama flooded Jack's mind. He worked his jaw, chewing on several retorts— counterarguments that if things were really going to be as bad as Al was suggesting, it was only right that he stayed and helped fix them. Al's unwavering stare provided a silent rebuttal to each one.

Al smiled. "Good." He gave Jack a gentle push and together they walked toward the door. "Find Morelli, get the deal made with Cleary, and take some time down there." He stopped Jack with a firm hand on his arm. "We'll take care of things here."

"And Norma? I want some guys on her."

Capone's eyebrows raised. "You do?"

Jack knew what Capone meant by the question. "She's my wife," he said tightly.

Capone sighed. "We'll take care of her. Don't worry."

Jack paused at the door. "It's going to be fucking miserable down there. Hot."

Capone waved a hand, dismissing Jack. "You can send word when you have it all straightened out. I'll let you know when it's clear to come back."

4

Harlan Gibbons let the wicker creel's strap slip from his shoulder, then placed the basket next to the bottom step. He leaned his two bamboo fishing poles against the uneven wall of his cabin. They shifted before settling against the rounded pine logs, and when he was satisfied they weren't going to topple completely to the ground, he set the metal tackle box atop the creel. The contents rattled like rocks in a tin can until it was steady atop the basket. He took a moment, placing his hands on the small of his back and leaning against them. The joints and muscles stretched, popped, and brought some measure of relief— the only good thing about the whole damned afternoon.

His hand was on the knob of the door when he realized his mud-caked boots were still on his feet. For a brief moment, he considered leaving them on, no matter what Harriet said. He'd built the damned house—well, he and Walter and Smokey—so he should be able to tread mud throughout it if he damned well pleased. But the last time he did that, and it was a much smaller amount of mud and dirt then, Harriet had rained holy hell down on him. That woman had a tongue sharper than a butcher's cleaver, and she knew how to use it to cut a man to the bone. After the tongue-lashing, she'd stopped speaking to him for three days. On the surface he liked to joke that the silence was a lovely vacation from her nagging, but deep down it had hurt him. For his wife to act as if he were a ghost in his own home was disconcerting. Harlan let out a long, weary sigh and bent to undo the laces, then kicked out of his boots and continued into the house.

The smells and sounds of his family enveloped him, and the frustrations of the day fell to the floor like clumps of mud breaking free from his soul. The house wasn't large, only three rooms, but the essence, the vitality of his family, filled every inch of it. Harriet stood at the stove stirring something. The small cook surface held three pots, flames licking the bottoms of each, sending curtains of fragrant smoke into the air. Harlan's mouth watered as he recognized the meal. She was making her pork stew with plenty of greens. His stomach, having only had a tin of sardines and a pack of crackers earlier in the day, gave a ravenous lurch.

On the floor of the main room, Benjamin and Cora sat cross-legged, playing a quiet game involving a teddy bear and a wooden train. Ben leapt to his feet excitedly as his father entered. Harlan pulled his son close, but only for a moment before Cora was there, squeezing her way between the two as she prattled on about her teddy bear.

"Y'all leave your daddy alone," Harriet scolded as she crossed the room. She flapped a kitchen towel at the children playfully and they cried out and ran back to their game. Harriet leaned close for a kiss but winced and pulled back sharply. "You smell, Harlan Gibbons." Her eyes did a quick up and down appraisal of him. "And you're filthy."

"Rough day," he said, and considered telling her about the condition of the water, how brackish it smelled and how no matter where he repositioned, the surface was dotted with the bloated corpses of dead fish. Then there had been the strange, blackened plants; ones he'd never known to grow in the woods, their leaves furred with some kind of mold that stunk worse than the river. But that would only worry her and she had enough to deal with. "I fell down the embankment over by Graddy's Cove."

"I can see. Looks like you took half the mud on the riverbank home with you. Any luck otherwise?" He shook his head, pushing down the images of distended fish bellies and disturbing dead eyes. Her face softened; she knew what a bad day's fishing meant to him, to their livelihood. The moment was over quickly and she smiled, putting on a brave face. He loved her more in that moment than he had before, even though he had the same feeling only this morning and at least four times the day previous. "Well, it's a good thing we live outside of town," Harriet said. She fanned her hand in front of her face mockingly. "Because you smell ripe as a rotten tomato. Now go get cleaned up. Supper's just about ready."

Harlan retreated to the back room, stripped, and cleaned himself up using the basin of water on the dresser. Not for the first time, he cursed himself for moving outside of the town to start a life of self-reliance. He'd been able to build the house and furnish it fairly well. The stove was one of the amenities he was most proud of, despite the bitch of a time he had moving it out to the cabin. However, the lack of running water was a real inconvenience.

But what the hell were those plants? And what about the fish? Had something died in the river and poisoned them? He dried his hands quickly and left the questions behind in the quiet stillness of the room.

When he returned to the main room, the children were seated at the table and Harriet was serving the stew from a large cast-iron pot. Harlan took his seat and waited for his wife to finish. As she settled into her chair, Cora pointed to the window. "It's so dark?" she said it like a question, and Harlan angled his head to see. His eyes narrowed in confusion. It was late spring, the days wouldn't start getting longer for another couple weeks, but at—he checked his Timex—6:47 p.m., it shouldn't be *that* dark. The view through the window was murky, the light saturated with shadows. What little of the sky was visible through the trees looked a bruised purple. The trees themselves appeared as dark sentinels, motionless against the encroaching night.

"That's odd," Harriet said. "Maybe a storm's coming."

Harlan nodded. A storm would explain things, certainly. But he'd read of no such thing in the almanac. And he certainly didn't smell rain at any point in the day. He held his attention on the window as a cold feeling settled in his chest, worming its way to his guts. Harriet cleared her throat, a soft noise that broke his momentary stupor.

Turning back to his family, he forced a smile. "Let's pray. Mother, will you do the honors?" Harlan always liked when Harriet said grace. She put a musical lilt to the words that were like a balm to his soul. Some of the other men, the older ones especially, didn't like it when a woman led the family in prayer, but Harlan always quietly maintained that the words to God came better from a woman, a fellow life-bringer.

The family joined hands, Harlan smiling as the small, fragile, and wriggling fingers of his children's hands grasped his own. They bowed their heads and Harriet began to speak, "Heavenly Father, we thank You for this meal before us, for the roof over our heads, and for the love that fills this home. Keep our family strong and safe, guide our steps, and bless Harlan's hands with good work. Grant him health and a bit of luck with his fishing. Let the bones in the deep crack spill their secrets. Let the shadows beneath the spoiled earth open their eyes. Let the hook sink into flesh not yet dead, and the net come up writhing."

His head still bowed, Harlan's brow furrowed as the word "writhing" came out thick and garbled, as if his wife were suddenly choking. She drew in a long, ragged breath and in the same clotted voice, continued. "Let the worms fatten on the screaming babies, and the earth drink deep of what's to come. Let the sky close its eye, and the trees forget our names. Let the doors stay unlocked. Let them come hungry."

Harriet, her head still bowed, spasmed in her chair with quick jerking movements. Her shoulders rolled as her neck strained first toward the table, then to the ceiling. Her lips pressed tightly together, going white from the pressure. A moment later, her mouth yawned wide.

"Honey?" Harlan still grasped the hands of his children and stared as Harriet continued to struggle. His mind searched for the word that he'd heard Doc Powell use to describe similar fits. It came to him: seizure. Panic flashed, hot and electric. If she were having a seizure, he had no idea what to do about it. They had a truck, but it was still a forty-minute drive to town. Would they be able—

Harlan leapt back as a deep, growling scream tore its way out of his wife's mouth, followed by a torrent of black liquid. The stream of vomitus hit the bowl of stew in front of her, sending broth and bile splashing across the wood. Harriet's hands scrabbled at the edge of the table, her fingers knocking utensils to the floor. She backhanded her glass of tea and it shattered when it landed by her foot. The children screamed and leapt from their chairs, huddling close behind Harlan who remained seated.

The stream of black liquid continued to pour from Harriet's mouth, her entire body shivering as she convulsed to expel it all. She planted her hands firmly on the table, fingers gripping the wood so tightly Harlan expected to hear it snap. She leaned forward, putting all her weight on her arms as she continued to shake and vomit.

Harriet's eyes shifted in their sockets to lock on to Harlan's face. In that look was sheer terror. The expression was so pure that it drove him to his feet before he knew he was in motion. He had to do something, and he searched the room for anything to trigger a plan of action.

When the children began screaming with more panic than they'd initially shown, Harlan abandoned his quest for aid and watched in disbelief as the waterfall of black fluid changed as it spewed forth. In one instant, it was pure liquid and in the next, what poured up her throat and over her lips held shapes, landing with a soft clicking patter.

Insects.

Beetles, centipedes, flies, and spiders all careened out of Harriet and down onto the table. They landed in the thick black liquid and attempted to crawl away as more of their horrific brethren fell on top of them.

Harlan screamed his wife's name, his arms sweeping out and behind him as he gathered the children and herded them back from the table. Their hands clutched at his belt, the warmth from their bodies pressing against him as he shuffled back. He continued backing away until he was in the middle of the living room, where the children had been playing when he'd come home.

Harriet continued to shake and convulse by the table, her eyes locked on her husband's empty chair.

"The spoiled! The spoiled soil!" The shrieks came from Cora, and Harlan diverted his focus from his wife to the panic-stricken face of his daughter. He gaped, unsure of where to tell her to go. The house was small, so there weren't many places for her to be that—

"Our blood will rot!" the little girl shouted, but this time the voice that bellowed the question was deeper, almost a man's voice. "Our blood will rot! Our blood will rot! Our blood will rot!" the girl chanted, screaming at the top of her lungs, each word pitched differently. First the deep growling of a man who had spent his life smoking and drinking, abusing his throat, then the plaintive, terror-filled tones of Harlan's youngest child, and finally an otherworldly cry so high-pitched it sounded as if she were shredding her own vocal cords. Harlan spun, eyes searching as he braced himself to witness his six-year-old daughter vomiting a nightmare plague.

Instead, she held out one arm and a long, inch-wide strip of her skin peeled up and away, exposing red muscle. Blood cascaded out of the strip and landed on the floor with soft splatters that were drowned out by the cacophony of screams. The strip ran from Cora's wrist to an inch below her elbow. Something deep in Harlan's brain clicked into place at the sight of the blood. This was a wound he could deal with. He stripped off his shirt and reached for the girl's arm. As he brought the fabric close, another shriek of pain burst out of her.

"Holy Jesus," Harlan gasped, finally finding his voice, as a strip of flesh peeled off Cora's face. The new wound ran from her temple and along her cheek. Another appeared on her other arm, yet another high on her shoulder. The girl ripped out of his grasp and she ran in panicked movements around the living room as more and more strips of skin ripped free.

"Dear God, what is this?" Harlan shouted as he looked from his blood-soaked daughter to his wife. Harriet's mouth hung open and Harlan saw the last of the insects—a thick black millipede—drop from her bottom lip. The table and floor were awash in crawling black and brown creatures. Harriet's head shook as if she were straining to turn it, but after a moment's resistance, her body gave out and she fell seemingly boneless onto the table. She stared, eyes sightless and glassy.

"Dad!" Benjamin shouted, ripping Harlan's focus back to his children. Cora was still screaming in pain, the girl's entire upper body covered in blood, her light brown hair matted and dripping. She collapsed on the hearth, crying and whimpering. Harlan took a step toward her but stopped when a sudden pressure ballooned up from his stomach. Pain slammed into him, doubling him over and driving him to his knees. He pushed one hand against his abdomen while holding himself upright with the other. A crawling tickling worked its way up his throat, sending tendrils of revulsion through him. As the first exploratory touches of legs and antennae drifted against his soft palate, something moved in the darkness of the fireplace.

A hand, blackened and gnarled, reached down from the small opening that was the chimney. Long, bony fingers unfurled, each one ending in an obsidian claw. The hand reached forward and grasped his daughter by the head, the claws sinking into the bleeding and torn skin. Cora shook with the contact but didn't cry out, her body too exhausted. Harlan vomited, bugs forcing their way past his teeth to bounce off his supporting hand as the clawed hand pulled his child up into the small space of the chimney with shocking force.

Harlan tried to scream his daughter's name, but only worms and spiders came out. He closed his eyes as a deluge of blood poured from the chimney to splash against the stone of the fireplace. A powerful wave of pain rolled through him and he collapsed. His cheek crunched atop the brittle insects. Harlan lay on the floor, head to one side and mouth agape, as more and more vermin flooded from his body. Around him, the interior of the cabin wavered, shimmering and darkening, as if someone were placing a filter over the lanterns.

Over the sound of small legs scurrying across the floor, Harlan caught the plodding shuffle of footsteps. Despite the fuzziness that consumed his thoughts, one word glowed in his mind.

Benjamin.

With great effort, Harlan raised his head enough to turn and find his son. The boy stood between his father and the table where Harriet still lay sprawled. Ben walked slowly, as though he was sleepwalking, his arms limp by his sides, feet barely lifting. He angled around the table and his dead mother, approaching the window that overlooked the woods at the front of the house. Harlan's throat twitched as he struggled to clear it of the continuing rush of bugs.

Benjamin paused, his head angling to regard something next to his foot. The boy bent and picked up the wooden train and held it, considering the toy. With a vicious movement, he hurled it at the window. Harlan blinked reflexively at the sound of glass shattering. Benjamin resumed his slow progress and a muffled mewling escaped Harlan's throat as the boy climbed through the window, heedless of the remaining shards that cut across his body. His shirt and pants tore, blood spilling and soaking the surrounding cloth. One long, wicked-looking fragment at the top of the frame cut across the child's head, parting the hair as it dug deep into the scalp. More blood streamed down Ben's neck and shoulders, yet he continued through the window as if nothing had happened.

Harlan summoned the last of his strength, pulling from reserves buried deep within himself, and managed to rise to his knees. Everything within him was on fire, a twisting, pulling, crawling pain that filled every inch of him. His abdomen convulsed, forcing more of the living bugs up and over his lips, yet Harlan's sole focus was on his son's back as the boy walked slowly through the darkening day toward the trees.

To the black figure that stood at their edge.

It appeared human, but was bent and twisted, as if the very act of standing was painful. Ben walked in that same shuffling slowness directly toward it, and the dark thing raised an arm, beckoning the child closer.

Harlan managed a scream, the expulsion of air sending ants and crickets across the room. The sound died after doing so, as the fuzziness in his vision darkened and closed down.

The last thing he saw was the flash of sharp, wicked teeth as the dark figure smiled in predatory anticipation.

5

Benjamin Gibbons's skin buzzed with painful fire as he plodded through the woods, following the shadow. His clothes were soaked, though he couldn't remember being in the rain. His hands and feet were numb with cold, but still he walked. The dark figure ahead of him flashed in and out of sight, one second within arm's reach and in the blink of an eye, so far away he could barely make it out among the night-shrouded trees.

He didn't want to follow the thing in the woods; his mind screamed at him to stop, to turn back and go help his family. He was the oldest and knew that Cora would be scared if he was gone too long. He didn't want to make his parents worry. He really didn't know how he had gotten outside in the first place. He was hungry, and Mommy had been making stew all afternoon. The smell of it, greasy and fragrant with spices, had hung heavily throughout the house. His stomach had been grumbling all afternoon waiting for it. He was going to have two bowls.

But now he was out in the woods at night. He'd never done that before. Daddy wouldn't allow it. It was too easy to get lost and hurt. But that wasn't a worry now, as the shifting dark figure blurred in front of him. He was following *her*. She wouldn't let anything happen to him. If only he could make the pain all over his body go away. If only he could stop and get something to eat. That would help, and then he could find his way back to his house and keep his family from being afraid.

The figure flashed back into view, this time inches away. Benjamin stopped walking, his feet ceasing their movement automatically. He tried to turn his head to see her face, but his body wouldn't cooperate. Instead, he could only stare straight ahead, into the infinite blackness of her body.

She shifted, a long-fingered hand drifting to the figure's waist. Benjamin continued to stare, his brain registering a quick movement that his eyes couldn't make out. Then came a wet ripping noise, as if a bedsheet were being torn. It came in short bursts, like the fabric didn't want to part but the hand was forcing it.

A smell pushed into his nose and Benjamin's empty stomach twisted and rolled in rebellion. He'd never smelled anything so awful, even that time last summer when he'd found the pile of fish guts his father had tossed into the bushes behind the house, leaving them to rot in the hot August sun.

Powerful fingers probed his lips, their tips elongated and sharp. New pricks of pain lit up along his mouth, tongue, and cheeks, and he tasted hot salty liquid. Instinct wanted him to push away, to clamp down on the violation, but once again, his body refused to work. Fear blossomed in his mind like a candle lit in a pitch-black room. The fingers probed deeper, their nails scraping the back of his throat, holding his tongue down.

A new pressure forced his jaw open wide, and something foul, rotting, and meaty was shoved into his mouth. Benjamin gagged, his throat finding some measure of independence. The wet strip filled his mouth, lying atop the fingers that continued to hold his jaw open.

I won't swallow. I won't. I—

The figure hissed something, a word or phrase in a language that sent spikes of pain through Benjamin's ears. He winced—or tried to —but his eyes remained wide and fixed on the figure in front of him.

His throat opened and he found that he didn't have to swallow the thing that lay in his mouth like a fat, dead worm.

As soon as the tissues of his neck relaxed, the thing twitched and slid, crawling, to the back of his mouth. A gentle, terrible tickling probed his throat as the thing felt around. In a single rush, it uncoiled from between his cheeks and slid down his throat and into his stomach. He felt it moving in there, swimming around and settling into its new home.

Tears streamed from the corners of his eyes, tracing hot across his cheeks, but Benjamin was unable to blink them away. The fingers withdrew from his mouth and his jaw slowly closed. He swayed on his feet for a moment. The fear and nausea sending the earth around him seesawing as the thing in his stomach continued to writhe and twist.

Benjamin's eyes rolled back in his head and he crumpled to the bed of pine needles covering the earth.

He was awakened by an impossible weight over his entire body. It pressed down everywhere, from his feet to his thighs to his arms and head. Benjamin wiggled his fingers through the thick grittiness of dirt. Realizing that somehow he'd fallen into a hole, he gasped, sucking in nothing but soil. It filled his mouth, bringing back images of the fingers and the horrible thing that had been in his mouth. Benjamin tried to sit up, but the weight was all-encompassing.

Despite being only seven, he knew immediately what had happened.

I've been buried.

His brain and lungs screamed for oxygen, convulsing in an attempt to pull in air, only to be rewarded with more stinking, choking dirt.

Mommy! Daddy! Help me!

The thing in his stomach shivered like an eel in response, as if rejoicing in his terror.

Despite his lack of air, Benjamin Gibbons screamed into the earth that surrounded him as his body was racked by a new pain. Things bulged within him, along his thighs and back, from his shoulders and neck. The skin tightened and swelled, stretching painfully outward until it cracked, giving birth to the things. Benjamin could feel them spreading out, spearing through the ground, growing like the roots of a tree.

They devoured, chewing through the living things they encountered, growing more powerful with each foot they extended. Consuming, killing.

Corrupting.

He felt all of this, understood it all, and as the candle in the blackness of his mind dimmed, he continued to scream into the earth.

6

"Sir, we're five minutes from the station." Beneath the hat he'd placed over his face, Jack blinked awake to the rocking and rattling of the train. He mumbled thanks to the attendant who, satisfied he'd roused the man as asked, continued along the aisle.

Outside, the Alabama landscape slid by, farmhouses in the middle of large rolling fields. Next came a large swath of woods, the trees passing in a green and brown blur. Jack watched a cluster of grain silos give way to a collection of brick buildings separated by both paved and hard-packed dirt streets.

The train shuddered as it slowed with a whining squeal of brakes. Jack stood and pulled his suitcase from the overhead compartment. One hand on the seat back, he leaned forward and watched the city surround him. Advertisements for cigarettes and laundry detergent were painted on the red brick facades of buildings in front of cars parked along curbs, sunlight glinting off their bodies. Down side avenues, he caught glimpses of street trolleys moving slowly while people strolled along sidewalks, crossing the avenues as cars wove in and out and around the crowds. The men wore mostly denim overalls but he spied a few sporting dark suits and hats. The women wore light colored dresses and hats. Many pushed black carriages as they went about their errands.

This may not be so bad, he thought, noting the hemlines of several of the dresses. The city and its inhabitants didn't appear quite as desolate or inbred as he'd imagined them to be. In fact, there was a lot of similarity to Chicago. Birmingham was much larger than he'd anticipated, and stores and people abounded, just on a slightly smaller scale than what he was accustomed to. His stomach grumbled as his eyes took in the red and white sign of a diner before it was obscured by the train station and platform.

Jack pushed ahead of an older man struggling to fold a newspaper and moved along the aisle to the door at the far end of the car. He pulled it open and stepped out onto the metal platform as the train slowed to a complete stop. Instantly the warmth of the day pressed against him, sending beads of sweat sprouting on his forehead and temples.

The platform was crowded but not nearly as bad as Dearborn or the new Union Station would be. A couple dozen people milled about, suitcases in hands or resting by their feet as they waited for the passengers to disembark. Jack scanned all of them, his gaze lingering on a woman who stood alone near the next car. *Mousy* came to Jack's mind at the sight of the woman. She was short and small with long, black hair. The resemblance to Norma was so uncanny that he'd taken three steps in her direction before he realized it. The woman must have sensed him because she lifted her face from reading her ticket, her lips parting in a small moment of surprise.

It wasn't Norma. Of course it wasn't Norma. She was back in Chicago in their small apartment on State Street. Probably still listening to that goddamn Clarence Williams record and drinking the whiskey he'd kept in the back of the pantry. Her reaction to his announcement of his immediate departure had been less than ideal, to say the least.

After leaving Al's, he had one of the guys from the lobby drive him home. As soon as he climbed the stairs to the fourth floor, he could hear the sounds of jazz drifting through the door and into the hallway. Hand held over the dark brass knob, Jack took a moment before opening the door. Jazz meant only one thing. He swallowed back anger and let out an ineffective calming breath.

As expected, his wife was slouched low in her favorite chair next to the window overlooking the street. Her arms dangled over the sides, fingers tracing lazy patterns in the air as the music crashed around the room. She wore a dark blue dress patterned with light green flowers. Her legs were crossed, one stockinged foot bouncing rhythmically. Her dark hair had fallen forward, covering most of her face.

The gramophone sat on a table a few feet away, next to a large, graceful fern that Jack had brought home last month. The plant was already drooping, the edges of its leaves a rusty brown. Next to the record player lay a small syringe, the inside of the tube discolored by the heroin it had recently contained. The rest of the evidence—the bottle containing the powder and the metal cap used to melt the powder—was missing, which meant that she'd prepared the hit either in the kitchen or the bathroom. Jack's jaw tightened as he forced his gaze back to his wife.

Norma peered at him with glassy eyes through the curtain of her hair. One corner of her mouth curled up in a wry grin as her drug-addled brain registered who was standing in front of her.

"What are you doing here?" she asked with painful slowness. The words came out thick and pressed together. With little effort, Jack crossed the living room, his feet muted thunder on the red and gold rug—a Christmas gift from Al.

"What . . . why are you here?" she repeated. The hand not flicking patterns in the air plucked a green tumbler from the other side of the chair. The cut glass drinkware held a finger of brown liquid. Norma finished the whiskey slowly, like a child consuming a late-night drink of water. When she was done, Norma regarded the empty glass with the curiosity of someone viewing a never-before-seen wonder at a museum.

"I have to get some things."

Her upper lip curled in a sneer, revealing white teeth. "Going someplace?"

"Business," he answered as he reached the bedroom door.

"Maybe you won't come back this time," Norma said. The words were sharper, clearer than her earlier question, and they hit Jack like small stabs in the back. He paused, one hand on the doorframe. He could hear the spiteful smile on his wife's face. Instead of responding, he entered the room and pulled his battered tan suitcase out from under the bed. Moving quickly, he threw several shirts and other items inside, then pulled together a few toiletries. Whatever else he needed, he could get on the road or when he got down south. The need to get out of the apartment filled him with a thrumming that reverberated in his fingers. He shut the lid and hauled the suitcase into the living room.

Norma remained in the chair, but she'd clearly gotten up at some point because her glass was full. Instead of the liquid bleariness that usually came with her heroin use, her gaze was colder, more solid.

"You'd like that? For me to go away for good?" he asked and inwardly winced. That was exactly what she wanted, to goad him into a fight.

Norma shrugged. "Wouldn't matter. You're never really here anyway. You're certainly never around when I actually need you."

"I've done nothing but take care of you," he said, forcing the words past his tightening throat. "Or tried to, despite the way you've treated yourself."

Norma rolled her eyes. She spoke, the words a low mumbling.

"What?" he asked. He didn't want to know, not really. For the past several months, Norma delighted in trying to hurt him. Why would he want to hear more of it? Besides, he didn't have time for this. He needed to be on the road.

With a languid rolling movement, Norma turned her head to face him. "You have never taken care of me. Not like you should. A husband is supposed to protect his wife. Or have you forgotten that? You weren't here." Her voice hitched, the words catching in her throat. She swallowed thickly and pressed on. "You weren't here when I needed you. You weren't here when I was bleeding out in our goddamn bathroom. You weren't here when I lost our baby. No, you were out there,"—she flapped a hand toward the window—"somewhere. Doing God knows what."

The declaration cut into him, spilling his emotions out in a hot rush and leaving behind only a hollow anger. "How dare you blame me? I wasn't out of the city. I was six fucking blocks away. Tony and the others knew where I was. All you had to do was call and they would have gotten me. I would have been here. I could have—"

Her shoulders rose and dropped in an apathetic shrug. "Wouldn't have mattered. It doesn't matter now," she said in a dreamy voice. She sipped her whiskey and flapped her hand dismissively. "Go on, then. Go on to whatever vile act you have to do now for your masters."

Jack stared, his mouth open in surprise. Norma continued to observe the cars on the street below. The chair swallowed her diminutive frame. When had she gotten so skinny? What had happened to the affectionate, confident woman he'd met in the night-club three years ago? The woman who performed on stage with the attitude of a ruling queen? His eyes drifted once more to the empty syringe, then back to Norma. It was as if the heroin had burned away everything that had been good and loving, leaving an emaciated shell full of despondence and black hate.

"You weren't always like this," he said.

Norma's laugh was brittle, like dead sticks breaking. She twisted to face him, her body stretching lazily like a cat sunning itself. "Yeah? And what was I like?"

Jack looked at her, noting the sharp elbows, the angles of her shoulders beneath the fabric of the dress, the small knobs of her knees along the narrow lengths of her legs. Legs that used to be toned from years of dancing. Legs that used to wrap tightly around his waist, urging him to go harder, faster. He studied her face, found the light dusting of freckles along her cheeks. Those cheeks used to color to the shade of apples as she teased him for always being so serious. Her eyes, blue with small flecks of hazel, used to focus on him as if he were the only thing in the room.

He thought of the small glass vials stashed in her dresser drawers behind blouses and hosiery. The faint smudges of powder on her mirror and how she used to swear it was only a little, just to take the edge off after a long night of dancing.

Until she stopped dancing, and the vials continued to show up empty.

He answered her question, "Not this."

Norma smirked and lifted her glass once more. Around the rim of it, she said, "Well, sweetheart . . . This is all that's left." As the words filled the space between them, something inside Jack broke and fell into the abyss.

He hefted the suitcase and started for the door. When he spoke again, the words were scratchy, their edges sharper, "I'm not sure how long I'll be. But I'll be out of Chicago. There's going to be some trouble." Norma coughed a laugh into her glass. "I talked to Al and he's going to have a couple guys close, keeping an eye on you. Just for your protection. You can still come and go as you please. If you need anything specific, call Tony."

Norma had turned back to the window, her fingers once more swirling in the air as the music continued to fill the apartment with its frenetic chaos. Jack stood, silently willing her to break through her hatefulness and say something, anything that would tell him that there was still a chance, that there was still something to be salvaged, that she still loved him.

Without turning from the window, Norma snarked, "And Tony will be the one to tell me when they find you in a ditch somewhere?"

The last vestiges of hope that Jack had been clinging to fell away with a tangible lurch. He let out a soft, shuddering breath and reached for the door. As he pulled it open, Norma said, "I hope they don't make a mess of your face. Would be a shame, after all."

Jack paused, stuck in the heavy silence that stretched between them. He closed his eyes and walked out of the apartment, shutting the door gently behind him.

On the platform, Jack jostled violently as a man shoved past him to climb the steps into the waiting train car. Jack recovered, the heat of anger rising in his neck. His fingers twitched, itching to grab the man by the collar, pull him back to the platform, and drive his fist into the guy's soft belly. Before he could, though, the man reached the top step and pushed his way down the aisle. A blast of warm smoke flowed up from beneath the train, stinging Jack's nose.

On the platform, he noticed a trio of men wearing dark pants and white cotton shirts watching him. All three had dark gambler hats cocked back on their heads. They stood in the shade of an overhang near the ticket window and spoke softly to each other as they watched the flow of people on the platform. Something about their body language didn't sit well with Jack and he tensed. The weight of his .45 under his left arm was reassuring. *Christ, I've only just arrived here.*

"Carmelo?" A voice pushed its way into the moment and despite his instincts telling him not to take his eyes off the three men, Jack turned. A blond-haired man with deeply creased skin dark from the sun stepped close, a warm smile on his face. He wore a blue cotton shirt underneath sun-bleached light blue overalls and heavy black boots. A wide-brimmed straw hat sat on his head, throwing a shadow across his face. The man fished out a crumpled pack of Lucky Strikes from a chest pocket, shook it, and pulled one of the white sticks out.

"Yeah," Jack answered.

The man offered a bent cigarette. "Smoke?"

"Who are you?" Jack's hand crept to his holstered gun.

The man smiled, his blue eyes almost black beneath the craggy shelves of his eyebrows. When he smiled, the leathery skin on his face wrinkled like a piece of paper being wadded up. He pushed his hat back on his head. "Randall Trask. Mr. Cleary said you'd be arriving today, although I expected you a couple hours ago. Told me to come get you, take you out to his place."

"There was a delay getting out of St. Louis," Jack said. Trask nodded, and Jack noted that his eyes had found the trio of men.

"Happens. You got bags?" Jack hefted the one suitcase he held. "All right. Come on. Let's get out of here before you attract any more attention. Truck's out this way."

Jack followed the man through the stifling air of the station and out to a gravel parking lot where a battered, red Model T Roadster sat baking in the oppressive heat. "Who were they?"

Trask took Jack's suitcase, his rough calloused fingers brushing over Jack's during the exchange, and tossed it in the wood slat bed before moving to the front of the truck and working the hand crank to start the engine. Once it was purring, he climbed behind the wheel. Randall Trask wasn't a large man, but the truck's chassis shook and groaned in protest as he settled behind the wheel.

"Members of the local Klan chapter and not folks you want to trifle with if you can avoid it." Seeing Jack's face, Trask patted the black cushioned seat. "Ain't as fancy as some of the things you probably ride around in up there in Chicago, but it'll get us where we're going and it won't leave your ass bruised."

Jack settled on the hard leather seat and adjusted himself in a vain attempt to find a comfortable position. With the door closed, his leg was less than an inch from Trask's. The heat intensified inside the truck and his shirt stuck to his back with every movement.

As if reading his mind, Trask said, "It'll get a little cooler once we get going. I can drop the top if you'd like. That'd give us some wind, but the trade-off is we'd be in direct sun most of the way."

"I don't mind the sun. How far is it to Cleary's office?"

Trask regarded Jack with a bemused expression. "Office? We're going to his home. It's about twenty miles away. We should be there in an hour or so."

"I thought ..."

Trask laughed, a rattling sound that blended with the rough cough of the engine, as he stepped out of the cab and lowered the collapsible roof. "You thought that someone in Cleary's business had an office building in downtown Birmingham?" When the top was secured, he slid behind the wheel and put the truck in gear. The vehicle lurched forward and Trask fought with the steering wheel as he directed them onto the street. "I don't know how they do things in Chicago, never been outside of this state in my whole life, but down here, people who don't want trouble with the law tend not to advertise that they're doing bad things."

"You know who I am?" Jack asked, putting an edge to his voice. This hillbilly was starting to act like he was the bigger of the fish in this truck.

Trask simply nodded and continued to drive, taking them beyond the city limits. Although the air that rushed over them was still warm, the flow of it provided some cooling relief to the heat of the day. The road's rough pavement eventually gave way to compacted dirt that wound through alternating patches of woods and farmlands, bringing with it the thick, green smells of trees and hay. Jack watched cattle milling about or huddled beneath a single tree in a pitiful vie for respite from the heat. Finally, Trask said, "Yes, Mr. Carmelo, I know who you are. I know what you do for a living and I know why you're down here."

"Why am I here?"

Trask refused to look over at his passenger. Instead, the man stared straight ahead, his head rocking and rolling gently with the motion of the truck. "Well," he started as the fingers of his left hand once again dipped into his chest pocket and produced a cigarette. He placed it between his lips and passed the pack over to Jack, who accepted. "I figure you're down here because we ain't producing as much as you fellas would like. So I guess your bosses told you to come down here and see what was going on, what the holdup was. Probably told you to bust a few heads if you had to. Maybe use that hand cannon you got under your arm." Jack stiffened at the mention of the weapon but realized that, of course, the man assumed he was armed. Men in this business would be.

Jack watched the dark shape of a bird angle away, heading for a copse of trees in a field. "And what about the man who was here before me? Morelli? Nobody's heard from him in a while."

Trask's eyes slid over to Jack for a quick moment, then returned to the road. He shook his head. "I'm not going to be much help there. I met the guy once, when he first came to talk to Elmer. Mr. Cleary, that is. He made the first deal, and other than a few small conversations, I hardly ever saw him."

"He didn't come back to Chicago," Jack said.

"No. What I mean is, he started spending his time with the crews, watching them work. I have other responsibilities, so our paths didn't cross often. One day I hear that he'd gone missing." Trask hesitated, his lips pressed tightly together. "They said he wandered into the woods."

"Just 'wandered into the woods'?"

"We sent people out looking for him but . . ." he trailed off with a sad shake of his head. "I'm sorry, but that's all I know."

Jack sucked on the cigarette and watched the skinny blond man. Trask's body was tight, his knuckles white from the way he gripped the knobby wheel. The man wasn't saying everything he knew. That made sense, Jack reasoned. Maybe Trask figured Jack would shoot him if he said the wrong thing. He decided to let it go for the moment. "You care to save me some time and tell me why you haven't been producing what was agreed to?"

For several long moments, the man driving the truck didn't answer. His face was pallid, as if the blood had seeped out of it. *Christ, he looks terrified*, Jack thought.

"No, sir, I don't."

"Don't or won't?" Jack asked.

Trask shrugged, keeping his attention on the road. "Wouldn't matter much either way," he replied softly.

Jack let the conversation die and focused on the passing land-scape. It all looked the same: rolling hills and forests, the occasional farmhouse or barn, wide fields full of livestock or crops that, other than the tall green stalks of corn, he couldn't identify.

Twenty minutes later, they passed a small wooden sign sprouting from the roadside weeds. Carved and painted lettering on the white slab of wood proclaimed:

Welcome to Jericho Springs
Est. 1728

Neat rows of buildings lined a series of sun-hardened dirt streets. A few vehicles, mostly trucks, crawled along the avenues, engines chugging throatily. Men dressed in farmers' overalls and women in long, flower-patterned dresses walked along the raised plank sidewalks.

"Bigger than I thought," Jack said. He almost made a joke about the dirt streets—Chicagoans had been walking and driving on paved roads for quite a while—but held his tongue.

Trask gave a gruff chuckle. "We do all right." Lifting one hand from the wheel, he pointed. "Just over forty-two hundred people. Got a Methodist church down there. And over there"—he shifted his arm to point across his body—"is the First Baptist that Pastor Sam McCauley runs." He turned a toothy grin to Jack. "Heck, we even got a laundromat. We're small compared to some, but downtown runs a few blocks. There's a couple blocks of houses just outside the main downtown blocks, but most live a little farther out. Farthest are the farms like the ones we just passed. Livestock, soybeans, corn, few cotton fields, couple orchards. Apple and peach, mostly."

The trip through town took only a few minutes. As they passed through the main thoroughfare—a road aptly named Heart Avenue —a building off to the right, just before thick trees regained control of the landscape, caught Jack's eye. It was a single-story brick building and with the glare of the sun on the glass, Jack couldn't make out what the business actually was. But what held his attention were two long ropes of black vines that snaked their way out of the grass behind the building and up a part of its rear wall.

"What's that?" he asked. Trask didn't answer; he instead jerked the wheel violently, causing the whole truck to shake and lurch. Jack's shoulder bumped painfully into the metal of the frame.

"Sorry. Bad patch on the road. You were saying?"

"I was asking about the vines growing on the building back there."

Once more, a shadow passed over Trask's face. "There's a blight right now. It's affecting some crops and killing some patches of woods." He pressed the gas a bit more and the truck lunged forward, speeding down the road that cut through the forest. Jack studied the shadowy terrain but couldn't make out any signs of blight.

Not that I know what blight looks like.

The forest opened up once more to expansive farmland, all of which looked the same as what they'd seen earlier. Jack had a fleeting moment of concern that at some point Trask had circled around and was taking him the way they'd come. But after a couple of minutes, the skinny man braked gently and turned down a narrow dirt path, its opening practically hidden between two clumps of thick grass.

"Here we are," Trask said, sleepily humming the announcement. Brush and thick grass hissed and scraped along both sides of the truck. Jack saw nothing beyond the tall vegetation and trees. Just as he opened his mouth to question Trask's proclamation, the thick greenery ended and the truck was cruising past open fields.

Beyond several neat rows of trees to the right of the dirt road and past a massive oak enclosed by a sagging, broken picket fence, its splintered boards like shattered teeth, stood Elmer Cleary's house. It was an old, large, two-story structure with a porch that wrapped around the left side, where chairs allowed a view of a dirt field.

Two other Model Ts sat parked in front of the porch. A man stood to the right of the stairs, working to attach a slab of plywood over the gap-toothed frame of a busted window. He glanced over his shoulder as Trask's truck entered the open space of the property. Letting the plywood slide to the ground, the man climbed the steps and disappeared into the house.

"What happened there?" Jack asked, looking at the empty socket of the window.

Trask sighed. "Deer tried to come in. Busted the glass."

"You're kidding."

"Must have been sick or something," Trask said. The words had the stiff, awkward edges that indicated a lie but before Jack could press him about it, Trask pointed at the neat rows of trees to the right. "Peach trees. Still a bit early, though. Another month or two and they'll be ready." Jack eyed the bent and rough angles of the branches as they passed. Several had black patches of what, from this distance, looked like mold growing along them. Many of the leaves were black and sagging as if overburdened by their very existence. The ground between many of the trees was muddy, almost swampy. Strangely, the nearby oak seemed devoid of the blight. It cast a wide pond of shadows across three small stone markers spaced evenly apart on one side of the tree.

Elmer Cleary's farmhouse loomed at the end of the dirt road, its white wooden siding flaking like sunburned skin despite the large shade trees that loomed over it. Green shutters, a few askew with paint nearly faded to white, framed the grime-covered windows that gazed out onto the pitiful land like tired, cataract-clouded eyes. The porch steps were worn soft in the middle, flanked by a railing bowed in places. Near the front door, a clutter of rusting buckets, empty feed sacks, and forgotten tools sat in a haphazard pile, as if Cleary had started a chore and never finished.

The land around the house was worse off. Once-fertile fields stretched out in dead, brittle patches, the soil gray and cracked. The massive hardwoods shading the house bore the first signs of sickness —leaves curled at the edges, bark peeling in places to expose dark, weeping wounds.

Several large patches of grass near the forest edge were blackened and slick in the sunlight. A few long tendrils of dark vines, like the ones Jack had seen in town, extended from the thick leaves of the undergrowth. They lay in the open like fat snakes.

The yard was a wreck. Where the lawn had once been, sunken

pits of stagnant dark water festered, their surfaces broken by the occasional sluggish ripple. A rank, swampy odor clung to the air, thick and sour.

"The fuck is that smell?" Jack asked, pressing the back of his hand to his mouth.

"You'll get used to it," Trask answered, turning his attention to the dirt field. "He plants corn out there. Lost that crop, though. Fucking blight," Trask said. "Behind the house are a few more fields, beans, lettuce, things like that."

Jack swallowed thickly against the smell that was pushing its way into his throat. "He supplies his own grains for the whiskey?"

"Nah. Elmer has his own way of doing things. He contracts with some of the other families around here and pays them well for their product and their discretion. Although . . ." he stopped, shaking his head in disgust.

"Although what?"

"He'll tell you. Come on, I'll introduce you." Jack stepped out of the truck, placing his feet carefully to avoid the foul, spongy patches of earth. Out of the confines of the cab, the smell intensified, exacerbated by the heat and thick humidity.

Movement inside the house, dark shapes shifting slowly through an equally dark screen door, caught Jack's eye. The door pushed open with a squeak of rusted hinges and Elmer Cleary stepped onto the porch. The moonshiner walked with a slow, shuffling gait, bent forward ever so slightly at the waist. His head held a wild mass of dark hair going to snow, and a thick patch of snowy beard covered most of his lower jaw. Seams and lines in his sun-cooked face were evidence of a man who'd spent most of his life, if not all of it, working the earth.

"Mr. Cleary," Trask started as he walked around the front of the truck, "I brought that fella from Chicago like you asked. Jack Carmelo."

Cleary stepped to the edge of the porch and observed the men in his yard with deep-set eyes. There was a hardness in them that Jack recognized and immediately respected. The old farmer raised a hand whose thick fingers Jack thought were showing just the earliest hints of arthritis, and waved them to follow.

Jack entered the house as the worker returned to the plywood and the busted window. The front room was tastefully decorated, if somewhat sparse. A single table with a lamp on it and a couple of chairs, the fabric of one starting to show some fraying at the seams. A painting of Jesus hung on a wall, surrounded by smaller, round frames displaying images of what Jack assumed were family members. Next to the chairs were several stacks of newspapers, magazines, and books. Jack glanced at them, surprised that Cleary and most of the people down here could read. The room held the soft, velvety smell of pipe smoke.

Wordlessly, Cleary crossed the room and entered a hallway lined with doors. The old farmer turned right at a junction halfway down and Jack found himself in yet another corridor, this one seemingly longer. They passed an opening that gave a view of a stairwell leading up, then they were in what had at one time been a formal dining room. The decor was still there: a large table surrounded by chairs, another piece of furniture that held old dust-coated dishes sat against one wall, decorative dinner plates and more religious pictures on the other walls. Atop the dining table lay several pieces of machinery in various states of repair, along with the tools needed to continue the work.

Just beyond the dining room was a kitchen where several large pots sat on top of a black potbelly stove. The air in the room had a sweet, bready hint that made Jack's stomach rumble again. A smaller dining table was positioned in the center of the room, its surface marked and scarred from years of regular use. Jack noted two doorways out of this room other than the one from which he had entered. One led to a utility room, the other to yet another screen door through which he could see a smaller porch and the fields beyond. More trees in the yard provided deep pockets of shade, and from the branches of one hung an old tire tied to a thick cord of rope. Cleary settled into a chair and motioned for the others to do the same.

"Something to drink?" he asked in a deep, leathery voice.

"Coffee would be nice," Jack answered as he pulled out a wooden chair. Trask moved to the stove and began making coffee. For a moment nobody spoke, then Cleary broke the silence.

"So. What is an upstanding young Italian," he pronounced it eye-talian, "from Chicago doing all the way down here in Jericho Springs?"

7

"I think you know why I'm here," Jack said. He kept his eyes fixed on the older man while Trask placed a cup of coffee on the table in front of him. Jack sipped it, wincing not only at the extreme heat but the acrid taste. *Jesus wept. These yokels can't even make a decent cup of Joe.* He sipped again, missing the quality of the coffee at Valois, and placed the cup back on the table. He crossed his legs and leaned back in his chair.

Cleary made a noise that could have been an acknowledgement or disgust. "I suppose your boss sent you down here to, what, take over my operation?"

Jack smiled. *The old man wants to dance around it a bit.* "My boss has no interest in taking over the operations that you have established. Let's be honest, I wouldn't know the first thing about making liquor down here. Ingredients, still operations, competition—"

Cleary grunted a laugh at that.

"—and the Prohis. Not to mention what your man there said on the drive over"—Jack noticed a slight stiffening of Cleary's eyes—"about the Klan being a pain in your side." The eyes softened, and Jack continued. "Now, I could figure it all out, of that there is no doubt. What I lack in local knowledge *at the moment*, I might add, I make up for in resources."

"You mean money," Trask said from where he leaned against a counter.

"Among other raw materials."

Cleary picked up a spoon and stirred his coffee despite not having added anything to the sludge. "You think a sudden influx of Italians and Chicago dollars down here in Jericho Springs would go unnoticed by the local authorities? As well as our"—he waved a hand vaguely—"competition?"

"I'm sure it wouldn't. Which is why I have no desire to take over the operations. However, my employer—"

"Capone," Cleary interrupted. "I know who you work for, Mr. Carmelo."

"You made an agreement with him, with his organization, to produce a certain amount of product per month. Thirty-five thousand gallons, to be exact. But, due to circumstances beyond our control back in Chicago, our supplies of Canadian whiskey have been impacted and will be reduced for a time. As such, we need to maintain a level of supply to meet the demands of Chicago and customers beyond. At the same time, although the original agreement was for thirty-five thousand gallons, so far we've only received just over twenty-three thousand the first month and only twenty thousand last month."

"You want me to increase my production."

"I want to find out why you haven't been meeting our agreed numbers. But yes, we need you to increase to fifty thousand gallons a month. We are prepared to pay you fifty-five cents a gallon in compensation. I understand this is going to be taxing to your current production and feel the price is more than fair."

Cleary stared at Jack. The silence stretched out between them. Finally, the old man asked, "Do you know how many stills I have?" Jack shook his head. "I have seventy-five spread out over a fifty-mile area in and around town. I employ just shy of a hundred men who operate those sites and transport the product. My whiskey is distributed from Atlanta to Louisville to Jackson. And, for the last two months, Chicago. With that number of stills, we can produce between thirty and forty thousand a month. That is with every still working at full capacity. But we only run at night, and I won't change that."

"Why only at night?"

"Smoke," Cleary said. "To run a still you have to burn a fire, and for quite a long time. Smoke's not visible at night. During the day, the Klan, even the occasional revenue man, can see the column out in the woods and just walk right up on the site."

"There's the other problem too." Trask cut in but was silenced by a sharp look from the older boss.

"What problem?" Jack asked as he took a sip of coffee.

Cleary kept his angry gaze on Trask before shaking his head and letting out a long, resigned breath.

"Someone's been attacking my stills. Over the last three weeks, I've lost twelve men. The stills were left untouched but the men . . ." He shook his head and sat back. "The ones we've found . . . it's bad."

Jack frowned. "The ones you found? What happened to the others?" When nobody answered, he continued. "Did this happen to Morelli? Was he at one of these stills that was attacked?"

Cleary's bearded jaw rippled as the man mulled over the question. Finally, he wagged his head, neither an affirmation nor a declination. "He was at one of the stills, yes. Your guy liked being on-site, watching the crews work. He was interested in the process, and although he wouldn't admit it, I think he liked being out in the woods. The forest calls to some people. Brings them a sense of peace. Morelli was working one of the sites when it was attacked. Now,"—he held up one large hand—"before you start firing a ton of questions, let me be clear. This is all I know. There was a single survivor. Man named Landry. Poor bastard was almost incoherent when we found him wandering along the shoulder of Pawnee Road. Covered in blood. He's lucky we found him before the law did. He told me that all he remembered was that they heard voices in the trees. Your guy Morelli went out by himself."

Jack leaned forward, rested his elbows on the table. "So, what, Morelli heard something and went out to handle it?"

Cleary shook his head. "No. Landry said that Morelli wandered off alone. Left his gun propped against a stump and just walked into the trees. They thought he was going to relieve himself. That was ten minutes before the attack."

"So where's Morelli now?"

Cleary sighed. "We don't know. After we found Landry, we sent a search party out. Never could find him, though."

Jack frowned. "How did this guy, Landry, escape? What else did he say about the attack?"

"He ran," Trask said. "Said he watched two of the other men die and that was all it took. He bolted."

"Did he say who attacked them? A rival gang? The Klan? Prohis? Surely with your resources you can track whoever it was down and take them out. Pay them off if it was the law. Come on, you're the biggest operation in the area, right?"

Cleary nodded. "We are. But what was done to the men running these sites . . ." he trailed off, staring into his coffee. "I ain't ever seen nothing like it." The large man took in a sharp breath and let it out just as quickly, breaking the moment he'd lost himself in. "But yeah, there are other . . ."—he searched for the word—"organizations, if you want to call them that. Small families or gangs that run their own sites either out in the woods or in their homes. They cause us problems from time to time, sure. They'll raid one of my stills, take the product, rough up my men. Couple of times they stole the entire still, and let me tell you, that ain't always easy to do. But no, this isn't that."

"How many attacks have there been?" Jack asked.

"There were two before Landry's. There's been four since."

Possibilities tumbled through Jack's mind. Who the hell would be attacking the stills and only killing the men? Something clicked and he looked at Trask. "Back at the train station, those men. You said they were Klan. I'm assuming you employ negros?"

"We do," started Trask, "but—"

"The Klan has been causing us problems for a while, that's true,"

Cleary interjected. "Ever since Volstead, the Anti-Saloon League and the Women's Temperance have used the Klan as a sort of police force. They haven't given up on their dislike of coloreds or anyone, really, that isn't white. They've simply added to their agenda. Until now, it wasn't a problem. The local Klan boys are bad cases, sure, but mostly disorganized, lazy, and stupid. But a few weeks back, they brought over a new guy from Atlanta to run the local group. Guy named Henry Dunn. Evil son of a bitch. Since then he's been running raids on stills, intercepting shipments, and threatening the people who supply the grains."

"How bad can this guy be?" Jack asked.

Trask answered, "A couple weeks back, Dunn caught a farmhand selling corn to one of our guys. Strung him up, cut him open, and left him hanging there as a warning. Boy was just sixteen. His daddy found him the next morning, still breathing. Didn't last long after that."

"As a result," Cleary added, "I'm not running in the day, and we've had to push deeper into the woods. Much deeper than we've ever had to. Plus, I've had to increase my payments to the ones who supply us and whose property we use for storage before shipment. All of that adds up to the reduction in supply that your boss is interested in."

"Tell me about the men you've lost. You said it was bad, and that some of them weren't found."

Cleary leaned back, the wooden chair creaking. "When I say that there were some men we didn't find, I mean just that. I have no idea where they went and nobody on my crew does either. I've had men run off before, sure. It's rare, but it's happened a time or two. But not like this. It's like they just vanished. The ones we did find weren't just killed by a knife or gun or even an accidental fire, which can happen. They were ..." he trailed off, shaking his head again. The skin around his eyes crinkled as he winced at the memory.

"They were mutilated." Trask finished. "Torn open."

"A wild animal—" Jack started.

But Trask cut him off, "No. Not like this. Some were up in the trees, their bodies completely broken like they'd fallen out of the sky.

Some had symbols cut into them. There were more symbols carved into the trees around the site or painted on the bark in blood. We found more symbols on the ground . . ."—he took a shuddering breath—"made out of their guts."

"What do you think did it?" Jack asked.

"Some of the men say demons," Cleary said. "Others are claiming witches."

Jack smiled, incredulous. "Witches?"

"What I know is that what I seen done to those men ain't natural. I think even an evil bastard like Henry Dunn has his limits, although only God knows what those are. There's been blights affecting crops in the area, which is another reason why you boys ain't been getting your full allotment each month. And it's not just my stills that have been affected. There's been talk around town of some people going missing over the last couple of weeks. Something is happening here, Mr. Carmelo. I don't know what it is. But it's bad."

Jack risked a sip of his coffee, his jaw clenching against the awful taste. He'd certainly seen plenty of mutilated bodies in his life. He thought briefly of the men just yesterday in that small basement, and in another dirty room in another part of Chicago, the boys last December.

Some men were capable of horrible things in the pursuit of what they wanted. It wasn't too far a stretch to think that the new ASL heavy was stringing bootleggers up, cutting them apart, carving symbols into their bodies. Especially considering what he was willing to do to a sixteen-year-old farmhand just for selling corn. It would be an effective tactic to try and scare the locals from running their sites. Probably more effective than just throwing them in jail, he had to admit. He didn't know what to make of the blight or other missing people, however. *Could be coincidence, could be this Dunn guy is poisoning farms and disappearing anyone who gets in his way.*

He'd deal with that later, he decided. Folklore and superstitions and the prospect of a lunatic Prohi wannabe could be set aside for the moment. What was important right now was getting production on track to the initially agreed-on levels and finding Carlo Morelli. They could worry about removing the threats and upping numbers to the new levels after that.

"I want to look at one of your current operations." He glanced at his watch. "It's still several hours before sundown, but would you have men at a site now, preparing things?"

Cleary shook his head. "Gave them a few nights off. After the last attack and what happened to that boy, they needed a break. I figured since you were coming down, I'd wait to see how you were going to handle things before starting back up."

Jack took in a sharp, irritated breath. "How many gallons do you have ready to send north right now?"

Trask answered, "I think we have about twenty-two thousand right now. But it's too late to organize crews to get them moving. Sun's going down in a little while and most of the guys will be with their families or tying one on in one of the few speaks we have around here."

"Tomorrow, then," Jack said. "And what about the survivor of the attack on Morelli? Can I see him tonight?"

Cleary's sleepy eyes fixed on Jack. "I suspect you're probably pretty tired from your trip. I think it's better for Randall here to drive you back into town, get you set up at the Holloway House. It's a boarding house near Mack's diner. You'll be comfortable there and we'll arrange for you to have a truck to get around in."

"I'd rather talk to Landry tonight."

"I think that's something better left to when the sun is high in the sky," Cleary drawled.

"You want to explain to me why that is?"

"Whatever George Landry saw that night messed him up something fierce. If you go out there tonight, he's not going to ask who you are. He's not going to invite you in for a cup of coffee and a chin wag. He's going to shoot you. If any of my guys are with you, he'll shoot them too. So no, Mr. Carmelo, I think you're going to want to wait until the sun is up and George Landry can see who's calling on him."

Jack bit back the rush of insults that filled his mouth. *You just got here. You don't know how these people work yet.* "Fine," he said. "I'll expect Trask or someone to come get me first thing."

Cleary chuckled, a deep sonorous rumbling, and sat back in his chair. "I'll be happy to have someone come fetch you, but it won't be until right after noon."

"Are you serious?" Jack blurted. "You expect me to sit around, waiting and wasting half the day? The hell for?"

"I don't know about you people up in Chicago, but down here, we go to church on Sundays. I go to Providence Methodist. Randall here is a First Church of Christ man, though I still don't know why." He gave Trask a sly smile. "But as soon as services end, I'll have someone come get you. We'll get you to Landry and later in the afternoon, out to one of the sites. Show you around, let you talk to some of the men there. How's that sound?"

It sounded like shit, Jack thought but didn't say. Although it shouldn't matter whether Cleary liked him or not, Jack liked the old farmer and found himself not wanting to burn any bridges right out of the gate. There was a lot of work to do and he'd need all the cooperation and goodwill he could gather.

Jack went to bed with the day's frustration clinging to him like sweat. As the night wore on, it shifted into a crawling, buzzing itch that prevented him from sinking into a deeper level of sleep. Jack's mind bobbed near the surface of wakefulness, awash with shifting visions of Cleary, rotting trees, Norma's mocking smile, Patrick McCarthy's severed head, and a dark figure that watched him with savage patience, eyes shining from the shadows between trees.

Jack awoke with a sharp breath and the image of long, bony fingers reaching for him quickly receding like a snake into tall grass. He held his breath for several moments, his eyes trained on the angle of a shadow along the ceiling. Slowly he let the air out of his lungs and his racing heartbeat calmed. He twisted on the thin mattress, bunching the pillow into a tight ball beneath his head. Finding some modicum of comfort in the new position, he closed his eyes and took several breaths in an effort to quiet his mind. A nagging feeling crawled its way across the nape of his neck, slithered between his shoulders. Jack, keeping his body completely still, opened his eyes.

Someone was in the room with him. He stared at the dark bulge of a head and shoulders, unmoving but unmistakably human, silhouetted between the dresser and the hall door. Beyond the single window, clouds over the moon threw most of the small bedroom into shadows. Jack's hand twitched with the need to grasp his pistol before he remembered leaving his shoulder rig hanging from the back of the chair. Taking his eyes from the motionless figure, Jack found his weapon. It was at least five feet away. Returning to the man—he was positive it was a man—he calculated the odds of climbing out of bed and reaching it before the intruder either crossed the room or fired his own weapon.

How in the hell did he get in? Jack had locked the door, remembered doing it. When he'd first checked into the room, he also recalled noting that the door's hinges needed a good oiling. Any attempt to enter would have been announced by the grating squeal.

Why hadn't the guy already attacked? The distance wasn't a factor and Jack was clearly at a disadvantage lying on his side in bed, unarmed. Not to mention the fact that the man had probably been there for some time. So why hadn't he attacked yet?

"You just gonna stand there all night?" Jack asked.

The figure didn't move. No answer floated across the room from the dark corner.

With the groan of springs, Jack sat up and swung his feet to the floor, the blanket puddled in his lap. A prickling, crawling sensation worked its way across his skin as he watched the figure. Outside, the clouds drifted clear of the moon and pale light flooded the room.

Carlo Morelli stood by the door, his dark eyes locked on Jack. In the moonlight, they were black pits in the round white of his face. Jack stiffened as recognition took hold of him. "What the hell are you doing here?" he asked. "Where have you been?" Relief flooded into him and he breathed a thankful sigh.

Morelli stepped forward, his footsteps like wet slaps. Jack glanced down. The man was barefoot. His fat, wide feet like slabs of turkey as they connected with the dirty floor. Each step left a slick of blood smeared across the wood. "Jesus, man, are you hurt?" Jack asked.

Morelli stopped halfway to the bed and stood, swaying slightly as he continued to stare at Jack. Something beneath the man's shirt moved; the fabric rolling, the buttons straining as whatever it was passed beneath. More undulations followed and Jack had the insane thought that several snakes were crawling across Carlo Morelli's rotund torso.

"The hell's wrong with you?" he demanded and stood up.

Carlo opened his mouth to answer, and Jack's legs threatened to give out beneath him when Morelli's jaw unhinged but kept going, yawning to an impossible angle. In the gaping hole, the Italian's teeth reflected light like small white stones in a field. His tongue lolled, fat and red. It jerked, and the man's throat shifted with a quiet gagging, gulping noise.

"Morelli?"

Something filled Carlo's mouth, emerging from the back of his throat, pushing up from deep within. It covered the man's teeth and obscured his tongue. The thing hesitated and for a moment, Jack thought Morelli had gotten himself under control, but then it rushed forward, spilling past his lips and dangling in the air.

It was a blackened, twisted vine. The rotting stench of it washed out of Morelli's guts and filled the room, sending Jack staggering back against the bed. His knees gave out and he sat down hard as the vine writhed slowly, a searching nightmare appendage. The gagging noises continued as Morelli's throat swelled and wrinkled as more vines forced their way out. His cheeks split with the sound of a wet cloth tearing and the new vines, their surfaces coated in a strange translucent moisture, extended into the air like tentacles.

The buttons on Morelli's shirt popped and scattered across the floor with a dry clicking that brought images of bones being tossed onto a table to Jack's mind. The shirt flapped open, revealing Morelli's fish-belly-white stomach. Red mouths opened across the flesh, the skin ripping as more of the putrescent vines forced their way free.

A scream clawed its way up Jack's throat as Morelli's feet slapped on the floor, bringing the large man closer. The vines wriggled eagerly, flinging droplets of the clear ooze to splatter on the floor, the bed, the ceiling. With each step that brought Morelli closer, more of his skin tore open, birthing innumerable tendrils of the reaching rot. The room swam around Jack as the stench of decay intensified.

The first tentacle-like vine touched him, its tip brushing across his collarbone. Jack winced, twisting away, his skin burning from the contact. His scream burst out of him like a caged animal finally freed. It exploded into the room and when he opened his eyes, he was alone. Jack, his chest heaving, gripped the mattress and scanned the room. There was no sign of Carlo Morelli. The floor was devoid of the bloody, smeared footprints, the furniture and ceiling held no traces of the foul-smelling sap from the vines.

Jack jolted up and propelled himself across the room. He ripped the .45 from its holster and staggered to the spot by the door where Morelli had first been. He pushed the barrel of the gun into all the corners of the room, then pulled the door open and glared into the hall.

"Morelli?" Jack didn't bother keeping his voice low.

Only silence answered.

8

Henry Dunn sat in the cramped cab of the Ford Model T, his eyes fixed on the pale sliver of road illuminated by the half-moon, and massaged his aching leg. Despite the late hour, the air was still warm and sweat tickled its way down his back and chest. The hard angle of the pistol tucked in the waistband at the back of his pants pressed into his flesh, uncomfortable yet reassuring. A warm breeze drifted in and across the cab, pushing the stink of sweat and body odor out into the surrounding landscape. In the tall weeds alongside the road, grasshoppers and other small insects bounced and fluttered.

Henry's skin buzzed with the need for a smoke and more than once, his hand drifted from the hard metal of the steering wheel, fingers reaching for the pipe he kept in his pocket. Each time, he caught himself and forced his hand back to the wheel. The truck would be coming along any moment now and it wouldn't do to have the driver notice the flicker of a match as they crested the small rise.

They better be coming, he thought. He'd hate to have to pay Ronnie Durham a visit. *No,* he corrected, *Ronnie would hate to have* me *pay him a visit if it turns out the tip he passed along from the ASL was bogus.* But so far the Anti-Saloon League folks hadn't been wrong very often, which was good.

Uncomfortably close to him, Clayton George sat nervously chewing on a long stalk of grass he'd had since they loaded up to drive out here. Henry wasn't a skinny man and his bulk added to the tightness of the space. He didn't look over, but could feel Clayton's eyes as they twitched between him and the road. The other man's body odor filled the small cab, a miasma of sweat, sour milk, and dirt. Dunn wrinkled his nose at the cloying stink.

"Out with it," Dunn said.

Next to him, Clayton startled as if he'd been poked with something sharp. "Huh? What?"

Henry spat out the window onto the grass and said, "You been sittin' there twitching like a damned cat in a room full of rocking chairs. You got something on your mind, spit it out."

Clayton cleared his throat and adjusted in the seat, his hip brushing against Henry's. At the contact, a shudder of irritation rippled through him and he fought down the urge to drive his elbow into his passenger's ribs. "It's, uh, just that, I was wondering . . ."

Dunn stared at Clayton's shadow-striped face. Under the intensity of the larger man's glare, Clayton kept his own eyes on the road. The man's Adam's apple bobbed up and down, up and down as he worked up his courage.

"You was wondering what?" But Dunn had a good feeling what the scrawny dirt-streaked man next to him was going to ask.

"I heard that kid didn't die right away. That true?"

Dunn thought about the boy, his legs kicking as his blood streamed from half a dozen deep cuts along his bare chest and sides, hands clawing at the rope around his neck. The swollen eyes. Cheeks beet red. "He died," Dunn said. "That's what matters in the end. That and the message it sent."

Clayton let out a low, slow whistle. "You're a hard man, you know that? Kid was sixteen. You think he really knew what he was doing? What he was involved in, just selling corn?"

Dunn studied the dark strip of road beyond the windshield. "He knew. Sixteen's old enough to know when you're involved in illegal activities." Dunn watched Clayton's pinched features as he absorbed the answer. *Guy looks like a fucking rat*, he thought. "Bootleggers and degenerates deserve swift and violent repercussions," he added.

Clayton chewed on that. "Ronnie said you was tough on them back in Atlanta. That's why he asked for you special-like."

Henry returned his attention to the road. A small shape, a mouse he thought, ran out from the weeds on one side, hesitated for a second before darting the rest of the way. His thick lips twitched in a faint smile as he thought about the last still he'd busted before receiving the request to come to Jericho Springs. He remembered the warmth of blood on his knuckles as the skin of the man's face split open. The screams of pain, the cries for mercy when Henry had picked up a log from a pile and slammed it against upraised arms and knees, shattering the bones.

"I've done what needed to be done," he said. "I've met resistance with what was necessary. I do what I need to in order to send the message that bootlegging won't be tolerated, that liquor is what is keeping white men feebleminded and unable to take care of themselves or their families. It makes them no better than the niggers. We can't be having that, can we?" He glanced at Clayton, whose teeth glowed in the light of the moon.

"No, sir. We can't."

Henry redirected his hand that had once more begun to creep toward the pipe in his pocket. A soft *thump* came from the bed of the truck where Gaylen and Joe Wallace sat waiting. The brothers seemed a little off, reckless in their eagerness to prove themselves to him—Gaylen especially. But Henry supposed you couldn't expect too much from a small backwoods town like this. When he'd been approached by William Adkins and that moonfaced mole of a WCTU woman, Florence Blankenship, the ASL representative had given Henry the impression that the entire county was overrun with corruption, the innocent citizens drowning in illegal booze. They'd both beseeched Henry to come help organize the local Klan members and lead the fight to enforce the Volstead Act. Local law enforcement, they'd said, was either woefully incompetent or on the payroll of the bootleggers. As such, it was up to the Klan to save the God-fearing white people from the evils of whiskey, gin, and beer.

Henry had been in town for three weeks and while he didn't find the streets to be under three feet of liquor, he did learn quickly that the rest of their pitch had been accurate. Ronnie Durham, the head of the county Klan chapter, confirmed the ineffectiveness of law enforcement, going on to say that even federal Prohis rarely came this far out. They preferred the larger cities and the pussy that tended to congregate in more substantial towns, he'd learned.

The deep grumble of a truck engine rose above the droning of crickets. A moment later, the horizon beyond the slight elevation in the road brightened as headlights approached.

A slow smile widened across Dunn's face. *Of course they'd be running with their headlights on. Dumb bastards had no idea what they were about to run into.* He slipped out of the truck, took a deep breath of blessedly clean air, and walked with a gentle limp—*Damn this leg and the Hun artillery!*—into the middle of the road and waited for the bootleggers to arrive. Clayton and the Wallace brothers gathered behind him as the night sky continued to grow brighter. Gaylen giggled in anticipation and his brother whispered for him to shut up.

Henry gave the men a sharp wave. "Get to the sides of the road. Wait until I've stopped them." The brothers scurried to the left side of the road, stepping into the thick brush while Clayton hurried off to the right, his baseball bat clutched nervously.

Henry raised one hand to shield his eyes as the Model T rumbled into sight. The road around him lit up in the twin beams of the head-lights as the truck slowed, brakes squealing. He couldn't see them but could imagine the driver and passenger exchanging nervous, confused looks. The truck stopped a few feet shy of where he stood and Henry quickly stepped to one side and out of the direct beam of the headlamps. He gave the dark shadows of the men in the cab a warm smile and a half wave.

"Either of you fellas got any gas to spare?" He gestured a hand irritably at his truck. "This bastard give out on me and I've been sittin' here half the damn night hoping someone would come by." The back of the bootleggers' truck was filled with boxes, their angled edges creasing the tarp that covered them. Behind the wheel, the driver mumbled something to his partner, then looked at Dunn through his open window.

"We don't—"

Henry pulled the pistol from his waistband and shot the driver. The bullet punched into his face just above his mouth and to the left of his nose. The man's head snapped back, a splash of blood and brains slopping across the passenger's stunned face. Before the second bootlegger had a chance to blink in surprise, Henry put a round through his right eye.

"Holy shit! What did you do that for?" Joe Wallace asked as they stepped onto the road. Henry ignored the question and pulled the tarp back, revealing the wooden crates. Each held eight bottles with hay stuffed around them as insulation. He picked one up, wrenched the cork out of the neck, and sniffed. The tang of whiskey tickled his nose and he smiled in satisfaction.

"Break them all," he told Clayton, who stood staring at the gore in the cabin. The boy didn't respond so Henry pushed the bottle at him, breaking his focus. Clayton took it automatically, his eyes drifting away to settle on Henry, who pointed to the bed of the truck. "Break them all. Drain the booze but leave everything else in place."

"What about them?" Gaylen asked, nodding at the dead men.

"Once you've busted all those bottles and let that shit drain into the dirt, we're leaving. We'll leave this truck and those sons of bitches here as a warning." He looked back at Clayton. "That's how you clean up a town, boy."

Henry moved back to his truck and leaned against the tires. He pulled his pipe out, loaded it, and puffed happily, sending plumes of smoke into the humid night air as he watched the other three men break bottle after bottle, spilling the whiskey onto the dirt.

9

George Landry lived in a small, three-room shack that, to Jack, looked like it had been hit with at least two tornadoes. His first thought as Trask steered the truck along the rutted and uneven dirt path that served as a driveway was that if the home had been a person, the only humane thing to do would be to put a bullet in their head and end their suffering.

The house was made of ancient slats of wood long since turned gray from time and weather. In several places along the exterior, gaps between the boards gave a peek into the home. There was no porch, only a grassless dirt patch surrounding the walls of the structure that served as a yard. A short, ringed wall of stones stood off to one side of the yard, a bucket tied to a wooden rail over its opening. A few feet from the well lay a misshapen brown and white lump covered in flies. An old door, its paint streaked and peeling, stood partially open. The roof sagged like a moth-eaten blanket on an ancient bed frame. Dirty windows, covered by mismatched scraps of cloth affixed to the glass from the inside, blocked any potential view into or out of the house.

"He lives here?" Jack asked, unable to hide his disgust.

Trask opened the door and climbed out of the cab. "With his son, yeah. Wife and daughter died a few years back."

"The hell is that?" Jack asked, looking pointedly at the fly-covered mass.

Trask glanced at it, his eyes lingering for a moment. "Deer," he said, then moved to knock on the door.

As Jack followed Trask, he noticed a tree on one side of the house, the ground around it a wide shadow. A moment later, he realized that it wasn't shade thrown by the tree but rather a patch of blackened soil. Trails of dark matter ran up the base of the tree. Parts of the trunk glistened wetly beneath twisting limbs that held blackened leaves. Jack started to ask Trask about it when the sound of the other man knocking on the ancient door interrupted him.

"George!" Trask called. "Randall Trask. Don't shoot! I'm just here to check on you." A muffled voice answered. Trask indicated for Jack to follow and opened the door.

The inside of the home was worse than the outside. Old, moldy furniture—nothing more than a torn sofa and a dining table with two chairs—sat covered by piles of garbage. Stacks of newspapers, wads of dirty clothing, empty flower pots, and various tools all filled every conceivable space. The floor was uneven, the planks soft and yielding as Jack and Trask stepped into the room. The entire place was coated in a smell somewhere between weeks-old body odor and spoiled food. Jack's eyes watered as the stench assaulted him.

The shadowy form of a rail-thin man moved through a doorway to the right. He stepped closer, crossing a window through which only the faintest light passed around the piles of refuse. In the muddy illumination, Jack noticed a skeleton of a man wearing only a dingy pair of overalls. One arm crossed over his stomach, dirty fingers scratching absentmindedly at the opposite forearm where a dirty, stained bandage was wrapped.

"You doin' all right, George?" Trask asked. The skeleton man didn't answer, only stood in the ochre light, his gaunt face covered in days-old scruff. A white film of spittle had settled at the corners of his dry, cracked lips, which moved rhythmically as the man mumbled softly to himself. In the dirty light, they looked to Jack like slugs that had been doused with salt. His eyes seemed unfocused but at the same time, Jack could tell that George Landry was aware of them.

Trask indicated Jack with a wave. "This is Jack Carmelo. Come down from Chicago to help with the operation. He wanted to talk to you about what you saw that night." The mumbling continued, a slurry of words that Jack couldn't make sense of.

"He ain't gonna talk to you," a younger voice said. A boy no older than fifteen entered the room. He was just as dirty as Landry and wore a pair of overalls with one of the straps hanging, his thin tan chest and shoulder exposed. He had a shock of straw-colored hair that fell in untamed waves about his head.

"You his son?" Jack asked. Instead of answering, the kid spat a wad of phlegm onto a pile of cordwood stacked along the wall near the fireplace.

Jack glanced and nodded at George's bandage. "What happened to his arm?"

"Come home like that," the boy replied. "Can't seem to get it to scab over."

Jack stepped closer to Landry. The older man didn't seem to notice, just continued mumbling and staring off into space. Carefully, Jack reached out and peeled the bandage away. George twitched at the touch but otherwise allowed it. The wound was grotesque. A gouge in the flesh about four inches wide and deep enough that Jack was surprised he didn't see bone peering through. "He needs a doctor." He started to say more when the skin around the edges of the wound fluttered. Jack peered closer, but pulled back sharply when the outline of something small and slender writhed beneath the man's parchment skin. The dermis pulsed, bulging and shifting as the thing continued to move, pushing itself deeper into his arm. Jack took another half step back.

The old man stared at Jack. His eyes were clear and focused. In a voice as thin and papery as his skin, he said, "They's still out there. I hear 'em, whispering. Gettin' closer all the time."

"Who?" Jack asked. "The Klan? Prohis?"

"The trees was whisperin'. It . . . they were telling us . . . fillin' our heads with . . ." Landry's head jerked to the cloth-covered window as if he'd heard something. His mouth gaped, giving Jack a clear view of a gumline struggling to hold on to the last few decaying teeth. "They whispered to Eddie. And then, then he started bleedin'. Nose, eyes, ears. He was, he was laughin'. Laughin' like . . . like it tickled. Till it didn't."

"What about Morelli?" Jack asked. "Did they whisper to him too?"

At the mention of the missing Italian, Landry jerked back, staggering until he connected with the wall with a *thump*. He shook his head.

Jack took a step closer. "What do you mean no? You said they were whispering. Who are they? Did you get a look at them?"

The man's eyes lost focus again and he returned to staring at some faraway point. "He went into the woods," he said. "He wasn't laughing. Not like Eddie."

"Did he say anything? Before he went into the woods, did he say anything?" Jack reached out and gripped the man's shoulder, giving it a rough shake. His patience was wearing thin. If the old prick didn't start making sense soon, Jack was going to end up smacking him, like a broad who's gone hysterical.

"The trees were whisperin' . . ." Landry repeated. "They're"—he blinked, a sluggish movement—"ancient. Christ, they're older than the mountains." His gaze turned once more to Jack, crawled over his face. "They're hungry," he said, the words barely audible.

Something popped outside. To Jack it sounded like a limb snapping. Landry's body went rigid. His head whipped around and he stared slack-jawed at the window. The older man's chin trembled and he stepped back, stumbling deeper into the shadows of the doorway. As his features fell into darkness, his head twitched from side to side.

"Get out!" Landry shouted. The command blasted through the quiet of the shack like a rifle shot. "Get out before they hear you! They's out there!" A gnarled finger pointed at the window. "They's out there and they's comin'! Gonna kill us all! Turn us inside out like they did Eddie!"

"George," Trask started, but the dark form of Landry moved, the man reaching for something behind the door. Jack's hand went instinctively to the .45 beneath his left arm. The pistol cleared the holster as Landry pulled a shotgun up and pointed it at the two men.

"They killed everyone! Your friend too!" Landry said with terrifying urgency. He pointed the shotgun at Jack. "Whispered to him and made him go off into the woods. He's dead. Just like all the others. Burst Eddie like a tomato. I heard the two niggers screaming, and I ran. I heard men scream before, but not like that. I ran. And you need to run too. Now get the fuck off my land before they hear me talkin'!"

Jack started to say more but the metallic *click* of the shotgun hammer pulling back stopped him. He patted the air with one hand. "All right, just lower that cannon. We're going." The shotgun didn't waver. Slowly, Trask and Jack backed out of the shack and into the bright midday sun. He didn't return his pistol to its holster until they were in the truck and quickly backing away.

Neither man spoke until they were on the main road. Trask fished a cigarette from a crumpled pack and after lighting his, passed the pack to Jack. "Did you get what you thought you would?" Jack noted the underlying mocking tone.

"Son of a bitch is full of prunes," Jack responded and blew bluish smoke out the window. "Trees whispering. Did he say that stuff when you guys found him?"

"Some, yeah. Mostly he just screamed and cried." He squinted through the smoky truck cab at Jack. "You don't think he's telling the truth?"

"Not at all." Jack thought about what Landry had said. "My money's still on this Dunn guy and his Klan friends. Based on what you said about that farmhand, it's clear that he will do almost anything to disrupt operations. No,"—he shook his head— "I'm thinking Landry back there experienced a pretty bad attack, saw his buddies die, and snapped." He paused, cigarette perched on the edge of his lips. "The wound was strange, though."

"He couldn't remember how he got it," Trask said.

Jack shrugged. "A branch probably stabbed him as he lammed it."

The image of something squirming beneath the skin around the wound lingered in his mind. "No," he said with a resigned sigh, "I'd bet a case of cigars that it was Dunn who killed your men."

Trask silently steered the truck through back roads for several long minutes, his brow furrowed in thought. "What about Morelli?" he asked finally.

"What about him?"

"Landry said he went into the woods right before the others were attacked."

"So? He must have heard Dunn and the others coming up on the site and went out to investigate."

"Then why did he leave his gun behind?"

The question caught Jack off guard for a moment. "Landry told you that, didn't he? I don't think we should—"

"We found it," Trask interrupted. "Morelli's gun. The Thompson. He left it in the dirt next to a stump." Trask shook his head. "He didn't take it with him into the woods."

Jack didn't respond. He mulled over the revelation as Trask continued to steer the truck along narrow, rutted, and weed-choked paths. Just when Jack started to think that his spine couldn't take any more jostling, Trask pulled onto a rough, grassy patch of ground barely as wide as the truck. Trees and brush with thick limbs from which sprouted thorns the size of Jack's fingernails reached to within a few scant inches of his door.

To Jack, the place the moonshiner had chosen to park looked no different than most of the landscape of the last ten miles they'd traveled. But Trask seemed to know where he was going as he stomped into the tree line. Jack followed, stepping roughly through the thick grass alongside the road before entering the thicker undergrowth of the woods.

As they walked, Trask hummed a tune Jack didn't recognize. The man's voice floated above them, not wavering whenever he stepped over a fallen log or had to leap over a wide creek bed. For Jack, every step was like a full round in the ring with a shifty opponent. The heat pressed in on him, soaking his shirt. His suit coat clung to him like a heavy woolen blanket, pulling at the elbows and shoulders as more of his body became drenched in sweat. Branches, weeds, and brambles grasped at him like eager lovers desperate to hold him close. He couldn't see anything beyond the few trees on either side of them and after only a couple of minutes, lost sight of the truck completely.

The woods surrounding them were dark and infinite. They were not, to Jack's increasing stress, silent. Birdsong filled the air and unseen things scurried through the boughs overhead, occasionally sending pinecones or small pieces of loose bark showering down. The first time a pinecone landed nearby, crashing its way through the branches to land with a *thud* somewhere to his right, Jack whirled around, pistol in hand. His finger tightened on the trigger as he scanned the shadows between trees, expecting to see the hulking form of a bear or wildcat bearing down on him.

After the fourth, he stopped returning the pistol to its holster and just carried it by his side.

Trask cleared another creek bed, this one long dried up, and glanced back. "You good?" Jack started to fire a sarcastic remark when his attention was drawn to the ground. The land around and in the creek bed was a black, spongy quagmire. All the surrounding vegetation had turned dark, and the leaves oozed with a clear substance. The trees along the bank suffered the same level of rotting growth, their branches and trunks also seeping the strange liquid.

"Yeah," Trask said, noticing what had caught Jack's attention. "That's the blight. It's patchy in some areas, but it's spreading pretty quickly. Don't worry, the still doesn't have any around it." He waved a hand for Jack to follow.

When they stopped, Jack was panting as if he'd just run ten miles. His sweat-soaked clothes were torn in two places. His shoes, once nice, were now caked with dirt and scuffed beyond repair.

"This is one of the ones that's closest to town," Trask said.

I'd hate to see one that was farthest, Jack thought bitterly, and swatted at a bug crawling on his arm. He peered into the trees. Despite the sun shining through the boughs, shadows stretched and covered large swaths of the landscape. It took Jack a full minute of searching before he spotted a man sitting on a small boulder about forty yards away. He sat completely still, his ebony skin blending almost perfectly with the shadows that fell across him. The Black man smiled, brilliant white teeth in the murkiness. A second later, Jack was able to pick out the long shape of a shotgun resting on the guard's lap.

A limb snapped and with it, reality broke free from the frozen moment and Jack was able to make out the soft mumble of voices, the softer rattling of equipment, and deeper, the thumping of an axe. As his eyes adjusted, he realized that there was a small clearing beyond the trees immediately in front of him.

Trask dipped two fingers into the breast pocket of his overalls and fished out his crumpled pack of cigarettes. He offered one to Jack, then lit both with a silver flip top lighter. Jack exhaled and followed Trask to the still.

The clearing wasn't large, maybe fifteen feet square. The brush and weeds had long since been pulverized by human traffic until only dirt, dead leaves, and small sticks remained. But it was what stood in the center of the clearing that commanded Jack's attention.

The still was much larger than he'd expected, certainly larger than what the Genna brothers were selling back in Chicago. A massive copper pot sat atop a chimney made of stones. On the left side of that, at ground level, was an opening through which the undulating orange light of a fire glowed. The pot that sat on the chimney was fat at the bottom but narrowed to a thinner column before ending in a skinny copper pipe that sprouted like a malformed arm. This stretched across several feet of ground before dipping down into a large wooden barrel. Another copper arm rose from the barrel and, like its sibling, ran for several more feet before ending in the largest barrel Jack had ever seen. Around the site, several men moved like busy ants, each focused on his task.

"Ever seen one of these?" Trask asked. Jack shook his head. "Pretty simple, really. After we've cooked the mash—that's what we call it after we've mixed the grains and corn with water—we put all of that into a container and let it ferment. After a couple of weeks, we bring it to one of these and pour the liquid in that big bugger there." He pointed to the copper pot on the chimney. "Then we light the fire and let it cook until the liquid turns into vapor, which goes along that first pipe into the smaller barrel. That's what we call a thumper. The spirit runs through that and basically gets distilled a second time. Bumps up the alcohol content. Next it goes along that second pipe into the fat barrel. That's a cooling barrel. There's water in it and that copper pipe winds around and around inside it. The vapor cools and turns back into liquid, and on the other side, we have a guy who mans the output valve collecting that liquid. From there it's stored in barrels, bottled, and sent on."

Jack pointed at the still. "Didn't you say something about trouble getting grains?"

"Yeah. We're still able to get some but most of the farms around here, especially on this end of town, are getting hit with the damned blight. Between that and Dunn and his guys harassing the farmers, we're burning through the supply we had built up."

Jack scanned the woods. "And you're certain that we're deep enough that the law can't find us? Or the Klan?" *Or witches and ghosts and ghouls,* he started to add, but the memory of Landry saying the trees had been whispering muted the response. Standing here looking into the depths of the forest around them, Jack thought he could almost believe what the old shell-shocked man had said.

Almost.

Trask ground his cigarette beneath his boot. "Only four cops in town, including the chief. They're overwhelmed and underequipped to handle this. Dunn and his fellas are giving them more than enough to deal with."

"You'd think that they'd be looking the other way, considering the Klan's basically doing their job for them," Jack said, watching a man add a log to the opening in the chimney of the still.

"If they were just rounding people up and citizens arresting them, sure," Trask said. "But what they're doing . . ." He shook his head. "Anyway, we ain't gotta worry about them."

Jack approached another large barrel and lifted the lid. It was over half-full of small white and yellow kernels of corn. He reached in, grabbed a handful, and let it stream through his fingers. "What about this blight? Any chance the mayor, or whoever, is doing something about it?"

Trask spat in the dirt and drifted closer. "They don't have a damned clue. Cleary told me that he heard they were talking about asking the state for help; somebody to come and evaluate the land or some such. But who knows when, or even if, that'll happen. I don't know about Illinois, but the state of Alabama moves slower than ice in winter."

"So they're doing nothing else?" Jack asked as he put the lid back on the barrel.

Trask chuckled darkly. "They cancelled the festival that was coming up. Town's anniversary. I guess they figured having a celebration in the middle of a blight when people's livelihoods were rotting away wasn't such a great idea."

"Yeah, but they left the fucking fireworks," a man said bitterly from nearby. Jack turned and saw a short, stocky man with a pronounced chin and slicked-back brown hair ambling closer. His lip bulged with a wad of chewing tobacco and he spat off to one side. "Left them in that warehouse downtown. Ain't got a fucking clue as to what to do with them. Waste of money, you ask me." He grunted a sarcastic laugh. "Fucking idiots stored them down the damned street from Oscar Tanner's place."

"What's that?" Jack asked.

The man spat another wad of tobacco juice and wiped his mouth with the back of one wrist. "Kerosene and oil storage warehouse. Y'all got those up north, Mister Yankee Man?" The question came out mockingly, as if to suggest that anywhere outside of Jericho Springs was too fancy to have a central repository for kerosene and oil supplies.

"We have a couple, yeah," Jack said. He started to ask another question but a crashing in the brush beyond the clearing brought him and the others around. Jack pulled his pistol without thinking and noticed from the corner of his eye that two others had picked up rifles and were watching the woods carefully. The sound continued, a violent thrashing of something moving through the undergrowth. The stocky man with the wad of tobacco spat again and sniffed. "Just a deer."

Jack thought of the deer corpse back at Landry's, and the one at Cleary's house that Trask claimed tried to jump through a window. "Something wrong with the wildlife around here? Does the blight affect animals?"

The other men exchanged a brief, concerned look. Chewing Tobacco grunted. "Some of them have gotten sick, yeah. We find them dead quite often, all torn up."

Jack followed the diminishing passage of the unseen creature. "Could an animal be responsible for what's happened to the stills? One that's gone mad from the blight?"

"Nah," said Trask. "There's no animal big enough to do those things."

"What about bears?" Jack asked. "There's bears down here, right?"

"There are, but it ain't them we gotta worry about," said another man—this one older and sporting a beard almost long enough to tuck into his belt—as he rounded the other side of the still. "Didn't mean to eavesdrop, but I'm telling you, even with that psycho Dunn running around town, it's not bears or infected deer we have to worry about."

"Who is it then?" Jack asked. "Some rogue Prohi?"

The man stared into the woods for a long moment before answering. "We just shouldn't be this far out, is all I'm saying. Shouldn't be as close to old Providence as we are." He shook his head. "It's not right. None of this. There's something *wrong* in the woods."

"Shouldn't be out running at night, neither," said Chewing Tobacco.

"According to your boss, the Klan has trouble finding you this deep out and at night. Seems like a good idea to me," Jack said.

"It ain't the Klan." The Black man from the rock approached slowly, almost reverently.

"What, then?" Jack asked. The Black man only gave him a sad

look before returning to his post. Jack regarded Longbeard and Chewing Tobacco. "You,"—he turned to Longbeard—"you said something about Providence? What's that?"

"The old ruins," the man said. He tilted his head toward the trees. "A ways out that way. Nobody goes out there. Not if they care about living. Or keeping their soul."

Jack turned to Trask. "He's talking about ghosts? Demons? Witches? That shit you mentioned back at the house?"

Trask stared off to one side. Finally, he sighed and tried on a smile. It didn't seem to fit, so he let it go. "Jericho Springs has been around a long time. Originally it was a town called Providence. Settled back in the sixteen hundreds. Before that, Indians lived on most of these lands. Who knows who lived here before them? But there's always been stories. Legends. Folklore. You know."

"Ain't no ghost story what got them fellas the other night," Chewing Tobacco interjected, a look of frustration on his scruffy and soot-stained face. "Ghosts don't tear men to pieces and carve Devil symbols in their skin." He started to say more, but spat a blast of brown juice onto the dirt.

"Who do you think did it?" asked Jack, stepping close. Part of him, he was shocked to realize, was genuinely curious about what the man thought. But the rest of him knew that whatever came out of his mouth was going to be nothing more than superstitious hillbilly shit.

Longbeard answered instead, shuffling forward as he spoke, "These woods have been haunted since my great-grandfather was a boy. Those ruins"—again the head jerked in the direction of the trees —"have been there for hundreds of years. Nobody knows what happened to the town, not really. But around here, you learn at a young age that you don't go exploring. There's been things seen out here. Will-o'-the-wisp, ghosts. Worse. I heard once that there was a wendigo lived out by the ruins."

"A wendi-what?" Jack asked. The question came out as an incredulous, barking laugh. "Jesus, you hillbillies believe anything, don't you?"

Chewing Tobacco eyed Jack, irritation at being mocked by a

stranger—one in a sodden and torn suit, at that—hardening his face. "Just who the fuck are you?" he asked as he licked excess spittle from his lips.

Before Jack could answer, Trask said, "This is Mr. Jack Carmelo from Chicago. He's here as Mr. Cleary's guest. He's also here to make sure we continue to produce without interference." As the word "Chicago" was uttered, the eyes of the man staring at Jack flinched.

"That's right. You know what that means, don't you?" Jack asked. The other man nodded. "Good. Now I'll ask you again. And this time, try to dispense with the fucking ghost stories and keep it to things that actually exist. Who do you think did that to those men? It was the Klan, right? This Dunn fella I've heard about?"

Chewing Tobacco hesitated. He shifted from foot to foot, then his eyes flicked over Jack's shoulder to the other men. "Stop acting like a goddamned schoolboy asked to recite a poem you didn't memorize and answer my question," Jack snapped.

"We don't know," the man said, lowering his eyes to the dirt. "But there's something out there, and we don't have a name for it. I think we made it mad when we started running deeper into the woods, closer to the ruins."

Jack laughed, unable to hide his disbelief. He walked in a small circle to dispel his rising frustration. When he returned to his original spot, none of the men around the still would meet his gaze. "Christ on a cracker, you people really think it was some ghost or something. That wendi-thing?"

"I heard it was cannibals," another man standing near the output valve offered. "They been living out here for generations. Nobody knows who they are or where they hail from. But they staked a claim to this land long before we came. And now that we're pushing out here to run, they ain't happy."

Jack swallowed, giving himself a minute to regain composure before laughing at the man. "Witches and cannibals?" The words started to break up at the end, Jack's laughing disbelief showing through.

"Ain't no joke, mister," Output Valve assured.

"Harry," Trask said, "that's enough."

"Whatever it is," Harry went on as he placed a jug beneath the copper pipe to collect the clear liquid that had started to drip out, "it's been calling men out into the woods. They just wander off and never come back. And the others . . ." He shrugged as if to say, "You know how that went."

Chewing Tobacco spoke up, "And there was the Gibbons family. What about them, huh? Harlan Gibbons and his wife and daughter killed? His boy gone missing? They weren't too far from—"

"That's enough!" Jack snapped. His voice echoed off the trees, and the other men around the still stopped what they were doing and stared dumbfoundedly at him. "I don't believe you fucking people, afraid of ghost stories. Are you kidding me? No fucking boogeyman came out of the trees and killed those people. Whatever happened to them was done by a man, most likely this Dunn guy. I'm going to deal with that. In the meantime, you people will operate these stills and will double your output. In the next couple of days, I will get the supply of grains back to the levels you need. Now get back to work." The men hesitated, stayed by their shock at the outburst. Jack bellowed, "Now!" The hold on the men evaporated and they all moved quickly to resume their tasks.

"Come on," Jack growled, and without waiting for Trask, stomped back into the woods.

10

Palmdale Road was a craggy dirt path that at the best of times was likely to turn an ankle or snap a wheel, and a thick swampland after the slightest rain. Over the last few weeks, the already treacherous road had deteriorated significantly. Pastor Sam McCauley found himself weaving his bicycle around wide patches of black, swampy earth only to have to whip the wheel sharply back to narrowly avoid a rut or jagged stone on the opposite side. The tall grass, blackberry bushes, and other weeds that lined either side of the country road were a mixture of greens slowly turning black as the rotting blight advanced from deeper in the forest. More than once, he passed over a tendril of the strange creeping vines that extended into the path like a searching finger. The bicycle's wheels jolting over the growths with a quick squish that sent the hairs on his neck prickling.

The rot was everywhere, it seemed, and getting worse with each new day. For the past three Sundays, his sermon had, at first, flirted with the concept of "the enemy at the gates" and quickly moved into messages of dealing with hardships. But as more and more reports came in of crops and livestock dying, as more and more people—children included, God help them all—went missing or were found mutilated, Sam was quickly coming to the limits of his capabilities to find words of comfort in the Scriptures.

Another vine passed under his tires with the sound of a wet cloth being wrung, and a shudder rippled through him. His shadow stretched before him as if racing him to his destination. The afternoon was slowly waning and while he was certainly looking forward to the potluck dinner with his congregants—Grace would be there, of that he was confident—he knew that there would come the inevitable questions as people looked to him for answers to their troubles.

A pit formed in his stomach as he guided the bicycle off the road and onto the fringes of Jonas Robertson's property. Near the house, a massive white structure with a wraparound porch and thick trunk hardwood trees dotting the yard, dozens of people milled about. Several tables were lined in the shade of the trees, mismatched tablecloths fluttering like trapped birds beneath the weight of the plates and serving platters placed atop them.

Sam slowed his bike to a stop. What would he tell them? What possible comfort could he give? Already he saw signs of the blight creeping across the property, moving inexorably toward the house. *Those beautiful trees*, he thought, eyeing their widespread branches. Soon they would be blackened, their wood oozing the foul liquid that seeped out of all the plants once they'd succumbed.

He dismounted and took a moment to pull a handkerchief out of his back pocket, using it to blot the sweat from his face. He returned the cloth and walked ahead, pushing the bicycle through the grass. Around the tables, several people flitted about like bees around flowers, bringing chairs or plates. Anna Robertson, her dark hair tied back and a white patterned dress hanging over her ample frame, turned in his direction, one hand shielding her eyes from the sun. Her lips broke into a wide smile and she raised her free hand, waving it overhead. He returned the gesture.

"Pastor McCauley!" a young sandy-haired boy called out and sprinted in Sam's direction. An even younger girl stumped behind him, her small legs moving in that awkward cadence of those who have recently learned to walk and were still working out the kinks. She watched the ground before her as she hustled and cried after the boy to wait for her.

Charlie Robertson reached Sam before the little girl could cover half the distance. "You made it!" the boy said. "I saved you a seat."

Sam smiled down at the six-year-old. "Thank you, Charles. Would you mind terribly finding a place to park my bicycle?" Charlie's eyes went wide, the boy taken aback by the honor. As he moved away, the little girl reached Sam. Her cheeks were rosy and her lips were pursed as she huffed and puffed from exertion. Sam leaned forward and scooped her up. "And how are you today, Miss Lizzie?"

Sam crossed the yard, smiling as the young girl babbled happily about her day and how she helped prepare all the food until she had to chase a frog out of the kitchen. Sam's mouth watered as he neared the long table and caught the first greasy smells of the meal.

Anna Robertson approached him, her arms reaching for Lizzie. "Come on, girl," she said in a gentle scolding. "Let Pastor McCauley get settled before you start crawling all over him. Go find your mama and have her wipe your nose." Lizzie stumped eagerly to her mother, wrapping her arms around the woman's neck as she continued to prattle on about the frog. Anna watched the girl go. "We're so glad you could make it, Pastor."

"I wouldn't have missed it for the world," Sam said. "Although perhaps I should consider getting one of those motor cars. At my age, riding a bicycle this far in the heat isn't a lot of fun. Maybe I'll see about getting one in a couple of years for my fiftieth birthday." He smiled at the long table. "This is quite an impressive spread."

Anna blinked at the platters on the long series of tables. "It is quite a feast," she agreed. "Of course, Martha Dell and Catherine Dodson helped quite a bit too." At the far end of the table, Sam saw one of the mentioned women, Martha, arranging plates and cutlery. "I didn't expect them to be able to," Anna went on, her voice pitched lower, "considering what they're dealing with at home." She shook her head sadly. "I don't know what Martha and Robert are going to do. They've lost so much already."

Sam could only mumble an agreement. What could he say? He'd not had a second to cool off after the bike ride out, and he could at least use a glass of lemonade before being asked to jump immediately into the role of consoler. A small part of him bristled, a brief rising of irritation there and gone again.

Around the yard, four children, all considerably older than Charles and Lizzie but not quite teenagers, arranged things on the table. A few others shuttled into and out of the house, bringing food or pitchers of golden colored sweet tea. The screen door to the porch slammed like a gunshot as they came and went. From inside the house came a sharp, reprimanding voice.

"Where's Grace?" he asked and inwardly winced, fearful that his question had come off a bit too zealous.

The expression of anticipation of a sermon of solace slipped off Anna's face and was replaced by a tired smile. She waved a hand toward the house. "Inside helping with the food. She's been making pies all morning. Why don't you go find Jonas and the other men? They're just around the other side of the house, sitting and talking. I'll let you know when we're ready to eat."

Jonas Robertson sat with Robert Dell and Thomas Dodson, along with the two eldest Dell boys, Eugene and Stan, in old weathered wooden chairs covered by a large patch of shade next to the house. The air around the men was thick with pipe and cigarette smoke. They spoke softly as they watched a group of three chickens scratch and peck aimlessly in the dirt a few feet away.

"Pastor," Jonas said, "have a seat." He snapped his fingers at Eugene. "Get up, boy, and let the pastor have your chair."

As the young man stood, Sam held out a hand in protest. "No, please, there's no need." Eugene stepped a few paces back, clearly indicating that he wouldn't be returning to the chair. Sam nodded a thanks and lowered himself onto the warm wood.

"Storm's coming," Robert Dell said, eyeing the clouds in the distance.

Jonas grunted. "It'll hold off for a while. I ain't smelling it too close just yet."

"You got a good sermon ready for us for Sunday?" Thomas Dodson asked around his pipe.

Sam sighed. *Here we go.* "I believe so."

Robert Dell spat onto the dirt over one shoulder. "I hope it's got some answers for everything been going on." His eyes were dark with frustration. *And fear,* Sam reminded himself. *He's terrified. As is everyone else.*

Jonas held up a wide, calloused hand. "Pastor here ain't the one responsible for the blight so don't go acting like he's going to have all the answers."

"Thank you," Sam said. Turning to Robert, he continued. "I have to admit, I've been thinking and praying on that for a long time and I don't understand any more than you do what has caused these troubles. But I do know that we'll find our way through them with prayer and perseverance. My talk on Sunday will highlight that." A tiny white lie, but one he felt would be overlooked. He'd not started to actually prepare his sermon yet, but did have some vague ideas of how to frame his message.

The group of men fell into silence. In the awkward moment, Sam watched the chickens scratch and peck at the dirt. He couldn't help but notice the parallel in their actions and his own attempts to bring peace to his congregation. In each sermon he was doing little more than scratching aimlessly in the dirt, trying to find even the smallest seed from which hope would sprout. In the end, however, the best he could come up with was more calls to prayer, to continue to beseech the Lord for guidance and mercy. What else could he do when his parishioners came to him talking of rotting crops, missing livestock, or disturbed sleep due to hearing voices whispering in the dark?

"Pastor McCauley?"

The voice sent a bolt of electricity through him. His skin tingled and his heartbeat increased. Grace Robertson's light brown hair hung around her shoulders, framing her features. She wore a yellow sundress with a clutch of small red flowers embroidered on the breast. The girl smiled, one hand flashing up to sweep a lock of hair behind one ear. She held out a glass bottle.

"Thought you might like a cold drink."

For a long, breathless moment, Sam's mouth was as dry as the Sahara. His tongue sat against his teeth like a piece of driftwood. He swallowed hard, aware of the thumping in his throat as his pulse raced. "How thoughtful," he managed to say, then took the cold, slick glass bottle. The dark, carbonated liquid inside scorched and soothed his throat. "Thank you," he said. Heat rose on the back of his neck and Sam resisted the urge to glance at the other men. He was certain they were watching the exchange carefully, and the last thing he wanted was to see their suspicious expressions. As Grace stepped back, Sam rose out of his chair. "Actually," he started, "I have something for you. A gift, to thank you for all the work you helped me with in the church garden."

The young girl's face wrinkled with confusion. "I don't need a gift, Pastor McCauley. I was happy to do it."

"Still," Sam said. He stood and walked toward the large oak tree where Grace's brother had leaned the bicycle. "It's right here in my satchel."

Sam's fingers fumbled with the buckle and strap. He was painfully aware of the girl's presence nearby and when he pulled the book from the pouch, he found her only a foot away, her hands clasped at her waist.

"A Bible?" Grace's eyes went wide at the present. "I couldn't possibly— This must have cost a fortune."

"It's a gift," he said again. "I know you don't have one of your own, and I hate to see you stretching your neck to look over your mother's shoulder during services. Please,"—he held the book out—"I want you to have it." Grace's eyes lingered on the Bible for a long second, then rose to meet his.

"Thank you." She took it from his hand and a tingling raced up his arm as her finger brushed the back of his own in the movement. Her cheeks blushed as she stood, holding it to her chest.

"It's not just a frivolous gift," he said. "I admit, there's a bit of a selfish nature behind it as well." Grace looked up at him sharply, confusion and surprise in her eyes. Sam chuckled. "When you turn sixteen, which I believe is in a couple of months, I plan to ask if you will help lead the Sunday school classes for the little ones. That"—he pointed at the Bible—"should help with the lessons."

Grace breathed a long sigh and grinned. "I would be happy to help Mrs. Golding."

"Oh no," Sam corrected. "You would be taking over from Mrs. Golding. I think it's about time she retired, don't you? Just last week I heard that she had confused Peter and Luke."

Grace giggled, the sound as musical as the early evening notes drifting from the grass as the crickets warmed up for their nightly concert. "That's so bad," she said.

"Not only that," Sam went on, aware that Grace's mother was drifting closer, "I heard she fell asleep in the middle of the story about the loaves and fishes." Grace laughed again, but the moment was cut short as Anna reached them.

"What's so funny?" she asked, placing a hand on Grace's back.

"Just a little anecdote about loaves and fishes," Sam answered.

"Look what Pastor McCauley gave me," Grace said to her mother, holding up the Bible. Anna's eyes went wide.

"Pastor," she said, "that's too much. A book like that must have cost you a month's wages."

Sam waved a hand dismissively. "I'm a pastor; I get a discount." He smiled and gave Grace a wink, happy when her cheeks flushed red. "I don't suppose you've come to tell us that it's time to eat?"

Anna gaped at the Bible in her daughter's hands for a moment longer. "I have, actually. Would you mind leading us in grace?"

"I'd be offended if you hadn't asked," Sam said. At the table, a woman lit several lanterns that hung from the thick branches of the sheltering tree. They cast a soft glow that in the early evening haze was inviting and comforting but would deepen to magical as the night darkened around them.

Moving to an empty chair next to Charles, the boy practically hopping with excitement over the prospect of sitting beside the pastor, Sam hesitated. The flickering light of the lanterns threw shifting shadows across the tables, their sphere of light extending a few feet beyond the seated guests. His eyes locked on a spot just behind the chair where Martha Dell sat, her face a sour mask as she talked to the ancient Eugenia Murphy. A single dark finger stretched into the light from the deeper mass of shadows. At first, Sam thought he was seeing one of the rotting vines creeping along the ground. But no, he corrected. He could see *through* it. It was a shadow. The shadow extended against the flicker of the light, pushing smoothly into the area of illumination. As it drew closer to the two women, its pace increased, as if it were a living thing emboldened by hunger. Sam blinked and when his eyes refocused, the shadow was gone. He searched the murky ground, watching the dark patches moving like disturbed water, but the strange finger of shadow didn't return.

The heat of the ride over must have really gotten to me.

Taking his seat, Charles's excited babbling buzzing like a distant fly, Sam glanced along the length of the table. Grace sat opposite him and down five seats, her hands in her lap and a pleasant smile on her beautiful face as she listened to her father. A gentle wind whispered through the tree, sending the lanterns into a lazy rocking. More shadows pulsed about the table and those gathered. Patches of gloom waved across Grace's face. Sam stared, transfixed by the curve of her chin and the rounded edge of her nose above her full lips.

As another shadow drifted over her, Grace turned to look directly at Sam. Preternatural eyes glowed from beneath the momentary veil of darkness. Cracked and bleeding lips peeled back, and a row of sharp, jagged teeth gleamed at him.

A snarling, screaming voice, something ancient and born from a place more horrifying than hell, smashed through Sam's mind. Growling words in a language older than the mountains ripped apart his thoughts and chewed at the ends of his sanity. Sam gasped and brought his hands to cover his ears just as the lanterns overhead lazed in a new direction, removing the mantle from Grace's features.

The girl continued to smile beatifically at her father. She answered a question that Sam couldn't hear, gesturing toward the fields in the distance as she spoke. Sam gaped. The cacophony in his mind was gone, leaving behind swirling eddies that made coherent thought difficult.

"Pastor, you gonna catch a fly if'n you don't close your mouth." Charlie Robertson laughed. The boy's high-pitched, humorous admonishment broke the spell, and Sam closed his mouth and let out a long breath. His racing heartbeat was already slowing, leaving a trembling feeling in his extremities.

He forced a smile. "That's a good idea." He glanced once more at Grace before forcing his attention to the others taking their seats along the table.

"I'm telling you," Robert Dell said as he pulled his chair out. "Just you watch. It won't be long and they'll be wanting to come to ours. Or build their own next to it."

"You've lost your mind," Thomas shot back. "Ain't no way. You think Mayor Huffman would actually let them build in the town proper? And as for attending our own church?" The grizzled man barked a laugh, then looked at Sam. "Would you tell this idiot that there's no way?"

Sam, puzzled, shook his head. "What's that?"

Thomas jabbed a finger at the other man. "He thinks that the way things are going in this country, pretty soon the niggers are going to be attending our church or wanting to build their own next door to ours." A hot wave passed over Sam as the faces of the others gathered turned in his direction.

"I . . ." His throat constricted, choking off words. Despite his own feelings about the negro race, Sam understood where he was and who he was speaking to. Who made up his congregation. He understood their opinions, as close-minded as they may be.

"Sam," Grace whispered. Her voice was close, her warm breath caressed his ear. Sam flinched, jerking his head in surprise. Grace remained in her chair, her attention on placing a napkin in her lap rather than on the conversation. The glowing eyes and sharp teeth that had gleamed through the shadow flickered through his mind and he swallowed a thick lump.

The adults nearby, and more than a few of the older children, regarded him curiously. Before Sam could fully brush off the moment of confusion, Anna Robertson stood and cleared her throat. "We're not going to have any discussions of race, politics, or anything of the like at this table. We're here to celebrate good friends and the blessings of family." Thomas seemed about to say something else, but clamped his teeth against the words and gave a sheepish nod. Anna smiled and looked at Sam. "Pastor?"

Sam clutched his hands into fists and released them, letting go of the last tendrils of tremors. When he was steady, he stood and launched into a prayer that despite the rumbling in his stomach lasted several minutes. When he was finished and the murmurs of "Amen" had faded, conversation rose like a humming wave punctuated only by the scraping of utensils.

A plate was passed to him, piled high with smoked ham, steaming greens, a single cob of corn slathered in butter, and black-eyed peas. A biscuit sat atop it all, runnels of butter oozing over the edges. Sam's stomach gave another grumble in anticipation and he happily began eating.

He had pushed three forkfuls into his mouth during the time his eyes had flicked half a dozen times to where Grace sat talking quietly with Helen, the middle daughter of another family who lived a couple of miles away, when, next to him, Charles made a sound. "What's wrong with the peas?" the boy asked, his voice thick with disgust.

Sam, still chewing a piece of ham and enjoying the sweet and salty flavors, looked at his own plate where only a few peas remained. He swallowed and asked, "What do you mean? They taste fine to me." He picked up the large biscuit and bit into it.

Charles's face screwed up and he pushed his plate away. "They're nasty."

Something writhed in Sam's mouth. A quivering squirming, pushing half-chewed biscuit against his tongue. In a panicked rush, Sam leaned forward and spat the food onto his plate. In the mashed, wet remains, a thin pink worm twitched, its body cleaved in half by the pastor's teeth. Black liquid seeped from its torn body and soaked into the masticated dough.

Good God.

As the thought crossed his consciousness, Sam's attention was drawn to the other end of his plate where the slices of ham lay stacked. The pink slabs twitched, bent, and relaxed as if trying to crawl. Blood welled between the fibers of the meat. Only a few tiny droplets at first, but soon thick rivulets poured over the fatty edges to form a growing puddle on the plate.

A few chairs down, Jonas Robertson stood quickly, sending his chair tumbling back. He slapped at his arms, his ribs, his stomach. With each blow, he gave a grunting cry of panic. "Some . . . something's in there! They're in my skin!" He stumbled back from the table, hands beating at his own flesh.

To Sam's right, more people cried out in horror and threw their utensils down or violently pushed their plates away before turning and spitting mouthfuls of food onto the ground. Chairs crashed to the ground, utensils rattled against the table, and more than one glass of tea was knocked over in the havoc. Sam sat, fork in one hand, bewildered as women clutched at their children or buried their faces against their husbands' chests. The men glared at the meal on the table with a mixture of fear and loathing. Sam forced his attention back to the platters of food, and as his mind scrambled to make sense of what he was seeing, he let the fork fall from his numb fingers.

All the food was rotten. Massive spots of mold covered whole cobs of corn, and the closest platter of carrots looked to be wearing a blanket of gray and black mottled fur. Writhing white maggots slithered in and around a bowl of peas. Another deep bowl containing collard greens oozed a black ichor that overflowed the edges of the bowl and ran in thick streams along its white ceramic surface to pool on the tablecloth.

People around the table backpedaled away, shouting curses and cries to God. Amid the chaos, Sam remained glued to his chair. Everywhere he looked, food decayed and oozed with a sickening putrefaction. Flies covered everything, crawling and vying for the juiciest pieces as they lay their eggs, only to have the milky white larvae spring forth seconds later to writhe in search of sustenance.

A face, distorted and fat, stared at him from a bowl of strawberries. The visage was off-kilter, with one eye higher and wider than the other. It leered at him with a crooked mouth from which seeped a thin sheet of blood. The fat, fleshy lips peeled back, revealing tiny, sharp teeth. More faces appeared in the bowls and platters around the strawberries. Each one a demonic mask of jeering malice.

William Bryant, his chin covered in a slick of grease, stared with wide, petrified eyes at his wife. Sam couldn't see Nadine's face; she sat with her back to him. But William's expression of horror and revulsion was clear. The young livestock farmer raised a hand and hesitated, fingertips trembling only inches from his wife's cheek. "What's wrong with you?" William breathed.

Sam stood. His entire body hummed with the need to see what William saw. He took a tremulous step in their direction when a screeching, animalistic cry brought him spinning around, Grace's name forming on his lips instinctively. There she stood, the Bible he'd given her held protectively against her breasts as she stared at some commotion across the table.

Others pressed back in confusion, jostling against one another, the wave colliding with Sam and nearly sending him tumbling over a toppled chair. He gripped the edge of the table to steady himself and pushed his way through the confusion to where a flurry of activity flashed near the ground.

Martha Dell lay there, her face bleeding from a series of parallel furrows torn across her forehead and cheeks. She slapped in a panicked defense at Eugenia Murphy who knelt atop her, dress bunched above her knees. Eugenia's hosiery was torn, fish-belly-white skin streaked with blue varicose veins peeking through the ripped fabric. The old woman's face was a snarling mask of hate. In her hand she clutched a table knife. Sam could see the smears of butter across its dull silver blade as she raised the instrument overhead.

She's going to stab Martha Dell with a butter knife. Sam's brain registered this lazily as the muscles in Eugenia's arms and shoulders tightened in preparation for the killing blow. Then Sam was leaping forward, throwing himself at Eugenia. He connected with the octogenarian, her body crumpling like a dead leaf under a boot, and sent her tumbling to the ground. The knife flew from her fingers and bounced against his own back. He landed, throwing one arm out to not only break his fall but to prevent the bulk of his weight from crushing the frail woman.

Instantly hands were on him, pulling him up, separating him from Eugenia. Sam allowed himself to be guided to his feet. Eugenia remained on the ground, eyes squeezed tight and gasping for breath. Her face was screwed up in a pinched expression of fear and regret. Sam bent and with the assistance of one of the older children, he helped Eugenia to sit.

Martha Dell slapped away the offered hands and stood, her hair hanging in limp clumps across her face. She watched the old woman sitting in the dirt with a hateful, confused glare. Her chest heaved and for a moment, Sam thought she was going to hurl herself, clawing and biting, at the old lady. Instead, she remained where she was until her husband approached her and took her by the shoulders. He turned her and together they walked stiffly to the house.

"I don't know what—" Eugenia said. She turned her scared face to Sam. "How did I get on top of her?" She glanced at the others gathered around, as if pleading for someone to explain what had just happened.

"You had a knife," Sam told her. Eugenia flinched as if the words had physically slammed into her.

She shook her head emphatically. "I've never hurt anyone in my life. I-I was sitting there eating and then . . . it was as if I was watching someone else." Tears spilled over her eyes and ran down her wrinkled cheeks. "Please, Pastor, you have to forgive me. Please. Something darkened my soul. I—" She broke down, giving way to sobs. Sam knelt in the dirt and did his best to console her until Anna Robertson and two other women approached, saying they would get Eugenia home and cleaned up.

Later that night, Sam sat on the screened porch of his small parsonage, rocking gently as he stared into his night-shrouded yard. His mind was a maelstrom of images, of memories of the rotting food and the screams of fear. Every time he closed his eyes, he saw the glinting white of the teeth within the shadow over Grace's beautiful face, the expression of pure, seething hatred in Eugenia's look as she raised the knife, or the appearance of stark horror in William Bryant's eyes when he asked his wife, *What's wrong with you?*

"What has been done to deserve this?" Sam asked. The words disintegrated in the night air, unanswered. All the way home he'd prayed, his words coming in sync with the pumping of his legs on the pedals, yet by the time he'd gotten to the church, he was no closer to a feeling of salvation. What more could he do? Why was God testing him and the good people of Jericho Springs? What was the path forward? If prayer wasn't working to reach God, what would?

Sam remained in that state of foggy confusion until well after the rain started to fall. When no answers came from the pulsing drumbeats of thunder, he went to bed as he had for days, with the hope that God would speak to him while he slept. He disrobed after mumbling his nightly prayers as he'd done since he was a child in Pinecrest, Mississippi. Despite his racing mind and the trembling fear that remained in his extremities, Sam McCauley drifted off to sleep.

By two thirty in the morning, he was fully immersed in a deep slumber. He didn't stir when a shadow detached itself from the wall beside his small bed. The shadow solidified, and the figure, its body all sharp and twisted angles, its eyes glowing silvery blue, crossed the wooden floor soundlessly and stood over Sam's unconscious form.

The figure leaned over and whispered. At first, Sam flinched, moaning and thrashing as the ancient, unknowable language squirmed into his mind, violating his deepest consciousness. But after a few moments he settled, his breath falling back into a slow, steady rhythm.

In the darkness of the bedroom, the figure continued to whisper.

Deep in his mind, Sam listened.

11

Jack dug in his pocket, his fingers brushing against the smooth ridges of the trolley coin before finding the money clip. He peeled off a dollar, left it on the table, and gave the morose waitress behind the counter a vague wave of thanks. She glanced up from the coffee mug she was cleaning, her heavy eyes fixing on him for just a moment before returning to her task. Leaving its thick, greasy smells behind, Jack stepped out of the diner and onto the sidewalk where the evening air was heavy with the wet, electric smell of an oncoming thunderstorm. The leaden sky was filled with dense, shifting clouds dark with rain. A quick gust of wind whipped his hair and he clamped his hat on, fitting it snugly.

He stood just outside the door to Mack's for a few moments, breathing in the smell of the storm and trying to shed the feelings of sadness that had plagued him during the meal. The food was wonderful, something called "chicken fried steak." The breaded meat had been smothered with a thick peppery gravy and served with mashed potatoes and green beans glistening with bacon grease. The only thing missing had been a beer or glass of wine, but the waitress with the dishwater-colored hair had told him in a soft, distracted tone that they upheld the eighteenth. She'd shaken her head dismissively when he'd produced a five, surreptitiously sliding it across the scarred wooden tabletop.

But despite the food and his repeated attempts to focus on Cleary, Trask, and the bootlegging operation, Jack's mind continued to bring up the last conversation with Norma. Her words, *Maybe you won't come back this time,* and *This is all that's left,* echoed like drumbeats in the darkness. The sentiment and the look in her eyes told him everything he'd been trying to deny for the last few months.

Norma was gone. He'd lost her long before the miscarriage; hell, he probably never truly had her. He knew she'd been using when they first met but had chosen to believe her lies: it was only just to take the edge off when performing or to help her get through long nights. He'd ignored the empty vials around their apartment and willfully overlooked the nights she came home with unfocused eyes and slurred speech.

Of course she blamed him for the miscarriage. And to an extent, he blamed himself. He knew her habit was getting worse but hadn't been able to do anything about it. Work for the Outfit had kept him out of the house more often than not.

He should have been there for her. It didn't matter that what he'd told her was the truth: he was only six blocks away when the miscarriage happened. He could have gotten help or been there for her, but he had been overseeing the card game and was none the wiser.

Because she hadn't sent for me. Because she was fucking high.

Jack let out a deep sigh. That was enough. He'd deal with the death of his marriage later. Right now he had more immediate things to contemplate and very little time to address them. He considered lighting a cigarette but the wind whipping along the streets made it clear that any attempts would be in vain. He shoved his hands into his pockets, chose a direction, and began walking.

Across from the diner, the low brick structure of the Holloway House stood sandwiched between Whitlock & Thread Tailors and Boone's Apothecary. Both businesses were closed, the space behind their windows dark. In fact, he noticed, all the stores along the street were completely buttoned up. He checked his watch: *6:37. What kind of place rolls up its sidewalks at fucking six thirty?* But, he reminded himself, it was Sunday. He remembered Cleary's insistence that nothing would be done that morning due to church services, and Jack assumed that businesses closed earlier than normal on Sundays, if they opened at all. Despite the dark windows in most of the shops along the street, there were a few people moving about, couples hurrying home before the rain arrived, and a gang of young boys no older than ten walking with baseball gloves and the cockiness of the very young.

Jack strolled, turning corners at random, getting a feel for the streets and the businesses. He pushed his thoughts to the immediate problems of the operation. On the drive back from the still, Trask had attempted to bring up the superstitious belief the men held but Jack hadn't allowed it. There was no room for that kind of shit in an operation like this. Especially since supply levels were not being met and there was a threat of a rogue Klan member killing bootleggers.

Jack glanced along the street before crossing. He turned left, moving back in the general direction from which he'd come, and thought about Elmer Cleary. There was a quiet gruffness to the old farmer that Jack liked. It was unlike the brazen outspokenness of Capone or others in the crew back in Chicago. Cleary ruled his operation firmly, that much was evident, yet he did it with what appeared to be a softer touch than Capone.

But I bet he's got one hell of a bite, push comes to shove, Jack thought. He considered once more the possibility of a rival gang killing the men. That would make a lot of sense despite Cleary saying confidently that it wasn't. But Jack assumed it would be pretty hard for someone like Cleary to admit he was getting the business from lower-level punks. Competition like that was something Jack himself was familiar with. He could operate within that arena with confidence. Even if it wasn't a rival operation but the Klan or even the Prohibition officers, that was still something Jack had familiarity with. Bribes or even outright threats to reduce the heat brought on by law enforcement weren't anything new for him.

But still, something niggled at the back of his thoughts. Rival gangs wouldn't have just killed the workers but would've either stolen or destroyed the actual stills. And the Klan or Prohis would absolutely have busted up the equipment. Yet in no reported attack had anyone touched the still.

Who would do that?

There's something out there, and we don't have a name for it. I think we made it mad when we started running deeper into the woods, closer to the ruins.

Jack's lips puffed in a quiet laugh at recalling those words. The level of superstition running through these men was insane. He understood it coming from women passing gossip during a sewing circle, or kids. He'd bet a whole month's salary that those boys who had been playing baseball had all sorts of stories about ghosts and witches and wendi-things stalking the ruins of the old town. But for grown men—men who were operating a highly sensitive and illegal operation, no less—to talk like that was laughable.

Jack's money was on that Dunn fellow and the Klan, supplied and backed by the ASL in Birmingham. It made sense. The Klan was trying to send a very clear message: stop bootlegging or die. Ambush attacks and the story of Dunn stringing up and gutting the young farmhand made sense in the context of the level of violence described in the wake of the attacks. Further, if the Klan wanted to really throw an extra level of fear into the men they were fighting against, carving symbols into the bodies and trees would do it. Everyone in town seemed to be religious, so it made sense that seeing a body torn apart and carved up with strange ciphers would elicit fears of the Devil or those who did his business.

He would have to pay them a visit soon. Let them know they were barking up the wrong tree. Jack decided he would try the carrot first rather than leading with the stick. Wave enough money in front of these hillbilly racists, more money than they'd make in a year, and surely they'd come around. Even a man with Dunn's tendencies would be enticed.

And if not, there was always the stick.

Another blast of wind rushed past him, throwing his suit jacket behind him like wings. Jack squinted against the ferocity of it and decided the time had come for a smoke. He ducked into the small alcove of a shop's front door and dug his cigarette case from his inner pocket. Leaning against the brick wall, he blew smoke and watched it whip away on the breeze. The storm was growing closer now, faint rumblings of thunder starting to come with increasing regularity.

As he smoked he thought about his immediate next steps. The first was to find a reliable supply of grain. On the drive back to town, Jack had asked Trask about local supply levels and outlying farms or neighboring towns. He had mentioned Elden Mills, a textile factory town several miles away that could be a possibility, and promised to look into it. If Elden Mills turned out to be the option, that would get them running at acceptable levels, assuming the shipments of grains weren't interrupted.

But still, the idea of the blight was worrying. Already he'd seen how the plants and trees in the woods were affected, and more than once he'd spotted blackened patches of road. What kind of blight affected a goddamned dirt road?

Jack put it out of his mind. He wasn't a plant doctor. He didn't know or care what was causing the blight. If Elden Mills turned out to be a viable option for grains, then the blight could eat everything in the county for all he cared. He flicked the butt onto the street, where it kicked up a flare of sparks before scuttling away on the wind.

Once Trask left for Elden Mills, Jack's primary focus would be on locating Morelli. He couldn't believe that Carlo, a forty-seven-year-old man who had survived a hell of a lot growing up in Sicily before making his name in the streets of Chicago, would have just wandered off into the woods at night. Hell, as far as Jack knew, Morelli had never been in the woods. Did they have woods in Sicily? While Jack's family was from Italy, he'd been born in Chicago and until just a few hours ago had never been in woods thicker than the trees in Lincoln Park.

Maybe he had heard something, Jack reasoned. That nutjob Landry had said he'd just wandered off. Of course, he'd also said the trees were whispering, so Jack had to take whatever else the man had said with a grain of salt the size of Tony Detti's ass. But Trask said that Carlo had left the Thompson behind. And Jack had no reason to believe that Trask was feeding him a line. So why the hell had Morelli left?

An answer occurred to him, but everything in him rebelled against it. What if Morelli was working with the Klan or had been pinched and turned by the Prohis? No. That wasn't possible. Jack had known Carlo Morelli all of his life and the man was loyal and on the level to a fault. The answers would be somewhere in those woods, and tomorrow, as soon as Jack had breakfast, he was going to take some guys and go find those answers.

He needed to call Capone and give him an update, letting him know an expected timeframe for the next shipment. He checked his watch. There was plenty of time to catch Al. He took a longer route back to the hotel, enjoying the feeling of the pre-storm air and thinking through scenarios of when he visited with the Klan members.

On the next block he found himself on a wider avenue and after a moment, recognized the main street, Heart Avenue. The buildings here were taller and he spied the Jericho Springs First Bank and Trust, an attorney's office whose name he couldn't make out, and a grocery store called Rangle's. Over the street, colored streamers attached to buildings sagged like thin, dead snakes. At the far end, where the lane dead-ended into a cross avenue, sat a large wooden stage. The platform and stairs were complete but the top portion— what Jack assumed was for some kind of enclosed canopy—had been abandoned, leaving the structure to look like the skeletal remains of some ancient creature. He turned in front of it, angling down a side street and a massive brick building with shuttered windows propped open. Large yellow block letters across the facade identified the building as a kerosene warehouse. Jack's nose wrinkled against the sharp, acrid smell of oil and kerosene as he passed.

He strolled past closed stores, dark behind their front windows. He could make out some things inside: tools, dresses, a bicycle. Most sported signs for the upcoming Summer Festival, which had been cancelled, he recalled. One window was filled with placards demonizing alcohol and reminding people to keep an eye out for bootleggers.

SHALL THE MOTHERS AND CHILDREN BE SACRIFICED TO THE FINANCIAL GREED OF LIQUOR TRAFFIC? one sign screamed. Another defined the drunkard as someone at risk for tuberculosis and venereal disease; his children at risk for insanity and rickets.

Christ save us from the WCTU, Jack groaned inwardly and continued on. Two doors down from the shop sporting the propaganda, a store's light winked out. Moments later, a woman backed out of the door, leaning forward to lock it. The tail of her dress fluttered in the wind like a trapped animal. She turned and drew up short with a gasp.

"Lord almighty, you scared me," the woman breathed, one hand drifting to her chest. "What's the big idea sneaking up on someone like that?"

"Sneaking up on you? You're the one who practically walked into me," Jack replied. "Here I was, minding my own business, taking in the evening air after a fine meal, and what happens? A dame like yourself comes barreling down the sidewalk and almost knocks me into the street. I could have been run over." He gestured to the empty road as if to indicate the flow of rush hour traffic.

The woman stepped closer and Jack's breath caught. Her dark hair was pulled back and pinned up under a fashionable hat. Her figure was evident beneath the dress that ended just below her knees. Shapely legs ran down to dark high-heeled shoes. The absolute fact of her beauty rocketed across his brain and slammed into his chest, sending his heart into a triple beat.

She smiled and the world lit up. "If you got run over after eating at Mack's," she said, "the car would be doing you a favor."

He frowned. "I don't know about that. Seems the meal was pretty good. The coffee, not so much."

She cocked her head slightly. "You're not from around here, are you?" The soft twang of her accent was intoxicating.

"No." He took off his hat and leaned forward in a slight bow. "Jack Carmelo. Chicago."

The woman blinked in mild surprise. "Well, Jack Carmelo Chicago, what dark forces sent you to our little neck of the woods?"

He looked around as if he were in the finest European city. "I've always heard that Jericho Springs is amazing this time of year. Had to come see it for myself."

She laughed, a light, tinkling sound that sent ripples of pleasure through him. "Well if that's the case, then I'm pretty sure you're going to be let down."

"How so?"

She wrinkled her nose in a playful gesture. "Tell you what . . . if you're able to walk tomorrow after eating at Mack's, maybe I will tell you."

"Maybe I will listen. That your business?" He gestured at the door from which she'd appeared.

"All mine. Florist. So if you need flowers . . ." Jack's mind drifted back to the last time he'd been in a florist. It had been just last year, when he and Frankie Yale and a couple others paid Dean O'Banion a visit.

"Well, if that food's so bad, maybe you can show me a better place," he said.

The woman smiled her brilliant smile again and stepped around him. "Maybe I can. See you around, Jack Carmelo Chicago."

He watched her move down the block, all curves and sultry swinging. Just before she turned the corner, he called out, "What's your name?"

She paused and glanced over one shoulder. "Evelyn Marrow. Call me Evie." She wiggled her fingers in a playful wave, then stepped around the corner and out of sight.

Jack stood rooted for several seconds hoping she would reappear, but when it became clear she had moved on, he pushed his hands into his pockets, touched the trolley token—*Good looking out, Bobby!*—and continued along the street. A gentle whistle rose to his lips as he moved.

He made his way back to his room just as the rumbling of thunder grew to angry smashing and the sky flickered with the strobe effects of lightning. The rain fell in a gushing torrent as he crawled into bed and blew out the bedside oil lamp. He let memories of Evie Marrow carry him down into sleep.

Not once did he think that he'd forgotten to call Capone.

12

Hymie Weiss shuffled the papers on his desk and shook his head. "Fucking O'Banion," he grumbled.

In a comfortable but well-worn leather chair opposite the wide mahogany desk, Adrian Turski blew a ring of smoke into the air. He watched it wavering as it rose before breaking apart. He grinned around the cigar, the scar that ran across his cheek and over his ear prevented one side of his mouth from forming a smile. "Left you with a mess, huh?"

Hymie dropped the papers and sat back heavily. "My fucking kingdom for some semblance of organization. The disorganized fuck." He let out a breath. "God rest him, of course." He plucked his cigarette from its perch at the edge of a blue glass ashtray. After tapping the ashes from it, he glanced at Turski. The Polish man was large. His muscles pressed against the wool of his jacket's sleeves and the buttons of his shirt strained against the expanse of his chest. Hymie had known a lot of Polacks in his life but never had he seen one as huge as Adrian Turski. *Fucking guy must eat a whole cow for breakfast.* "How you guys do at the docks the other night?" Hymie asked.

Turski shrugged and Hymie thought he heard the seams on the

big man's jacket tear. "Did all right. Caught a little skip trying to sneak in about twenty crates. Little fucker thought he could slip in without anyone seeing."

Hymie nodded. Twenty crates was good. It wasn't huge, but every little bit helped. "And the boat captain?"

Turski smiled wide.

Mother of God, Hymie thought, *even his teeth are fucking huge.*

"It'll be a while before he can hold a steering wheel, if you know what I mean."

"Good." Hymie pointed to the papers on his desk, scribbled numbers and abbreviations for warehouses or the names of items. All of it barely legible and most of it in O'Banion's secret code. "I need you to get me an accurate count of the shit we got up around Lawrence and Belmont. I can't read any of this."

Turski's face darkened, his eyes narrowing. "That ain't my job."

"I didn't say for you personally to fucking do it," Hymie snapped. "Get one of your goons to handle it. I need to know what we got and I ain't got the fucking time or manpower to do it. Not with shit blowing up with those palookas on the South Side."

Turski sucked on the cigar, its tip glowing bright red. Fingers of smoke trailed out of the corners of his mouth and he stared at Hymie with tight, dark eyes. "I'll throw a couple guys at it," he said as a soft knock sounded on the office door.

The dark wood swung in a few inches and Will Crowe poked his ginger-hair-framed face into the crack. "Sir, there's a George Lafferty to see you."

Hymie's brow wrinkled. "Who the fuck is George Lafferty?"

"Cop. One of ours."

Hymie waved a hand and Will's face disappeared. The door opened wide and the young Irishman gestured for a darker silhouette in the hall to enter. George Lafferty moved slowly, hesitantly, into the office. He looked like he was in his late twenties, with dark hair and a heavily freckled face. He wore a plain wool suit and held his hat in front of him, his spidery fingers playing along the wide brim nervously. Turski's chair creaked uncomfortably as the large man twisted to watch the cop.

As Will shut the door, Lafferty's shoulders twitched, but to his credit, he didn't turn and run. He kept his gaze fixed on Hymie, although he could tell the cop desperately wanted to look over at the Polish gorilla sitting only a few feet away. The young man's face was covered in a thin sheen of sweat.

"What do you want?" Hymie asked, putting a little impatience on the question.

Lafferty finally allowed his eyes to flick to Turski, then back to Hymie. He cleared his throat and shifted his weight from side to side. "We, uh, got a call earlier today. To the, uh, seventeen hundred block of Clark."

Hymie's face twisted into a sour look. "The fuck does that mean? Why do I care?"

Lafferty cleared his throat. "The call was to the Bell Warehouse," he said, letting the unspoken statement hang in the air.

Hymie pointed a finger at the cop. "You need to start making sense, boy."

The officer took in a steadying breath and said in a quick flush of words, "We were called to the location because the remains of several bodies had been discovered in a basement room. It seems they'd been playing cards. It took us a while but we were able to identify the bodies. The McCarthy brothers were among the dead." He cleared his throat and again glanced at Turski. This time the look lingered. "I'm sorry to tell you that one of the bodies was Jacob Turski."

Adrian remained very still as he processed the statement. His knuckles were white as they strained against the arms of the chair, the soft grinding of the wood filling the silence. "You're telling me," he said in a very quiet, measured tone, "that my sister's kid is dead?"

Lafferty's head bobbed like a chicken pecking corn. "Yes, sir. I'm terribly sorry. I—" The rest was choked off as Adrian exploded out of the chair and wrapped one massive paw around the cop's throat. His momentum propelled Lafferty across the room and slammed him against the wall to the left of a window. Turski loomed in front of the man, massive and hulking yet still a few inches shorter than Lafferty. His face was a red mask of fury. Spittle flew from his lips and dotted the cop's face as he snarled, "You're sure of this? You'd better be. If this is a joke, I'm going to break you and mail the pieces to your family once a year. Who did it? Huh? Who?"

Lafferty's face was turning purple, his eyes distended and lips trembling as he fought for even the tiniest sliver of oxygen. His feet and hands tapped a skittering rhythm on the floor and wall.

"You gotta let him breathe if you want him to answer you," Hymie said, lighting another cigarette. Turski considered the suggestion, and with a mechanical motion, he relaxed his grip. Lafferty sagged and dragged in a heaving breath. He tried to raise a hand to his bruised throat but Adrian's mitt remained poised to clamp shut once more.

When he'd gathered himself enough to speak, although the voice came out pinched and wheezing, Lafferty said, "We don't have anyone in custody. There were no witnesses. Not yet anyway. But we're searching."

"How?" Turski asked. For a moment, Hymie thought the idiot cop was going to be so stupid as to ask what Turski meant.

Lafferty swallowed, grimaced, and said, "They were killed with what is believed to be an axe or some other sharp-bladed weapon. They were . . ." He gave a pained expression that said, "Please don't make me describe it."

Adrian's glare never wavered. He stared at Lafferty so hard and for so long that Hymie thought the Polack had gone into a trance. That, or he was going to explode again at any second and hurl the cop out of the window just for delivering the message. Finally, Adrian said, "Any information you get comes to me first. Not your lieutenant, not your sergeant, not even your fucking wife or priest. Me. Understand?" Lafferty nodded. "You will not arrest this piece of shit. You'll let me handle it. Do you understand?" Once more, the cop nodded, eager to agree with the raging bull. Turski jerked his head toward the door. "Get the fuck out of here."

While the cop scrambled to get out of the office, Hymie reached into a lower drawer of his desk and pulled out a bottle of Canadian whiskey. He snatched two lowball glasses from the credenza behind him and poured a hefty bolt into each. Adrian remained where he had been, facing the wall and taking long, slow breaths. His cheeks and neck were still a bright angry red. Hymie held a glass in front of the man.

"Here. Drink this. I'm sorry for your loss." For a moment, Turski didn't react, only stared at the blank wall where Lafferty had just been. Hymie bumped the glass into the big man's chest. The contact broke the spell and Turski blinked down at the offered booze. Slowly he took it.

Hymie raised his own glass in a salute. "To your nephew. He was a good kid." He swallowed down the liquor and after a moment of staring at his own glass, Turski mumbled something and tossed his back. "Sit down," Hymie said. "Let's have another round and figure this out."

Adrian moved back to the chair, quietly and slowly like a schoolboy who'd just been scolded in front of the class. Hymie refilled the glasses. "I'm gonna find the lowlife," Turski mumbled.

"I almost feel sorry for the son of a bitch when you do." Hymie thought for a moment. "You have any ideas?"

Turski said nothing. The steady rhythm of his breathing was the only sound. Frowning, he shook his head. "Not yet. But I will. I'm going to get Eli Kinnerk and Frank Ryan." He swallowed the whiskey and set the glass gently on the desk. "We'll find him."

Frank Ryan, Hymie thought, and his stomach curdled. *If he's using that animal, it's going to be ugly.*

"Do you need anything from me?" Hymie asked. "Anything I can—"

"No." The interruption was soft but solid. Turski raised his eyes, met Hymie's. "I'm going to kill him and everyone in his family going back six generations."

Bit stiff, Hymie considered, but then again, family ties were important to the Polish and who was he to argue with vengeance? Hell, the McCarthys were a loss, but at least they weren't family. He rapped a knuckle on the desk. "I'll let you get started. Let me know if there's anything I can do to help."

Adrian Turski peeled himself out of the chair and moved to the door, his footsteps heavy tolls of an oncoming executioner's bell. He paused with one hand gripping the knob. "I'm not going to apologize for the mess I'm going to make."

"I wouldn't expect you to," Hymie agreed, but before the sentence was even complete, Turski was gone and the door closed.

13

Jonas Robertson lay in the dark room and tried to focus on his wife's soft snores. She snored every night but adamantly refused to admit it, and Jonas had lost sleep on more than one occasion due to the noise. Tending to crops after only a couple of fitful hours of sleep was never an easy task, and it often left him in a foul mood come supper time.

Not that the crops had needed much tending lately, he thought. They'd lost almost all the corn, and that was before they gave Elmer Cleary the portion promised to him. The few cows the Robertsons owned were down from a herd of twenty-five to only twelve. The rest had died, either from a sudden and vicious wasting that occurred in a matter of days and left their corpses emaciated husks as if they'd been starved for weeks, or in the case of three of the poor creatures, from horrible mutations. In the darkness of his bedroom, Jonas squeezed his eyes shut and denied himself the torment of remembering the growths, the disfigured limbs.

Across his chest, the fingers of his left hand twitched as if in response to some crawling sensation. The movement forced another memory: the sensation, the *certainty*, of things crawling beneath his skin on the evening of the potluck dinner. In his mind, he saw himself leap from the table and slap at his body, trying to crush the small, writhing things as they burrowed deeper. He'd felt them all over, in his legs, his buttocks, his back, crawling within his chest and up his neck, winding around the tendons and veins like horrible children around a maypole.

The illusion had been broken when Anna finally managed to grab hold of one of his flailing arms, clutching it tightly in her own hands. As soon as her skin made contact with his own, the crawling stopped, leaving him panting, his skin buzzing with pain from where he'd hit himself in desperation.

The feast had ended with a whimper, confused and scared people clutching one another and shuffling slowly to their own homes. Steering Jonas like he'd been on a bender, Anna had taken him inside and gotten him into bed. Grace and Charlie had understandably been concerned but Anna quelled their nervous questions, saying only that their father wasn't feeling well. It didn't take much to convince them, Anna had said. They'd been rather upset after the events of the night anyway.

That night, though, Jonas hadn't slept. Anna had fallen asleep easily, but he'd lain there staring at the dark shadows across the ceiling, his fingers plugging his ears against the strange whispering voices that filled the entire room. How Anna hadn't heard them was beyond him. They were soft, nearly inaudible at times, but never gone. They whispered in a strange language, in different voices. He had not understood any of what they said, and spent all of the next day, Monday, in a fog. He'd been left with a lethargy that pressed heavily against his body. That morning, even the simplest act felt like wading through mud. He'd practically sleepwalked through his chores and when he finally collapsed into bed just a few hours ago without eating dinner, he found he couldn't remember the day at all. To his relief, his mind had shut down and he fell asleep instantly.

Tonight he had burst into wakefulness with a scream dying to a brittle, raspy whisper on his lips. It hadn't been the whisperings this time but rather fitful dreams; swirling dark clouds of visions that vanished like fish darting through murky water. But the dreams left something behind, like a glistening slug's trail across his brain.

A dark sense of need.

Of hunger.

The feeling was intense, akin to a person denied food and water for days on end. Jonas lay in the quiet dark of his bedroom and grimaced against the greasy film the dreams had left on his soul. In the wake of the nightmares, his thoughts constantly scattered, breaking apart like a flock of birds startled from a field, only to coalesce moments later with the same meaning.

Something was hungry. A hunger that was a clawing, screaming need. And Jonas knew exactly what had to be done to satisfy the feeling of hunger.

Anna's snoring receded to a sound no more noticeable than the buzzing of a fly's wings as understanding took root in Jonas's mind. The knowledge was overwhelming, a vicious tide that battered the part of his brain that railed in horror at the idea, pushing it violently down, muting it until the idea wasn't even an idea any longer but a deeply rooted, immutable fact.

Jonas pushed the blanket back and swung out of bed. The movements were automatic, the sensations muted. The entire experience was as if he were standing to one side observing the actions. He dressed, and on stiff legs, crossed the small bedroom and entered the main living area where he stopped, head tilted a fraction as though he was considering.

Or listening.

The silence in the house stretched as Jonas remained motionless. For long minutes he didn't shift, didn't twitch, didn't even blink despite the burning irritation in his eyes.

Another corridor, longer, branched off the main room. Along that hall stood three doors, all closed. One led to the bathroom, the others to Grace and Charlie. Jonas, still feeling as if he were observing his actions, approached the doors to his children's bedrooms. He hesitated outside of Grace's, one trembling hand reaching for the knob.

Something passed over his thoughts like a cloud scudding across the moon, obscuring the idea of the girl.

Jonas turned his head, his eyes settling on Charlie's door.

The six-year-old was a curled ball beneath his sheets, the blanket wadded around his small form. Charlie had always been on the thinner side, a little frail for most farm chores, yet the boy attacked every task with the intensity of a grown man. On those occasions when Jonas grew overly frustrated with the boy for a hastily and sloppily done job, Anna reminded him that Charlie did everything with such intensity to impress his father. Her words were always a balm on his inflamed nerves, and after a time, Jonas could see his son's intentions.

Charlie, normally a deep sleeper, roused surprisingly quickly as Jonas's hand fell on his shoulder. The boy rolled over, hair jutting out wildly from his scalp, and screwed a fist into one eye.

"Daddy?"

Jonas's voice was low and gruff in the quiet room. "Get dressed. Come with me."

The child wasted no time, throwing the blanket back and scrambling out of bed. Jonas watched as his son pulled on pants and a shirt, threw suspenders over his shoulders. "Where we going?" An overwhelming urge to reach out and smooth the child's hair, to pull him close swept over Jonas. Yet despite the need, he couldn't manage to bring his arm up. His fingers twitched with the effort. The moment passed, pushed aside by the same dark tide that had caused him to dismiss Grace's bedroom.

Instead of answering the question, Jonas left the room and moved through the house to the back door. He slipped his feet into his boots. Charlie did the same, then the two exited the house and stepped out into the dew-soaked grass. The three-quarter moon bathed the lawn in a silver glow, the moisture reflecting like glass shards. Crickets chirped in concert, unbothered by the man and boy who passed close by.

Jonas led his son to the edge of the lawn and along a knobby path that stretched between the two closest fields. The trail was used by

Jonas and his tractor frequently, the grass beaten down. Wide swaths of the ground were inky black spots in the moonlight where the creeping rot had taken hold. He walked quickly, Charlie's footsteps a soft whisper behind him. Within minutes, both reached the edge of the field that abutted another wide patch of grass. This one ran perpendicular, giving access to the other dead and rotting fields farther on. The swath was about thirty feet wide with a thick line of pine trees marking the boundary of the woods.

Jonas stopped at the edge of the clearing, his eyes locked on the slender, dark forms of the trees. Inside his mind, thoughts and garbled voices swirled, collided, and twisted around one another. The din was a painful pressure that sent a sharp ache along his skull and down into his neck and shoulders. Dimly aware that Charlie stood beside him, small face turned up in eager expectation, Jonas took a step and the pressure in his head changed. Instead of receding, it morphed into a pulling, spiraling whirlpool, urging him forward. With each step the pull intensified, filling him with a sense of right. He had a sensation, not exactly an image but the *feeling* of an image, of a dark figure, starving, watching as a tray of food was brought close.

"Daddy?" Charlie asked, and Jonas stumbled to a halt. "We going in the woods? Do you need me to go get the shotgun?" The question was painted with eagerness. Charlie hadn't yet been allowed to go hunting with his father despite begging every time Jonas pulled the shotgun from the rack over the fireplace.

The child's voice cut through the maelstrom in his head like lightning splitting the night and for that brief instant, fear and panic spiked into Jonas, pinpricks rippling through his hands. He opened his mouth to tell the boy to turn back, to run to the house and lock the doors, but as soon as the moment of clarity had come, it was gone. The night closed in on itself and the pulling, urging need filled him once more.

Jonas raised a hand, one thick knuckled finger indicating the trees. "Go," he said. The word was deep, almost a growl, and Charlie took a half step back.

Yes! The part of Jonas observing screamed. *Go! Run home!* But the thoughts were as effective as pipe smoke against a brick wall.

"Sir?" Charlie asked. His voice wavered from confusion and worry.

Jonas's mouth opened, closed, opened again as he struggled to make the words. "In . . . woods. Go."

"Why? What about you?" Charlie twisted and looked at the house.

To his horror, Jonas heard himself say in a calm, controlled voice, "I need you to go into the woods. Do you remember the hickory tree we cut down last fall?" Charlie shifted his attention to the dark trees. "Go there and wait for me. I have to go get something. When I come back, I'll tell you why I got you out of bed. Go on, now."

"But I ain't got a light," the child protested.

"Moon's full enough. You'll be fine. Go on."

Charlie gave his father one final uneasy look, set his jaw, and walked into the trees. Jonas stood watching as his son's form slowly faded from view, the darkness of the woods enveloping him slowly as if the boy were wading into a lake. The cacophony in Jonas's mind reached a crescendo, the feeling of joyful eagerness almost orgasmic. He couldn't see more than a couple of feet into the woods, but sensed the presence of something waiting by the old hickory tree.

Jonas remained where he was, listening to the rustling of his son picking his way through the brush. He didn't move until those sounds faded completely. Only then did he start walking back to the house.

He stumbled once, when Charlie's screams pierced the night. But as the wet sounds of flesh tearing and frenzied chewing drifted out of the trees, Jonas's stride strengthened.

By the time he reached the house and stepped into the kitchen, the screaming had stopped. Jonas undressed and climbed back into bed. He fell asleep instantly, a smile on his lips.

14

The waitress, the same woman with dishwater-colored hair that had been on shift Sunday night, placed the large platter before Jack while her other hand poured a refill of steaming black coffee. His eyes twitched at the prospect of drinking more of the sludge but found his attention drawn back to the plate before him. Three scrambled eggs, four fat sausage links, and somewhere under a pool of whitish gravy the size of Lake Eerie were two of what the menu listed as "cathead biscuits." The gravy looked thick enough to choke a train engine and was dotted with large flecks of pepper. Small boulders of crumbled sausage sat like animals stuck in the tar pits Jack learned about in school as a child.

"Need anything else?" Dishwater asked in a flat voice.

"Not a thing," he said and picked up his utensils. The waitress drifted away to serve others and Jack ate with singular focus. As the items on the plate dwindled in size, he turned his thoughts to the business of the day.

Trask had left the previous afternoon for Elden Mills to secure more grains, returning late last night with good news. Jack had spent the day around Cleary's kitchen table getting a clear understanding of the current logistics from numbers and locations of stills to output volumes and storage locations.

That handled, Jack turned his focus to the search for Morelli. His plan was to have one of the other men drive him out to the site where Carlo had last been seen. Jack didn't know what he expected to find out there; he certainly wasn't a detective, but he figured that at least standing in the same dirt where the missing Italian had stood might help. If it didn't, he would organize some of the men into a search party and scour the woods. Cleary had said that they'd searched the surrounding forest, but based on the way some of the other men had looked and spoken about it, Jack guessed they hadn't searched long or hard.

The repugnant question floated back into his thoughts like a rotting fish bobbing just beneath the surface of the Chicago River. What if Morelli had been working with whoever attacked the still? It would explain why he walked alone into the woods before the attack started, why he left his weapon behind, and why he'd not been seen since. But besides infringing on the memory of a damned good man, it made no sense. The still hadn't been a massive one, it hadn't even been the only one in operation. Killing the men running it, while psychologically effective, didn't stop its operation or even hurt Cleary's business overall. And since the still itself wasn't touched, there was nothing to be gained by the attack. So Morelli working with whoever was behind the attacks made no sense. Now, if they had attacked Cleary's farm, Jack reasoned as he choked down another mouthful of coffee, that would make sense.

So, no. There was no way Morelli was in bed with the people attacking Cleary's operation. If Jack was lucky, he'd find the man, or at least evidence of where he'd run off to. *The prick better have a good reason, too*, Jack thought. Either way, he wanted to be back in town by midafternoon. He had an urge to go flower shopping.

Jack smiled in spite of himself at the thought of Evie Marrow. *She'll probably be impressed with my new duds*, he thought. That morning there had been a package waiting outside his door. Brown paper tied up with simple twine had contained a set of bib overalls, a white T-shirt, and a pair of worn, scuffed leather boots. A note tucked into one of them read *Sorry about your clothes.* It was signed by Elmer Cleary in large, loopy letters. Jack considered for a moment not putting them on; there was a certain image and reputation he needed to uphold around town and with Cleary's men.

But, he reasoned as he sat on the edge of the mattress, his experience Sunday had taught him that clothes perfect for Friar's Inn were woefully inadequate for slogging through the thick woods in rural Alabama. The downside was that, while roomy and surprisingly comfortable, the overalls left little by way of places to put a pistol. Not able to don his jacket with the new clothes, wearing his shoulder rig wasn't an option. The waist of the overalls was loose, so his .45 had to go in one of the deep hip pockets. He felt ridiculous with it there, but after a few minutes in front of the mirror, he was able to angle it so that it wasn't overly noticeable and still easy to reach.

Jack finished his food and waved for a refill on the coffee. Around the diner, a few other patrons sat idly picking at their own plates. Most wore the rugged overalls of farmers or laborers, but a couple sported slacks and jackets. All, though, sat with an exhausted slump, their movements sluggish and morose. Dishwater refilled his cup and was clearing away his plate when the bell mounted over the door chimed.

"Oh no," she mumbled and backed away, moving toward the kitchen like a beaten dog that just caught sight of the belt again.

Five men stood just inside the diner's door. Four of them wore outfits similar to Jack's, overalls and hats, but the fifth wore dark pants and a white cotton shirt with suspenders over his shoulders. Jack's first thought about the man was *He looks like a toad.* He was short and pudgy, his belly and flabby breasts pressing against his shirt like cancerous lumps. His face was wide and round, his thick cheeks drooped and pulled his fat lips in a permanent frown. But it was the eyes, Jack noticed, that told the real story. Small, dark, and set close together, they watched everything and everyone in the diner with calculating intensity. The toad man waved one hand, indicating to his compatriots that they should take up seats around the room.

They settled into chairs or on stools at the counter and watched Jack with drowsy interest.

His men positioned, Toad approached Jack's table, his body moving with a gentle roll as he favored one leg. He pulled out a chair and poured himself into it. Up close, the man smelled of aftershave, a cloying scent applied too heavily as if to mask something worse. To keep from recoiling, Jack raised his coffee to his mouth, eyes locked on the man's wide, pale face.

"You must be Henry Dunn," Jack said and took a tentative sip of the coffee.

The other man smiled and the gesture confirmed Jack's impression of a toad. All that was missing was a tongue to dart out and pull the mug out of Jack's hand. "Now how'd you figure that out?" The voice was sharp and clear, not the garbled, clotted string of sounds Jack had expected.

Jack set his coffee down. "I'm a good guesser. It's why my dad always took me to the casinos. Said I could guess whether he should hit or stay every time."

"Your daddy a good gambler?"

"He was."

"What happened to him?"

"Got killed."

"Yeah? Got caught cheating?"

Jack gave a quick shake of his head. "Hit by a train."

Dunn laughed at that, a nasally, pinched sound that resonated like nails on a chalkboard. The laugh died, choked off, and Dunn leaned forward. "You're from up north. Chicago, I hear." Jack said nothing. He'd learned long ago that when a man started talking like this, he'd keep going just to fill the air.

Dunn tilted his head, as if observing a rare artifact. "You from Chicago originally?"

"Nope," Jack lied. "I'm from here. Alabama. Moved to Chicago when I was three."

"Moved when you were three," Dunn repeated through a wide "I don't believe this shit" smile. "What brings you down here? This doesn't seem like the kind of place a guy like you would just pop into."

"Nope. Came to see my cousin."

Dunn's eyebrows rose in surprise. "No shit? Now, Carmelo don't sound like any Alabama family name I ever heard of. Where abouts in Alabama you from?"

"Downtown. You looking to write a book?"

"Naw," Dunn said. "It's just that, well, I'm sure you're aware, being from Chicago and all, that we have a strict policy banning the manu-facture—"

"That's a big word."

The Southerner let it slide, but his eyes flinched at the insult. He finished his sentence. "Sale and distribution of alcohol in this coun-try. Not to mention the consumption of it. And it seems strange to me that— And pardon me saying so, but if you're not a wop, I don't know what one is. It seems strange to me that a wop like you come to our town"—he waved a thick arm to indicate the men behind him—"right when we're having a problem with illegal alcohol. You wouldn't happen to be involved in anything like that, would you?"

"Not at all."

Dunn's tone changed instantly, swinging from joking affability to sharp and menacing. "Good. Because we're . . . call us concerned citi-zens. We want to make sure that everything in this town stays on the straight and narrow. It's our job to ensure that the people aren't both-ered. And having a dago like you, a fucking Yankee no less, suddenly roll into town, throws our harmonious society out of balance."

"You're full of big words," Jack said. "Your mom must be proud." When Dunn still didn't react, Jack faked being deflated and put on a mock pained expression. "So you're saying I can't visit my cousin?"

Dunn's jaw worked, sending the pudgy cheeks wiggling. Inwardly, Jack smiled with satisfaction that he was starting to frustrate the man. He'd seen men like Henry Dunn before. They were used to getting their way, to having people cower before them at the slightest threat of a beating. The problem was, Jack had found, most of these men were hot air looking for a place to blow. If you stood firm and didn't waver under their speeches, they tended to back off. There were exceptions, though, and a small voice in the back of his head reminded him what Henry Dunn was said to have done to the sixteen-year-old farmhand.

"I want you to get the fuck out of my town," Dunn said, his voice low and firm.

"What I hear, it's not your town," Jack responded. "I heard you came over from Atlanta. Why do you care so much about Jericho Springs?"

"I care about this white community. I care about the good white Christians who live here and who don't want or need a Yankee Italian down here causing problems. I care about getting rid of all the booze according to the law and ending its negative effects on those same good Christians. I fought for that in France, and I'm only too happy to continue that war here where it really matters."

Jack thought back to the posters he'd seen the night before. "Tuberculosis, venereal disease, and insanity. That about right?"

Dunn didn't answer, only stared at him.

Jack drank his coffee. Henry Dunn may be full of hot air but considering what he'd heard about the man, Jack knew there was a hard edge to him also. But hard-edged men weren't anything new. He'd dealt with them his entire life. The Irish had some of the hardest he'd gone up against and all of them died just the same, screaming and bleeding. Hell, Jack himself had put several bullets into Dean O'Banion's body. There was no way this shitkicker hillbilly was going to make him flinch.

Tony Detti's voice floated from an old memory. *Watch it with this one, Jackie. Somewhere out there a village is missing its idiot.* The thought made Jack smile, the smile snowballing into a chuckle before avalanching into a full laugh. Dunn's men looked at each other, then back at Jack. Henry, however, only sat staring intently at the man laughing hysterically.

Jack managed to get the fit under a semblance of control, the laughter now only low waves of giggles that ebbed and flowed over him. He flapped his fingers in a shooing gesture. "Go on, I need to finish my breakfast. This has been fun, though. Thanks for coming by, fellas, I appreciate it. I needed the laugh." Without actually taking his attention off Dunn, Jack searched for the waitress. However, both she and the cook were nowhere to be seen.

The Klan members stared at each other, confused. Dunn leaned forward and hissed, "I'm not fucking around with you. You're not wanted here. So I suggest you pack up and get out."

This sent Jack into another gale. He rocked back and forth in his chair, unable to contain the huge peals of laughter that poured out of him. Finally, red-faced, his lips drawn into a thin hard line, Henry Dunn turned and stormed out of the diner with his gang following like a bunch of beaten dogs. The sight of Dunn moving as quickly as his short, heavyset frame would allow brought on a renewed fit of hysterics, and it took several minutes to compose himself. When he did, Jack wiped the tears from his eyes and blew his nose into the napkin. He was fishing in his pockets for money for the meal when Dishwater approached him and said, "Don't worry about paying. Considering who that was you just laughed at, I figure you getting a last meal for free is the least I can do."

Jack threw a few coins on the table regardless. Outside, he scanned the street, using the act of lighting a cigarette as a guise. Henry Dunn and his Klan brethren were nowhere to be seen. Jack put one hand in his pocket, the one with the pistol, and casually walked in the direction of the hotel.

The truck that Cleary had promised him sat parked at an angle near the pharmacy. Inside the shop, a small elderly man with a thick mustache and round spectacles leaned over the counter reading the paper. Jack started the truck and drove through town, turning randomly for several minutes, watching his side mirror to see if Dunn or any of his friends were following. When he was satisfied he wasn't being tailed, he steered toward Cleary's farm.

He found Elmer sitting hunched over a long wooden table in what had once been a dining room. The table's surface was covered with newspaper and bits of cloth. The old farmer was focused on cleaning the breech of a .30-30 Winchester. Scattered about the table were several shotguns and half a dozen revolvers. Cleaning pads and rods and a can of oil sat near the man's elbow. Jack breathed in the pleasant smell of gun oil.

"Rot's getting worse out there," he said, tossing his hat on a clear spot of the table.

Cleary grunted, his attention focused on the rifle. "Lost the peach trees. Probably going to lose the oak tree out by the cemetery too. It's oozing some kind of liquid. Ain't sap, neither." He pulled the cleaning cloth out of the rifle and glanced at Jack. "You're getting a late start on the day."

"I caught a later breakfast at Mack's. Had some interesting company while I ate."

"That so?" Cleary returned his attention to oiling the lever of the Winchester.

"I met Henry Dunn and some of his buddies."

The statement stopped Cleary cold and he glanced up at Jack. "You don't say."

Jack pulled a chair out and lowered himself into it. "I'm a little disappointed. The way you guys talked about him, I expected a hard-faced man, all muscles and sharp angles and a smile like a snake. But he looks like a fat toad."

Cleary grunted a short laugh and went back to the rifle.

Jack continued. "But talking to him confirmed something that's been on my mind since I got here. I'm going to have to do something about the Klan."

The farmer's head shook, his thick white hair wavering with the movement. "People been trying to do something about the Klan for years. Well, maybe not actually trying, more like just talking about it when they know weren't nobody listening." He paused, swapped the rag for the can of oil. "You think Dunn's going to take a bribe?"

"I do not. He's a crusader. He believes wholeheartedly in what he's doing. Went on and on about saving the good Christians of Jericho Springs from the evils of alcohol. No, he's not going to take a bribe. He wouldn't flinch if you put that Winchester to his head."

"So what are you thinking?"

"I'm going to find the man who was in charge before Dunn showed up. Find him and the guys who followed him and make *them* an offer. I figure once they understand that supporting Dunn in his mission isn't in the interest of their health and well-being, that'll be that. Dunn may still cause some problems, but by himself he'll be much easier to deal with. Or make disappear. Cut the legs off the toad, he won't be able to hop anymore. And we'll be back in business."

Another grunt of acknowledgement. "The man you're looking for, in that case, is Carl Stott. He was the head of that group of idiots before Dunn. Lives over on Walston. When do you think you'll be paying him a visit?"

"Tonight. Tomorrow night at the latest. I'll probably take one or two of your guys with me, if you can spare them."

"I can."

Jack leaned forward, placed his elbows on the table. "You don't think it's going to work, do you?"

Cleary let out a long breath and sat back. "I hope it does. I just know that the kinds of people who are involved with that organization aren't the smartest. They feed on hatred, and even flashing around some money isn't going to quench that hunger. But, maybe it'll be enough to stop the . . . problems." Jack could see that Cleary believed there was something more to the attacks.

Christ, he actually thinks it's some supernatural thing. Witches or that wendi-thing.

"So what's your plan in the meantime?" Cleary asked, diverting Jack from his train of thought.

"I need a few of your guys for the day. Five should do. I want them to take me to the site where Landry was attacked. I'm going to see if I can find Carlo Morelli."

15

"**A**re you sure this is it?" Jack asked.

The man who had driven him to the still, Louis Ware, spat a wad of tobacco juice onto a pile of pine needles and rubbed the back of his hand across his lips. "Yep."

The remains of the still looked like the site of ancient ruins. Strange weeds grew thick around the shattered remnants of the equipment. Dark vines oozing an even darker sap twisted through and around the pipes emerging from ragged holes in the copper pots.

"They said the equipment wasn't damaged in the attack."

Louis jerked his bony shoulders toward his pockmarked cheeks.

"How old is this site?" Jack asked.

The skinny man's eyes roamed the broken pieces of equipment. "Few weeks."

Jack turned to the man and pointed at the ruins. "You're telling me all this shit grew up around it in just a few weeks?"

Again the shoulders jerked.

Jack gave an inquiring glance at the other three men who had ridden out with them—two Black men and one white standing several yards away, hands in their pockets and nervous expressions on their faces. Jack raised his eyebrows to them questioningly but none responded. Instead, they shifted their eyes to their feet like children being scolded for tracking mud into the house.

"And what is that smell?" Jack growled. A heavy stench of vegetative rot hung in the air like smoke over a poker table, thick and layered.

"Whole parts of the woods been smelling like that lately," Louis said and spat again. "Parts of town too. Ain't you noticed?"

"It's the rot. Whatever we disturbed out here sent that plague," one of the men mumbled.

Jack pointed at the small group. "I don't want to hear that shit, understand?" The men kept their eyes averted and Jack returned his attention to the site.

The space had once been a clearing about fifty feet across and slightly larger than that wide. A few stumps dotted the area where trees had been felled to make room for the equipment. On the far side of the site stood the remains of a small shelter built from tree limbs; a place for shade and rest when the men weren't chopping wood or working the whiskey. Weeds and thick brambles covered the ground, and they pulled at his feet as he stepped closer to the destroyed still.

Jack moved to the equipment itself. As he neared, his throat tightened against the wet stench. The main pot was a large angular piece that sat atop a partially collapsed pile of rocks. The metal was badly dented and had long, ragged gashes through which the foul-smelling vines grew. Jack circled the collapsed rocks and noticed a small opening at the base where a few half-burned logs protruded. The barrel into which the pipe running from the main pot emptied was nothing but splinters, revealing what used to be the copper coil of the cooling arm.

The stones and the main boiler were painted in an erratic pattern of dark blood. Jack ran a finger along one stain across the sun-warmed metal pot. The digit came away clean, as he expected. The bloodstains were old. Stepping back he examined the ground, kicking aside leaves and the thick weeds to reveal the sticks, rocks, and bare dirt beneath. He continued this motion, circling the ruins.

When he returned to his starting point, he scowled. There had been no other splashes of blood, not on any rock or piece of wood. More disturbing was the lack of shell casings. Cleary's men typically only carried shotguns, but a few had bolt-action rifles or repeaters. For a group of men that found themselves attacked by the Klan, it seemed not a single one had gotten a shot off. Frowning, Jack turned in a circle, his eyes drifting along the ground.

"Mr. Carmelo?" Louis asked from across the remains of the cooling arm.

"There are no flies," Jack said softly.

"Beg pardon?"

Jack pointed to the bloodstains. "There's blood. It's dry, but still. There are no flies." He searched the equipment. "Not a single one. I've seen flies at sites where the blood was weeks old. But there are none here. No birds either. Why do you suppose that is?"

Louis searched the trees and shook his head. "Symbols up there. Few on some of the other trees too."

The bark of the large pine tree had been removed, exposing a swath of pale yellow wood about six inches square. Slashes in the bare trunk stood bright against the darker bark. Jack ran his finger across the rough gouges. His skin came away tacky with sap. The symbol was an intricate pattern of intersecting circles and sharp angled lines. Jack had grown up Catholic, but despite all the symbology within that religion, he'd never seen anything like this.

"What is it?" he asked over his shoulder. Louis didn't reply and after a second, Jack turned to the man. "Well?"

Louis spat another wad of tobacco juice. "You told us you didn't want to hear it."

More symbols were found on other trees, just as Louis had said. Jack counted six in all, each one different in size and complexity. He spent several minutes studying them, trying to make sense of them. Why had the Klan carved them? Was it just to sow fear and confusion in the superstitious hillbillies Cleary employed? Make them think that some demonic force was responsible? It made a certain kind of sense, but at the same time, based on his knowledge of the Klan, it didn't. Most of the men in the Klan were deeply devoted to the Christian faith, even if they didn't always practice the Gospel the way Jack had been taught. That men who viewed the white race to be God's chosen and alcohol to be an instrument of the Devil had now employed the use of dark rituals as a means of intimidation was a bit of a stretch. The Klan tended to stick to brute violence to get their point across.

This was much more sophisticated, he thought.

"We done here?" Louis asked.

"No," Jack said, still studying one of the symbols. "We need to search for Morelli."

"We did," Louis protested. "Day after the attack, when we found Landry and what was left of them other boys. Your guy weren't anywhere."

"How far did you look for him?"

Louis flapped a hand at the trees. "We went a ways in. Figured if he was dead, he'd be close by. Never saw no blood leading off nowhere. If he'd been wounded, we'd have found him."

Jack considered the forest and reminded himself that just because neither a body nor blood was found didn't mean Morelli was involved with the attack. The trees grew thicker after several yards, their canopy filtering the sunlight to a muddy haze. "What else is out here?"

"Ain't nothing else out there," Louis said. "Just them woods for miles. Some hills, few hollers, maybe a crick or two." With some effort, Jack suppressed a mocking smile at the pronunciation. "But otherwise, ain't nothing out there."

"All right," Jack said. "Let's get moving. We'll start over here."

The men looked at each other. *If they're going to buck and jump me, this is when they'll do it*, Jack told himself. He brought his right hand slowly into the pocket of his overalls and let his fingers rest against the rough metal of the .45.

"What?" Louis asked.

"You heard me. I came down here to find Carlo Morelli, in addition to getting you mooks back on track with production. This is where he was last seen, and I don't trust that anyone looked for him very well. So come on."

Louis gaped. "How do you know where to look?" He raised a hand, indicating the expanse of forest around them.

Jack pointed in the direction of the mostly destroyed shelter. "That direction. The Klan guys would have come from the road like we did. You said there was nothing else out here, so it's not like they had a base of operations close by. So they came from there." He pointed past the three men still standing several yards away. "Morelli would have been here,"—he jerked a thumb at the shelter—"watching. Probably sitting on his ass, smoking. He was never the most energetic sort. So when the attack came, whether he was wounded or not, he would have figured that Dunn's guys wouldn't pursue him. So he would have gone that way. Now come on."

Still, the men hesitated. They threw worried looks at the trees. "What the hell are you waiting on?" Jack asked.

One of the Black men spoke up, "We ain't supposed to go out there. Being this far's why those boys got killed."

"What are you talking—" Jack stopped himself. "The fucking superstitions again? Jesus Christ. You're grown men. There are no ghosts or demons, or whatever the hell you want to call it, out here. Those guys got killed because the Klan is working with the Prohis to stop bootlegging. It has nothing to do with these woods or, what's that old town out here called?" He snapped his fingers, remembering. "Providence. Is it out this way?"

The nervous looks of the men turned immediately to naked fear. Two of them shook their heads and moved several steps back. "We don't go there," Louis said, putting a little steel in the declaration.

"Did you know Morelli very well?" Jack asked Louis. He raised his eyes questioningly to the other men. "No? Okay. I did. I've known him my whole life. Worked with him a few times on some things. The thing about Morelli is, he's really, really close with his family. I mean, family's the most important thing, wouldn't you agree?" Jack focused on the men in an effort to ignore the images of Norma that his mind conjured. "Morelli's got a brother. Few years younger. Name's Gino. We call him 'Guts.' Not because he's brave, although he is. He survived France and a whole lot worse before that growing up, if you can believe it. No, we call him Guts because his favorite way to kill a man is by cutting his guts out. He uses a knife that he had made special. It has a hook on the top edge of the blade and he uses that hook to tear open the stomach. It's fucking awful. Because the person is aware. Screaming. Begging for their mother the entire time. And Guts, he just doesn't care. Just stares at them like they're a fly and he's pulling the wings off." A couple of the men's faces paled. "I tell you this because if I have to report back to my boss-and I do-that nobody down here would help me find Carlo because you were too scared to go to some old abandoned buildings, then Guts is going to hear about it. Right now he doesn't know his brother is missing. But when he does, Guts is going to come down here and pay all of you a visit. And he takes that knife with him everywhere."

Looking at the near panic on the faces of the men, Jack was proud of himself. He'd never been much of a storyteller, so to come up with such a whopper out of the blue like that was impressive. Carlo Morelli had been born an only child and raised by his grandparents after his parents died when he was two.

"Now come on. We'll spread out in a line and start searching."

Louis and the other three grumbled their reservations but under Jack's unrelenting steely gaze, gave in. Louis took position at Jack's left, the other three men to his right. They spaced out so there was about ten yards between each of them. Carefully they picked their way through the thick brush and trees, stepping carefully around the patches of ground and vegetation that had withered under the blight's effects.

Two hours later, Jack saw the first signs of the house.

He called for a halt and the men sank to the ground with relieved sighs. Jack's entire body was covered in sweat and his forearms burned from dozens of small scrapes and cuts. At least two places on his neck itched maddeningly from insect bites, but all of that receded to a minute hum as he stared at the house. He picked his way toward it, eyes searching the jagged, rotting, vine-covered ruins as he neared. "You know what this is?" he asked Louis.

"Never been this deep before. Probably one of the houses left from Providence. They was the settlers back in colonial times."

"Why would there be just a single house this far in the middle of nowhere if it was part of a larger town?" The house was once a two-story structure, but part of the roof and second floor had collapsed. A tree, bent and twisted, its trunk shimmering with a patina of some sludge that assaulted Jack's senses with a sharp acrid stench, grew from the center of the house, rising above the fallen roof. Its limbs extended over the remains of the home like the protective arms of a mother shielding her child from rain. Black moss hung from the branches, a few of the thick clumps dripping a foul liquid into the exposed house. Along the shattered walls, timbers jutted like the shards of broken bones. On the side of the house where he stood, a few windows were still intact, their leaded glass dulled by years of grime. "It's in better shape than I'd have imagined, considering how old it is." He glanced at Louis. "You sure this is part of the original town?"

"Hell if I know," Louis snapped. "Maybe we come in on the edge of town and the rest of it is out there somewhere. Maybe it belonged to some old hermit who liked living way the hell out here until he pissed off the wrong *ghost*." He gave Jack a pointed look as he emphasized the word ghost. "Now me and the boys have been more than accommodating, Mr. Carmelo, but it's getting late in the day and we need to be heading back. Besides,"—he threw a fearful look at the vegetation around the house—"this ain't natural."

Jack had to admit the man was right about that. The deeper they'd moved into the woods, the worse the signs of the blight had become, until everything as far as they could see was blackened, oozing, and dead.

Now, as he stood next to the ruins of the house, the dirt beneath his feet was spongy. Each step seemed to disturb something long since dormant on the top layer, sending the vegetative rotting smell wafting up.

Jack didn't respond to Louis's insistence. Instead, he moved along the side of the house until he reached the broken edge of the wall. Peering around, he saw what he assumed had once been the family room, now a jumbled mass of stones and rotting wood. Weeds sprouted in the cracks. The remains of the roof and walls lay against the base of the tree that forced its way out of the rotting earth like an abscessed tooth from a diseased gum.

The rest of the house stood open to view beyond the fallen roof. He could pick out the shadow-draped rooms on the second floor. More rooms were visible on the ground floor, and he stepped into the house and began moving toward them. Beneath his boots, stones shifted, threatening to turn and break his ankle. Jack stayed close to the exterior wall as he progressed, one hand touching the wet and rot-softened wood for balance.

The first room he came to looked to have been a study. A lone, simple, wooden chair sat in a corner. Although no other adornments hung, sagging shelves lined three of the four walls. To his surprise, a couple of books, their covers furred with mold and pages thick and yellowed from time and weather, lay on one shelf. Curiosity urged him to inspect them, but after his first step in that direction yielded a concerning *creak* from the floor, Jack decided not to risk it. He turned and left the room via an open doorway, passing along a short hallway and into the kitchen.

The smell of rotting meat hit him as soon as he crossed the threshold. Jack's vision swam in the small, hot room as the stench washed over him, and he threw one hand out to steady himself.

"Holy Mother of God," he whispered.

Carlo Morelli was three feet off the floor, pinned to the wall by iron spikes. His hair had been ripped out in patches, the waxy pale skull visible beneath surrounded by small tufts of dirty, blood-matted hair. His head drooped to his chest, obscuring his face. Thick ropes of rotting vines extended from the man's ears and his downturned face. The skin of the chest was flayed open like the covers of a book, exposing the red meat within. The flaps of flesh were held back, pinned to Morelli's sides by something Jack couldn't see. His abdomen was a gaping hole, the intestines and other organs removed. More black vines grew out of the orifice, winding around each other and off into the shadowy recesses of the house. Morelli's viscera lay on the dirt- and leaf-covered floor beneath the dead mobster's feet. His bare legs suffered more open cuts, the skin streaked with dried blood. The flies were here, jostling against one another for the best parts.

It took Jack a long moment to realize that the cuts on Morelli's skin weren't just claw marks or gashes from a knife or razor, but symbols. Dozens of the strange images covered the man's legs and arms. The exposed muscles of Morelli's chest were scored with even more glyphs. Deep grooves cut across the red tissue, lines that at first glance seemed the chaotic hackings of a maniac. But on closer inspection, Jack saw the patterns, the triangles, the circles, the small half-moon curves, and jagged contours all intersecting to form complex arrangements.

He took a step back. Morelli had been a larger man, not fat by any means, just a beefy guy. But the figure that hung now in a horrible parody of a crucifixion was considerably more slender, almost emaciated. "What the hell did those Klan boys do to you?" he whispered.

Only the droning of the flies answered.

16

Something was wrong with the cows in William Bryant's field. The farmer stood on the top stoop of his porch, a coffee cup held loosely in his left fist, and stared into the small pasture. He couldn't see the cows but could hear their fearful, grunting moans. They'd made that noise only once before and at the time, he'd rushed out to find a couple of coyotes moving lithely through the grass, tongues lolling in anticipation of finding an easy meal. He finished the last cooling dregs of the coffee and placed the cup on the railing of the porch.

"You be careful," Nadine called to him from beyond the screen door as he plucked the shotgun from where it leaned against a support post. William flicked a hand in acknowledgement, then trotted down the stairs and across the scrubby grass of his yard. He threw an irritated look at the blackened patches that had started to appear at the edges of his property. Damned blight was getting out of hand. Already he'd had to move the cows to the field closest to the house because the acreage at the edge of his property, where he needed the cows to cull some of the grass, had become a rotting bog.

On the other side of a large oak tree, William slipped a loop of wire off a vertical fence post and pushed the makeshift gate inward.

He left the pasture open and walked quickly to the top of the small rise. The smell of wet grass mixed with the musky stench of the cows filled the air as he pushed deeper into the field, shotgun held across his body and his eyes searching for the herd.

He found them gathered in a shifting, nervous cluster near the fence line that marked the separation between the last untouched field and the ones consumed by the blight. He watched the moving bodies, searching for the slender forms of coyotes. Seeing none, he moved closer. A few of the cows noticed him and trotted steadily away, their tails swishing irritably.

William moved among the cows but found nothing amiss. There were no wounds, not one lay sick or dead. Yet there was a fearful energy among the herd and they continued their lowing despite his gentle hands on their backs and necks while mumbling reassuring words.

A sharp, sour cry drew his attention from the cows surrounding him. He waited, ears straining until it came again. At once, he understood the herd's concern. A calf was somewhere beyond the fence, deep in the black sea of dead, seeping grasses. How it managed to get through the damned barbed wire was beyond him. Grumbling a curse, William climbed the fence and entered the dead field, trying his best to ignore the horrible odor and squelching that his boots made.

Pausing every few steps to reorient himself to the sounds of the calf's cries, he crossed the area quickly. As he moved deeper into the field, a sinking feeling grew in his chest. He had an idea where the calf was. He prayed he was wrong.

He wasn't wrong.

The old well had been discovered fifty years ago when William's father expanded his farm to encompass this field and was clearing the land in preparation for planting. The well sat flush with the ground, the stones that had once ringed it long since crumbled and fallen into the throat. Knowing he had a small child at home, one on the way, and plans for more if God was kind, George Bryant had boarded over the opening to the well.

After taking over the home and farm, William had, on occasion, replaced the boards as they became weathered, brittle, or broken. But he'd not done so in the last five years, having always had something else come up that demanded his attention. Moving from crops to cattle would do that to a man. So it was with a general disgust at himself that he stood in the rain-and-rot-softened earth and stared into the black mouth of the well, listening to the pained bleatings of the calf trapped somewhere in the darkness below.

"Son of a bitch," he grumbled, looking at the jagged ends of the broken boards through which the pitiful creature had fallen. "Just wait a minute," he called down and stomped back to the house. He returned with two lengths of rope, a heavy mallet, and a long metal post he'd found in the back of his barn. He drove the post deep into the ground until he was certain it was solidly held, then tied the ropes off. He threw the leading edges of both lines in the well, and with another grumbled curse, began the arduous climb into the earth.

The well stank, as if the rot that plagued the trees and grass had sent its corrupting roots deep into the soil. William didn't think the well held water, but after the rains, it was possible. It couldn't be much, he considered, or else the calf would have drowned. In the narrow confines, the young cow's cries were amplified and thundered off the rough stone walls. Between exerted breaths and teeth clenched against the effort of lowering himself, William spoke to the animal, trying to let it know he was coming.

One foot brushed against the calf and it screamed and thrashed and splashed in its panic. William planted his feet in the cold water and breathed a gentle sigh of relief that it only came to an inch above his ankles. He grasped for the cow and in that moment, cursed himself for forgetting to bring a flashlight to check it for injuries. There was enough sunlight to allow him to see the animal and the moss-and-slime-coated rock walls surrounding them, but it wasn't enough to allow for a close inspection of its legs.

The calf fought, bucking against his touch, and William quickly gave up. Instead, he snagged one of the lengths of rope and tied it around the animal, just behind the front legs. The wee thing shivered against his body as he worked and William, despite his irritation at having to climb into a goddamned well, felt a pang of sorrow for the pitiful beast.

When the rope was secured around the calf, William grabbed the second rope. He would climb out before pulling the cow up. He placed his feet against the rough stones and worked his toes into the soft mortar. As he pushed off, reaching higher on his line, the well filled with a grating rumble. The rocks beneath his boots fell away and his legs lurched awkwardly as a section of the well's wall collapsed, splashing into the water and sending the calf into a new spasm of terrified cries. William's hand slipped from the rope and he landed against the opposite wall, a flash of pain in his lower back as he collided with the stones. He screamed a curse, his hands balling into fists with the urge to beat the goddamned cow. How could it be so fucking stupid as to fall into a well? A well it had no business being near, at that. The calf, sensing his anger, uttered a soft low and pressed itself against the wall.

William pulled in several slow, deep breaths to calm himself. There was no point in losing his temper, not here, not now. What had happened had been an accident.

He was reaching for the rope when, in the soft light from above, he noticed a pale shape in the dirt and mud exposed by the wall's collapse. Curious, he reached for it and brushed away the grit and grime. His breath caught in his throat.

A small pile of bones lay in the dirty hole. Several were broken into fragments, and his fingers had touched metal while clearing away the mud. "What in the hell?" he whispered. A few more moments of scraping and a loop of heavy, rough iron chain loosed from where it had been coiled around the bones. It slid over the rocks and landed in the water at William's feet like a petrified snake. He paid it no attention. His entire focus was on his find. He noted arm and leg bones, the broken curves of ribs, and peering through the muck farther back, the rounded shape of an eye socket.

The light in the well dimmed, bringing a wave of cold washing over

William. It pressed against him, icy fingers probing for any way to burrow into the warmth of his flesh, sending creeping tendrils of shivering fear through his muscles. William stared, fixated on the bones, distantly aware that the calf had stopped its crying and stood rigid next to him.

William's arm raised, fingers outstretched and reaching once more for the bones. His fingertips caressed their brittle smoothness, and the contact sent a charge through him, a flaring idea bright in his mind.

Take them.

He needed them. But needed wasn't the right word, he thought. He *craved* them. His hands ached to hold them. His blood boiled with a lustful hunger. The urge was all-consuming. Images of taking the bones into the house, sitting in a dark space alone with them cradled in his lap, and running his hands over them and over them filled him.

So focused was he on the bones and his compulsion to have them, William never noticed the dark figure standing only yards above, peering into the well with silvery glowing eyes. He didn't hear the barely audible words. Words in a language so old not even the trees had heard it slipping past blackened, cracked lips.

After a moment, the figure drifted back from the well, leaving the man and calf in the dark below. A calm quiet settled over the field, the black and rotting grass oozing its foul fluids barely moving in the breeze. In the sky, the sun had gained its confidence and begun its climb through the blue expanse.

The fields lay silent, spread out from the hole in the earth. Nothing moved. In the lush field, the cows remained motionless near the fence, as if they were afraid of disturbing something that would turn its vile, malevolent eye in their direction.

From the depths of the well came gentle, furtive sounds: scraping, muffled protests amid quick gasps of panicked breath. Then, a voice pregnant with despair.

"No."

The calf gave a single long scream of panic. With a series of wet thuds, its voice was silenced.

Once more, the land fell quiet. Once again, everything froze. Not a blade of grass or single leaf quivered. No insects crawled, no birds took flight or gave song.

A hand, its skin split and bloodied, slapped against the rotted earth beside the well's mouth. A moment later, a second hand reached out of the darkness and grasped, fingers digging deep into the rancid earth. The form of William Bryant pushed itself out of the darkness, soaked in blood and covered with mud.

He remained on his hands and knees, head bowed and chest heaving from the effort of climbing out of the well. His entire body was awash in fiery pain and deep within him, something rotten grew, expanding like a cancer. His stomach spasmed and he dry heaved, coughing and sputtering as his muscles contracted, sending spears of pain lancing deep within him.

His eyes opened and he stared at the ripped skin along the back of his hand where he'd inserted the bone. The skin puckered as something moved beneath the surface. The sensation of things crawling through the meat of his hands and arms rippled through him. He opened his mouth to scream, to vent the pain that chewed through every inch of his being, but only a strained gagging came out. William's muscles seized, throwing his body into an arcing, distorted pose. His eyes bulged, his tongue protruded from his lips. A subtle series of grunts bubbled from deep within his throat. The pressure in his head grew as if he were caught in a vise that was slowly closing. The whites of his eyes burst a crimson red as the vessels within ruptured. Blood seeped from the corners of his eyes and from his nose, painting the decaying grass.

William Bryant remained this way for an hour before he died. His body collapsed to the earth, the muck pressing lovingly against him as the day stretched on. Not once did his wife think to check on him; she'd long ago learned that William did what he wanted and worked on his own schedule. If he wanted contact with her during a workday, he would come to the house.

When the sun completed its snail crawl and the sky took on the muted blues and purples of early evening, William's body twitched. His bones and joints popped and broke as his skin bulged and split.

A dark figure, a shadow against the shadows of the dying light, uncurled itself, rising to stand in the decaying field. It stood, head bowed, for several minutes before lifting its head and opening its silvery eyes. The figure felt the presence of its sister, nearby and watching with infinite patience.

But it detected the presence of warm, living flesh even closer.

With steps that at first were somewhat uneven, the figure crossed the field. By the time it reached the porch of the house, windows glowing warmly from the lamps and the sounds of a mother singing a soft hymn drifting into the late spring night, its gait had grown firm and confident.

In the darkness at the base of the stairs, a strip of white split the blackness of the figure's face as it smiled in anticipation.

With fluid ease, it climbed the steps and entered the home.

The singing turned to screaming.

17

It waited while the last of the muffled screams died within the dwelling. The scent of blood and suffering was intoxicating, filling it with a sense of elevation, of power. At the same time, the blood brought an increase in hunger and rage. It smiled blackly at the thought of the corrupted flesh within the walls. More was needed. What it had accomplished thus far had only been a teasing, a tickling that hinted at the greater need.

Beneath its feet, the rotting corruption coursed through the ground, spreading slowly but steadily as it ate through the living soil, tainting the ground, poisoning the water, and altering the living. That was good. That was beautiful.

The spreading decay was a paltry salve on the seething, burning pain it felt at the continued existence of the land and those that dwelled upon it. Now that one of its sisters had been found, that pain receded.

But not entirely.

There was more to be done. Another to be found.

Its sister appeared at the top of the steps, a crooked form bathed in hot blood. They looked at one another, and each sensed the other's thoughts. The shared memories of a different race of people, dirty pitiful things wearing furs and screaming for power against the dark. The demands *turning to horrified shrieks as the truth became clear and the world filled with blood.*

The rebirth into a changed world, and the agonized return to the void. But greater than that pain was the torment of separation, the breaking of their coven. That absence ate at it as it did its sisters—a constant raw wound that never healed; a madness that consumed, regurgitated, and consumed again.

Now the two perversions of nature stood bathed in pain and madness and hate, and drank it in. Beneath the silver glowing eyes, a blackened split formed a malignant grin. They were reunited and soon, following the pull of their sister somewhere in the town, they would sing their dark songs of corruption and death.

18

While Jack Carmelo was leaving Mack's and thinking about Henry Dunn, and William Bryant was tying a rope around a post above a well, Pastor Sam McCauley was humming in his kitchen as he waited for the percolator to finish its job. The small kitchen of the parsonage was filled with the savory scent of coffee, and Sam added the heavy aroma of frying bacon to the mix. He stood over the stove, poking absentmindedly at the fatty strips with a fork as he thought about the day ahead.

It was going to be a good day. The prospect filled him with a ballooning sense of joy. He had some chores to tend to, of course: a quick run to Rangle's for some vegetables, and he needed to see to the loose hinge on the back door. However, the thing that warred with the needs of his errands, the thing that teased him with feelings of euphoria, was the time he planned to dedicate to documenting his new path forward.

His path to deliver the town from the torment of the blight.

The feeling of invigoration was one he hadn't been familiar with in quite some time, having lost countless hours of sleep to worrying about the concerns happening in and around town. For the last several days—weeks, really—he'd been frazzled, hanging on by a thread. As he prayed deep into the nights, he could feel his community slipping away, pulled under the rising waterline of fears and doubts. The blight affecting the crops and large sections of the surrounding forest, coupled with the deaths of livestock and humans, had entwined around the collective consciousness of the town like choking vines.

Sam had been the one most people came to for help, for guidance, for grounding. But what had he been able to tell them? To keep praying? To read their Bibles? Most did that anyway, and a redoubling of those efforts had yielded no noticeable effects.

Then, on Sunday at Jonas Robertson's farm . . . Sam shook his head as he flipped the bacon, his eyes squinting against the rising splatter of grease. What he'd witnessed there had been terrible. For some time after, he was convinced it had been a hallucination—a mirage brought on by stress and the heat of the day. But for so many others to have experienced it as well? And the incident with Eugenia almost stabbing Martha Bell? No. That had been no hallucination. He had experienced it. They all had.

He'd awakened Monday morning feeling as if he'd barely slept, but also with the sense that something, some idea, had begun to form deep in his mind. However, the harder he tried to focus on it, the more elusive it became, dancing just out of reach the way dreams do after waking. So, he had continued to pray for guidance and not answered the door every time people came calling. Eugenia Murphy was the most vocal of them, banging her palms against his door and begging for his help, begging him for forgiveness and to save her soul from eternal damnation. But Sam had no answers to give, so he'd remained quiet and still, only his lips moving in silent prayer until the pleas slowed and finally drifted away. Yesterday morning, the feeling of an idea was still there. It didn't vanish when he turned his thoughts to it, but instead remained locked behind a cloudy, fuzzy casing he couldn't break through.

But it was there. Reinvigorated, Sam continued to pray and read Scripture, and when the impenetrable haze didn't crack after a full day of reflection, he went to bed hopeful that another night's rest was all that was needed. He'd fallen asleep, the words of a prayer drying on his lips as his brain finally, mercifully, shut down.

In his sleep, the veil broke away, flecking apart like ash lifting from a charred body, fluttering away on the black wind of dreams. In the swirling darkness, Sam watched as shapes—figures of people but with all the solidity of smoke—gathered and prayed. They brought forth sacrifices: bleating goats, screaming horses, even other people struggling against bonds. The visions broke apart like clouds before he could get a full sense of what he was watching. With each dream, a foul feeling wormed itself into his body, filling him with a sickening cold.

Then the whispers came. The words at first made no sense, the language something he'd never heard. Each syllable sounded strained, painful, as if the speaker had to force their mouth to stretch and fit around the jagged edges of broken letters in order to expel the words. But the whispers cast the horrible visions away, replacing them with calm and clarity. Their words coalesced into a rhythm, a pattern that in his deep level of sleep, Sam was able to decipher.

At first, his mind rebelled at what they suggested. The concepts were anathema to his core beliefs. In his bed, Sam's body twitched and twisted as he struggled against the ideas that surrounded him, finding cracks and filling him. But as the late hours ticked on, his struggles lessened. After a time, he stilled. When the sun's light spilled over the sill of his window, filling the bedroom with gauzy warmth, Sam opened his eyes and smiled.

He lay in bed for some time, enjoying the sensation of the sheets against his skin and considering all that swirled in his mind. When he'd finally gotten up, the sight of the strange carved wooden box sitting quietly atop his dresser cast away any leftover fragments of doubt about what he'd learned while asleep. The box was black wood, a type of dark hardwood he'd never seen in his life. The symbols—twisting, grotesque filigree—filled him with a cold, clammy sensation. There was something ancient and terrible about the box.

What was inside was even worse.

Sam recoiled, staggering back, one hand rising to his mouth to stifle a scream. What *was* that?

Then, clarity. As the idea settled into his mind and took root, the sickening wave that coursed through him dissipated. He took another glance at the thing amassed within the box and frowned at himself. His initial reaction must have been fueled by the last vestiges of sleep still clinging to his mind. There was nothing wrong with the contents. They were but a furtherance of God's love and assistance.

Now, standing at his stove and picking at the frying bacon, he remembered being resistant, at first, to the words and the path laid out to him. But he remembered the moment, as if it had been a conversation around his small dining table just the day before, that his fear had fled and he understood. These weren't evil ideas, nor heretical as they had seemed at first.

Anything new, he reasoned, had the risk of feeling wrong. It diverted from the old, the comfortable, the familiar. In doing so, in the act of treading new ground, a sense of fear and distrust was natural. But deep down, Sam understood that what he had been told while he slept was the right path forward.

God had spoken to him. In the middle of the night, God had finally answered his prayers and delivered a way for Sam to help lead the town and its people through this ordeal.

He transferred the bacon to a plate, poured a cup of coffee, and moved to the small table that sat against the wall beneath a paper calendar depicting a picture of a hillside overlooking a cloudy sky, the sun's rays spearing through the clouds to bring light to the people below. He sat and ate and considered the new rituals and prayers. Despite never having seen or heard them before, they were as clear and familiar as the ones he'd studied since he was a young boy.

Still, it could be difficult to present these new concepts to the townspeople. There was a risk that they would reject his plans outright, possibly going as far as attacking him in their fear of his words. But how was that any different than the veritable slings and arrows that Jesus himself suffered when preaching His approach to acceptance and love to everyone?

Sam chuckled to himself. Of course he wasn't comparing himself to Christ, that would be ridiculous. But there was a similarity in what he was facing and what the son of God endured. People were already terrified by the current unnatural happenings and if that fear was compounded by the prospect of a new way of worship, there was a chance that Sam could find himself nailed to a board. Instead of Golgotha, he would most likely wind up dying in a field full of rotting corn somewhere east of Jonas Robertson's barn.

He finished his meal and dressed for the day. He decided he couldn't wait any longer; he would tend to the door hinge and market later in the afternoon. Sam wanted to spend most of the morning and early afternoon in his small office in the church, transcribing the words that flowed through his head like a river. He needed to map out the rituals and plan the best way to introduce them.

Four people, two men and two women, stood by the front doors to the church when he turned the corner of the building. Jonas Robertson was the first to see the pastor and the man hurried down the short flight of brick steps. Sam couldn't help but notice that they all held the same expression on their faces. Fear. This wasn't the same guise of concern over their lands that he'd seen from the pulpit for the last several sermons. This was new, deeper, more pure.

"Sam," Jonas said curtly in greeting.

"Jonas," Sam answered, forcing a smile. He said hello to the others, his eyes lingering on Anna Robertson, still at the top of the stairs where her husband had just stood. "How can I help all of you this morning?"

Jonas glanced back at the others briefly. "Something's happened."

Concern gnawed at Sam's chest. *Please don't let it be Grace.* "What? Has something happened in town? Should we call the police?"

Two of the people, Jonas and Robert Wolfe, spoke at the same time.

"Tell him, Alma. Tell him what you—" Robert said.

"He's gone," Jonas said in a weary, thin voice. "Just . . . gone."

Confusion locked his smile in place and Sam gestured to the door of the church. "Why don't you all follow me. We can talk about whatever it is. I will do everything I can to help." He unlocked the door and stepped inside, waiting for the small group to file in.

The nave was unnervingly quiet. Despite the thousands of times he'd been inside a silent, empty church, to Sam it always felt like trespassing. Especially when he was the only one inside. It only seemed slightly less so now as he went about lighting candles and flaming the lanterns. The deep shadows banished, Sam walked to the front of the pews and gestured for the foursome to sit while he lowered himself to the top step of the chancel.

The others sat, fidgeting with their hands in their laps, eyes downcast. Sam spread his hands. "Who would like to start?"

Alma Wolfe looked up, her tight black curls forming a heavy helmet against her scalp. There were dark bags under her bloodshot eyes and her lips were pressed tightly into a thin line. Her husband sat hunched like a boulder next to her, refusing to raise his head to look at anyone. The muscles in Alma's face shifted and jerked as she warred with the need to speak and the clear fear of saying whatever it was that bothered her.

Finally, she spat it out, "I killed all our chickens. I didn't mean to —" She stopped short, lowered her head, and gave it a shake as if admonishing herself. "That's not true. I did mean to. Last night after Robert went to bed, I stayed up sitting out on the porch, knitting. I couldn't sleep. Don't know why." Her small shoulders jerked up and down at that. "But as I sat there working the needles, I smelled it. It was rotten, like something dead laying in the sun for days. It was coming from the chicken coop. I've worked in and around that coop for the last fifteen years and never smelled anything like that. You find dead chickens from time to time, but they never smell like that. Not even in August. But when I opened the door, the entire coop was filled with dead chickens. Every single one of them. Bloated and dead. Some had burst open. It was . . ." She shook her head again, as if denying the memory. "My first thought was to wake Robert. But what would he have done? I was still thinking I needed to wake him when the heat of the flames forced me back. I don't even remember getting the gas can from the garage, or pouring it into the coop and throwing in a match. I was standing there thinking about waking my husband, and the next thing I knew, the entire chicken coop was covered in flames."

Sam leaned forward, held out a sympathetic hand despite the distance being too far for him to touch her. "I'm so sorry. I can't imagine losing—"

Alma cut in. "They were still alive." Sam leaned back, his brow furrowing. Alma sniffed, rubbed her nose with the back of one hand, and continued. "They were all screaming in there. I didn't even know chickens could scream. I saw them, running around, crashing into each other. They were on fire. They—" Her voice tightened, pitching higher as she spoke until it cut off with a soft wheeze. Her lips quivered and she began to cry. Anna Robertson wrapped one hesitant arm around the woman. Alma leaned into her, sniffling.

Sam listened with growing fascination. The events described were horrific, there was no doubt, but he sensed that horror, his revulsion, as if through a thick batting of cotton. What he really felt, what filled Sam with a warmth that he hadn't experienced since the first time he knew—truly knew—his calling was to be a shepherd for the Lord, was a sense of connection. Of rightness.

Jonas held his wife's hand in his own large one as he spoke. Tuesday morning he had gotten up, and as he started his chores had noticed that Charlie wasn't in bed. After a search of the house and surrounding barns turned up nothing, he, Anna, and Grace—Sam's heart gave a quick flutter at her name—spent several frantic hours searching the property.

"When we found the torn scrap of shirt," Jonas said, "it came back to me. I had no memory of it until I touched that piece of cloth. I . . ." His voice broke and it took him a long moment to gather himself. "I remember leading him there, sending him into the trees. I couldn't stop it. I *had* to. Something made me send my son into the woods." Jonas had kept his eyes cast toward the floor while he spoke, but now he raised them and fixed his sorrowful gaze on Sam. The man looked like a hound dog who knew he'd let the quarry get away and was due a whipping. "I just don't know what to do," Jonas said. "I need to let Chief Dickerson know so he can—"

"No," Sam interjected. His body was humming with excitement. Jonas's eyebrows raised in surprise and even Alma stiffened at Sam's brusqueness. The pastor let out a long, calming breath. "Sorry. That came out stronger than I'd intended. If you go to Dickerson, with everything that he has going on, these things will just be added to the pile and forgotten. But they're not meant to be forgotten. They're meant for something greater, as truly awful as they may seem right now. What I mean is, and I mean this for all of you, I believe that you were called to do what you did. Called by God." The faces in the pew darkened with confusion, and Sam pressed on. "What all of you did, while shocking and at the moment horrible, is, I believe, the best thing you could have done."

"What in the hell are you talking about?" Robert asked angrily. "How can you sit there and tell us that killing our livestock and Jonas's boy being left out in the woods is a good thing? How is either possibly a good thing?"

Sam steepled his hands beneath his chin, resting his head on the fingertips. "I have prayed, like all of you, for weeks now. Asking for a way through this plague. Seeking any sign, any hint of a path forward. And for the longest time, nothing came. But then I experienced my own . . ."—he looked to the ceiling, searching for the right word—"event. At the potluck." The farmer and his wife nodded, the memories bringing frowns to their lips. "After I got home, I spent the next two days and nights praying and thinking on what I'd seen. What we'd all seen. Last night, in my sleep, God came to me."

"He came to you?" Anna asked, her words colored with hope and suspicion.

"He did. Not in the sense that we've read about in the Good Book. Not as a flaming bush, or by proxy of one of His glorious angels. He came and showed me the path forward. It's a new path. New to us, at least, but old and all but forgotten to mankind. It's a path requiring sacrifice, such as the ones you have just made. There will be new prayers for us to learn. There will be new hymns to sing. I promise, I will make everything clear at Wednesday night's sermon, when I can address the full congregation. But these new ways are exactly what we need to do in order to gain the Lord's favor, and to deliver us from this evil that has beset us."

The others were silent for a long time. Sam's heart raced. They would either accept the truth as he'd delivered it, or they would call him a madman and storm out, dooming themselves. He didn't want that to happen. He genuinely cared about each and every one of them and wanted only to protect them and guide them to salvation. And this new way *was* the way to that redemption. He knew it as certainly as he knew he breathed air to live.

"What should we do?" Anna Robertson asked hesitantly. The faces of the others shifted from concern to open hopefulness.

"I will lay it all out at Wednesday's service. But for now, will you pray with me? It's a new prayer, so I will lead it." The group bowed their heads. Sam took a steadying breath and focused on the words that had been floating in the back of his mind since waking that morning. He spoke, his words part of a strange language whose origin he didn't know. Sam's eyes watered as he formed each syllable, the action, the words themselves painful in his mouth. Yet with each agonizing utterance, Sam's body tingled as a surge of renewing energy rushed through him. As he pushed the strange phrases out, tears spilled along his cheeks. Warmth, coppery and salty, tickling his tongue as his gums bled. He let them, ignoring the tickling on his skin and dull ache around his teeth. Those things didn't matter. Nothing else mattered.

This was the first step to salvation.

19

"You listening to me?" The question cut through the haze in Jack's mind and pulled his attention from the truck's window. Behind the wheel, Elmer Cleary watched the uneven road ahead, steering smoothly around patches of blackened, swampy rot.

"What?" Jack asked.

Cleary's eyes slid to Jack and back to the road. "What's got you all tied up?" He paused before answering his own question. "Your man Morelli."

Jack thought of Carlo hanging, flayed open, crawlers of dead vines running out of his hollow abdomen, his mouth, his eyes. "Yeah," Jack said. "They did a number on him."

Cleary was quiet for several seconds. "You're still thinking Dunn and his guys did it?"

"Who else? Prohis wouldn't have done that. They would have arrested him. *Maybe* shot him dead. But that?" He looked out the window at the shifting greens and browns of the passing landscape. "That was . . ." Jack's fist tightened and he thumped it once against the door. "After what you told me about Dunn killing that kid, this level of violence makes sense for him."

"Even those symbols?" Cleary's doubtful tone wasn't lost on Jack.

"Considering the rumors your men have been spreading— something in the woods, something unnatural—the Klan carving up Morelli like that would be a smart move. Kill someone horribly—a known gangster from Chicago, for example—carve symbols into his body, and let superstition run rampant. It's a perfect tool." *To attack simpleminded people.* He finished to himself. No point in insulting Cleary.

He continued. "Dunn's the wild card. The man who approached me in the diner is certainly an up-front type of guy. But there was something in his eyes. He's not your average thug. He's calculating. Mean. The guy has seen death."

"That don't mean much," Cleary said. "Most men these days threw a bit of lead across the trenches in France."

"Yeah, but there's something about Dunn," Jack said. "Something darker. That guy, he's always got something going on in his head. 'Working out the angles,' as a friend of mine back home likes to say."

Cleary nodded. "He hit one of our trucks just the other night. Killed both guys. So what are you going to do? Still think visiting Carl Stott is going to work?"

That was a question Jack had been debating ever since finding Morelli. His first instinct was to hit back against Dunn, hard and fast. Send a clear message that the toady little shitkicker had seriously fucked up by bumping off a member of the Outfit. But that could escalate into a war that he didn't need. Cleary's operation was large, but the majority of the people working for him weren't hard men ready to do what was needed. Not like the guys Jack worked with in Chicago. And Dunn and his people had already shown they were willing to go to extreme lengths to intimidate and achieve their ends.

So, no, hitting back immediately wouldn't achieve anything.

Jack thought about the McCarthys and that Polish kid, Turski. He thought about Eamon Flynn and Cormac O'Shea, the other two in McCarthy's little crew. He'd waited for years to get his revenge on them for what they'd done to Bobby. Waiting wasn't a problem for Jack. Dunn was going to get what was coming to him for Morelli, that was a certainty. But the plan to speak to this Stott guy and the lower-level hayseeds was still very much on the docket.

"We'll see." Jack lit a cigarette and gestured at the road ahead. "So what's the deal with this guy?"

Cleary paused, his seamed face creased deeper by irritation that Jack had changed the subject. "William Bryant. Good guy, has about thirty acres. Used to grow crops but switched to cattle a few years back. We've been using his old barn for a while now to store bottles before shipping. He's got a place dug beneath the floor in some of the old stalls to hold them. Probably fifteen hundred gallons there now."

"And they'll be okay after the storm?"

"Should be. But it's always good to check. Besides, if what you were saying about altering our routes turns out to work, we'll need to coordinate with him so he knows we're coming out in the middle of the night and won't shoot us."

"You've lived here all your life?" Jack asked.

The big farmer gave a grunt of assent. "Family's owned land here for generations, going back to Providence."

"What's the wire on that place?"

"Wire?"

Jack rolled his eyes. "What do you know about it? Why are your men so terrified of it? I practically had to threaten to shoot them to get them to go out there looking for Morelli. It was luck that we found him in one of the houses farther out. I don't think even the threat of a bullet would have gotten them to go any farther."

"Providence was around back in the late sixteen hundreds. Sometime around the turn of the century—nobody really knows when, there's no record of anything—Jericho Springs came into being. Story is—and nobody knows this for certain, it's all just word of mouth—most of the people left Providence and started Jericho. The rest stayed behind and eventually died out."

Jack frowned. "That doesn't make sense. Why would half a town relocate, what, five miles or so away?"

"No idea. Like I said, ain't no record of anything, far as I know." He lifted a massive hand and pointed. "Here we are."

Cleary turned onto a wide dirt road. On the left stretched rolling hills of farmland segmented by barbed wire fencing. A large barn, its wooden facade gray from decades of weather, sat sagging and forlorn beyond a single-story farmhouse near the road. A few chickens pecked listlessly in the front yard until Cleary pulled the truck onto the grass and sent them scurrying. Across the road several homes were spaced evenly apart, all lacking the fields of their neighbor. An old Black man with a snowy beard sat on what looked like a wooden crate on the short porch of one of the homes, a knife in one hand and a small piece of wood in the other. He paused his whittling to watch as Cleary raised an indifferent hand in greeting. The man spat to one side, narrowly missing a dirty brown dog sleeping nearby. The sickly smell of rotting vegetation was a thick grease in the air. Jack caught several blackened patches of trees behind the row of homes and in the grass before he turned to follow Cleary toward Bryant's house.

"William hired some of them to help on his farm. That's the start of their part of town," Cleary said and stepped around a putrid spot of ground.

"Bryant doesn't mind living next to them?" Jack asked.

Cleary ignored the question and mounted the few steps to the porch. He brought the side of his fist against the door, rattling the wood in its frame and sending heavy booms through the warm afternoon. When no answer came, he repeated the process. Again no answer. Cleary turned his heavy eyes to Jack. "Let's try around back."

They found the rear door of the house, a flimsy wooden-framed screen door hanging by one screw that opened onto a shadowy porch filled with piles of junk. The screen mesh was ripped, the flaps hanging limp. Blood smeared the doorframe. Red footprints criss-crossed the steps, the trail leading both across the porch to the kitchen door and through the dry grass. Jack's eyes followed the splotchy tracks on the ground. He lost sight of them near the fence that marked the boundary of the pasture, but picked it up again as it wove up a gentle hill and deeper into the field. From somewhere beyond the rise came the occasional *moo* of cows.

Jack pulled open the remains of the door and stepped carefully onto the closest clean patch of floor. The shadows did nothing to quell the heat, and sweat sprang out along his head, neck, and back.

"William!" Cleary called out from the bottom of the stairs. "Nadine? Y'all in there?"

As Elmer spoke, Jack approached the solid kitchen door. It hung open, the knob smeared with blood. Through the gap came the soft droning of flies, the buzzing drifting on a tide of air tinted with a familiar smell. Jack withdrew his pistol and glanced back at Cleary. "Something's dead in there."

The bootlegger, preparing to call out again, closed his mouth. His eyes took on a hard edge. "I'm right behind you," he said and mounted the steps. The ruined door rasped weakly as he stepped onto the porch. In the hot confines, Cleary's bulk towered over Jack, pressing him uncomfortably toward the house. Jack pushed the kitchen door open, and after a quick peek, stepped inside.

Before his foot touched the wooden floor, the familiar odor of blood and death rushed at Jack like a desperate lover, wrapping him in a stifling embrace. Jack's throat tightened and he forced a swallow. His eyes watered, the moisture spilling down his cheeks. He pushed the door open the rest of the way, bracing himself in expectation of seeing the staring dead eyes of the McCarthys. Instead, he stepped into a simple kitchen. Sunlight angled in through a pair of windows to his left, the light muddied by the detritus piled on the porch. His eyes drifted over a simple table with two chairs, a wooden icebox, and a squat black stove. The only signs of disarray were a pot lying on the floor on its side, a slick of some lumpy food he couldn't identify, and a single bloody handprint on the open doorjamb leading out of the room. The print was smeared, the finger marks stretching impossibly long. Flies danced greedily around the cold food as Jack thumped softly across the floor. A gasp and soft retching sound told him that Cleary had crossed the threshold.

Jack pointed to the handprint. "They're probably in the hall."

Cleary didn't answer. His short gasps told Jack that he was fighting to keep from vomiting. Jack peered through the doorway, ignoring the dried smears of blood inches from his head. The hall was short and narrow. A second doorway framed the opposite end of the corridor, hazy light from more windows giving the impression of a living room.

A dark shape lay among the darker pool of shadows in the hall. The smell of dead flesh and blood was impossibly thick and once more, Jack's mind conjured images of the tiny basement room back in Chicago.

"Is there a lantern?" he asked, not taking his eyes off the inert form on the floor. Cleary gave a soft sound, what may have been acknowledgement, and thumped his way through the kitchen. He returned a moment later and passed a wire-handled lantern into Jack's hand. He held it while Cleary lit the wick. In the weak glow of the match, Jack glimpsed the breadth of the damage done to the body. When the lantern was fully lit and held before him, the total vision was astonishing.

"That's Nadine." Cleary's voice was firm, the man having found some measure of control over the situation.

Nadine Bryant lay sprawled in the hall, her body twisted where she had fallen. But that wasn't quite right, Jack noticed. The lower half of her body faced the floor, her knees resting against the wooden slats. But her back and shoulders were also pressed to the floor, as what was left of her face gaped at the ceiling. The woman had been broken in half and twisted like a chicken bone. Her dress was covered in blood. More of the red fluid covered the floor and coated the walls in arcing sprays as well as fat smears. Jack glanced at the patterns and could almost picture the frenzied level of violence that had taken place in the small space. When his gaze returned to the corpse, a stillness settled over him.

Her skin, what he could see of it, was gouged and slashed, the cuts forming patterns. Instantly he thought of the symbols he'd seen cut into Morelli's body where it hung in the remains of the house deep in the woods. Tearing his attention away, he saw that some of the blood patterns on the walls were crudely drawn symbols as well.

"William?" Cleary called. In the tomb-like quiet of the house, his voice was a cannon blast. Jack fought the urge to tell the man to shut up, that whoever did this could still be there. Gripping his pistol, he stepped quickly past the body of the woman and into the rooms beyond. All were empty and showed no signs of violence. He returned to the hall. Cleary remained in the kitchen, his body filling the open frame as he stared at the corpse.

"Nobody else is here," Jack said. "There's no sign of Dunn or any of his guys or of the husband."

Cleary dragged his attention from Nadine. The man's face was pale with shock. "William wouldn't have allowed this. He'd have fought."

"So where is he?" But as Jack asked the question, he remembered the bloody tracks leading into the field. Hurrying through the hall and past Cleary, he made for the back door.

Blinking in the glare of the afternoon sun, Jack followed the trail to the fence. He lifted the wire latch and started into the field, following the faint smears. When he reached the top of the hill he paused, surveying the expanse of the farm. The cows he'd heard earlier were gathered in a cluster at the far edge of the fenced plot of land on which he stood. They shuffled against one another, ears and tails flicking nervously. The field beyond was blackened with rot, but the trail of blood led directly to it. Jack approached the next fence line and studied the ground. Against the glistening black blades of grass, the blood was invisible. But where that trail ended, another in the form of trampled grass started. Grimacing, Jack climbed over the fence and stepped into the muck. His feet sank slightly in the rotted earth and the grass squeaked wetly beneath his soles as he continued on.

Moments later, he noticed the pole driven into the ground, two ropes tied to it leading into the grass. As he grew closer, he saw the hole in the earth into which they dropped. The decayed ground on one side of the hole was broken and smashed, as if someone or something had fought to climb out. He'd left the lantern with Cleary but didn't need it to understand what the hole was. Jack put his hands on his knees and leaned over, peering into the black depths of the well.

Even with the sun high overhead, he couldn't make out anything at the bottom.

"Jesus H," Elmer said, his voice thick with disgust, his attention focused on something to one side of the well. Following Cleary's line of sight, Jack grimaced.

A pile of bloody clothes and red pulpy meat lay on the dark ground. Jack was able to pick out a finger and a patch of hair no bigger than a baseball. The rest looked like it had been put through a grinder.

"Any idea who that is?" he asked. "Bryant maybe?"

Cleary shook his head and turned from the grisly scene. "No clue." He approached the pole and the attached ropes. "I bet we tug on one of those, we'll pull up the cow."

Jack pointed to the trampled ground leading to the house. "So, what? Bryant starts to rescue a cow and for some reason changes his mind? Goes back to the house?"

"Would make sense if your theory of Dunn and the Klan holds up. If they came here, William would have gone back to deal with them. That don't explain what that is," he said, gesturing weakly at the pile of ruined meat.

"What do you mean, if my theory holds up?"

Cleary turned his sad, hound dog eyes to the well, the blackened fields, and finally to Jack. "Maybe it wasn't the Klan." Jack started to answer, to rebuke the hint of superstition, when a piercing cry echoed across the fields. "Hawk," Cleary said softly, then started back toward the house. "I'm going to check the stores."

Jack held back, his heart hammering in his chest at the screeching of the hawk. His eyes scanned the dark length of trees beyond the pastures. He couldn't shake the feeling that something was watching him from the woods.

20

"Get in the truck," Carl Stott growled and shoved the crying woman. She stumbled forward, tripped over her feet, and dropped to her hands and knees. A sharp cry of pain and fear tore from her throat. She stayed on the ground, her hair hanging like dark curtains on either side of her face. Her back hitched with shaky breaths.

Henry Dunn leaned against the front fender of the truck, a pipe clenched between his teeth as he watched the woman struggle to untangle her dress from around her feet and stand. Stott's slim, muscular form stood over her, fists clenched and his face screwed up in anger. *He's trying,* Dunn thought. Of all the local Klan boys that he'd been working with, a small handful had quickly adopted Dunn's way of doing things. Carl Stott had been the fastest and most ardent.

The longer the woman took to recover and stand, the more Dunn felt the urge to pull his pistol and place it against the back of her skull. All the people they'd gathered so far had resisted and it was starting to piss him off. *I should have shot that first bastard right away. That would have sent the message that I'm not to be fucked with.* Of course, the man in question had been colored, and Dunn doubted that shooting a nigger in the street would have had much of an effect on any of the white people.

The woman pulled herself up and glared at Stott with a mixture of defiance and outright fear. A clump of auburn hair lay across her face at an angle, but she ignored it. Before she could say anything, Stott shoved her again. "Get in the fucking truck." The woman looked at Dunn, although whether seeking aid or confirmation, Henry wasn't sure. He gave neither, only watched her coolly and sucked on his pipe. The woman hitched up her dress and with the aid of the other three people in the back, climbed up. Stott waited until she was settled, then waved to Clayton George. The kid grinned wickedly and pulled a pistol from his waistband before boarding the truck to guard those clustered in the small bed.

"Anyone else?" Stott asked. Dunn considered the people gathered in the two trucks. Six people—four men and two women—sat huddled together, fearful, their eyes darting from the hard, silent men guarding them to Dunn and Stott.

"Is that all from the list?" he asked softly. Earlier in the day, after he'd calmed down from his interaction with Jack Carmelo, Dunn had told Stott to put together a list of people either known or heavily suspected of involvement with Elmer Cleary's operations. These were to be either people who supplied material goods to support the manufacture of moonshine or those who actually ran the stills or delivered the product. The woman they'd just rounded up was the spouse of one of the suspected bootleggers. The man hadn't been home, and according to his wife, she had no idea where he was. She claimed that he'd not been home in three days. Dunn had ordered her onto the truck in his place. If she was married to a bootlegger, she was guilty by association.

"Yeah," Stott said. "Well, except the husband." He turned his blue eyes to the sky. "It's getting late."

"So?"

Carl Stott wasn't a large man, just average height. He was in shape, his body hardened from long days working as a hay farmer.

He had sandy hair and a face covered in an early growth beard. The look of nervousness on his features soured Dunn's stomach.

"It's just that,"—he paused, swallowing thickly— "considering where we're going . . ."

The pipe stem creaked under the pressure of Dunn's teeth. "Out with it, man."

"Some of the other guys get a little nervous being out that close to the woods at night. Especially with, you know, some of the things that's been going on."

Dunn's eyes narrowed and he leaned in close enough to smell Stott's sour body odor. "Ain't nothing out there you need to be afraid of other than me, if you don't get moving." Stott's throat bobbed again and he hurried to the driver's side of the truck. Dunn signaled to the other men and they drove into the approaching darkness.

As Stott steered, Dunn rested one elbow on the door and leaned his face close to the opening, enjoying the air against his skin. The grumble of the truck's engine and the rattling of the vehicle over the uneven, rocky road drowned out the pleas and questions of the people in the bed of the truck. Dunn allowed his thoughts to drift, finding that they settled, as they had frequently since that morning, on Jack Carmelo.

He reminded himself, not for the first time that day, that the gangster from Chicago had been lucky Dunn hadn't shot him right then and there. If they hadn't been in the diner with other patrons and staff, he would have. He'd always found it best to do the killing first and fast. Doing so left no room for anyone to question him, to try and talk or worm their way out of the trouble they'd found themselves in. It had been a lesson he'd learned in France while fighting the Hun, and it had been one he'd continued to follow while working with the ASL.

Besides, he'd always told others when they expressed shock at his sudden, vicious actions, "If you kill the other bastard first, there isn't anyone to contradict your version of the story."

In the few moments he'd spoken to Carmelo, Dunn had gotten the full measure of the man. It wasn't hard with people like that.

Foreigners like Carmelo were all the same. They came over here and spread their seed, propagating their kind. That they wanted only to change America into a version of the place they'd just left never made any sense to Dunn. And naturally, with them came the violence, the booze, the drugs, the diseases. Sure America had violence and booze, but the violence had been born out of necessity; a country fighting to stand on its own against a world determined to control and subjugate it.

Booze was a different story, though. Dunn had spent his entire life watching as alcohol slowly ate away at his father, like a self-inflicted cancer that took and took and took until all that was left was a weak, incoherent shell of a man. A man who could barely stand and who pissed and shat himself most days.

When the Volstead Act had been implemented, Dunn had allowed himself a moment of happiness, a few minutes to cheer the bravery of those who fought for the new direction, who had struggled to take such an important step toward saving the soul of America. Then he had gotten to work, hunting down anyone guilty of violating the law.

Jack Carmelo represented the worst of that kind. He was an extension of a disease that was growing unchecked in other parts of the country. A member of a gang who only preyed on the weak, taking whatever they wanted and giving only pain, addiction, and death in return. And now that same cancer had spread its tentacles to Jericho Springs. Of course, Dunn had no deep ties to Jericho Springs; it was just another small town on the map. But it was a community of God-fearing and mostly law-abiding white citizens who needed his help scraping off the wart of booze. Dunn had to dig deep to cut out the affliction and give the good Christians a sense of peace and prosperity.

Over the course of the day, Dunn had come to understand why Carmelo was in town. It made sense, with the headlines Dunn had read about the gang wars in Chicago and other cities like New York and LA, that those involved would look to expand their reach, increase their business, and by extension, their coffers.

Which meant that Dunn would have to step up his efforts as well. With the arrival of Carmelo, the production of illegal whiskey would increase. Even with news of some of the stills being attacked and those working them killed, with stories of a blight affecting some crops, Dunn knew that the people caught up in the thrall of illicit activities would only continue until they were stopped.

Night had fallen by the time the headlights of Stott's truck splashed on the old barn, sending a flash of a memory ripping through Dunn's mind like lightning.

The woman, her face screwed up in terror, eyes squeezed tight beneath his hard stare and wide grin. Her eyes springing open wide as the knife penetrated her skin.

"You coming?" Stott asked, pulling Dunn back to the moment.

"Get them inside," he said, still staring at the barn.

He waited until the men had forced the six lawbreakers off the trucks and herded them at gunpoint toward the barn. One of Dunn's men trotted ahead and pulled the large sliding door aside, revealing the black maw of the barn. As the door reached its terminus on the track, the man recoiled, raising a hand to his mouth. He said something to his crew that Dunn couldn't make out. Stott and a couple of the other Klansmen exchanged words. A few threw glances back to where Dunn sat in the truck, before Stott barked a command and they entered the barn, shoving the prisoners before them.

Dunn waited until the interior of the barn glowed with lantern light before getting out of the truck. The volume of those they'd rounded up swelled—panicked questions and sharp demands to be released, threats of retribution when others found out. He drifted through the wide, open doorway and inhaled deeply. The air was a thick perfume of the wet, musty odor of stored hay, dirt, and sweat. Yet something lay beneath that heady smell. It was an acrid, sour stench that reminded Dunn of bodies left to rot at the bottom of a trench, the exposed flesh bloated and cooking in the sun while the rest of the corpse was submerged in the ever-present ankle-deep pool of water that filled most of the dugouts. It was the fetid smell of putrescence, of oozing decay. His own nose wrinkled in disgust. His stomach gave a lurch, threatening to send his dinner up. Dunn paused inside the door and looked curiously around the wide space, searching for the source.

The barn was large, with stacked bales of hay along the opposite wall. More were piled to the left and tendrils draped over the edge of the loft overhead. A series of tools hung from pegs, while others leaned against the wall to his right. The floor was covered with loose straw and dirt. The six people he had arrested stood in a clump in the center of the space, surrounded by Stott, Clayton, and Dunn's other thugs. A couple of the armed men glanced nervously at the dark corners of the barn.

"The fuck is that smell?" one asked.

"The wood's rotting," another said, pointing. The section of wall showed the boards blackened with mold and rot. A greasy moisture leaked out of the wood, sliding along it like a slug trail.

One of the men stepped closer to the wood, reached a hand toward it, then stopped short of actually touching it. "This ain't right. This is my brother's place. He only built it three years ago. I know. I helped him. I don't—"

"Get your ass back over there," Dunn said. The man flinched, gave the wood a final concerned look, and returned to his original spot. Dunn approached the cluster of scared-looking people. The men had positioned themselves in front of the two women. The largest man, a thick bull of a white guy, glared at Dunn with one good eye. The other was a large, swollen, purple mass. Blood smeared on his chin from a busted lip was further proof of the struggle he'd put up. Next to him, the Black man stood, eyes directed to the floor.

"I know who you are," Black Eye said, pointing at Dunn. "I've heard about you."

"That so?" Dunn asked, slightly amused.

"Yeah. I heard you killed people back in Georgia and have the law after you." The mention of murder caused one of the women to begin crying. The other men's faces darkened and even the Black man risked glancing at Dunn.

"Oh, I've killed a lot of people," Dunn said matter-of-factly. "Most were in France in service to this country. And a few were here after the war, also in service to this country."

"That's murder," Black Eye spat.

"Doesn't matter what you call it," Dunn said. He raised a hand, curled the fingers in, and inspected them as if looking for dirt. "Violence like that is the only thing that people like you understand. It's the only message that can cut through the addiction that fills your head and blackens your heart and soul. People like you and *you*"—he shifted his eyes to the Black man— "are rotting this country. It's luck, you see, that has brought me here. Jericho Springs is a black hole of rot. And I'm the knife that is going to cut it out." He looked at Stott. "Tie them."

Stott grabbed one of the men. The group shrank back, the women crying out as Black Eye rushed forward, one meaty fist coming up to connect with the side of Stott's head. Before impact, the upper side of Black Eye's head blew out in a wet splash of blood, spraying the women's faces. Dunn suppressed a smile at the sight of a couple of small pieces of bone sticking to the cheek of one, held in place by a large piece of what could only be brain. As the man's body crumpled to the ground, Dunn lowered his pistol and sucked on the pipe. He gave Stott a "What are you waiting for?" look.

When the five remaining men and women were secured, hands bound together behind them, Dunn instructed his men to line them up and drop them to their knees. The sounds of crying intensified while two of the three men began what Dunn knew to be the bargaining phase of the event. They offered money, they offered the deeds to their land. One even offered his wife, saying she could bake a peach cobbler that would make the angels weep with envy.

Dunn ignored it all. He stood back and off to the side as the five were forced to their knees. The only one who made no sound and offered no resistance was the Black man, which to Henry, stood to reason. The Black race, as he understood it, was made to do as it was told. Subservience was its natural state. A niggling feeling settled in the back of his mind. He almost wished the man would struggle. It would do no good, of course, but even a trapped rabbit fights until the very end.

When all five were kneeling on the straw, Dunn stepped in front of them, hands by his sides, and studied each in turn. He adjusted his teeth around the pipe stem, thankful for the fragrant smoke that made the stench of the barn somewhat bearable.

"All right," he said. "Let's do this."

21

Jack never would have admitted it to Cleary, but seeing the Bryant woman dead had stuck with him. Every time he closed his eyes—and more often than he'd like when his eyes were open—he saw the blood-soaked body in the hall, its spine broken and twisted. In every image, it wasn't Nadine Bryant's face that stared up stupidly shocked in her final moments, but Norma's. His wife's small, perfect features staring at him with hateful accusation from beneath the deep cuts of the symbols etched into her face.

A painful spasm wrenched its way across his chest and he slowed, ignoring the suspicious looks thrown by a pair of women as they passed. *It hadn't been Norma,* he told himself. *I saw that woman's face clearly. It wasn't her. Norma's back in Chicago.*

Of course she is, a cold voice whispered in the back of his mind. *But what if she's dead? What if she's slumped in that chair, needle sticking out of her arm, foamy spittle oozing from her lips, dead eyes looking out at the street?*

Jack pulled in two deep, powerful breaths, exhaling forcefully. Of course that was possible, but if that were the case, Tony would have contacted him. So no, she wasn't dead. The discomfort in his chest faded and as he started walking again, a flash of anger replaced concern.

Why did he care? She'd made it clear that she had no interest in whether he lived or died. The only thing she cared about was the heroin and maybe the pipe dream of returning to the stage. An emaciated nightclub dancer gyrating her bony, skeletal hips while a quartet played a jazzy tune wouldn't exactly do wonders for the nether regions of club patrons.

She was done with the marriage and with him. They'd not had a civil word between them in months, and hadn't gone to bed together in over a year. Every time he was with her, her disgust with him radiated off her like heat waves off pavement. So why did he care?

He lit a cigarette and forced himself to admit the truth. He didn't. Not really. He cared because of who she had once been, what she had represented: A happy life with children and security. Love. Comfort. But all of that had never really been an option . . . He'd picked the flower that was beautiful on the outside but filled with a cancerous rot on the inside. A hungry disease that was never satisfied. It never allowed Norma to fully love no matter how hard he'd tried in the beginning. Her personal blight was always going to win. It was always going to consume her. Admitting what he'd always known didn't mean it hurt any less.

He sighed, the gears in his mind switching and settling on a decision. When this job was over and he returned to Chicago, if Norma was still above ground, he would give her the freedom she wanted. She could even keep the apartment. He'd take his things to the Hawthorne and focus on moving on. Al wouldn't like it; the man was a staunch family guy and liked his men to be hitched, too, but he'd understand because he knew about the heroin. And as much of a family man as Capone was, the man hated heroin more.

"Fuck," Jack whispered in resignation. He turned the corner at the end of the block and stood a moment, his attention distracted by a building with black vines creeping up its facade. It wasn't the one he'd seen when Trask had first driven him through downtown Jericho Springs. *Harplee's Woodworks*, the sign over the door read. Vines, their surfaces knotted and shining with the stinking clear ooze they secreted, covered the *P* and one *S*. Jack thought about the men he'd seen clearing the vines from the first store and wondered why nobody had bothered with Harplee's. The store was still functioning, rocking chairs and desks could be seen through the single picture window to the right of the door. He studied the vines, following their length across the building and around the corner where they vanished in the darkness. Jack didn't know anything about blights, but couldn't help wondering if this type of thing was normal.

Well, he told himself as he continued on, what happened to some of the buildings here wasn't his problem. Now that Trask had secured a new supply of corn and grains from some of the farmers around Elden Mills, and once a visit was paid to Carl Stott, Jack's mission would be back on track. That was what was important. He spent half a block practicing blowing smoke rings while one hand dug in his pocket and fingered the trolley token. Smoke rings were something Al could do—Bobby also, he recalled—and Jack had always wanted to be able to do the same. He managed one lopsided ring that broke apart inches from his lips.

At the end of the block, the door to Evie's flower shop stood flanked by two windows full of greenery and colorful petals. A small sign hung on the inside of the glass of the door, its message—that the shop was open, he assumed—invisible from where he was and in the fading light of the day. Evie stood behind the counter, a lantern nearby providing the light by which she worked. Her hands moved fluidly as she trimmed the stems from some yellow and white flowers with a pair of shears. Her hair was tucked behind one ear and she worked with a singular focus, never once looking up from her task.

What about Norma? asked that cold voice in the back of his mind. *She's still your wife.*

Not anymore, Jack answered. The only thing still holding him to Norma was a matter of paperwork. He cared, of course he did. He always would. But no, that was a dead end and a path he wasn't going to continue to tread. There was a new trail to follow, and it started in a flower shop. Whistling a light tune, he started toward the store.

When he was a few feet from the door, Jack flinched at the sudden rumble of several trucks thundering from somewhere on the road ahead. Evie seemed to hear them as well. Through the glass of the door, Jack saw her drop the shears and stare, her eyes falling on him.

From around a corner came three trucks. They sped past the shop, dark smoke belching from their exhausts. Henry Dunn sat in the passenger seat of the lead truck, arm cocked out the window, his hat angled back on his head. As the vehicle barreled past Jack, Dunn's eyes flicked to him. Then the convoy was down the street before Jack could see if there was any reaction on the toad-like face. The beds of each truck were filled with people. Jack caught the fearful expressions on some, the hard-eyed stares and weapons of the others.

An image came to him, as clear as the sun on a cloudless summer day. The teenage farmhand hanged, still alive while his guts pooled on the ground beneath his boots. Not hidden somewhere but displayed out in the open air for God and everyone else to see. Sending a message.

Dunn was going to send another message, this time more brazenly. He was going to kill those people, carve symbols into them, and leave them somewhere public, somewhere that not only Cleary's men would see them but also the people of the town. He was ramping up the intensity of his crusade.

Jack glanced back at Evie. Their eyes locked and despite the surprise on her face, he thought her lips twitched into a smile. She raised one hand in a wave, but Jack was already turning and sprinting to where the truck Cleary had loaned him was parked. He cranked it and slammed the pedal to the floor, hoping he would be able to catch up to the small convoy before it was too late.

22

Jack had not seen Dunn's convoy for some time and was starting to think he'd lost them when a spot of soft light to his right caught his eye. The barn was set a distance from the farmhouse, both separated from the main road by a wide lawn so large it could have been a pasture itself. The house was dark; the occupants either asleep or participating in whatever was happening in the barn.

Jack pulled the truck to the side of the road, branches and tall grass hissing along its side. He climbed out, leaving the door to the cab open, and crept along the thicket. The three trucks he'd followed were parked in front of the open building. Soft amber light filled the interior of the barn and he could see the vague movements of people within, but the vehicles blocked any clear view. Stepping from the cover of the thick roadside brush, he hurried across the field, hunching as if he were crossing No Man's Land, charging for the enemy trenches. Patches of ground that had surrendered to the creeping rot squelched disturbingly beneath his shoes. Just as he reached the rear of the trucks, a gunshot as loud as cannon fire ripped through the night. Jack pulled his .45, thumbed back the hammer, and peeked around one vehicle.

Henry Dunn stood in front of a group of five unarmed men and women, his smoking pistol held by his side. One person lay in front of Dunn, not moving. Dunn gave a command and one of his men tied the arms of the others behind their backs as they stared in shock at the dead man.

Jack counted ten armed men, including Dunn. With those numbers, he guessed he could take three of them before they recovered and returned fire. He considered the hostages—three men and two women whose hands were secured with rope. The defeated, terrified expressions on their faces told him that any hope of them helping overwhelm their captors was out of the question.

Once the prisoners were securely bound, Dunn snapped another instruction, his words muffled to Jack. The women were openly sobbing and cried out when rough hands grabbed their shoulders, forcing them down. The bound men were dropped with kicks to the backs of their knees. They tried bargaining with Dunn, offering money and other things, anything to cut them loose and spare their lives.

Jack thought he recognized one of the hostages; someone he'd seen around Cleary's farm. A delivery man, he recalled, but couldn't think of his name. The others he had no clue about, but assumed they were, in Dunn's mind at least, associated with the bootlegging operation in some way. His suspicion was confirmed when Dunn began pacing in front of the kneeling, weeping people like a general inspecting his troops.

"I want you all to take a good look at that piece of meat there," Dunn said, pointing at the corpse. "That is what is waiting for you. That is the end you come to when you choose to participate in the evils of liquor, of willingly breaking the law. You and your kind are a scourge on this town, on your fellow Christians. Your selfish actions, your greed, speaks to the evils within your hearts, the blackness that consumes your souls."

Dunn continued, raising his voice to be heard over the pleading. "I have been brought here to eradicate your kind. It does not matter to me that your skin is white. To me, you are all niggers and no better than those Black sons of bitches. Once you crossed the line into violating the law, you gave up all your rights as Christians and human beings. You chose to run and lay with dogs, and dogs you became. And as dogs, you will be put down."

In two quick steps, Dunn placed himself in front of the first woman, a pretty young girl with reddish brown hair and a smattering of freckles across her cheeks. She flinched, too afraid to even look at the fat, jowled man. Dunn growled something, the woman shook her head and twisted her shoulders, trying to turn away. Dunn grasped her chin and forced her head back, tilted it up to glare into her eyes.

Jack heard a plaintive "P-please." Her body jerked as Dunn's pistol barked. He then pushed the body back. She fell in a limp heap on her side, twisted at the waist. The woman next in line screamed, horrible, gut-wrenching screeches of pure terror, over and over and over until Dunn shot her through the eye.

Before the second body had even slumped to the dirty ground, Dunn shot the Black man. He carried out the execution with bored detachment, pointing the pistol and squeezing the trigger quickly. The second of the three men died just as insignificantly, his eyes squeezed tight, lips fluttering in hasty prayers cut short by a fast bullet.

Dunn positioned himself before the last man and pulled the trigger. The pistol gave a dull *click* instead of the life-shattering roar. He scowled at the gun and thrust it at the nearest guard. While he inspected the weapon in an attempt to clear the jam, Dunn stepped past and out of Jack's line of sight. He returned a moment later with a pickaxe.

The kneeling man saw what Dunn had, and despite the bevy of heavily armed men standing around, he fought to stand. The man working with Dunn's pistol saw the attempt and brought the gun up quick and hard in an arc. It connected with the side of the man's face, sending him falling back, dazed. Before the guard could do anything else, Dunn said something in a low voice to him before standing over the writhing, bound man. The pickaxe raised high over Dunn's head, he hesitated for the span of a breath, then came down. It slammed into the prisoner with a meaty *smack.*

Dunn hit the man ten more times before he tossed the pickaxe aside, legs wide, his shoulders and back heaving from the exertion. Jack eased the hammer down on his own pistol but kept the weapon in his hand. Moving as quickly and as quietly as he could, he jogged across the dark lawn to his own truck.

His thoughts were a whirling hurricane. *Henry Dunn wasn't just a bully hired to stop illegal booze. He was deeply dangerous and beyond reason. No amount of money or strong-armed threats would cut through the deep fanatic beliefs he held.* At the center of the chaos, the calm eye of the storm, was a single clear thought. *The only way Dunn would cease to be a threat was when he was killed.*

Jack never looked back at the barn. If he had, he would have seen the dark silhouette of Henry Dunn standing in the doorway, watching him.

23

The fat balls of dough plopped into the pot, sending a splash of steaming liquid across her knuckle. Grace hissed and sucked on the reddened digit as she dropped the rest of the dumplings in. The kitchen was filled with the mouthwatering scent of chicken cooking and her stomach gave a gentle burble of anticipation. As she stirred the pot, mixing the dumplings into the broth, a lump rose in her throat. Chicken and dumplings was Charlie's favorite meal, had been ever since he'd started eating solid food, and making it without the small boy at her elbow staring at the pot with excitement was soul-crushing.

Where was he? Where had he gotten off to? It made no sense that he would've just wandered out of the house in the middle of the night. Yet that seems to have been what happened. Her parents maintained that they'd not heard or seen Charlie sneaking out, and Grace certainly hadn't. So what had possessed him to do it? Not for the first time, she wondered if someone had come into the house and taken him. But that idea was dismissed as quickly now as it had been the first time she'd thought it. If someone had come into the house, Father would have known. The man knew every creak, even the smallest noise was familiar to him, so the sound of a stranger invading their home would have roused him immediately.

She crossed the room to retrieve a half loaf of day-old bread. When she wasn't out searching the woods or the rest of the town for Charlie, Grace spent her time in the kitchen. Cooking was a comforting act, and it helped keep her busy, occupying both her hands and her mind. Besides, ever since waking to find Charlie gone, her parents had fallen into a lethargic existence. If Grace didn't cook for them, she was certain they'd simply starve. Providing meals filled her with a sense of purpose and of action, so she'd taken on the role wholeheartedly.

In the next room, her parents sat at the small table where the family took its meals. They kept their voices low, but occasionally their excitement would swell their volume and Grace could catch bits and pieces of what they were saying.

"... new path. I think it'll be good ..."

"... he'll know exactly what to do ..."

" ... in good hands."

Grace took a large knife and sliced the bread. The morning Charlie had gone missing, she and her parents had rushed about the property in a confused panic. She'd followed her father into the woods to search. After only a few dozen steps, he had stopped and plucked something from the branches of a bush. He'd stared at it for a long moment, shoved it into his pocket, and stood, his breath pluming in the unseasonably chilly morning air, a pale, scared look on his face. Of course he was scared; his son was missing. But even before she could say anything, her father's expression had changed. His features hardened, his eyes growing darker. He set his mouth in a hard line and turned back to the house, telling her in a sharp, clipped tone to come with him. Grace had hesitated, alternating her gaze between her father and the dark woods. When she had asked him why they weren't searching because Charlie could be out there hurt, her father barked to get her ass back to the house.

Later that morning her parents had left, speaking to each other in quiet, fearful voices. They'd instructed Grace to stay home and that under no circumstances was she to go into the woods searching for Charlie. When they'd returned hours later, something had changed within them. Gone was the humming scared energy. In its place was a calm sedateness that extended even to their eyes, giving both her parents a sleepy look. Grace had asked them where they'd been and if they were going to continue looking for Charlie, but her mother simply shook her head and said it was in God's hands. Grace pleaded with them, not understanding how, in such a short time, they could have given up on searching for their child, but neither would be swayed. She grabbed her coat and made for the door, intent to continue the search herself, but her father's tight hand around her arm and the expression in his eyes stopped her.

She'd never seen him look at her with seething hatred before. But that's what she saw in his face, in the curl of his upper lip, in the furrowed brow over his hard eyes. At that moment, he *hated* her. And she knew with absolute certainty that if she continued to search for her brother, her father would put a stop to it. Violently.

So she'd focused on cooking, on doing small chores around the house, and using the opportunity when she had to tend to something near the barn to search the grounds for Charlie. So far, nothing had turned up, but Grace was far from ready to admit defeat. She would search for her brother until the day she died or until he was found. The thought of the small boy, his light hair tousled and jutting in a chaotic mess as he giggled, burned brightly in her mind and brought a tremendous ache to her chest. The knife tumbled out of her numb fingers as she thought about how Charlie's eyes danced whenever he babbled about a frog he'd found or how he thought a band of murderous Indians was creeping across the fields and only he could scare them off.

Grace blinked the thoughts away and gathered plates from the cupboard, stacking them against her chest. On her way into the dining room, she plucked a white ceramic pitcher of water from the table. Her parents sat in their customary seats at the table that practically filled the small room—her father at the head, her mother to his left. Neither acknowledged her as she edged around the room placing bowls for each diner and filling water glasses. As she started to lower a bowl in front of her mother, Grace paused, heart hammering. Her eyes drifted over to a spot in front of an empty chair.

Charlie's chair.

She'd placed a bowl in his spot habitually. Her hand trembling, Grace lowered her mother's bowl to the table at the same time that her father reached out, picked up Charlie's setting, and stacked it under his own bowl. He performed the movements almost subconsciously, never taking his focus off his wife who continued to talk about Pastor Sam and the special worship session later that night.

Grace's cheeks warmed at the sight of the casual removal of her brother's place setting. Neither of her parents batted so much as an eyelash at the silent acknowledgement of Charlie's absence. It was as if the boy simply didn't exist. Grace began to speak up, to ask why her parents had given up so quickly, but the fact that neither one had even noticed her froze the words in her throat.

As soon as their last bites were consumed, both parents stood and hurried away. Grace cleared the table and started the process of cleaning up, listening to the sounds of them preparing to leave. She moved slowly, taking her time washing the dinnerware to avoid an awkward exchange with her parents.

Minutes later, they were gone. The firm *thump* of the door closing was the only indication that they'd exited the house. Grace let out a long breath and gripped the edge of the sink. She leaned forward, her hair hanging on either side of her face like curtains, and forced herself to take long, slow breaths. Her fingers pressed against the sink so hard her flesh whitened. Small vibrations of frustration and anger rippled through her, causing her arms to shake.

God, why is this happening?

Grace closed her eyes and prayed, reciting the familiar and comforting words of the Lord's Prayer before moving into a more personal beseeching. As she spoke, the trembling in her lips and heat in her chest slowly subsided. The words soothed her nerves, and she was able to press her anger and fear down, bottling them and placing them on a shelf in the corner of herself where they couldn't cause any more problems.

When the last of the bowls and utensils had been dried and put away, Grace went onto the porch, down the steps, and into the yard. The night air was cool, the last few days of spring slowly dying under the relentless assault of summer. She let herself wander the familiar path toward the fields. The smell of rot reached her, cloying and throat-tightening as she drew closer to the pastures and the woods beyond. Grace moved along the path between the rows of blackened soil and rotting crops, her eyes fixed on the black wall of trees.

Near the last row of dead crops, her foot scraped across something in the grass. Nudging it with her toe, Grace's breath caught in her throat when she saw the reflection of moonlight on a piece of blue glass. It wasn't large, about the size of her thumb, its edges worn smooth.

Charlie had found it one day half-buried in the silt along the bank of the Shadako near the spot everyone called Graddy's Cove. The way the light appeared, filtered through the blue curve, had fascinated him and he'd carried it everywhere he went.

Grace closed her fingers around the shard and held it tight to her chest, feeling the vibration of her heart against her hand. "I'm going to find you," she said softly. "I'm not going to stop looking. I swear."

But the trees were thick and dark and as she stood at their edge, something told her that entering them now, tonight, wouldn't be wise. It was more than just the fact that she didn't have a light; there was a cold sense of malice seeping from between the silent trees. A feeling of something watching from the darkness, waiting with the infinite patience of a snake watching a mouse slowly creep closer.

Grace retreated, unable to tear her focus from the lightless mass of forest. She knew with absolute certainty that if she turned her back on it, that thing waiting inside would burst out, leaping through the air, all fangs and claws and killing fury. She wove slightly along the path between the rows until the full length of the field was between her and the woods. Only then did she turn and make her way back to the porch, where she settled into the soft and well-worn cushion of her father's rocking chair. She pulled one leg up, wrapping her arm around it while her other foot pushed off against the porch floor, sending the chair into its lazy motion. Her fingers turned the piece of glass over and around, feeling its gentle edges and remembering Charlie holding it up to his face as he gazed at the sky.

Tomorrow, she decided. Tomorrow she was going to go into the woods and search. Maybe start near Graddy's Cove. As soon as the sun cleared the trees, she would set off.

In the dark something screamed. The cry was distant, hollow-sounding as it echoed across the landscape. "It's just a fox," she told herself, but the words were bitter on her tongue. They held no truth or conviction. The sensation of being watched returned, slipping its icy fingers along her back, running them up her spine to her neck and sending a wave of goose bumps tickling across her scalp.

From farther along the road that ran in front of the property came the throaty chug of a car engine. It swelled and faded as the vehicle continued along, moving through the night toward town. Grace breathed a smile, quietly laughing at herself for allowing the darkness to scare her. She had nothing to be afraid of, beyond her worry over Charlie and the encroaching blight and its effects on her family's farm. She pocketed the piece of glass and padded inside to prepare for bed.

Pausing in the doorway, Grace allowed herself one last look across the fields. The property was covered in total darkness, the fields and even the barrier of trees invisible. She stepped the rest of the way into the kitchen and closed the door. Then, for the first time in her life, she thumbed the lock into place.

24

When Sam emerged from the tiny office in the rear of the building, he was overwhelmed by the energy that flowed through the congregation, filling every inch of the chapel. The space was imbued with a sense of belonging, of rightness. The light from dozens of candles and the low rumbling of voices from those gathered transformed the church, elevating it into so much more than a simple place of worship. It was a bastion of hope against the pressing darkness that threatened to swallow them all.

He stood off to the side of the chancel, just behind the piano. There were more people in the pews than Sam had expected. The candlelight pushed shadows to the ceiling where they pulsed and rippled. The pews were just over half-filled with faces he knew. Faces that all wore similar expressions: curiosity, exhaustion, and worry etched in deep lines across brows; dark circles around eyes; thin, downturned lips.

Jonas and Anna Robertson sat in their usual places at the front of the congregation. With a pang of disappointment, Sam noted that Grace was absent. Anna held a kerchief in her lap and twisted it around her fingers obsessively. Sam wondered what was going through her mind. He couldn't imagine the pain and anguish of losing a child, even though the loss would bring them one step closer to salvation and freedom from the curse that affected the town so awfully.

Sam's grip tightened on the carved wooden box. Faint pulses radiated through the thick wood and its textured scrollwork, the power of the contents within vibrating into his hands.

"Give me strength," Sam whispered and approached the chancel. He placed the box on a shelf within his pulpit. As he drifted to the front edge of the chancel, the crowd fell silent and every face turned to him, hopeful and expectant. Sam waited as a few coughs floated up from farther back, and the occasional *creak* of a pew signaled someone adjusting to find a slightly more comfortable position.

"My friends," he began, holding his arms out invitingly. His voice quavered, nervousness suddenly there, settling high in his chest. He cleared his throat, surprised at himself. He'd given countless sermons and stage fright had never been an issue. The church pulpit was the one place he was truly at peace. He put on a smile, the act quelling the slithering eels of nerves. "I'm so glad you came. I know that Brother Jonas and Brother Robert told you about this special meeting, and I want to go a step further and explain everything. We've all been suffering lately. Our crops are showing signs of rot. Our livestock are behaving unnaturally or dying. Our friends and neighbors have started acting strange or going missing. Some have died." He had considered pointing out that most of those folks who had been found dead or gone missing occurred while in the employ of illegal bootleggers, but decided that wasn't necessary. In rough times, people did what they had to in order to provide for their families.

"I know it sounds upsetting. I know that it can be distressing to hear of such atrocities. But I ask you, are we not in terribly strange and stressful times? The things that beset our town, our friends and neighbors, are not simple invasions of a criminal element. They are not the things that a small group of law officers can handle. No. They are older, they run deeper. They are malevolent. They are the works of Satan himself and are brought upon us because we've been weak.

It's this weakness that has opened our town and our minds to evil influences. But I'm here to tell you that we can prevail. We can break through these constricting chains and save ourselves, save our livelihoods.

"The other night I was up for hours praying for guidance, just as I have been every night for the last several weeks. However, my heart wasn't in my words because I, too, had fallen prey to weakness. I feared, deep down, that my prayers would not be heard or heeded. I feared these plagues would continue to beset us regardless of what I said or how fervently I voiced my pleas. But brothers and sisters, that night while I slept, God spoke to me."

The admission sent a fresh wave of conversation through the crowd, rolling back to the far end of the church before rebounding and returning even louder. Sam continued on, riding the wave of excitement. "He showed me all the ways we have strayed from the path despite our—your—adherence to our regular services, your dedication to prayer and Scripture. He showed me how such wandering opened the door for these dark forces. He told me that the current ways of tradition and worship were no longer the way forward. A new path was shown to me by His loving hand. A path along which I can lead you all. This path calls on older conventions, practices lost to history. These new customs will seem strange to us, being modern people in modern times, but our Lord has promised me that following them will bring us the salvation we all desperately crave."

"Why you?" The voice filled the nave, cutting through the air like a scythe through dried stalks of wheat. Sam raised his face, searching for the man who had spoken.

"Who said that?" he asked. Realizing his own question had sounded like a rebuke, Sam softened his tone. "It's perfectly okay, my friends. I simply would like to know to whom I'm speaking." Slowly, hesitantly, as if he suddenly regretted the attention, Clyde Hensley, the owner of Springline Dry Goods, stood. Sam smiled and angled to face the man.

"Brother Hensley, what is your concern?"

Clyde licked his lips, a furtive gesture that made Sam think of a lizard sunning itself on a rock. "I was just wondering, why you? Why is it that God spoke to you and not Reverend Mullins over at the Church of Christ or Preacher Michaels down the road at First United Methodist?" Murmurs of questioning agreements drifted through the congregation.

Sam nodded. "You ask a great question. It's one that I myself have pondered since my visitation. The answer is simple. In times of great trial, God has always chosen someone. Moses. Elijah. Paul. Not the strongest, not the holiest, just someone willing to listen. I don't ask why He chose me. I only pray I'm worthy." Sam paused. A small part of him expected applause and shouts of approval, energetic reactions of people eager to begin this new way. The congregation, however, remained silent and still. Clyde Hensley took a seat. Throughout the room, plain, uncomprehending, or confused faces stared back at Sam. More than a few brows furrowed skeptically.

Sam continued, relating to them the visions he had while sleeping, the words he heard in his dreams. He told them how this new path required sacrifice, purification. That the land upon which they all lived and from which they drew life was a holy place that could only be purified through sacrifice and new prayers. He pulled the wooden box from the shelf and held it up so they could see. "We have been given a new Host, a new rite of communion. Through this we will—"

"Absolutely not!" The objection was so sudden and sharp that for a long moment, Sam was almost convinced he'd imagined it. Another parishioner rose from the pews to stand, an older man with a scowl on his face and one gnarled finger jutting accusingly at Sam. "You speak of blasphemy!" Turning to look at those seated, he asked, "How can you consider this? New rituals? Purification? It's madness!" Yet another soft rhythm of whispers filled the air. "We should stick to the prayers and Psalms we know, that the church is built on, that are in the Good Book!"

"Where has that gotten us?" Jonas Robertson asked suddenly, rising to face the man. His hands were clenched into fists at his sides.

"We've done nothing but pray and beseech, reciting the same old passages over and over. Where has that gotten us? What has changed? This"—he stabbed a finger in the direction of a window—"has only gotten worse. You know I'm right. You all know that things are only getting worse. God has spoken to Pastor Sam. Are you saying He didn't? Are you?" Jonas glared at the man, practically daring him to contradict Sam's proclamation. "God spoke to him and has offered us a guiding hand into salvation. He's offering us hope. Are you really going to stand there and say that it's a lie?"

Jonas's shoulders raised and lowered as he took a deep breath. "The Lord called for my own sacrifice the other night. Some of you know what I'm talking about. For those who don't, He came to me as He came to Abraham." A few of the women covered their mouths in stunned surprise. "And He took my Charlie into His loving arms. God accepted our sacrifice. And the blight has slowed on our property."

At that declaration, a chorus of gasps flew out of the congregation. Sam watched the interaction with mute wonder. Had Jonas really noticed a slowing or reversal of the creeping rot? He blinked away the doubt. Of course he had. Why would he lie? In a church, no less. In accepting his act of sacrifice, Jonas Robertson had seen the fruits of accepting the new ways.

Around the nave, the mumbled conversation slowed. The dissenter's face shifted from hard lines to the wide-eyed look of hope and promise. "Say you truth?" he asked Jonas, who nodded. The dissenter raised his eyes to Sam. "Have you seen this, Pastor?"

The tiniest knot of reluctance formed at the base of Sam's throat, but he spoke around it. "I have. Brother Jonas speaks the truth. He sacrificed a tremendous thing and God has rewarded him." A small lie, but he believed the Lord would forgive him such a minor detail in the larger scheme of bringing the town into the fold. Sam went on to explain that he had been entrusted by God to lead them from these dark places, that these events that the Robertsons and others had endured were only the first drops in the bucket, that they were part of the sacrifices that would be required of many of the people.

He saw that the majority of those gathered were following along, rapt. "Will you pray with me now?" he asked. The responses were quick and enthusiastic.

"Yes!"

"Lead us!"

"Take us from this darkness!"

Sam bowed his head and prayed, using the new language that he'd never learned but which came to his tongue as easily as apples bobbing in a tub of water. All he had to do was pick each one up.

His lips stretched and struggled around the words, and their eldritch sounds filled the chapel. As the prayer continued, the light of the candles muted as the flames shrank beneath the shadows that expanded down from the ceiling. The congregation listened to the harsh, strange prayers, letting the words fill their minds and bodies.

Sam didn't even notice that as he fought to push the ancient language out, his gums began to bleed. When the prayer was finished, he opened the lid of the box. A putrid stench wafted up and sent his eyes watering. "Please, come forward and receive the Host. Come and accept the new embodiment of Christ and our salvation."

Jonas and Alma Robertson were the first to reach the foot of the stairs. Sam's fingers pulled the Host out and held it over Jonas's mouth. He placed the wafer on the outstretched tongue. Just as Jonas retracted his tongue and closed his mouth, the wafer changed to something black and slimy and rancid. It writhed ever so slightly when Jonas's lips came together and he swallowed.

"Praise God," Jonas breathed and moved aside for the next person to receive their communion.

25

Jack's lips parted in a smile as Evie stepped close to the glass of her shop door, breaking apart the reflection of the late afternoon sun. He raised a hand in a wave, but Evie's attention was focused on something across the street. Jack followed her gaze to the same vine-covered building he'd noticed upon his arrival in town. The creepers had increased, both in number and coverage of the building, as if the forest were wrapping arms around a present beneath a Christmas tree and eagerly pulling it closer. In the spaces between the encircling arms of black vines were what looked like spots, as if the whole building had come down with a case of the measles. The distance was too great, so Jack couldn't be certain, but it looked like each spot glistened with some kind of moisture.

Standing on the sidewalk before the doomed building were two men. A scattering of tools lay next to one of them: hatchets, hammers, a saw. The pair were arguing. Well, one of them was arguing, the other just stood there laughing maniacally. As Jack drew closer, he could make out a portion of the conversation.

". . . can't! It's our salvation! Our transformation! Don't fucking touch it! I'm warning you!"

At that, the man who had proclaimed salvation lashed out with a vicious left hook that snapped the other's head back. Scarlet spatter dotted the air and streamed down his chin. Jack noticed small flurries of movement as a few of the laughing man's teeth bounced across the planks. He paid no attention to them, only continued howling with laughter, blood spraying from his mouth with each exhalation, speckling the face of his attacker.

Before another punch could be landed, both men spun and sprinted away down a side street like children suddenly called to dinner, their tools and teeth left forgotten. Shouts of laughter and threats of death trailed behind them, dwindling as they vanished around another corner.

"The hell was that about?" Jack mumbled.

"This whole town is losing its mind," Evie said. Jack snapped out of his daze. She stood in her shop entrance, looking worriedly down the street where the men had run. Her eyes flicked back to the building and a shudder rippled through her. "It's starting to show up on more buildings."

"What's with the spots?" Jack asked.

Evie shook her head. "I won't get close enough to look. Someone told me that they're leaking something. Like the building has sores. How is that even possible?"

Jack ignored the urge to glance back at the building or any of the dark patches of swampy ground that had begun to creep along the edges of the streets. "How's business?" he asked, following Evie into the store.

She waved a hand, deadpan. "Totally tapped. Sold out completely."

Jack glanced at the shelves and tables displaying green plants and colored flowers, then back at her face, flat as glass but with a flicker of mirth in her eyes. "That's unfortunate. I was hoping to find something to mask the smell of my hotel room. And to distract me from the diner."

Evie's eyebrows raised. "So you finally understand what I was trying to tell you about the place? Fair enough. I'm pretty sure we can find you something for nausea. As for your room . . ." She shook her head. "Don't know if there's much to do about that. I heard the person who was there before you kept chickens in there."

"Chickens."

Evie bobbed her head forward in a campy parody of a bird pecking. "Feathers and all. Bible truth. You'd need every flower in the joint to come close to erasing that smell." She frowned. "What the hell are you wearing?"

Jack glanced at his overalls. "You don't like it? I was told it was the height of fashion around here."

"Maybe if your job is farming pigs."

"What's wrong with pigs? Everyone likes bacon."

"I'm not especially fond of it."

"I don't know, Mack's has some good bacon. And those biscuits and gravy . . . to die for."

"They'll kill you, that's for sure. And wouldn't that be a pity, you croaking because of lard-filled biscuits and bacon."

Jack was entranced by the crinkling of the skin around her eyes when she smiled, the way her nose wrinkled at the mention of lard-filled biscuits. Good Christ, she was beautiful.

"You did say you knew of better places."

Evie's head bobbed. "I know a few."

"Maybe you let me take you tonight. Since you're about to close—"

"Oh, I can't close up now, it's the height of my busy time."

Jack glanced around. "You're right. I completely missed all the people over there by those . . ."—he frowned—"what do you call those?"

"Flowers. Sorry, I'm not free tonight. Gotta get ready for the night shift."

"The night shift," Jack repeated.

Evie's short dark hair swayed as she nodded. "You may not believe it, being from Chicago and all, but there's a booming night scene here in Jericho Springs. It'll be all I can do to maintain some semblance of order in here come midnight." Her smile faded. "Wait," she said. "What happened last night? With those trucks?"

Jack's mind filled with images of the people in the barn begging and crying as Henry Dunn methodically shot them. "I couldn't catch up to them. I don't know all the roads." Evie watched him, and he was certain she knew he was lying.

"So," she began, stepping back behind the counter, "you're on your way to Mack's, I assume? I told you, the food there is going to kill you."

He glanced at his watch. "I have to meet a guy at the diner. Let me buy you a cup of coffee before that. To help prepare you for the night rush. You can keep me company while I wait."

When they settled at a table in the front area of Mack's and ordered coffee, Evie asked, "So how are the shipments going?" At Jack's startled expression, she gave a light, tinkling laugh. "I've been in this town for a long time, Jack Carmelo Chicago. You think I don't know what's going on? Hell, my daddy used to make and sell whiskey before Volstead."

"He doesn't anymore?"

A dark cloud settled over her. "No. Not anymore."

"What happened?"

Evie's fingers danced around the silver fork on the table, spinning it, stopping it, spinning it. Her eyes were far away. She blinked slowly. "My dad used to own the store. Like me, he wasn't segregated. Daddy never thought Blacks were any different than the rest of us. They were just people trying to live their own lives when they were hijacked and brought over. And now that they were here and finally free, they were once more just trying to survive. Like the rest of us."

"Not a popular belief."

"You could say that, sure." She was quiet again. Jack sat patiently, fingers wrapped around the small coffee mug, and waited. "One night he was making a delivery—we used to do that; I would prepare the flowers and he would deliver them. Anyway, he was delivering some gerbera daisies to Edith Green—not that you know who that is—and he saw some men pulling a Black man out of a truck. These men were all holding bats and a couple had knives. There were four of them. They pulled the guy out of the truck right there and had started to kick and shove him when Daddy pulled up. Unfortunately for them, Daddy had been rabbit hunting that morning. He pulled out his shotgun and very calmly told them to leave the man alone."

"They didn't take that too well, I guess?"

She turned her lips into a sour frown. "One of the men was Carl Stott. He's been the ringleader of the Klan around here for a while. Until Dunn showed up, that is."

"I know of him."

"Do you?" Her eyes were wide in surprise. "Well, yes, I suppose you must. So, after Daddy stopped them from killing that man in the middle of the afternoon. . ." she trailed off, her voice pinched. "A week later, they found my dad on the tracks. The cops told me he must have gotten drunk and fallen or stumbled in front of a train."

"I'm sorry."

"He wasn't a drunk. My dad drank, sure, but never to excess. The only time I ever saw him drunk was the night after we laid Mama to rest. He sat in his rocking chair by the fire and drank until he passed out. After that, he only had a sip or two, usually to celebrate something. Birthdays, holidays, small things."

"You think Carl Stott had something to do with it?"

Evie's eyes flashed fiercely. "I know he did."

"How do you know?"

She let out a long breath. "He's hinted about it, just never outright said so. But I know in my heart it was him."

A silence fell between them, Evie returning her focus to spinning the fork, Jack clutching his mug and watching the lines on her face. After a few minutes, she smiled. "I can't believe I just told you all of that. I'm so sorry. I didn't mean to unburden myself like that."

"It's quite all right. For what it's worth, I'm sorry."

She smiled appreciatively. "So I imagine the Klan is giving you a bit of trouble, if you're familiar with Carl Stott."

"They don't seem to look kindly on people engaging in certain activities, that's for sure."

Evie snorted. "Or on anyone else around here who's tried to make a living in the last couple of years. I suppose in the larger cities, some people have a small army to help keep the Klan at bay. But the small operations, the farmers who have to do it to help supplement income, they don't. They can't afford to take their operations deep in the woods, not that anyone in their right mind would want to, so they run it in their homes or in their barns. Dunn, he finds them and . . ." She shook her head. "He's a bad man. If you have any sense about you, you'll keep far away from him."

A much younger waitress than the usual server approached, her attention on Evie, who shook her head. "I'm not staying," she said, and the girl melted into the background. Jack sipped his coffee and studied the woman across from him. Her hair was pulled back as it had been the first time he'd met her. Her eyes, a dark hazel green, flicked back and forth as she watched him in equal measure. She'd stopped chewing her lip and the urge to kiss her, to feel her lips against his, to feel them parting, overwhelmed him. By Christ, she was beautiful.

"So you're having some trouble?" she asked. "I've heard about people going missing. People rumored to be working stills."

Jack's neck warmed. Once again, the woman had surprised him with her knowledge. "It's nothing. Business."

"From what I've heard, what's been happening in those woods the last few months isn't business. It's got people scared. Even people who aren't in the trade." She shook her head sadly. "Nobody in their right mind would be out there, running stills or not."

"'In the trade'?" Jack smiled. "We're handling it. But what do you mean, that nobody in their right mind would run out in the woods?"

Evie hesitated, her eyes flicked over his shoulder and she shook her head. Then her lips parted as she started to speak, "It's nothing, just a figure of speech. Your friend is here."

The man Cleary had sent to meet with Jack was less a man and more a slab of beef with eyes. He ducked to step through the diner's doorway. Once fully inside, the man filled most of the front dining area. Huge arms hung by his sides, and the straps of his overalls strained against his immense chest. The guy had short blond hair and a smattering of freckles across a shockingly boyish face. When he saw Jack he smiled wide, revealing a few missing teeth.

"Looks like they sent the goon squad," Evie said with a chuckle. "Jesus, that guy looks like he eats freight trains for breakfast."

"Mr. Carmelo?" the man asked in a soft, nasally voice.

"Yeah, one sec." Jack turned back to Evie. "I have to meet with this guy."

She was already starting to stand. "Of course. I have to get back to the shop anyway. There'll be hell to pay if people can't buy their ferns at two in the morning." She started away but Jack caught her wrist.

"Have dinner with me tonight."

"Here? You're crazy."

"I'll pick you up when you close shop. You can tell me where to go then. But I . . ."—he glanced back at the young bull of a man who was within earshot but staring at a small framed picture of a windmill—"I really want to see you again." Evie's cheeks colored and she lifted the corner of her mouth in a smirk.

"Seven. Bring your appetite." Jack let her go and she left the diner, smiling a greeting at Cleary's man, who paused to watch her exit.

When she was gone, Jack waved the large man over. He approached with a sheepish grin on his face. "I'm really happy to meet you, sir," he said, extending a hand the size of a picnic ham. Jack shook it and considered the chair Evie had vacated.

"Can you sit without breaking that?"

The man laughed, a lilting noise. "Gosh, probably not."

"What's your name?"

"Curtis Jemison."

"Did Cleary tell you what we're doing?"

The boyish features hardened, and Jack saw steel in the man's eyes. "He did."

"You're okay with that?"

Curtis nodded. "I ain't got no love for them Klan guys. Some of the best people I know are colored."

"I'm not sure where the house is. You got someone to drive us?"

"Yes, sir. Mr. Cleary told Legs to do it. He lives near the place."

Curtis paused and gave a questioning look. "Are you sure we don't need more guys?"

Jack waved off the waitress who had started to drift their way, coffee pot in hand. "No. Best case, Stott will be the only one in the house. Worst case, you're the size of four guys. And if things go south . . ." He let the rest go unsaid, but the thought was clear. If Carl Stott had everyone in his house, including Dunn, tonight would not be a very pleasant experience for the Italian and the big man.

"If you don't mind me asking," Curtis said, "what are you planning?"

"Hopefully just talking. Make them an offer."

Curtis blew out a long breath, his cheeks puffing wide. "Better be some offer. You think they'll take it?"

"Never can tell. Most of those guys are just idiots and racists. But there are some that are devoted." He thought about the men standing over the kneeling, crying people in the barn. Pushing the memory aside, Jack flashed a grin.

To which, Curtis leaned back and said, "I can be quite persuasive."

Jack finished his coffee and paid the bill. He and Curtis stepped outside where a thin, bald Black man stood on the sidewalk shuffling nervously.

"You Cleary's boy?" Jack asked.

"Yes, sir. Name's Legs."

"Legs?"

"I'm a pretty fast runner."

"You got a piece?" Legs raised his dirty white shirt to reveal the butt of a pistol jutting above his dark pants. "Good," Jack said. "Let's go."

Carl Stott's home was on a dirt road at the southeastern edge of town. They parked several lots away, but even from a distance, thanks to the fact that there weren't houses close to either side of it, Jack could see it clearly. It looked more like a small barn that had suffered too many storms. The roof sagged on one edge and there were broken windows along the front, some covered over with wooden slats. An uneven porch propped up by columns of bricks led to a door that held on to the frame by sheer stubbornness. The yard was a weed-choked patch dotted with trash and other detritus. Parked haphazardly in the yard were three cars.

Jack noticed a pile of dead pine trees, the largest not bigger than a baseball bat in diameter, stacked near one side of the home. Beyond that, where the yard faded into a larger field, the remains of a tractor peered through a choking, twisted patch of brambles.

"If you can avoid it," Legs said from close behind Jack, "don't go back there. That's snake city."

The thought of dozens, probably hundreds, of deadly snakes all coiled throughout the field sent a cold shiver across Jack's neck, and he struggled to restrain the physical reaction of shuddering. "Stay by the trucks, keep an eye out. We yell, you come blasting. Got it?"

"Yes, sir."

"Lay on the horn if you see trouble."

Curtis stood nearby. He held a shotgun like a toy in his hands. "You sure Stott's in there?" he asked Legs, his voice all business.

"Yes, sir. Seen 'im myself not twenty minutes before I went and brought y'all out here."

"Any others?"

"Four. Playing cards, I think. Mr. Stott has a regular poker game with"—his lips turned down in a sour frown—"his friends."

Jack studied the house. "What about Dunn?"

Legs shook his head. "No, sir. That new guy don't hang around with the others very much. Least not that anyone's ever seen. Unless they're out on business, you know?"

"How long have they been in there?"

"Creeping up on an hour, I suppose."

Jack said to Curtis, "Let's give them just a couple more minutes. Make sure they're really into that game."

Curtis continued to stare at the house. A breeze swept down the street and rustled his blond hair, and for a brief moment, Jack found himself wondering what the huge man had been like as a child. He imagined a locomotive-sized child trying to round the bases, or playing with wooden trucks on the floor of his room.

"How do you want to handle it? I know we need to send a message, but what's your plan?" Curtis asked.

"What would you do?" Jack asked, genuinely curious what the soft-spoken man would suggest.

Curtis sucked on his bottom lip, thinking. "We could just burn it down. Lock the doors and light it up."

Jesus. "How would that get our message across?"

Curtis's face showed genuine confusion. "How would it not? People know the Klan been messing with our operations. Then all of a sudden several of them are roasted alive, and you don't think that'd be a pretty clear message?"

Jack chuckled. "Okay, you have a point. But something that big would also bring local law down on us. And if not them, the staties."

"You got a better idea?"

"It's coming to me. Come on." Jack crossed the yard and carefully stepped onto the porch. Through the flimsy door drifted the slow strains of Vernon Dalhart lamenting how he wished he had someone to call his own.

"Good song," Curtis said in a low voice. Beyond the music, Jack heard other voices but was unable to make out what they were saying.

"Sounds like maybe four or five, but . . ." He shrugged. He pulled out his .45 and Curtis gripped the shotgun. In one quick motion, Jack shoved the door open and stepped inside, his weapon coming up as he moved.

Inside the house the air was thick and musty, and for some reason had the sickly sweet smell of manure or hay turned to rot. The room they were in comprised the main living space, with a small sink and stove in a far corner serving as a kitchen. There was a doorway to the right, which Jack assumed led to a bedroom. The floor was bare warped wood and just as dirty as he'd expected. Littering the space were clothes, pages of newspapers, old rusted tools, and dirty plates —the ghosts of meals past still clinging thickly to them.

In the center of the room, five men lounged in chairs or on old wooden apple crates, smoking cigarettes and playing cards gripped in dirty hands. A small crate sat in the center of them, cards and pennies scattered across its surface. Behind one of the men, a phonograph sat on the floor, the record moving in a wobbly circle beneath the needle. Jack recognized three of the men as those who had been with Dunn in the barn the previous night.

The poker players stared in stunned surprise at the weapons pointed at them. One stood, fists clenched. Another leaned to one side and reached to pick up a shotgun from the dirty floor.

"That'd be a really stupid move," Jack warned, thumbing back the hammer on his weapon. The man froze and Jack could see the warring of thoughts in his eyes. Jack shook his head slowly. "Stand up. All of you. Slow and with your hands where I can see them. That goes double for you," he said to Shotgun. The man licked his lips and glanced at Fists. *May have to shoot both of them*, Jack thought.

When all were on their feet, Curtis moved forward and collected the shotgun. He hastily searched the others and found two knives and an old, rusted pistol. "What were you gonna do with this?" he asked, waving the relic.

"The fuck you think?" the man he'd taken it from growled. Curtis just shook his head and chuckled, tucking the pistol away.

"Which one of you is Carl Stott?" Jack asked, bringing the group's attention back to himself. Nobody moved or spoke. "Do I need to start shooting you one by one until I get my answer?"

"That'd be me," said Fists. Stott was good-looking. Sandy hair over blue eyes and a lean, muscular physique that probably drove women crazy.

Until they learned what kind of a shitkicker he really was, Jack mused. "You're an ugly son of a bitch, aren't you?" For a long moment, Jack was sure the man wasn't going to answer.

Stott stood there, glaring at the Italian, his jaw working as if he were chewing nails. Finally, through clenched teeth, he asked, "What do you want?"

"You know who I am? Of course you do, I remember you and

those two"—Jack pointed the barrel of his gun at two others to either side of Stott—"from the barn." Stott's eyes went wide and small coughs of surprise flew from the others. "You weren't as alone as you thought," Jack said.

Stott recovered. "They knew what they were doing was wrong. They were contributing to the . . ." He faltered, searching for the right words, "They were poisoning the good white Christians of this community. And so are you, Mister Yankee. If you have half a brain, you'll take Henry's suggestion and get out of town."

Jack ignored the threat. "I doubt seriously those women were doing much poisoning. But that's only a part of why I'm here. As you've ascertained, I'm here representing certain business interests. I've been sent to assist in certain operations. Now, I know the Klan is being used as the army of the ASL, busting stills, intercepting shipments, that sort of thing. But I figure you fellas don't really care all that much about a few people having some fun or making a little extra cash to put food on their tables. Not really, do you?"

"Dunn won't—"

"I don't give a wet shit about Dunn," Jack said. "I'm talking about the men in this room, and any other friends you may have. The way I see it, the ASL realized you weren't really doing much to stop things. Which makes sense, who wants Prohibition anyway? So they send over this ballbuster, Dunn. He gets here and starts bossing you guys around,"—he looked directly at Stott—"taking your job away, probably making you look weak in the process, am I right?"

Stott didn't answer, only continued to grind his teeth.

"Which is why I'm suggesting this to you. You let Henry Dunn continue his crusade. Let him do whatever he wants. But don't help him. You let most shipments slide, you let stills go unmolested. In return, I will occasionally pass information to you about some shipments or stills you can bust."

The Klansmen were quiet for a while, eyes moving from Jack to Stott and back. Stott asked, "What kind of deal is that? We're supposed to keep allowing those heathens to continue poisoning white men? We're supposed to just let niggers—"

Jack pointed his pistol at Shotgun, who had slipped a knife from some secret location and was starting to inch toward Jack. Their eyes met and Jack saw the hatred mingling with shock—what Tony Detti liked to call the "oh shit moment"—just as he pulled the trigger. The blast was cannon fire in the small house and most of the man's face and head vanished in a spray of blood. The other Klansmen stared, struck dumb by the sudden violence. In that moment, Jack moved swiftly forward and grabbed Stott by the hair, pulling his head roughly to one side. He screwed the hot barrel of his pistol into the man's cheek. Stott howled in pain as the metal seared his skin. Jack's nose wrinkled at the smell of burning hair.

"Don't fucking move," Jack growled to the others. "Now that I have your attention, we're going to get a few things straight. That"—he pointed at the dead man lying in a spreading pool of crimson—"is a warning. A reminder of what will happen to all of you if you don't stop these attacks."

"Mister, we—"

"Bullshit. Of course it's you. Sure, it's Dunn leading the charge, but you pieces of shit are causing the problems. So what you're going to do is tell all the others in your little playgroup that if one more still is attacked that I didn't authorize, one more shipment interrupted, or one more man is killed, me and my overly large associate over there are going to come back. If that happens, not only are we going to kill all of you, we're going to find your families. We're going to tie them to their beds and light their fucking houses on fire. Do you understand?"

"Yeah," Stott answered. "Yeah, we get it."

26

Evie directed Jack to a small steakhouse in Birmingham. The restaurant, Arthur's, had polished wood booths and dim electric lights that cast a soft glow over the dining room. Waiters moved smoothly about, weaving between the tables and vanishing into the back room like apparitions.

"Are you ready for this?" Evie asked playfully as Jack held the door. As she passed, Jack breathed deeply, inhaling her perfume—an intoxicating scent that mingled flowers with something he couldn't quite put a finger on. It conjured images of lace and pouty lips, of legs intertwined.

"It took an hour to get here," he said. "At this point, I'd eat the maître d'."

The man in question was tall and thin with jet-black hair slicked back and a small tuft of facial hair beneath his lower lip. He smiled widely and welcomed them to the establishment with a flourish and a bow. Jack held up two fingers with one hand, while the other reached into his suit coat pocket for the cash to get them a choice table. Despite the hour and the restaurant being situated on a high hill that offered a breathtaking view of the rolling, tree-carpeted landscape beneath a sky slowly turning to purples and pinks, there weren't but three other tables occupied.

The maître d' led them across the floor, winding around the other tables with practiced ease. He stopped at a small table against the glass and pulled back Evie's chair, gesturing for her to sit.

When they were alone, Evie turned and took in the sunset. "Isn't it absolutely beautiful? I love sunsets. And it's so nice to be somewhere that the land isn't turning black." She glanced at him and smiled. "You're not looking."

"I've got the best view right here."

Her face lowered, her cheeks coloring. "You talk like that to every girl you meet?"

"Only the ones that nearly run me over the first time I meet them." The waiter appeared and Jack ordered a whiskey. The man's face tightened.

"I'm sorry, sir, but we uphold the eighteenth here." Jack slid a ten-dollar bill across the table. The waiter eyed it, plucked it up, and in the blink of an eye deposited it into his pocket. "And for the lady?"

"Same," Evie said, her lips working to suppress a smile. The waiter vanished as quickly as he'd appeared.

"Ten bucks, eh?" she asked when he was gone.

Jack shrugged. "It's nothing."

When the food arrived—their drinks concealed in ceramic coffee mugs—Jack raised his eyebrows appreciatively at the size of the steak on his plate. As they ate, Jack said, "Tell me something. I asked you earlier what you meant by nobody in their right mind would run their stills out in the woods. You dodged it. What did you mean?"

Evie chewed, her eyes shining in the light. Finally, she shrugged and said, "I told you, it's just a figure of speech."

"I don't believe you. You know why I'm here."

"Because you're addicted to biscuits and gravy?"

Jack ignored the joke. "And you, like everyone, know about the attacks. Is that what you meant? That people are crazy for continuing to do business with these attacks happening?"

Evie took her time answering. She spread softened butter on a corn muffin as she mulled over her response, "I've lived in town most of my life. I was born here in Birmingham, but Mama moved us to Jericho Springs when I was seven because she wanted to run a flower shop. She couldn't afford to open one here, and the smaller town had better opportunities. It was good business until she got sick. Daddy didn't know how to run it himself but after Mama passed, we figured it out. That was two years ago." She sipped her whiskey and asked, "What about you?" Irritation formed a tight knot in Jack's chest. She was taking a roundabout way of answering his question, but he figured he'd play along.

"Born and raised in Chicago. Parents are from Sicily. They came over for the same reason most people come. Land of opportunity and all. They stayed in New York for a while, then hopped a train to Chicago." A smiling image of Bobby, his dark hair mussed and sweat-matted to his head after a day of playing baseball, flashed in Jack's mind and a lump formed in his throat.

"They're still around, your parents?"

Jack coughed to clear the lump. "No. Lost Mom a couple of years ago. Dad went a few years back. Tuberculosis. What's this got to do with—"

"How'd you get into"—she wiggled her fingers at him—"all this?"

"All what?" Jack asked, knowing exactly what she was suggesting.

"You know. Being a gangster."

"I'm a businessman," Jack corrected. The old party line came as naturally as breathing.

"Right," she said, eyes wide mockingly. "And I'm a nun."

"My brother," Jack answered truthfully. "Bobby. He was three years older than me. After Pop died, we did whatever we could to help Ma put food on the table. I sold newspapers, shined shoes, whatever. Pop knew some people who were connected and occasionally they'd come around and check on us, make sure we had things we needed. Bobby ended up working with them. Lots of kids in the neighborhood did. Running errands, things like that."

"What about you? Did you work for them too?"

"Not then, no. I followed Bobby everywhere, though, so it was like

I did. I got to know most of the fellas that way. Most ignored me, but some were decent guys and didn't mind me hanging around."

"Is Bobby still working with them?"

A stillness settled over Jack. Evie noticed the change and slid a hand across the table. Her fingers were a soft heat against his skin. Swallowing, Jack said, "When he was fifteen, so this was about four years after he started running jobs for the crew, Bobby met this girl. He had been delivering payments and met her on one of his routes. Caroline McCarthy. Irish girl. Real pretty. Had a brother, Patrick, who ran with the Irish North Side Gang. Anyway,"—Jack lit a cigarette and blew the smoke up to the ceiling—"they started seeing each other a little here and there. She took his virginity. A few days later, Bobby's running payments and I'm following like a puppy. I'd been sick that week but couldn't stay cooped up in the house any longer. I knew Bobby would've beat my ass for getting out while I was sick, so I stayed about a half block back.

"Patrick McCarthy and a few of his pals jumped Bobby. Pulled him into an alley and beat him pretty bad. Patrick couldn't stand the thought of an Italian with his sister and kept screaming at Bobby about it. Then he shot my brother."

"Jesus," Evie whispered. Her fingers tightened on Jack's hand. "I'm so sorry. What did you do?"

Jack shook his head. "Nothing I could do. I was twelve. Not to mention, still sick. If I had come out from behind those garbage cans, they'd have shot me too. After the funeral, I found one of the guys Bobby worked with who had always been nice to me. Tony Detti. Told him I wanted to take my brother's place. As the man of the house, I had to do what I had to in order to help provide. Tony knew I wanted revenge, it wasn't like I hid it. Not at first, at least. The gang wouldn't do anything because Bobby hadn't fully earned his spot yet. Low-level runners like that get pinched or get themselves dead sometimes. It's the cost of doing business."

"Did you ever find Patrick McCarthy and the others?"

"Finding them wasn't the problem. I wanted them to forget all about it. So I waited. I'm a patient man. I found two of them a few years back. But Patrick and one of his closest friends, I found just last week."

"What did you—" The question died on her lips as Jack gave her a hard look. He held her gaze, and after a time she nodded, understanding, and redirected her eyes to her plate.

"That's how I came to be here." Jack continued. "The boss needed me to get out of town for a little while, let things cool down. Plus, he had this thing down here he needed taken care of."

The waiter appeared and cleared their plates. Jack ordered desserts and while they waited, Evie dropped another loaded question. "What about a wife? Here we are at dinner and I don't even know if you're married."

Jack's mouth dried up. His tongue sat behind his teeth like a mound of sand. He drained his whiskey, caught the waiter's attention, and indicated his mug. "I . . ." he started, letting the word drag out. "I was."

Evie leaned forward, resting her chin in her hand. Her eyes narrowed as she studied him. "What happened?"

The memory of Bobby was replaced by Norma. Norma in their bed, smiling up at him; Norma sprawled on the couch; Norma stumbling around in the dark of the living room, slurring curses as she knocked items to the floor in search of her vial and needle.

This is all that's left.

Jack shook his head. "It's not polite dinner conversation. But it ended quite some time ago. She made her choices."

Evie continued to examine him, as if she were trying to decide something. "I understand."

The waiter placed a fresh mug of whiskey next to Jack and slipped silently away. Jack forced himself not to down it in a single go. "So, about these attacks? You were saying?"

Evie sat back. "I'm sure that even in a city as big and modern as Chicago, people have superstitions."

Jack thought. "Ma wouldn't let Dad bring any garden tools in through the house, said it would bring bad luck. And I remember one of my neighbors pulling on her baby's hair because she believed doing that would make him grow up tall."

Evie giggled. "I've heard of that one. Down here we have superstitions, too, only they're a little more rooted in religion."

"You mean angels, demons, things like that? I know about those." He smiled at her raised eyebrows. "Catholic. Somewhat lapsed, but still."

"Exactly. But a little different here. A lot of them—the superstitions, I mean—are tied into crops, into livestock health, but others are deeper than that. Have you seen any houses with blue porch ceilings?"

"One or two. Couple of businesses too. Is that significant?"

"Down here, we paint porch ceilings blue if we want to scare off evil spirits."

Jack couldn't hold in the laugh. "Is that serious? People believe that?"

Evie's face was all fact. "We don't play around with haints."

"Haints?"

"Restless spirits of the dead who haven't moved on. The blue protects the people inside the home from being taken or influenced by evil spirits."

"What does this have to do with the woods?"

"We burn fields and patches of woods. Once a year, usually in the early fall, people will burn a section of woods or one of their fields. The smoke is believed to drive away evil spirits and bring good luck the rest of the year. I'm telling you this so you'll understand that there is a deep-rooted history of people believing in things, in evil spirits and such. Often those are connected with the woods around town. As far back as I can remember, people have told stories about seeing things in those woods. Goblins, demons, monsters. There's even a story about a really large pond somewhere out there that has a serpent creature in it. Everyone knows someone who claims to have seen it, to have lost a pet to it, but I don't know anyone who has personally laid eyes on it."

"But surely people realize that there aren't monsters? There are no such things as ghosts and ghouls."

She cocked her head slightly and squinted. "You're a Catholic. You believe in the concept of a virgin birth of the son of God, but you can't accept that there may be other things?"

He spread his hands. "What can I say? I always had a hard time swallowing the Virgin Mary pill too. But to think that something supernatural is out in the woods and is attacking men running stills?" He chuckled. "That's a bit much."

Evie leaned forward, wrapping both hands around the mug, staring into the liquid within. "Mama had a friend, Mrs. Stewart. She's passed on now, and was older than the hills when Mama knew her. Mrs. Stewart used to come around to the house a couple times a week bringing canned preserves or something she'd made. We weren't struggling, it was just her way. Never come empty-handed, I suppose. She'd sit in the front room with Mama and the two of them would talk for hours. Sometimes they'd knit, sometimes just sit and chat. I asked her, my mother, that is, why she was friends with someone so much older than her. Mama told me she believed Mrs. Stewart had nobody else, and that in addition to Mama actually enjoying the company and conversation, she felt it was her Christian duty to be Mrs. Stewart's surrogate family. We'd invite her over for Thanksgiving, the Fourth, all that."

"I feel you're getting off the subject," Jack said with a small smile.

"No," Evie said with a gentle shake of her head. "I'm not. Mrs. Stewart had been in Jericho Springs all her life. Her entire family was from here, going back generations. All the way back to the original settlement of Providence."

"Cleary said something about Providence, that it was back in the sixteen hundreds. Some of the guys working for him act like they're terrified of it."

"It's got a place in local legend, that's for sure. Providence was settled by people looking for new farmland and trying to get away from the crowded East Coast cities. But something happened to Providence and the people in it."

"Is that why some people moved just down the road and founded Jericho Springs? Wait a minute. That was a couple hundred years ago, wasn't it?" Jack asked. "How do you know what happened there? Cleary said there weren't any records."

"I don't. Not for certain," Evie conceded. "And he's right, there aren't any records going back that far. But something went on. Had to, to cause most of the town to relocate to where Jericho Springs is now. Mrs. Stewart said that a few people stayed, trying to keep Providence going."

"What happened to them?"

"Nobody knows. But their houses are still out there, what's left of them anyway."

Jack had an image of Morelli hanging, his skin flayed open and symbols carved into his flesh.

Evie continued. "Since I came to live here, people have always talked about those ruins. How they were haunted, that the spirits of the dead settlers were restless, searching the forest for the living, to kill and eat them in hopes of gaining their life force so they can live again. There's stories about strange lights in the woods, especially the closer to the ruins you get. Hunters claim to have heard something walking around. Something big."

"Could be a bear," Jack suggested.

"That's what I always thought, too," Evie said. "My point is, superstition is part of the lifeblood of this town. Now with the blight and those men dead or gone missing . . . The Gibbons family all dying or gone missing from their cabin . . . All the livestock that have died . . . Something isn't natural about it all."

One corner of Jack's mouth slowly rose in a half smile. "I can't tell if you're serious."

Evie stabbed her finger at the table, rattling her silverware against her plate. "You can't tell me those vines are natural. You can't tell me that buildings sprouting what looks like open sores is natural. Or do you know something I don't?"

"I know nothing about rot or blights," Jack admitted. "I grew up in the city. The closest I ever got to blight is when Ma would kill a plant she'd tried to grow. Woman had a black thumb."

"So if it's not normal, what are we left with?"

"You're just a ball of sunshine, aren't you?" Jack asked with a grimace as he pushed his pie plate away. "I don't think it's anything supernatural. I think it's easy to point to strange happenings and with nothing else to blame, say it's ghosts or witches or something."

"So what is it?"

Jack told her about his theory regarding Dunn and the Klan trying to scare religious and superstitious bootleggers.

Evie's face soured. "Henry Dunn is a horrible person," she said, "but I don't think he has the capacity or the manpower to do what I've heard has been done to some of those people." Once more, Jack thought about the blasé way Dunn shot the kneeling and bound people before getting the pickaxe.

Evie continued before Jack could counter her statement about Dunn. "Don't get me wrong, those Klan boys are pure evil." Jack saw the cloud pass over her eyes and knew she was seeing the face of Carl Stott. "But I don't think they're the ones doing this. I can't imagine someone doing those kinds of things to another person, no matter what they believed."

Jack considered telling her about the things that went on in France just a few years ago, the stories he'd heard, but decided the evening had turned morbid enough already.

When their coffee was finished, Jack threw some bills on the table and led Evie out to the truck. The night had cooled considerably and he draped his jacket over her shoulders. It hung on her as if she were a child trying on her father's coat and she laughed about it, flapping the arm sleeves about as they drove back toward Jericho Springs.

Not wanting to end the night just yet, Jack parked three blocks from Evie's store. She gave him a knowing look, one eyebrow raised mockingly but said nothing. He extended his arm and she took it, slipping hers around the crook of his elbow. They walked slowly, neither wanting to break the quiet moment. Jack breathed deeply, a sense of calm and comfort filling him. The stores along the main street were all closed, dark windows reflecting the pale moonlight. They moved quickly past the buildings that had begun to succumb to the rotting vines.

As they walked, they came across streets lined with sagging streamers and banners affixed to store windows. A few blocks away stood the incomplete stage. "Technically, it's our Town Anniversary celebration, but everyone just calls it the Summer Festival," Evie said. "People come in from other towns, Elden Mills and even Birmingham. They fill the streets. There's music, dancing, food—oh God, the food—and on the last night, a huge fireworks show. They shoot them off the roof of the bank. But all that's cancelled."

"Mm-hmm," Jack hummed. He'd stopped listening soon after she'd started talking, his inner alarm drawing his focus from her voice to something else entirely. He'd caught a glimpse of it as they reached the halfway point of the block. It was just a smudge, a darkness against deeper shadows in a nook next to Williams Hardware. Jack gave no indication he'd noticed. He continued walking, one hand casually in his pocket, the other against his hip as Evie held on.

On the next block, he pretended to drop something and as he bent to pick it up, glanced at the hardware store. The smudge had moved. The man had slipped farther along the opposite side of the street, keeping to the shadows and deep doorways.

"Well, this is me," Evie said when they reached her store.

Jack frowned at the glass door. "Don't tell me you sleep in your store."

"Above it," she clarified as she slipped his coat from her shoulders and pulled a set of keys from her pocketbook. They rattled a metallic tune as she worked them against the lock. The door swung open a few inches and Evie turned to face him, her eyes searching his for just a moment. Then she stretched on her toes and kissed him. Her lips, as soft as feather pillows, pressed against him and beneath his feet, the earth shifted. Evie held the kiss for a long moment before breaking it off.

"I hope I'll see you again," she breathed.

Jack smiled. "I'll stop by tomorrow." Evie kissed him again, this time quicker, before slipping into her shop. Jack waited until she closed the door and threw the bolt. She hesitated just on the other side of the glass before raising a hand and giving her fingers a quick wag. Jack raised his own hand in response and she turned and faded into the blackness. For a heart-lurching moment, Jack anticipated a scream as she encountered something or someone waiting for her in the dark. He reached out reflexively for the doorknob but pulled his hand back when no such shriek came. He let out a long breath and gave himself a self-scolding smile before moving on.

By the time he'd taken his third step, Jack's mind had switched gears, turning from Evie to the dark shape of a man that now stood just inside an alley directly across the street. The guy was good, Jack had to admit. Disciplined. Most mugs doing a follow like that smoked, the cherry on the end of the cigarette giving them away. But this one was smarter. *Probably learned that in the war,* he thought.

Jack reached the end of the block and crossed to the same side of the street as his observer. As he hopped onto the sidewalk, he whistled a short, happy tune. He paused occasionally to peer into a dark storefront for the next block and a half, then he turned and entered a pitch-black alley. The notes of the song he whistled echoed off the brick walls as he strolled into the dark.

One corner of his mouth ticked up in a smile, then behind him, the soft scuffle of a shoe signaled Henry Dunn entering the alley.

27

From the darkness, Henry Dunn watched Jack Carmelo stroll, pretty as you please, into the alley. *The fuck was that idiot whistling?* The song had sounded somewhat familiar, but the name danced just beyond Dunn's ability to catch. *It doesn't matter*, he decided. The wop was going to die in a few moments, so if he wanted to go out whistling some stupid song, that was his tough luck.

Dunn had waited in the dark recess of a building across from the flower shop for a couple of hours. While he waited, he'd observed the building down the street slowly being consumed by the weird vines. He'd seen more and more of those things cropping up around town lately; this building was just the latest. It was unnerving, the way the things looked like they were covered in some kind of moisture.

Other than the strange sight several dozen feet away, Dunn didn't mind the wait or the fact that he'd had to remain relatively still. He'd learned patience a long time ago, sitting in the mud of a trench waiting for the inevitable roar of machine-gun fire or the ball-shriveling scream of artillery rounds descending on his position.

Ever since he caught sight of Carmelo scurrying back to his truck near the barn, Henry had known what needed to be done. He'd put his normal philosophy of shoot first, ask questions later on hold earlier when he'd spoken to the Italian in the diner. Everyone knew that Carmelo was part of the Chicago Outfit, and even Dunn had managed enough self-control to understand that if he'd walked into a public place like Mack's and started shooting, the retribution from up north would be more trouble than killing one lousy greaseball was worth.

When Carmelo had laughed at him, lips twisted into an aloof smirk, the likelihood of Dunn killing the man increased. But once he'd caught sight of Jack spying at the barn, the decision was made, consequences be damned. Sure, Capone would just send someone else. But until then, Dunn would have ample opportunity to eliminate the bootlegging operation in town. And, by the time Carmelo's replacement arrived, there would be no whiskey operation left for anyone to make money off of.

Dunn hesitated at the edge of the alley and pulled a pistol from his waistband. He gave it a quick check, ensuring it was loaded and a round was chambered. The alley ahead was long and narrow, like something meant to swallow a man whole. Carmelo's whistling continued, the trilling notes bouncing off the walls. Dunn shook his head, surprised at the man's carelessness. Of course he would consider himself untouchable. *Thinks he's a big fish in a small pond. Plus, he's thinking about that cooze in the flower shop.* Dunn had to admit, the dark-haired woman was attractive. Maybe when Carmelo was nothing more than cooling meat, Dunn would go and knock on that florist's door. He thought again of the French woman in the barn and his body flushed with warmth.

The backstreet was long and the opposite end opened to Oak Street, the wide road bathed in moonlight. Dunn could make out small clusters of trash cans huddled at irregular intervals along either side. As he moved slowly down the alley, the smell of garbage mingled with the slimy odor of rot filled his nose, and his eyes squinted against it.

As Dunn approached the first cluster of battered bins, he realized something had changed.

The whistling had stopped.

Dunn flexed his fingers around the grip of the pistol and seeing nothing around the cans, he moved on. His feet moved silently as he drifted to one side of the alley. He was so focused on the path ahead that he didn't notice the stinking wet slime seeping down the exterior of the building. Dunn hugged the brick wall, the sleeve of his jacket soaking up the fetid moisture. Every few steps, he threw a glance over his shoulder, making sure Carmelo hadn't somehow looped around and was sneaking up behind him.

A few feet later, Dunn froze, the pistol coming up quickly. He trained the barrel on another collection of trash cans several yards ahead. One of the bins lay on its side, the contents spilled out like a drunk's evening meal. Sticking out from the opposite side was a pair of legs. Dunn remained as still as a statue, watching as one of them shifted, the person pulling the limb in. The clothing looked like the dark outfit Carmelo had been wearing. Dunn didn't recall seeing the Italian staggering, but that didn't mean he wasn't drunk. Still, it made no sense that he would have been whistling his way through an alley moments ago, only to now be sitting behind some garbage cans in a dirty backstreet.

Dunn scanned his surroundings. Seeing nothing, he thumbed the hammer of his pistol back and approached the man. As close as he was to the end of the alley, if the person behind the cans wasn't Carmelo, Dunn would have to abandon his mission for the night.

Once more, whistling drifted up, the sound filling the alley. Dunn stepped wide of the bins and as the man came into view, pressed his finger to the curved metal of the trigger.

Bleary eyes peered up at Dunn above a thick snow-white beard. Equally white hair stood out from the man's scalp like porcupine quills. The old drunk's eyes swam for a moment before they fell firmly on Dunn. The beard shifted as the man opened his mouth and held up a hand. "Got a nickel to spare?"

Dunn considered shooting the old inebriate but the urge passed and he lowered his gun. He began to say something, a threat forming on his tongue when the hardness of a gun barrel touched the back of his head, just behind his ear. Panic flared white-hot in his chest, settling like a lead balloon in his guts.

"Don't move," Carmelo said. His voice was calm, even, completely devoid of any emotion. It was the voice of a man who had killed before and was comfortable with it.

"How the fuck did you get behind me?" Dunn demanded.

"A gun to your head in a dark alley, and that's your question?"

"Did you really think I was going to start crying and begging for my life?" Instead of answering, Jack ripped the pistol from Dunn's fingers and spun him around. On the ground behind him, the drunk man babbled to himself, a mishmash of nonsense words having to do with vines and shining eyes in the dark. Dunn shifted his focus from the black maw of the gun to the hard eyes of Carmelo.

"You were going to kill me," Carmelo said. It wasn't a question, simply a statement of fact.

Dunn angled his head slightly, jutting his chin out in defiance. "You're down here to poison the people. You think your mission is—" The words died in his mouth as brilliant light exploded across his vision. A sharp pain followed immediately and as his head rocked back, Dunn realized he'd been punched. He staggered backward, his feet knocking against the corrugated metal of the trash cans. They rattled angrily as he fought to keep his balance.

Another blow, this time to the other side of his face, drove him to the ground. Before he could even register the sting of rocks against his knees and palms, Carmelo's foot lashed out and slammed into Dunn's ribs. All the air rushed out of his lungs and something in his side cracked with another flare of agony. His entire world transformed into a thunderstorm of hurt as Carmelo smashed kick after kick into him. Dunn could only writhe on the ground, absorbing each blow with strangled gasps.

The kicks kept coming. Dunn lost track of how many. His own grunts, the dull thumps, the old drunk babbling nonsense, they all blended into a nightmare soundtrack. Carmelo straddled him, bending and grasping the front of his shirt. He lifted Dunn up and punched him three times, very fast and very, very hard. There was a blinding *crunch* as his nose shattered and his lips were coated in warm blood.

Carmelo let go and Dunn slumped. Through all the pain, he was aware that Carmelo had returned the barrel of a gun to his head. "I saw what you did in that barn," Jack said. His words were again calm and even, as if he'd not just spent the last several minutes beating the shit out of someone.

"Degenerates," Dunn spat. The words came out along with a spray of blood from ruined lips. "They deserved—"

"Shut up," Carmelo snarled. "Shut your mouth and listen. You're done here. Do you understand? You've caught me on a day when I happen to be in a good mood. I've dealt with your buddies already and now I'm dealing with you. Normally I'd put a bullet in your brain and just be done with it. Considering the trouble you've caused me and my business interests, that's exactly what you deserve. But I'm feeling charitable, and believe me, Mr. Dunn, that isn't a feeling I get very often. Certainly not toward self-righteous, small-pricked racists like yourself. But I'm going to make you an offer. You're going to stop your investigations into liquor operations. You're going to pack your belongings and move on to whatever shithole will take you next. It will be better for your health that you're not here anymore. How does that strike you?"

Dunn glared up at the man. The brim of his hat threw an angled shadow across his features, but within that darkness, he saw the gleam in Jack's eyes. A cold hatred settled in Dunn's chest like a snake coiling, pressing down the instinct to lash out, to fight back and return the beating. Instead, a calm settled over his thoughts, coalescing them into one central mantra.

Jack Carmelo was going to die, and he was going to die very, very badly.

"Yeah," Dunn said, putting a little quaver into the word, showing that he was beaten.

"Good. And just in case you forget." Lightning fast, the Italian bent forward and swiped the butt of his pistol across Dunn's face. Hot pain speared through his cheek and the world faded to a pinprick of light.

As darkness closed in on his mind and unconsciousness pulled him down into its swirling depths, Dunn heard Carmelo whistling again as he stepped out of the alley and turned the corner.

28

Tony Detti stirred the large pot of marinara sauce, inhaled the heady scent of spices, and smiled. Unable to resist, he dipped the tip of his pinkie finger and tasted the sauce. Couple more hours and it'd be perfect. He grinned around the fleshy digit. The key was anchovies. Mash them up into a pulp and let 'em cook down.

Leaving the sauce gently bubbling on the stove, Tony entered the living room. He picked up his cigar from the ashtray next to the sofa and took a long pull, tilted his head back, and blew a thick, gray, aromatic plume up to the ceiling. Marie would have a fit when she got back and smelled the smoke, but that was for later. For now she was gone, off to play Lost Heir with some of the other wives. Tony wasn't sure how much card playing actually happened; he was certain that when those birds got together, all they did was drink wine and talk shit about their husbands.

"Marko didn't come home last night."

"Robert said he was going to take me on vacation to Atlantic City. We were going to take the first-class train all the way, but that was six months ago."

He tucked the cigar into the corner of his mouth and moved to the bar cart, plucked a bottle of Canadian whiskey, and poured a generous helping. He held it up, swirled it, and admired the "legs" trailing down. It was good stuff and it made him think of Jack Carmelo and the trouble the kid had caused. Tony shook his head and took a sip of the whiskey, refilled the glass, then turned back to his chair.

And for Al to send the boy south . . . He shook his head again and chewed on the cigar as he flipped on the large radio. Bessie Smith crooning "St. Louis Blues" floated out as Tony settled in and let the music mingle with his thoughts. There'd already been an uptick in incidents with the Irish, even though it had only been two days since he'd found Jack standing in the middle of the mess in that room. Tony understood revenge, had done more than his fair share of exacting it over the years, and what Jack had done with that axe? That was some devious shit. But it was done and there wasn't any use crying over it. If it had been anyone else but Jack, Al would have caved their head in and had them dumped in the river.

Tony thought about Carmelo. It was a horrible thing to carry— watching your brother die the way Bobby had. Tony didn't know how Jack lived with it. And to resist the urge to hit back immediately took a special kind of resolve. But that's exactly what Jack had done. After Bobby's funeral, Johnny Torrio had asked Detti to bring Jack in for a meeting. The Fox had offered his personal condolences for Bobby's death. In a bold, but not totally unexpected move, Jack had asked to become a member of the group, taking his brother's place. The kid was only twelve, and only God knew what Torrio saw in him, but Jack had been brought on to make the same runs Bobby had been doing. The move was highly unusual, but nobody questioned it.

When Torrio had brought Capone over, Jack was almost twenty years old and well established as someone to call when certain problems needed to be taken care of. Capone, despite being only six years older than Jack, took an immediate shine to the quiet Carmelo and used him often on various jobs.

And now he's been sent way the hell down south to rub elbows with a bunch of hillbillies, Tony thought with a grim smile. He didn't know who he should feel sorry for the most, Jack or the hillbillies.

The sound of a car outside broke Tony from his thoughts and he got up to refill his glass. The whiskey wasn't as strong as it could be, a result of either rushed production or the Canadians cutting the spirit to stretch their volumes. He knew he'd have to drink most of the bottle to get where he was going, but that was all right. Marie would probably leave him passed out in the chair when she got home. He chuckled. It would save her the trouble of having to sleep with his loud, drunken snores.

When Tony turned back to his chair, it took him several long seconds to understand that he was seeing a huge man standing near the radio. Adrian Turski, his mind registered with the gravitas of a nail in a coffin being hammered home. Just inside the kitchen doorway stood two more men: red-headed Eli Kinnerk and the dead-eyed Frank Ryan. Tony let out a long, resigned breath.

"Don't do anything stupid," Adrian said. He leaned forward menacingly and Tony saw the white scar tissue that ran across the man's cheek and vanished over one ear. He moved his large, muscled arm and Tony saw the glinting metal of a pistol aimed in his direction. "You know why we're here?"

Tony took a sip of his whiskey. "I've got a good idea. Can't help you, though."

Adrian stepped closer. A lock of his dark hair lay across his eyes and he swept it aside in a smooth motion with his free hand. "Can't say as I believe you. You know how much I had to go through to get here? To you? Don't bullshit me. Don't play smart with me. I had to pull out a guy's goddamn fingernails before he finally told me it was Jack Carmelo you helped get out of that warehouse. So telling us you don't know anything rings a bit hollow."

The corner of Tony's mouth twitched in a half smile. "You have any idea what Capone is going to do to you for this? He's going to tear the North Side apart until he finds you. Brick by brick, and he'll use those bricks to bury you. What's left of you, that is."

Turski chuckled. "Yeah, Jack's junkie wife told us something similar, 'You know who my husband works for?' Blah, blah, blah. It got old really fast."

Tony's cheeks drooped heavily as the feeling rushed out of him. "You went—"

"Of course we did," Eli said in a voice like a weasel. "Went by there early this morning. Caught the bird making coffee. She takes it black. Strange for a broad. All the broads I know take it with cream and sugar out the wazoo."

"Jack wouldn't have told her where he was going," Tony said and inwardly prayed that was true. He knew Jack and Norma's relationship was basically dead but anything was possible. The thought made him think about Marie. How much longer before she came home? It was still early, so hopefully she'd be gone for a few more hours.

"Yeah," Adrian said. "Seems he didn't. Just told her he had some business out of town and that he'd be gone for a few days."

"And we asked really, really nicely," Eli said. He pointed to the chair Tony had occupied earlier. "Sit that fat ass of yours down and let's have a chat."

Tony hesitated but the soft *click* of the pistol being cocked broke that spell. He sat. Eli and Adrian pulled chairs over and straddled them, resting their arms on the thin backs. "So, here's how this is going to go," Eli said. "Adrian here is gonna ask you what you know about the hit and where Capone sent that scumbag Jack. If he doesn't like the answers you give, Frank over there is going to hurt you."

"What did you do to Norma?"

Eli smiled, dirty crooked teeth flashing. "Aww, ain't that sweet? You got a thing for that bird? I can't blame you. Easy on the eyes. Except for how skinny she's gotten. Heroin will do that, I hear. Say, you know anything about photography?"

Tony blinked, confused. The fuck was this Irish piece of shit going with that?

"The look on your face tells me you don't. That's okay. Frank here is a real big fan of it. It's kind of his hobby, you could say. Takes his camera everywhere he goes. You got it with you now, Frankie?"

"Yeah," came the low, toneless answer.

"He takes pictures of everything. Does it so much that he built one of them rooms where he can make the pictures and all. Whaddya call it, Frank?"

"Darkroom."

"Yeah, that's it. So he makes the pictures in that room, using all them chemicals and shite. I saw it once. Smells like the inside of a nickel hooker's asshole, but it works. Few hours later and you got a real picture you can hold. Hey, Frankie, show our pal here the pictures you took this morning."

Frank's shoes scuffled on the carpet as he crossed the room. Tony's heart rabbited in his chest, his sweat running in thin streams along his neck. Frank stopped next to Tony. The man's face was a pale, expressionless mask; his eyes reminded Tony of the dead, glossy black of one of the dolls Marie collected and kept on the dresser in their bedroom. Frank held up a picture between two smooth fingers.

Tony forced himself to look at the image. Incomprehension at what he was seeing slowly melted away as things took shape. His head shook slightly, refusing the images. No, this was impossible. That couldn't be a person. That couldn't be real.

"See?" Eli said, drawing the word out. "We tried real hard with her. We asked very nicely. And eventually, we had to stop asking nicely."

Tony struggled to tear his eyes from the picture, the image of what used to be a human being.

"We're going to ask you nicely now. And Frank even brought his camera for later."

29

"Do you mind if I put this in your window?" Grace asked, holding out the flyer. The dark-haired woman behind the counter took the slip of paper and scanned it.

"You did this yourself?"

"Yes, ma'am," Grace said. "I had to handwrite all of them. Did it yesterday. I should have been out looking, but Daddy wouldn't let me. Said to let the authorities handle it."

Under the hazel green eyes of the woman, Grace couldn't help but feel self-conscious, and she ran a nervous finger through her hair, tucking it behind her ear. Standing there in the flower shop wearing the same plain brown dress she wore most days, her hair in dire need of a good brushing and sleeplessness pulling her eyelids down, Grace knew she looked every bit the poor bumpkin that she was.

The woman smiled. "Of course you can. Put two, in fact. One in each window. Better yet, put a third on the door so we can be sure people see it when they come in." Grace's cheeks warmed with relief and affection toward the woman's willingness to help. The clerks at the last few stores, all men, had told her gruffly that they weren't allowed to put signage up that wasn't directly related to the business.

"Thank you, ma'am," she said and blinked away tears.

The woman, seeing the wetness on Grace's cheeks, hurried around the counter and pulled her into an embrace. The woman's body was soft and warm, radiating confidence and safety. The feeling reminded Grace of how her mother's hugs had felt before Charlie went missing. But in the last few days, her mother had grown distant and stiff, engaging with Grace only as needed to instruct her toward some chore or another. Grace leaned into the hug until she remembered she hadn't had a bath in a couple of days. She pulled back, worried that she'd gotten the brunette's nice blue dress dirty.

The woman held out a hand. "Here. Give me the other two and I'll put them up myself. And don't call me 'ma'am' again, okay? My name is Evie. What's yours?"

Grace cleared her throat. "Grace. Grace Robertson."

Evie took the flyers and gave Grace an appraising look. "Have you eaten today?"

"No, ma'am," Grace said. She'd not eaten anything since yesterday morning, in fact. Creating the flyers advertising her missing brother had taken all her concentration, and she'd fallen asleep at the kitchen table, waking in the late hours of the night. Her stomach gave a rumble as if it had been listening and was scolding her for ignoring it.

The pretty brunette slipped behind the counter littered with the detritus of cut flowers and random leaves. She bent, rummaged through something out of sight, and returned with a dollar bill. Grace's eyes went wide. A dollar was more than she'd had at one time in all fifteen years of her life. "Take this and go to Mack's and get something to eat."

Grace shook her head and took a faltering step back. "I couldn't possibly. I appreciate it, but—" Before she knew it, the woman was back in front of her and pressing the bill into her hand, wrapping Grace's fingers around it.

"I'm not asking you. I'm telling you. If you're searching for your brother, you need to eat. You need strength. Consider it my payment for hanging your flyers up." Grace opened her mouth to protest again but the woman gripped her by the shoulders and turned her toward the door. "I'm not discussing this. Go eat."

Outside in the warm sun, Grace turned back. "I'll bring your change."

The shop owner raised one eyebrow. "You'd better not. If I find out all you did was get a soda or a glass of water, I'll put my foot up your butt. You go and eat a full meal. If you have change left over, and it better not be much, leave a dime for the waitress. When you're done, come back and we can talk about the best places for you to put the rest of those." She gestured at the bundle of handwritten flyers.

Evie gave Grace a final gentle nudge, then returned to her work. Grace sighed and turned to cross the street. Mack's wasn't more than a block down; she could see the red lettering of the sign from where she stood. A few cars grunted their way along the street, their thin tires flattening the dark weeds that had started to grow out of cracks in the road. The strange knobby growths sprang back up moments after being rolled over, continuing to fill the air with their awful stench. Only a couple of people passed by, paying her no attention as they hurried to do whatever errands they had.

Grace jolted violently as someone collided with her. She took a wide, lurching step before she caught her balance, then looked to see who had bumped her. Her eyes found the form of a man she recognized. He was slightly younger than her father and she'd seen him often at church or in the aisles of Rangle's where he worked. Thomas Whittaker walked with a stumbling gait, his shoulders hunched and head lowered as if he were examining something in his hands.

"Mr. Whittaker?" Grace called after him. He'd always been nice to her and her mother when they saw him, so it made no sense that he would have knocked her half into the street and not apologized.

Thomas slowed and half turned to regard her. At the sight of his face, Grace's legs threatened to give out. Blood streamed from the man's mouth, running in thick rivulets along his cheeks and chin, soaking into the fabric of his shirt. Among the shining red was the glint of white and with sickening horror, Grace understood she was seeing part of one of his teeth, half buried in the meat of his lower lip.

"They're going to take us all," he said. His voice was guttural and phlegmy, and the exhalation of his words sent droplets of blood arcing onto the sidewalk. "We're their black flowers and they will harvest us all." His bloody mouth expanded into a maniac's grin and he resumed his path, chittering to himself as he walked on stiff, ungainly legs.

Grace stared after the man until he was around a corner and out of sight. Her heart thundered in her chest at the sight of all the blood, and for a moment, she warred with herself over the urge to follow him and see if he needed help. But the sight of the drops already drying to a dark maroon on the concrete settled the debate. There had been something in that smile that told Grace in no uncertain terms that she couldn't help Thomas Whittaker.

But she could still help Charlie. That thought galvanized her and forced her back to her original task. As she crossed the road, the familiar figure of Pastor McCauley stepped out of a shop. Despite the heat of the day, he wore his usual dark pants and white long-sleeved shirt, and he walked slowly, his head slightly bowed as if in deep thought or concentrating on the ground so as not to trip.

A shiver of revulsion went through her. She was young, but not so young that she was oblivious to the attention he paid her. Frequently she'd noticed the older man's eyes lingering on her, a glazed look in them. Each time she'd caught him, he'd shifted his attention else-where, and more than once she'd seen his neck redden with embar-rassment at being caught. But he'd always been nice and polite to her, had never tried to touch her other than the occasional handshake or gentle squeeze of the shoulders before or after a sermon. And if anyone in town, aside from Evie at the flower shop, could help her with her efforts to find Charlie and to rally people to help search for him, it was Pastor Sam.

Grace hurried to catch up. "Pastor Sam?" she asked as she pulled alongside him.

His head snapped up at the sound of his name and he blinked at her in surprise. "Hey there," he said. His voice was thick and some-what strained, as if speaking hurt him. She wondered if he had a toothache or perhaps had started to come down with a case of laryngitis.

Grace held up the papers. "I've made a bunch of flyers about Charlie. I've been trying to post them around town."

"That's good. I'm sure that's helpful."

They took a few more steps in silence. Grace's mind swirled with ways to ask him for help, but none seemed right. Finally, she decided to just come right out with it. "I was wondering if you could help. I don't know, I just figured people listened to you and respected you. So maybe you could, I don't know, talk to them?"

Sam stopped walking and turned to face her. His eyes bored into hers. "Talk to who?" he asked.

Grace shifted uncomfortably. One shoulder jerked up in a half shrug. "I don't know. The police? I've asked Chief Dickerson about what they're doing to find Charlie and he said that he had people out looking right now."

"That sounds like they're doing exactly what they're supposed to be doing," Sam said. His eyes drifted down her face and settled around her chest. They lingered there for a long beat.

"It's just that I'm not sure I believe them," Grace said. She lifted the flyers and clutched them across her breasts as if they were a shield. "He also said that it was likely Charlie just ran away, or was out exploring and avoiding his chores."

"How are your parents doing?"

The question caught Grace by surprise. "I don't know," she answered. "They've been worried since that morning we saw that he was missing. Daddy spent hours in the woods looking for him. He sat up most all that night crying." That had been as bad as her brother going missing. In all her life, she'd never once seen her father cry. To hear him sitting in the dark in the living room sobbing into his hands was too much to bear. "And today—" she started but stopped, considering how to describe the shift in her parents' attitude. "I can't say they're happier, but they don't seem to be as worried. It's like they just know that Charlie's okay even though he's not home and nobody knows where he is."

Pastor Sam absorbed her words without expression. After a moment, he took a deep, audible breath and said, "The Lord holds in

His hands the young, the weak, and the old. I've no doubt, and I told your parents this just last night at our special service, that Charlie is perfectly safe." He stumbled over the last word, as if he knew it wasn't true and had to force it out anyway. Grace's eyes narrowed at the thought. Before she could say anything else, Pastor Sam continued. "We're having another service tonight. You should come."

"It's not Wednesday or Sunday. Is this a service to talk about finding Charlie?"

"This is a new worship that I'm implementing. With everything that's been happening around town, I and the rest of the congregation feel that an increase in prayers will have a more positive impact than just once or twice a week. We're going to be meeting frequently, concentrating our energies so that the Lord will hear us and guide us to purification and salvation." He reached out quickly and grabbed her arm, his fingers pressing roughly into her. "You should be there, with your parents. With all of us. Together we will walk this new path and emerge in the light."

Grace's lips peeled back in a pained grimace as she pulled her arm free of the pastor's grasp. The skin and muscles throbbed where he'd gripped her. She took two quick steps back until the edge of the curb dug into her heel. She stopped, the flyers still clutched to her chest. Sam watched her intently, his mouth slightly open and the hand he'd held her with dangling in the space between them. "I have to be at home tonight," she said. The words came out in a hot rush. "In case Charlie comes back, or if anyone shows up with news."

Sam remained where he was, upper body angled slightly toward her, hand still hanging in the air for several seconds. Abruptly, he straightened. "I understand. But sooner or later, we're going to need you there. We're going to need everyone there. To participate. To sacrifice and cleanse."

"I'll be there as soon as Charlie is found," Grace said and stepped quickly away, her feet clicking fast and hard on the sidewalk. She looked back once, just before pushing open the door to Mack's.

Sam McCauley remained motionless, watching her with hollow eyes.

30

As Evie finished taping the last flyer to the store window, she noticed Grace standing across the street talking to the Baptist preacher, McCauley, then returned to the counter. Her heart hurt for the girl. Seeing the fear and exhaustion on her face, imagining how long it took her to write up each individual poster . . . it was heartbreaking.

She took a moment to reorient herself with what she'd been doing prior to the interruption. Her fingers drifted across the scattered stems of the tulips, trying to remember what her next step with them should be, but her earlier focus was gone. Instead, her thoughts continued drifting back to Grace's story about her young brother going missing in the middle of the night. It was just awful to think of a girl her age, not to mention the rest of the family, waking up to find a child gone without a trace.

It was all getting to be too much. All the strange occurrences in the forests and along the outskirts of the town. She thought of the reports of odd mutations discovered on rabbits and deer, the rotting fields of crops, the stories of men going missing or being found dead near the moonshine stills they'd been working. How people weren't up in arms about that, she couldn't understand. She'd asked Jack about local law enforcement looking into matters, specifically the dead men. He'd told her that the cops didn't have the manpower to investigate all of it. Between the blight and the Klan increasing their vigilante activities, there was little the tiny force could do. They were short on manpower, and to bring in reinforcements from larger agencies would take time.

Last night at dinner, he'd seemed convinced the attacks and deaths were a part of Henry Dunn and the Klan's operations, but as Evie glanced at the strange, mottled weeds growing out of the road, she had to admit she wasn't so certain. The Klan was capable of a lot of things, but growing never-before-seen flora or causing blights to crops went beyond their simplistic minds. Not to mention the animal mutations. A smile tickled her lips as she tried to imagine Henry Dunn struggling to hold down a panicked rabbit as he fought to sew on a fifth leg.

Evie's stomach rumbled, and she dropped the tulip she'd been holding and slipped behind the counter, moving to a dark stairwell that led up to her small apartment. She had some bologna and bread in the fridge, and a small sandwich with a glass of buttermilk sounded like a perfect lunch. After that, she'd be able to refocus on her work.

Her apartment was small but cozy. The main living area dominated the footprint and contained a sofa flanked by a couple of end tables. A set of two windows overlooked the street and she'd set a couple of comfortable chairs next to them with a table between the two, where an Agatha Christie novel sat beside a small two-arm candelabra and a book of matches. A fern hung from the ceiling above, the plant's sawtooth leaves drooping so low that they occasionally brushed across her head when she sat to read. To the left of the main door was a low, wide dresser with several framed pictures arranged on its top. A small gramophone in one corner and a radio situated across from the couch completed the layout of the room. A doorway to the right led to her bedroom and the bathroom, while another open door on the left provided access to the small, well-organized kitchen.

She prepared her food, then placed her lunch on a small plate and carried it into the living room, intending to eat while looking out over the street outside her shop. The sandwich looked pitiful: plain white bread and a slice of bologna on a plain white plate. Nothing like the meal she had enjoyed the night before with Jack.

The thought of the handsome gangster from Chicago made her smile and sent a warmth rippling through her chest. She'd known the instant she met him that she wanted him. All it took was a single glance. An idea came to her, sudden and raw. What if Jack had a girl back in Chicago already? He'd said that he wasn't married, but it was inconceivable that a man like Jack Carmelo, as strong and handsome as he was, would still be single. The thought weakened her, and the plate slipped from her fingers. It struck the floor, the sandwich tumbling away, bologna separating from bread to fall limply to the hardwood floor.

"Oh Christ," she gasped, a soft scolding to herself as she looked at the disassembled sandwich.

"He ain't got nothing to do with this," a man said. For a split second she thought it was Jack and she flinched, her mouth hanging open in shock and anticipation. But the feelings were broken apart as her mind registered what—who—she was looking at.

Henry Dunn limped into the apartment, one hand in his pants pocket, the other still holding the doorknob. He moved slowly, as if in great pain. His normally fleshy face was a swollen mass of bruises and cuts, and his nose looked like a tomato that someone had flattened with a pan.

"How . . ." Evie began. "What are you doing in my home?"

The sharp fear flared brilliantly as Dunn moved aside and another figure entered and closed the door. Carl Stott grinned coldly at her from around one of Henry's shoulders.

Dunn turned his fat, ruined face to survey the apartment. "You call this a home? Shit on a shingle, this is more like a broom closet than anything. You get a free dustpan with your rent? Christ, even Carl here has better digs than this."

Carl giggled, a high-pitched tittering. "It's what was left to her after her pa fell in front of that train."

Evie's mind clawed weakly to make sense of what they were saying, to understand how they'd appeared in her doorway, how Henry was now standing in her home, his hat spinning between his fingers.

With effort, Evie stood. "I didn't give you permission to come in here." Her voice was shakier than she'd hoped it would be and the words came out mousy. She cast a hateful glare at Stott. "And he's absolutely not welcome."

"But here we are, all the same." With a soft grunt, Henry paced about the room, turning his back to her as he looked at a small painting of sand dunes on one wall. Chills swept over her, the sensation of a thousand spiders crawling. Something about Henry Dunn gave her the impression of a slime-coated creature covered in glistening scales, a serpentine tail whip-cracking through mud, its oozing fingers reaching for her, waggling in eager anticipation.

Then there was Carl Stott, who had drifted uncomfortably close while Dunn peered around her home. Against her will she glanced at him. His yellow teeth showed through a hungry grin. Evie shuddered, cleared her throat, and ran a hand across her hair, smoothing it down. "What can I do for you?" She directed the question at Dunn and for a moment, he didn't speak. When he did, his words took the breath out of her.

"Where's Jack Carmelo? I know you two are"—he sneered—"seeing each other. Saw y'all last night."

"He's not—" Her throat closed to the width of a pea, cutting off her ability to finish.

Dunn stepped closer. His torn and swollen lips puffed small exhalations with every step he took. Evie, not understanding how the certainty came to her, knew in an instant that Jack had done this to the man. Had beaten him like a rented mule. With effort, she fought down a satisfied smile.

Without glancing away, Dunn tossed his hat onto the sofa where it landed with a soft *thump*, masked by the sound of his boot on the hardwood floor. Evie retreated and collided with the wiry form of Carl Stott. Hot breath tickled the nape of her neck and she groaned inwardly.

"Where would he be?" Henry asked. The lack of affect in his voice sent cold fear through Evie's guts. She looked into his flat eyes and realized that whatever made him human had stepped out.

Dunn was, without a doubt, a bully—someone who got their jollies through intimidation and occasionally violence, as was anyone who was a member of the Ku Klux Klan. But there was something about Henry that went far beyond just simple bullying. He kept it locked away, caged deep within him like a forbidden exotic animal, but sometimes you could see it reflected in his eyes . . . the monster struggling at its bars.

One day, while standing in the canned goods aisle of Rangle's, Milicent Sanders had told her about some of the people who came back from France changed in ways that were for the worse; men waking up screaming only to find their hands squeezing the life out of their wives was just one example. With a gleam in her eye and her voice cast low, Milicent had related the story of a man in Birmingham who woke up one morning convinced that the Germans were inside his trench. He took a rifle and walked through the streets shooting at anything that moved. He killed four people before the police showed up.

What Evie didn't know was whether Henry Dunn came home from the war like that, or if he had been broken before he left. Either way, it didn't matter now. She glanced down and saw his hands balled into fists.

"I haven't seen Jack since he dropped me off last night. We came back here and had a fight. He'd been drinking and tried to force himself on me. I threw him out and haven't seen him since." The lie felt weak on the surface and she could see in Dunn's eyes that he knew it was bullshit.

"That so? Carl, you believe that?"

"Nope," said the oily voice behind her.

Dunn's boots were soft, uneven thuds against the floor, each step like the tolling of a bell signaling an impending execution. Through tight lips, he grunted, "Where is he?"

Evie moved automatically, stepping around Stott and back until she bumped into the dresser. Behind her came the rattling of picture frames toppling over.

"I told you I don't know. What do you want with him?"

"I just want to ask him some questions, that's all. You tell me where he is, and I'll just go talk to him."

"Is that why you brought your lapdog? Didn't think you could handle the big words on your own?" She widened her eyes in mock surprise. "Oh, I get it. He's here to help you form complete sentences." The second the words were past her lips, Evie knew she'd gone too far. Dunn stopped, seemingly like he'd been punched in the chest. His jaw worked as though he was chewing on his anger.

"Where's Jack?" he whispered.

"I told you, I don't know," she said again.

Dunn nodded, his eyes narrowing and telling her in no uncertain terms that he didn't believe her. "I know you did. I'm just going to make sure. Carl." Hands like bands of iron clamped around her wrists and pulled her away from the dresser. Stott moved those bands higher, gripping both her biceps. Evie struggled but his grasp was stronger than she assumed it would be. Stott's hot breath was on her neck.

"You stand still while he's talking to you. You're gonna wanna listen good, bitch."

Evie froze, her body cold. As one meaty fist slowly drew back, Dunn said wryly, "This is going to hurt."

31

The Shadako River was smaller than Jack had anticipated based on the way Cleary had spoken about it when they set up the transport plan. About forty feet across, the river— "More of a creek," Trask had called it—was full of smoothly moving brown water. Gentle swirls and eddies patterned the surface and Jack watched a tangle of leaves, all seemingly connected as if some small being had used them to fashion a raft, gliding its way along to points west.

Nearby, sat a boat, its front half—he knew there was a name for it but couldn't think of it—resting on the muddy ground. The vessel was little more than a raft itself, made out of wood slats with low sides. A single plank stretched across the rear, forming a bench for someone to sit and operate the very small motor.

"She may look tiny but she'll get the job done," said a man clad in overalls, his tanned and seamed face covered in three-day scruff. He approached, wiped dirt from his palms, and extended one hand. "Edgar Monroe. I'm taking this load up." Jack shook his hand and watched as two Black men shifted boxes from a stack on the bank into the boat.

"They packed well?" Jack asked.

"We got plenty of wheat straw in there. They gonna be just fine. Got a secret compartment that stores more than you'd think."

Jack looked pointedly at the boat. "That thing going to hold?"

Monroe chuckled. "I've had this boat since I was a young 'un. Me and my pop built it and took it out fishing all the time. She'll hold. We could probably put about eight boxes more than what you're sending before I started having trouble. But for this?" He shrugged. "Easy as pie."

"And you know where you're going," Jack said.

"Sure do." Monroe dug into a pocket and pulled out a pipe, lit it, and puffed fragrant smoke into the air. "If you don't mind, I gotta keep an eye on them." He leaned his head to indicate the Black men. "They's usually good about things, but you don't want to leave 'em unsupervised too long."

Jack looked back at the boat where Monroe and the two Blacks were focused on their work, then thought about the beating he'd given Henry Dunn the night before. The fat fuck had seemed resigned by the end of it, but Jack wasn't so sure. He was fairly confident his message had gotten through to Stott and the others, but Dunn . . . "I don't know," he said in a low voice. He didn't think the Klansman was the kind to learn a lesson that quickly. If anything, Jack likely stirred up a hornet's nest.

When the boat was loaded, Monroe launched into the moving water. Jack watched until it was out of sight beyond a bend; the engine's high-pitched whine fading as it moved farther upriver.

As he drove back to town, he let his mind drift, his thoughts flitting to small details about the pipeline north, whether the boats he had Cleary arrange were going to be able to move up along the Tennessee River until it connected with the larger Mississippi. Getting the load to the Tennessee River would be tricky, too, relying on land transportation. He wished Al had agreed to send more men down for security the last time he'd spoken to him. Jack could have really used those bodies to guard the trucks as they moved north to the waterway.

He wondered if Evie would want to take a ride up north and

spend a weekend at the river, or maybe even go into Nashville. It was absolutely a hick city, but he thought they could have fun there regardless. Maybe see a show. With little to do for the afternoon, he decided to drop by and see how she felt about the idea.

Despite being past the traditional lunch hour, Evie was nowhere to be found inside the small shop. Jack stood in the middle of the store, breathing in the heavily perfumed air and listening for any sound of the woman. A soft *thump* drifted through the ceiling and he glanced up. The sound didn't repeat and after another few minutes, when Evie didn't emerge, Jack slid around the counter and into the back room.

The rear of the store was small and filled with shelves of supplies, including several open empty boxes. A table took up most of the space, its surface covered with flowers, trimmings, vases, and pruning shears. An open doorway to his left revealed a staircase leading up. As he peered into the darkness of the second floor, the familiar feeling of something not being right crept up his back, tightening his muscles.

At the top of the stairs, he glanced around the corner at the short hallway outside her apartment door. There was nobody waiting in the small space, but what held his attention and pulled a soft gasp from his throat was the door to Evie's living quarters hanging open a couple of inches. It was possible she just left it like that, being the only apartment up here, but a sour pit in his gut told him that wasn't the case.

He freed the pistol from his pocket and thumbed off the safety as he stepped slowly, moving with extreme care toward the door. His ears strained to hear anything on the other side, voices, a struggle, anything. There was only silence and the ever-so-soft tread of his own feet on the floor as he inched forward.

He reached out and let his fingertips brush against the smooth surface of the door. It swayed gently with the contact and after a deep breath, he pushed it open and moved quickly through, the .45 sweeping the small apartment from left to right.

In the main room, two large windows allowed bright sunlight in, highlighting the sofa where Evie lay, her back to him. She flinched and gasped in fear as he entered the room. Though he knew something was wrong with her, Jack quickly stepped through the rest of the apartment to make sure they were alone.

"Evie?" His voice came out dry and raspy. She only shook her head and pulled a knitted pink blanket higher over herself. Jack hesitated, unsure of his next course of action. "It's Jack."

The body on the couch sagged. "I'm not feeling very well at the moment. Would you mind terribly coming back tomorrow?" The words were thick, matted together, and seemed to take some effort to say.

"Why won't you look at me?" The fact that the woman he'd finally realized he was coming to care for, possibly even love, wouldn't turn and look at him had started to ratchet the tension in his body again. Evie had never hesitated to look him in the eye, usually with a mischievous grin on her face. He approached her.

"Don't." The force in that one word, barely whispered, stopped him like a punch to the chest.

"What's going on?" he asked.

Evie was quiet for a long moment and Jack had the irrational fear that she'd passed away. Panic flared in his chest and he took another step. "I don't want you to see me right now. I'm . . . I don't feel well."

"Let me help," he said. "I can get something from the pharmacy" —he stepped toward the kitchen doorway—"or I could make you some soup. Believe it or not, I have some sk—" He stopped as his toe connected with something small and solid on the floor. The object skittered across the hardwood with a clicking sound that filled him with images of spiders scurrying. Jack bent to pick it up. As his fingers neared it, he stopped, the breath evaporating from his lungs.

It was a tooth, patches of white peering out from beneath a film of drying blood. "What the hell?" he mumbled and moved to the couch. Evie's face came into view barely above the edge of the blanket, and Jack nearly collapsed. She looked at him with one good eye; a look of pity, sadness, embarrassment, and anger clashing in the glossy orb. The other eye was swollen shut beneath a hideous black and purple mound of bruised flesh. There were cuts across her cheeks and forehead, and her nose was a thick, bloody pulp. "How . . ." Jack whispered. He dropped to his knees and pulled the blanket back. Evie's fingers struggled to resist, to keep the cover in place, but ultimately couldn't maintain their hold.

Her lips were cracked, bleeding, and a thick line of blood trailed from the corner of her mouth and along her chin. One side of her face was swollen, the flesh bulging beneath cuts and scrapes. Her arms were covered in bruises and abrasions, most of them wide and giving the impression of fingernails raked across the skin. The hand that didn't hold the blanket was tucked against her chest, nestled between her breasts, and Jack could see at least two fingers bent and twisted at unnatural angles.

Evie watched him with the same puppy dog glare out of her one good eye. Her scalp was a menagerie of raw and bleeding skin where clumps of her hair had been pulled out.

"What? Who?" Jack wanted to know.

The cracked and swollen lips moved and Evie said thickly, "Dunn and Stott send their love." She paused to swallow and winced while doing so. "Wanted to know where you were. I had no idea. He . . ." she trailed off, and blinked hard. "They didn't believe me."

"Henry Dunn did this to you?" The steel in Jack's voice surprised even himself. "He came here and did . . . this?"

"Said to give you a message. Said to meet him at the gas station on Locust Road at midnight."

The rage that whipped through Jack's mind was something he'd not experienced since watching Bobby's murder. Even when he had stepped into the room in that basement and brought the axe up over Patrick McCarthy's head, he'd only felt a cold determination. The fury swirled in him now like a typhoon, its eye a cold, hellish resolve.

Henry Dunn was not going to see the sun rise tomorrow.

Pushing his hatred down, he bent forward and kissed Evie gently on the top of her head. "I'm getting you help. Is anything else—" He stopped, his throat closing again. "Is anything else broken?" He wanted to ask if they'd done more, but he wouldn't. He couldn't.

"Don't think so. My foot's bad. Twisted my ankle trying to get away. I don't think I can walk."

Jack bent and slid his hands gently under her. She whimpered, tensing at the contact, then nodded for him to continue. When she was ready, he lifted her and held her tightly against him. "I'm getting you to Cleary's. He has a doctor on call. You're going to be all right." Jack started toward the door. As he carried her out to his truck, Evie said something, the words muffled against his shoulder. "What?" he asked her, placing her onto the truck's bench seat.

Evie smiled through bloody and torn lips. "I got him one, though. I scratched the hell out of his face. With luck, he'll wear the scar for the rest of his life."

Jack paused, one hand on the door. "He won't have long to wear it. His ticket's about to be punched."

The soft, sweet smell of pipe tobacco drifting from deep in the house greeted them as Jack carried Evie into Cleary's front room. The sound of Elmer Cleary's boots, heavy on the wood floor, drifted from a long hallway. The large bootlegger appeared, wiping his hands absently on a light pink towel. Both hands stopped their twisting motions and the towel slid to the floor like a dead snake. His pipe dipped and toppled out, landing near his feet as Cleary's grizzled, sun-kissed features fell slack and he gaped a shocked O.

"Lord Jesus, what's happened?"

"Just help me, will ya?" Jack grunted. Cleary hesitated only a fraction longer before he lurched forward and helped Jack steer Evie to a battered and sad-looking couch near the smooth stone fireplace.

Once they had her situated, Jack lightly brushed some of her dark hair back from the black and purple mess that was her swollen eye. Wordlessly, Cleary retreated and Jack distantly heard a faucet running. A wet rag appeared. "Get her cleaned up. I'll send for the doc."

Jack took the cloth and Cleary hurried off, his deep voice booming through the small hallway as he called to one of his men. Carefully, using light and short movements, Jack wiped the blood from Evie's lips, nose, and cheeks. He cleaned the dried maroon streaks from her neck and wiped down her arms and hands, holding each one gently, as though they might turn to dust at any second.

When the majority of the blood had been cleaned away, he kissed her softly on the forehead and went to find Cleary. He found the farmer in the kitchen busy with something in the sink. "I sent for Powell. He'll be here soon," Elmer said. He gestured toward a cupboard. "Bottle in there. I'm washing glasses."

Jack retrieved the amber liquid and poured the whiskey. They stood there a moment, each regarding the drink in their hand. Cleary asked, "Who was it?"

Jack inhaled and exhaled a long breath. "Dunn. Him and that son of a whore, Stott." Jack tossed the whiskey into his mouth and waited as Cleary filled the glass again. He repeated the message Dunn had left.

Cleary's already red cheeks flushed a deeper scarlet, the color extending down the older man's throat. Jack watched the massive hand wrapped around the small glass and wondered how much more pressure it would take before the thing exploded in his palm. Cleary shook his head, poured another drink, and moved to lean against the sink.

"I guess your message to Dunn's underlings didn't stick. I won't say I told you so, but men like that don't typically take too well to threats. You have to beat it into them, and even then . . ." He shook his head. "You're going to go? To the gas station?"

"I am."

Cleary sucked in a slow breath. "I'll send a few of my boys with you."

Jack shook his head. "No. If I come with an army, he'll beat feet."

"You know Stott's going to be with him. Probably a few more of those shitheads."

"I suppose so. But Dunn's problem is with me. I'm the one who insulted him and removed one of his guys from the board. Him not being able to put a bullet in my head in that alley really pissed him off. He'll want to even the score."

Cleary huffed a chuckle. "You really think someone like Henry

Dunn has any concept of honor? You think he's going to stand there and tell his buddies to leave you be, while the two of you duke it out in the middle of the road like a couple of teenagers?"

"I'm planning on the son of a bitch not even knowing I'm there until I've opened up on him."

"You'd have to be a hell of a fast shot. You that good?"

Jack smirked. "Hell no. But I don't have to be. Not with what I have in mind. Now what can you tell me about this gas station?"

Fifteen minutes later, Doc Powell arrived, wearing an off-white linen suit with a thin black tie. Jack couldn't help but think he looked like a small walrus, all balding pate, bristling mustache, and wire-rimmed spectacles. The man went directly to Evie and knelt over her, hands probing gently, mumbling to himself as he observed each wound. After his initial inspection, he instructed Jack and Cleary to move the woman into a bedroom where he could treat her wounds and she'd be more comfortable with a modicum of privacy.

Jack paced nervously in and out of the kitchen, one hand buried in his pocket, his fingers twirling the trolley token incessantly. Every time his path led him to the hall he would pause, glaring at the closed bedroom door and the soft mumble of voices heard behind it.

After what felt like hours, Powell emerged and quietly shut the door behind him. He pushed the glasses up on his nose and entered the kitchen, where he accepted a small glass of whiskey. While the doctor swallowed the shot, Jack stood trembling with the need to grab the man and shake him until his teeth rattled. *If he doesn't fucking tell me how she is in the next two seconds, I'll do just that,* he thought.

Powell set the glass down and took a deep breath. "She's going to be fine, let me start by saying that much. None of her injuries are life-threatening. The ankle is badly sprained, and she took a hell of a knock to that eye, but the bone, the orbital socket, doesn't seem to be broken. We can send a prayer of thanks for that. The rest are bruises and cuts that will heal over the next several days. The swelling around her eye will probably look worse for twenty-four or forty-eight hours, but it too will subside. Now,"—he held up a finger, stopping Jack before he could ask a question—"she took a really bad beating. Especially to the head. It's hard to say what that'll do. She may be dizzy, confused. Could even act a little strange for a bit. I'm not saying she'll start speaking in tongues, but she may lose track of her thoughts or even say some weird things at times. Try not to panic if that happens. It's just her brain's way of rewiring itself. Just keep a close eye on her and don't let her wander off on her own until she's steady again."

The old, yellowing clock on the wall of Cleary's kitchen read *10:30* when Jack climbed back into his truck and pulled out of the yard. Through the evening, Cleary had tried to convince him to go with backup, and as Jack followed his headlights down the dark, tree-lined driveway, he was worried that Cleary would still send . . . what did they call it down here? A posse? Well, he reasoned, there was nothing to be done about it now. If Cleary sent men after him, they'd better pray they didn't get in the way.

He drove carefully, following the instructions Elmer had given him. Locust Road was a main thoroughfare that led out of town to the west. Cleary had drawn a little sketch of the station and the woods around it. He marked in his best estimation where Dunn would be waiting. Jack noted that he figured Henry would leave his car parked visibly, but he himself would be hidden nearby, probably just inside the trees around the side of the pump house. He assumed Stott would be there, too, or maybe he would be opposite the car in the main patch of woods.

It wouldn't matter.

Jack let his mind drift, thinking of Evie, of how terrified she must have been, of how she would have cried out, grunting in pain as each blow landed on her. In his mind, he could hear the laughter of the two men as they worked her over.

He let the sounds carry him forward into the night.

Toward Henry Dunn and death.

32

"Put that fucking thing out," Dunn hissed. Carl Stott squinted through the smoke from his newly lit cigarette, irritation furrowing his brow. He took another drag, slow and long. "So help me God," Dunn growled, "if you don't put it out, I'm going to put a fucking bullet through your eye."

"He ain't here, what's it matter?" Stott whined. "Besides, it fucking stinks with all that rot everywhere. Jesus, look at the pump. It's practically covered in those vines. The smoke helps."

Dunn stared. *Prick wasn't in the war*, he reminded himself. *Got himself excluded from service.* So there was no way for him to know things like light discipline: how far someone could see the glow of a cigarette in the night. It was so much farther than you'd imagine. He remembered using the small cherry glow across the desolation of No Man's Land to hone in on targets, aiming about three inches above the bouncing red orb.

Instead of replying with another scolding, he raised his shotgun and pointed it at Stott. Dunn could see the man trying to work out whether or not he'd actually pull the trigger. *Fucking right, I'd pull it. You risk fucking this up for me, and I'll blow your guts all over that pine tree.* Dunn's finger slipped into the trigger guard and rested gently on the grooved curve of the trigger. The metal was cool against his skin and he thought about how good it would feel to put just a little more pressure on the mechanism. The weapon would buck in his hands, expected but still surprising. There would be the briefest of flashes as the slug left the barrel and Carl's face would vanish into a red sludge of blood, ravaged meat, and splintered bone.

The thought sent a tickling of butterflies through his abdomen and for a second, Dunn was certain he was going to do it—pull the trigger and watch Stott transform into a wasted piece of hamburger meat. He caught himself, remembering where he was and what he was there to do. He lowered the shotgun. Stott exhaled shakily and dropped the smoke, grinding it out with the toe of his boot.

Dunn checked his watch, saw it was past midnight. From his vantage point in the thick trees to the left of the vine-covered gas pump, Carl had been right. The pump looked like it was sinking into the soft dirt, as if it were being pulled down by those things. He had a clear view of the path that broke from the highway, looped through the small shed-covered pump station and back out again. His car was parked near the pump, a hat resting on the back of the seat to give the impression that a man was inside. He hoped it would do the trick to lure the Italian. If it distracted him for only a second, that would be enough.

A soft cough broke through the night and Dunn winced, once again fighting the urge to kill the man who had disturbed the quiet. He peered through the moonlit trees, trying to spy the four men he had stationed across from the pump house, but couldn't make out any of them. He made a mental note to kick the shit out of whoever it had been when this was over and Carmelo lay dead out there on the dirt path.

He adjusted the grip on his weapon and again checked his watch. Time was slipping away, running beyond him like Turkey Creek did when he was a child. Usually following a beating from one of the boys in town or, worse, one of his parents after having seen him in the aftermath of one of the beatings, Henry would hide in a small copse of trees and throw leaves and small twigs into the muddy green water and watch them race quickly away, heading for an ending unseen. That's how it felt now, the night swiftly moving toward morning. But this time he knew the ending.

The problem was that it was now almost twelve thirty. Carmelo was supposed to have been here by now. Hell, this whole fucking thing was supposed to be over by now, the last of the gunshots long since faded in the midnight air. Dunn ground his teeth, his jaw flexing beneath his cheeks. *Maybe the Yankee prick has a yellow streak. Maybe after seeing what they'd done to that mouthy cunt, he'd—*

The rumble of a truck engine preceded the soft glow of approaching headlights, cutting through Dunn's thoughts. He risked a glance over at Stott, saw that the man had heard the vehicle and was crouched low, his own weapon gripped tightly. The truck approached slowly, as though the driver was looking for something. *An ambush?* Dunn wondered and smiled. *Come on, you prick, see my car and pull in. Pull in and park and walk over like the arrogant son of a whore you are. Fucking Italian gangster*, he thought, *all bravado.* He was certain that Carmelo, regardless of how mad the man was about what had been done to his girl, would approach in the open and demand a fight. Back in France, Dunn had served alongside a Brit unit that had an Italian in its ranks. More than once the arrogant shit had to be pulled back down into the trenches; the man screaming threats and dares to the Germans across the wasteland.

The truck reached the service road for the station and slowed to a crawl. *He sees my car. He sees it. Come on.*

The engine revved and the truck accelerated along the road, moving quickly past the station and disappearing around the bend, its engine rolling off into the night.

Dunn stood and stared through the skim of trees in the direction the truck had driven. His tongue sat fat and heavy in a dry mouth and he worked to muster saliva to spit out in frustration. A soft rustling drew his attention. Stott stared back, his body paused mid-step as if he were going to come over and chat. He hissed, "What do we do n—"

The entire world exploded with gunfire.

Bullets screamed through the night, taking Dunn by such surprise that he flinched with each deafening blast. He was temporarily stunned by how loud and amplified the shots were. That they were coming from a source unseen out in the dark made them all the more terrifying. The screams came, the voices small and pitiful in the brief pauses between the gunfire.

"He's here!" Stott screamed and fired his rifle blindly into the night. Stott's weapon sounded like a child's cap gun in comparison and realizing that, Dunn understood what he was hearing.

"He's got a fucking Thompson," he said to himself, a tone of admiration painted on the words. Stott continued firing blindly, his own frustrated and scared grunts accompanying the fight. Dunn leaned against the tree, ignoring the rancid moisture that leaked from various spots along its trunk, and stared into the woods beyond the pump, looking for the muzzle flash of the machine gun.

There. A brilliant tongue of flame like something out of a children's book about dragons lanced out in the blackness. Just as he saw it, it was gone and the silence that rushed in to fill the void was nearly as deafening as the Thompson had been.

Despite the ringing in his ears, he could still hear Stott's soft, panicky grunts as the man struggled to reload. Dunn ignored him and cupped a hand to the side of his mouth.

"Jack? You over there?"

The woods were stoic and dark in response.

"Harv? Milton?" Again no answer. The quiet confirmed what he already knew to be true. The four men he'd placed in the woods were all dead, their bodies riddled with holes.

"Henry?" Stott hissed. "The fuck do we do now?" Dunn ground his teeth again and considered his next move. He opened his mouth to answer, to tell Stott to creep up and take shelter behind the car and see what he could see, but the words never made it out. The Thompson roared again, and this time the tree that served as his cover vibrated with the thudding impact of the bullets. He cursed in surprise and hit the ground, his shotgun rattling through the leaves and sticks as he pressed his face against the dirt and waited for the barrage to end.

Bastard's gotta be out of rounds. He may have a Thompson, but Dunn was willing to bet that the son of a bitch didn't have another magazine. To confirm his suspicions, the smaller and comparatively softer sounds of a handgun ripped through the air. A few rounds whizzed overhead; their trajectory told him that Jack was moving, shifting position.

Dunn pulled himself to his feet, grabbed the shotgun, and pointed in the direction he guessed Jack had moved. "Shoot that way," he said in a low tone. Stott nodded, his face pale and eyes wide. "Keep shooting until I get to that other tree over there. Understand?" Stott turned and unleashed a volley of shots.

Henry took a breath, eyed his intended path, and pushed out from behind the tree. He had gone three loping steps when the bullet screamed across his waist. The force spun him around. He slammed down hard, the breath flying from his lungs. Dunn gasped and gulped for air, pressing a hand to his left side just above his hip bone. The bullet had gouged him, but hadn't gone too deep. Through the hot, sticky blood that poured over his fingers, he could feel a groove burned into his flesh.

Stott screamed as he fired. The rifle was a loud punctuation mark to the man's piggish blatting and it took everything Dunn had not to shoot the bastard and shut him up. He'd just about decided to do it— odds in a firefight be damned—when Stott's rifle clicked empty. He continued pulling the trigger four more times before his brain got the message. He looked at the weapon, confused.

Jack Carmelo stepped onto the service road. His pistol was held at his waist, the barrel pointed toward Dunn, who raised his own weapon with a grunt of pain, the wound in his side screaming in protest. Henry met Jack's eyes, saw the shade of hatred pass over his face. Deep in the back of his mind, he recognized that look on the other man. He'd seen it staring back at him from his own shaving mirror more than once.

Stott threw down his rifle and bolted toward the car, his trajectory taking him between the remaining gunmen. Dunn saw the movement out of the corner of his eye but ignored it, instead focusing on bracing his rifle against his shoulder and firing at Carmelo. Jack's pistol spat flame at the same time.

Henry didn't see where his round went, only knew that he'd missed. Jack's shot, however, did not. Carl Stott grunted in surprise and fell like a deer going down under a hunter's aim. He hit the ground, slid a foot or two, and his top half ended up on the solid dirt of the service road, gurgling and coughing in pain.

Jack's attention was focused on his own pistol, his hands moving through the process of reloading. Henry racked the slide on his shotgun and saw that the chamber was empty. His breath coming in panicked gasps, Dunn pulled himself fully upright. He threw one last look at Jack and ran as fast as he could through the trees. His feet slapped the road and he winced, expecting to feel the punch of a bullet into his exposed back. Then he was stumbling off the other side and plunging into the woods. His waist shrieked in pain with every step, but he kept a hand pressed to the wound and continued running, cursing the events that had just gone completely to hell.

33

Jack watched the fleeing shape of Henry Dunn as the man scrambled across the hardpan before crashing into the thickets beyond. Jack's hands completed the task of reloading the .45. He'd hit the bastard, he knew that much. The question was: how bad? There was a good chance that he could run Dunn down before the sun came up and finish this whole business.

Not that he wanted it over with too soon. He wanted to take his time with the toad-faced man, wanted to keep the bastard alive long enough to really feel what was being done to him, to make him suffer more than he'd made Evie suffer. Jack was nearing the road when the soft sounds of wet gurgling broke his trance and he blinked. Carl Stott crawled with agonized slowness along the dirt road. Jack considered retrieving the Thompson and beating Carl to death with it. But another idea came to him, sliding coldly across his mind like a grave worm eager to feast on rotting flesh. Jack holstered his pistol and pulled out a knife as he approached the man who had helped Dunn beat Evie Marrow to a pulp. The man who now stared up at him with all the wide-eyed terror of a trapped rabbit.

Jack held the knife tightly in one hand and bent forward to tend to Carl Stott.

34

Henry Dunn's brain swirled with pain signals from every inch of his body. His ribs white-hot, burning and pulsing with every step and stumble as he crashed through the blackness of the forest. The cuts on his face, his split lips, and the bruised eye were a constant murmuring of discomfort. On top of all that was the bullet wound, a ribbon of scorching fire across his waist that screamed at every bump and twist.

Worst of all was the shame, the embarrassment of failing yet again to kill Jack Carmelo. The humiliation burrowed into his mind, overriding all thoughts. As Dunn ran through the blight-chewed woods, dodging black and oozing bushes and careening off rotting pine trees in his desperate attempt to distance himself from the ambush, his mind returned to one image: Jack, pistol directed at him with a calm look in his eye. Dunn had no idea how the son of a bitch had managed to circle around and get the drop on them, much less how he'd managed to take out all five guys so efficiently.

It didn't matter. All that mattered was getting far away. Starting over. Finding a new way to hurt that bastard. There was an angle to that end. The woman he and Stott had roughed up was the key; they'd just not gone far enough. Something in the moment had pressed back on Dunn's natural impulses. The impulses that howled for more blood, to see her throat opened up and to feel the arterial spray across his face.

Yes, he thought darkly and stumbled to a halt. One hand reached out blindly into the blackness. His fingers scraped across the soft, festering bark of a pine tree, the wood like jelly. He ignored the feeling and leaned against it as he fought to control his breathing, sucking in deep breaths of the cloying air of the spoiled woods. Sweat streamed along his body. His shirt and pants clung to his damp flesh like a second skin and his hair was a matted tangle. He pressed a hand against the blood-soaked fabric of his shirt and a smile drifted across his face. He would find some place to let his wounds heal, to hole up long enough for Carmelo to think the matter was settled, that Dunn had been beaten into submission. Only then would he step out of hiding.

But not that the Italian would know it, of course. Not until Dunn wanted him to know. And that knowledge would come when what remained of that brunette whore's body, broken and skinned, was left hanging from a pole in the center of town. Dunn pictured the quivering agony he would see in her eyes as he cut into her, the shaking pain so intense she couldn't make a single peep. Instead, her mouth would gape wide, lips trembling as she tried to scream, *needing* to give voice to her agony. Dunn would keep her alive for a long time as he cut her apart and snapped her bones.

When Jack found her and understood what had happened and, more importantly, *why* it had happened, he would know with absolute clarity how deep into hell he had stepped.

A coughing laugh bubbled up Dunn's throat. He pushed off the tree and continued on, moving slower now, picking his way carefully across the uneven terrain. The thoughts of committing atrocities against that woman and later on, Jack, pressed Dunn's own immediate pains to the background.

Fifteen minutes later, the ground became soft. At first, he didn't notice the change; most of the rotting forest floor had a spongy feel to it that he was accustomed to. But after a few moments, he registered the wet squelching that marked each footstep. He paused, peering through the faint glow of cloudy moonlight in an attempt to get his bearings. There weren't any swamps out here, as far as he knew. At least none that Stott or any of the others ever mentioned. Assuming it was just a low part of the landscape where rainwater had accumulated and couldn't drain, he started forward. *That didn't account for the growing smell, though*, he thought. With the blight, the woods around Jericho Springs had taken on a sick stench, but this was somehow worse.

The toe of his boot caught on something hard and he fell, crashing to the wet ground. The sleeves of his jacket were soaked as he splashed into the mud. Dirty water sloshed against his raw wounds, lighting new fires of pain that screamed through him. Dunn grunted in frustration as he sloshed through the muck in an effort to climb to his feet. When he was standing, he peered through the dark to see what he'd tripped over.

It was a stone carved roughly into a rectangle. It jutted out of the dirt like a worn tooth. Peering at it, he thought, *That's part of a foundation. What's a stone foundation doing all the way to hell and gone in the middle of nowhere?* Nearby, another stone peeked from beneath a screen of weeds. He saw yet another beyond that. Soon he was able to make out the rough shape of the foundation. Was this the remnant of some old hermit's house? Or a hunting cabin? He took a few steps and paused as the moon slipped free of the clouds overhead. Dunn's breath caught at the sight of the hulking shapes of buildings throughout the patch of woods. They were in various states of ruin. Some, like the one he'd tripped over, were only the faint suggestion of foundations. Others retained their walls to varying degrees. All were covered in bruise-colored moss and runners of black ivy.

A wide swath of cleared land wound its way through the ruins. *Son of a bitch. Is this an old town?* The path led to a wide swath of muddy ground. At the far end of the patch of earth stood the remains of an old church, doors open, the sanctuary beyond shrouded in darkness. On either side of the double doors were lit torches mounted on posts. Their flames spilled arcs of pulsing light over the muddy ground and yet looked pitifully small and feeble against the rest of the dark forest.

In the paltry firelight, the walls of the church glistened. Symbols were carved into the old wood—strange curves and intersecting lines that sent a quivering nausea through Dunn. He blinked and turned away. Whatever the hell this was, he wanted nothing to do with it. This place had been abandoned by God. *Probably something to do with that fucking voodoo the niggers practice,* he thought, and searched for a better path. Seeing none, he decided to follow the main avenue back the way he'd come. If nothing else, he'd eventually come across the road near the gas station. Carmelo would be long gone by now, and Dunn could get the car and find a more suitable place to hole up.

He almost didn't notice the uneven, lumbering shapes drifting slowly through the trees until it was too late. The snapping of a branch off to one side brought him up short and after a second, he noticed the movement. "Hey!" he called out to them. No answer came back. The figures, he counted at least eight of them spread out on either side of the wide path, continued their plodding trek toward him. A chilly essence drifted ahead of the things and the irrational thought that it was the cold of the grave filled him, settling into his brain as an inarguable truth.

Suddenly Dunn didn't want to be anywhere near those things. There was something terribly wrong with them. About this entire place, really, but especially about the sluggish, waddling motion of their advancing that drove nails of panic into him. But where to go? None of the buildings offered adequate cover or concealment. And he was pretty sure there wouldn't be anything within them he could use as a weapon. That left only two options. Run mindlessly through the dark swamp and hope he didn't get even more lost or . . .

The church.

Dunn's face contorted into a pitiful, agonized frown. The almost childish reluctance to go into the old building was overwhelming. But the wet sounds of the dark shapes' advances were growing louder, and more than not wanting to be in a desecrated house of God, Dunn did not want to see what those things were when they got right up on him.

He turned and ran, the mud clinging thickly to his boots, sucking at each pounding step. His wounds thumped angrily in time with his steps and his chest burned from the exertion as he fought to put distance between himself and the nearing horrors. *Get inside and find a way to barricade that door,* he told himself in an effort to clear his mind and focus. *Once you have a barrier, find something, anything, you can use as a weapon.* Deep down he hoped that whatever those things were, they would be unable to enter a church regardless of its current state. It was a weak hope, but it was all he had.

The inside was worse than he could have imagined. Pews lay broken and jumbled with small candles affixed to them by puddles of wax. In their soft light, Dunn was able to see the symbols that covered the walls. Many were drawn in blood, but others were made of worse things. He fought back the urge to retch and searched for a pew that he could maneuver across the open doorway. His eyes flicked to the muddy expanse beyond the church door and saw the figures emerging from the tormented trees.

"Oh dear sweet God." His mind registered what he was seeing in strobe flashes of images: a torn throat, a missing jaw, a flayed face, a gaping chest filled with dark shining things that writhed and slithered around one another.

Forcing himself from the sights, he approached a pile of benches and reached for the closest. As his fingers gripped the wood, soft with moisture, its surface slippery, he froze. Something in the back of the church moved and for a heart-stopping moment, he was positive the things from outside had slipped around the building and entered through a rear door.

But it was worse.

Two figures detached from the shadows at the far end of the nave. They were tall and slender, but at the same time bent and twisted, as if misshapen by years of pressure against their bodies. They stood apart and yet very close to one another.

Two sets of glowing, silver eyes appeared in the middle of the rounded outline of each head. As those ethereal orbs focused on him, Dunn's head rocked back, his mind filling with hellish noise. He clutched his head with both hands and grimaced against the screams of torment and unending pain that echoed in his brain.

The agony was blinding, and Dunn crumpled to his knees. His breath came in short, harsh pants, whistling through teeth clenched so tight they creaked in his gums. Spittle shot from his lips and dripped down his chin. A wet tickling brushed his left ear as the pressure in his skull mounted, sending small ribbons of blood out and down his jaw.

On the verge of collapse, as he felt himself compressing into nothingness, the tenor of the voices and screeching torment within his mind shifted. The suffering transformed into a probing, violative exploration of his thoughts. Dunn's mind was subjected to a flashing display of his darkest, worst memories. He saw the animals he'd killed as a child, all the children he'd beaten as he grew up, the girls —some as much as ten years younger than him—he'd forced himself on. He saw all the men, women, and children he'd killed in the forests of France, their broken and savaged bodies on the battlefield and in the small towns. He saw the terror-stricken face of the French woman in the farmhouse and all the men, Black and white, that he'd killed since returning to Georgia and joining the Klan. Every single one was brought up for inspection, then tossed aside as if ultimately found to be uninteresting.

All the while, the two dark, anfractuous figures watched with cold indifference. The noise and images vanished, swept aside in an instant, and Dunn managed a quavering breath of relief. He stood and advanced through the church toward the figures and the small chancel. He was halfway there when his mind recovered sufficiently from the assault of sights and sounds to realize he hadn't moved intentionally.

A force like a massive invisible hand pulled him across the floor. He reached the single step to the altar and stumbled as he was lifted onto the platform. *I didn't do that,* his mind screamed. *I didn't do that. I didn't take a step. I didn't do that!*

One of the figures flicked a finger, a casual gesture. Henry Dunn's knees broke, the bones smashing inward, the joints reversing their natural angle. Before he could scream, the finger moved again and his hips shattered. The pain was a dull punch ringed with needlelike stabs of agony.

The finger twitched again and Dunn's torso was forced backward, his head angling to take in the dark, filthy roof, then farther so he was staring upside down at the open door. The nightmares that had herded him into the church stood in a line, viewing the events unfolding with dull expressions.

In the church, the black thing's finger continued to twitch, and his body continued to break, his bones splintering, shards punching through his flesh and stabbing deep into organs. His blood streamed out of him, spilling across the dirty floor like a waterfall.

Dunn's screams echoed off the walls and fell, dead, in the still night air as the things outside in the mud watched.

35

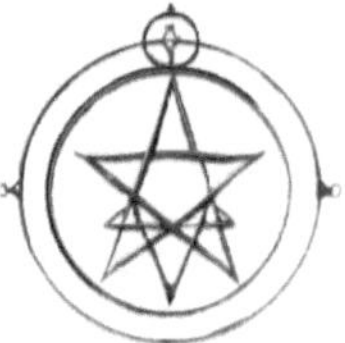

drian Turski stepped onto the porch of Tony Detti's small home and breathed in the clean air. "Christ, that fat bastard lasted longer than I thought he would." He chuckled, squinting in the midafternoon light, "You see the look on his wife's face when she came in and saw us standing over him?" He sighed as he closed the door. "But fucking Alabama?"

Eli dabbed at the blood on his face with a small towel he'd taken from the kitchen. "I'm pretty sure he wasn't lying. Did you think he was?"

Adrian coughed, something between a grunt and a laugh. "After what Frank did with those pliers? No. I just wouldn't have expected Alabama, you know? New York, LA, maybe even Seattle, you know? Somewhere big, somewhere Capone may have some connections to keep the guy safe." He shook his head. "But down south with those fucking peckerwood hillbillies? That don't make any sense. Let's go get cleaned up. I need to call a few guys; I don't want to be riding down there light." He looked at Frank. "You think you can get us a couple cars big enough to make the drive?"

"The hell? That'd take two goddamn days to drive down there!" Eli burst out. "I say we take the train. We'd be killing that rat bastard tomorrow."

Adrian met Eli's eyes with a serene look. "If we take the train, we can't travel heavy. There's law on trains. There's the porters. There's people, fucking nosy kids on trains. We're taking hardware and we're not taking a train."

Eli's lips quivered with a retort, but Adrian knew the Irishman saw the truth. Finally, the freckled face jerked in a reluctant nod.

Frank answered, "I can get a couple cars. How many guys?"

"I want ten, including us."

Frank shrugged placidly. "Okay.

Jack watched the men moving around the still, going about their tasks like ants working on a new hill. The night was coming on fast, the sky above the pines and hardwoods turning a bruised purple streaked with orange. A gentle wind pushed through the trees, sending the branches against one another in a chorus of whispers. When the crew had first reached the site after a twenty-minute hike through the woods, one of the men, a massively muscled brute with shoulder-length hair and a thick beard, turned his head up, his nostrils flaring.

"What are you doing?" Jack had asked.

The man gave another deep sniff. "Checking for rain." He smiled at Jack. "I think we're in for a dry night. The stink makes it hard to tell, but I think we'll be okay."

None of the others had asked or even suggested through body language that they'd expected Jack to participate in the preparation of the site. Instead, they'd immediately set about their work: pulling tarps off the copper pipes and wood barrels, connecting sections together, and applying a white paste made from flour and water to the joints. Two others faded into the trees, axes propped on their shoulders. Within minutes, the rhythmic sounds of blades biting into trees drifted over the clearing.

Jack sat on a downed tree that allowed him to view both the site and the forest through which they'd approached. He dug at the ground with the heel of one boot, the soil soft to the point of swampy. As he disturbed the dirt, more of the now familiar rotting smell wafted up. Most of the ground around the still was the overly soft blackened soil, the damage extending to the trees and brush surrounding the clearing. As the men lit the fires beneath the boil pot, Jack smoked and let his thoughts drift to Stott and Dunn's ambush attempt at the gas station. Then his mind turned to Evie.

Cleary's house and surrounding grounds had been crawling with armed men, a precaution the old farmer had insisted on after taking Evie in. Jack had spent most of the day sitting in a chair next to the bed where she rested. He brought her water and tended to the numerous cuts and bruises that marred her skin. She, for the most part, was alert and in good spirits, even teasing Jack somewhat about his bedside manner and nursing skills. To his relief, in the light of day and after Doc Powell had bandaged her, the wounds didn't seem nearly as bad as he'd initially thought they were.

When Jack had first entered the room, Evie had tried to climb out of bed to reach him, but Jack quickly guided her back. She wrapped her arms around him tightly and he pretended not to notice the hiss of pain she gave or the way her body stiffened as the hug brushed against the more tender spots. He held her until she broke the embrace. After she settled back against her pillows, Jack told her about the events at the gas station.

"It really wasn't well thought out," he said. "I don't think Dunn's a very smart guy if he thought putting a hat on the seat of a car would fool me."

"How many did he bring?" she asked.

"Five, including himself." He described how he'd snuck through the trees and took out the others. Evie's face went pale when he told her that Carl Stott had been one of the five. Her eyes widened when he described shooting at Dunn, only to have Stott get in the way.

"He sacrificed himself for Dunn?" she asked, incredulous.

"I don't think it was anything nearly as noble as that," Jack said. "He was trying to get the hell out of there and chose the wrong direction. Caught a slug in the guts for his dumb luck."

"Where is he now?"

"Dunn? I don't know. The coward ran off into the woods."

"I mean Stott. Did he get away?"

Jack's eyes went hard. "No," he said quietly. "He didn't get away." Evie's expression softened as the truth of the matter, the reality that Carl Stott died and had done so very badly at the hands of the man sitting next to her, hit home.

Jack ground the butt of his cigarette beneath the heel of his boot and stared at the large moonshine still without really seeing it. Night had fully fallen and the fire beneath the boil pot cast a pool of shifting tawny light that barely pushed the darkness back. He sat in the flickering shadows and thought about Carl Stott and the visit he'd paid the man the other night. Inwardly, he scolded himself for assuming his come-to-Jesus talk would have the intended effect of forcing Stott and the others to back off.

However, after the gunfight last night, it was likely that with Dunn in the wind and Stott dead, they'd slow their efforts to stem the flow of booze. At the very least, they would be in disarray until they found a new figurehead, he reasoned.

Or until Dunn pops his head back out of wherever he's hiding.

The memory of the pudgy Klan leader, hand pressed to his side where Jack's bullet had grazed him, plunging into the dark trees opposite the road, replayed in Jack's mind. Dunn hadn't even looked back to see if Stott was okay or if Jack was pursuing. He'd just sprinted into the woods in a blind panic.

But was he dead? That was the question. Jack felt confident he wasn't. He may have some busted ribs and a bullet graze to his side, but there was no way the man was dead. Unless, that is, he tripped over something or fell in a hole and snapped his neck. Jack smiled at the imagined scene: The toady bastard lying in a broken heap among dead leaves and windfallen branches, breathing his last shallow gulps of air as he wondered how he came to such an inglorious end. Maybe by now the crows and coyotes or whatever wildlife prowled the woods down here had gotten to him, and Dunn's half-eaten corpse would be found one day by a luckless hunter.

The better assumption was that he was alive and hiding somewhere, mending and resting. Considering how quickly after the beating in the alley he'd set up the ambush, it stood to reason that he wouldn't rest too long before trying again. And he would try again, of that much Jack was certain. Men like Dunn were cowards at their core, but surrounding that core was a rotten layer of pride. Henry's pride had been badly wounded twice now and Jack would have bet all of Capone's wealth that he wasn't done trying to kill him.

One of the men to the left of the still stood and turned to face the dark woods. He remained motionless for several seconds. Jack watched the man, not really seeing him but instead thinking about Evie and how he'd been considering taking her to Nashville. The idea of getting her out of Jericho Springs for a little while seemed even more appealing now than it had a day ago. Once Doc Powell gave her the all clear to travel, Jack was going to get her away from the many odd things plaguing the town. Between the strange symbols, the dead and mutated animals he'd seen on Cleary's property, and the weird vegetation and rotting smells of fields and buildings, there was no way she could truly rest and heal by staying here.

"Abner!" called the massive bearded man who stood by the condenser, eyes locked on his friend staring into the dark trees. Without acknowledging his huge companion, Abner moved toward the trees in stiff, jerking steps. "Where the hell are you going?" Muscle Beard yelled.

"Maybe he's gotta take a shit," someone else offered.

Muscle Beard ignored the joke and drifted closer, calling after Abner again. Once more, Abner ignored the voice of his friend and continued toward the trees. A steady, rhythmic pattern of noise drifted across the clearing. Jack sat up slowly, realizing the sound was coming from Abner.

The man was babbling something low and incomprehensible as

he slipped between a hickory tree and a pine. Jack's eyes met those of the other men, everyone exchanging questioning looks as Abner stepped beyond the paltry light of the cook fire. The shadows closed around his body like a cloak, enveloping him completely. The sounds of the man's rambling vanished at the same time as his body, cutting off with startling abruptness. Other than the crackling of the fire and the soft bubbling of the cooking mash, the clearing fell silent as all the men stared into the darkness.

Abner's scream ripped through the night, echoing as it bounced around the trees. It rose, climbing in pitch. If Jack hadn't known better, he would have thought a woman was being attacked. The shrieks were pitiful, full of pain beyond imagining and threaded with terror. The men around the still were frozen in fear for a long moment as the cries continued.

"Jesus Christ," one of the men gasped. The utterance broke the momentary paralysis and everyone moved at once. Three of the men grabbed the unburnt ends of logs from the fire and held the flaming torches aloft as everyone plunged into the trees, shouting for Abner.

Jack pulled his pistol and raced after the men, giving the woods opposite the still a glance to ensure there was no ambush happening. When no armed Klansmen or Prohibition officers came pouring out, Jack charged into the woods, following the shouts of the others and the glowing torchlight. He caught up with them after only a few yards, pushing his way past the men who stood staring dumbstruck at something on the ground.

A blood-covered mass sat atop the dirt and pine needles. At first, it looked like a pile of thick, twisted, and knotted rope, but after a moment, Jack understood what the pale purple and bloody mound was.

"Are those Abner's guts?" Muscle Beard asked, his voice thick with disgust.

"Can't be," another said. "Has to be a deer or something."

"They're fresh," Muscle Beard countered. "Look at all the blood. Ain't no deer carcass around here."

"Well it ain't fucking Abner either. You think he would have lost his intestines like that and still be walking around?"

"Shut up," Jack snapped. "Spread out, search the woods. He's out here somewhere and so is the son of a bitch that did this." Jack brought his weapon up, finger tight on the trigger as he scanned the trees.

The men hesitated, throwing uncertain looks at Jack. "Go," he commanded. Before they could fan out and begin the search, Muscle Beard grunted and fell to his knees. His mouth gaped in a silent yawn. He drew in a powerful breath and let out a strangled scream. His massive hands slapped at his body as if trying to kill a swarm of insects.

The others hurried to help but before anyone could reach out and grab him, he fell to the ground, writhing. His arms and legs kicked spastically. The man's face was a ghoulish mask of unbelievable pain and torment. His eyes bulged in their sockets, his lips pulled back in a tight grimace.

Just as the first tendrils of blood poured from the man's nostrils and eyes, another of the gathered workers shrieked. *It's smoking,* Jack thought numbly. *The blood is smoking like it's hot.* The rest of the men cried out in horror as vines and roots burst out of the ground and encircled the man like dirty gray snakes. They wrapped around his arms, his waist, and one leg. His screams climbed octaves as they squeezed. The sound of his bones snapping beneath the unrelenting pressure was like muffled gunshots. The vines continued squeezing, splitting the man's skin. Blood surged from the fissures, soaking his overalls and spattering on the dirt.

"Fuck this," one of the remaining men shouted. He turned and ran. A large shadow rose out of the ground, like a wave surging out of the ocean. It towered over the man as his momentum carried him into it. No sooner had he vanished from sight did the shadow crash back to the ground. The man—what was left of him—lay on his side, his body a dry, desiccated husk. The skin was sunken, brittle, and cracked. In the glow of the torchlight, Jack saw pieces of dried skin slough away, revealing dirty, rotting bones.

Jack whirled, searching for the remaining members of the crew. His eyes fell on two figures several yards back in the trees. They were dark shapes, mere suggestions of shadows in the surrounding night. They stood close to one another and motionless despite the bedlam happening all around.

One of the figures shifted, a gentle motion, and a pair of shining orbs—*That's its eyes! It's staring at me!*—settled on Jack. The connection brought a sensation of cold, of worms crawling over and beneath Jack's skin, writhing their way around his bones, finding passage deeper and deeper into his flesh. Jack's mind filled with screams and howls of torment above and beyond those of the dying men around him. He saw visions, flashes of images there and gone in less than a heartbeat. People dressed in rags worshiping at an altar of blood. The land decaying and rotting. Three dark figures standing in a loose group atop a hill. Their faces blackened not from skin color but from the malevolence that *was* them. Those faces looking down on the scene of people writhing in madness, bathing in blood, turning on one another with clawed hands and bared teeth. They watched as the world rotted and decayed.

And they smiled.

Jack screamed, rocking back on his feet under the assault. He screwed the heels of his hands into his eyes, pressing until the visions were replaced by bright blooms of light. The phantom screams faded, then surged forward once more with shocking clarity. In the same instant that Jack realized the sounds weren't coming from within his mind but were the anguished screams of the other men of his crew, the ground beneath his feet erupted in a shower of dirt and rocks. Thick vines shot out, whipping up and around Jack with lightning speed. They snugged around his legs, his waist. Several gripped his arms and one lashed about his neck.

The vines were rough, their sinewy bark etched in tight twisting spirals. Between the grooves leaked a thick, foul sludge, soaking into his skin with a horrible warmth. The instant they touched him, the vines tightened, the sounds of their constriction like the dry crackling of paper. The pressure was immense, his entire body sheathed in a crushing agony. His pistol thumped to the ground, his spasming fingers unable to curl around it. Jack's vision swam with wavering grays, the trees close to him fading into a hazy fog. He blinked, the movement fat and sluggish. Thin breath rattled past his lips like water from a faucet shutting off.

Two large trees sprouted in front of him. Again Jack forced a blink. The trees shrank, their branches pulling in and solidifying into the bent and broken forms of people. Silver eyes studied him with cold interest as the vines ratcheted tighter. Jack knew he was only moments from something inside him giving way to the pulverizing force. The knowledge of his impending death brought a calm over him. He'd always imagined that the end would be peaceful rather than a fit of screaming, but the suddenness of the serenity was surprising.

Among the chaos of dying men, the black things remained as still as ancient rocks. Yet there was something about them, a humming energy. *They're just going to watch me die the way a child watches a spider slowly die after hitting it with a rock.*

Over the raspy crackling of the vines and the blood roaring in his ears came the sharp bark of a gun. One of the dark figures flinched, winking out for a moment like a shadow dispersed against the flare of a match. In the split second that the thing was gone, the vines around Jack's throat loosened. Not much, but enough that he could claw a thread of air into his lungs. More gunshots cleaved the night, the muzzle flashes dull pops of light in the corner of Jack's vision. Then both things winked out of sight. When they reappeared, they were several feet farther away. Jack's restraints loosened incrementally with each flicker of their bodies.

A man's screams pierced the night, rising above the quick blasts of the pistol. The dark things moved toward the man, their movements smooth and even as if they floated over the ground. Jack twisted within the loosened restraints and managed to pull one hand free. It passed out of the loops of vines with a painful scrape, the exposed skin burning terribly as the thick sap touched raw flesh. Forcing that pain down, Jack hooked his fingers beneath the crawler around his throat and pulled. His strength was weakened but he managed a couple of good tugs. The vine came away with a wet, tearing sound.

The rest of the ramblers broke free reluctantly, like children dragging their feet when returning to the classroom from recess. Jack stood, his bonds lying about his boots like dead worms, his chest heaving, and an ache like a massive armored fist slamming within his skull. He searched for his pistol, found it beneath one of the tendrils, and snatched it up quickly.

The gunshots had stopped, as had the screaming of the man. In fact, Jack realized the forest had fallen silent. He held his weapon out, the gun feeling like an oversized club beneath his thick fingers. In the pale shreds of light that filtered through the trees, he saw hints of the carnage: a crumpled body here, the glistening wet pile of someone's insides there. He swept the quivering muzzle of the .45 in a wide arc but saw no evidence of the dark figures.

Jack trembled, the tremors rising through his body as the adrenaline flooded out of him. He took a faltering step, the toes of his boots dragging across the limp strands of vines. He called out, shouting for anyone still alive, but his voice was a dry husk that came out more like a cough than an earnest cry. He shouted twice more as he moved through the shadowy space between trees, threading his way carefully back to the clearing, now empty of life. Only the still remained, its cook fire a weak glow between the rocks atop which the boil pot stood. Jack passed a hand over his face, palming sweat and tears out of his eyes. They were all gone. Every single man who had been working only moments ago. Each of them was dead—crushed or torn apart.

What in the hell had those things been? He turned back to the forest as if the answer would be found standing before him. Only darkness and silence answered his unspoken question.

Then, faint, from deep within the trees came inauspicious laughter. It was a black laugh. Hungry and promising pain and suffering.

Jack turned and ran to the truck.

37

Sam's hand shook as he raised the match to the candle's wick. He let out a steadying breath, the air snuffing the tiny flame. Scowling, he pulled a second match from the small cardboard book and, holding his breath, managed to light the candle. That task done, he stepped away and ran the back of his hand across his forehead. It came away damp and he dried it absently on his pant leg while taking in the rest of the sanctuary.

As before, the room was bathed in the comforting glow of dozens of candles. The flames danced erratically as the small congregation filed in and took their seats. A few newer attendees entered near the rear of the nave, faces drawn and uncertain as they observed those who had attended the previous sermon, which had boasted, by his estimation, around thirty people. Tonight the congregation had swelled to closer to fifty. It was a pitiful gathering compared to the number of bodies that usually packed the church. But, he reasoned, some people needed more time to come around to new ways of thinking. And the ones that didn't would, unfortunately, come to regret it in the end.

And just like last time, Jonas and Anna Robertson sat in the front pew alongside Alma and Robert Wolfe. In the first few rows of pews, the faces were pale and drawn, cheeks hollowed beneath dull, bruised eyes. Their lips, cracked and dry, bore faint stains of red along the edges as if scraped raw. Sam returned to the pulpit. From the hall that led to his small personal office, a muted musty animal stench drifted by a closed door with a small porthole window at head height through which the wide-eyed, moonfaced Thomas Caldry fixated on Sam. The pastor gave the young man a patient smile and Thomas returned the gesture with a nod, indicating he was ready.

Sam's hands continued to shake with eagerness and excitement and he gripped the sides of the pulpit to keep them still. "Friends," he said, casting his voice out over the upturned faces, "it gives me such pleasure to see all of you here. And several new attendees. To you, welcome. I want to assure you that while our new practices may seem strange compared to how you've grown up worshiping, they are no less impactful. Even so, they are designed to cut through all the other tired prayers and pleadings and land straight in Our Father's holy ears. I know this because He has continued to visit me and has let me know that He hears us." At this, a wave of excited conversation rolled over the crowd. "Our Lord hears our new prayers and assures me that He is receptive to our needs. But He tells me that we still have a ways to go. He tells me that while the praying we did last time has reached Him, we have yet to, in a manner of speaking, prostrate ourselves sufficiently. Still, He has already begun to heal our town." Another wave of voices swelled, rose, and fell. Sam held out a hand to temper it and continued.

"I had a series of plants that I kept on the back stoop of my home." He extended an arm in the direction of the small parsonage. "They had begun to show signs of the rot and unusual weeds that we've seen throughout the town and the surrounding woods. Additionally, there's a small dogwood tree—many of you know the exact tree of which I speak—that had begun a few days ago to weep the most foul sap. That sap bled from the trunk and had started to work itself into the ground, killing the grass and turning the dirt to a malodorous muck." He paused, leaning forward and gazing intently at the congregation. "Since our first new sermon, that tree? The land?

My small plants? All have been healed." This time the excitement was too much for him to temper, and he let the parishioners clamor and feel the excitement. They beamed at one another and laughed. Several turned their faces to the large cross that hung behind Sam and dabbed tears from their eyes. Dimly, Sam was aware that some of the smiling mouths had begun to bleed, the cracked lips breaking open once more and small trickles of blood seeping across chins. Those people ignored the blood and continued to smile, their faces filled with a singular emotion.

Hope.

The smallest tickle of revulsion wound through Sam at the lie he'd just told, but he swallowed it down. He'd already decided that such a fabrication was but a tool to be employed in helping the people along this new path. In truth, those plants had died from lack of water and he'd replaced them a week ago. The dogwood tree had not yet suffered signs of the blight that plagued the fields and forests, but so few people ever found themselves on that side of his home that the story was easily sold. After the first new sermon, Samuel had seen that the parishioners had perhaps been teetering on the edge of uncertainty and doubt. He couldn't blame them; the prayers were strange, the words ugly and uncomfortable to say. The symbols he drew in the air as he recited them had been alien, and had he encountered them even a month prior without context would have been deemed blasphemous.

But now, with the "proof" of healing in the wake of the prayers, Sam witnessed those faces that had been somewhat doubtful only moments before as they entered the nave were now awash with joy and hopefulness. This is what he needed for them. He'd not lied when telling them that the Lord had continued to visit him. In fact, his dreams remained full of strange visions of people dressed in animal skins or heavy robes gathered in a forest that Sam felt was the same one that surrounded Jericho Springs. These people conducted these same rituals and saw their prosperity blossom.

Whispers had threaded through all of the visions, recitations of new prayers, descriptions of new sermons and declarations of sacrifices needed, of purification still required. Sam had awakened each morning rejuvenated and energized with the new message to spread to those in the town, but also understanding that while they'd taken the first step, more was still to be asked of them all before redemption was granted.

Eventually, the congregation calmed and Sam continued. "Friends, we have taken that all-important first step along the path. I'm proud of each and every one of you and know that with the small improvements gained already, we will be able to take the next step and the one after that until we reach full salvation and redemption."

He glanced at his hands, letting the silence that covered the sanctuary swell for a moment. "The one thing that God told me, the thing He was very, very clear about, is that we all must make greater sacrifices. We will continue to take the Host and will do so before concluding services tonight. But we must show Him that we are willing to lay ourselves bare before His might and give ourselves fully to Him. So before we begin tonight's ceremony, I task you with this: Go home tonight and consider what you have. What can you offer to the Lord in order to purify your homes and the land? This mustn't be some small trinket or paltry offering, no. This has to be something significant. It should hurt to give up. It is the proverbial pound of flesh. Only by giving that to the land, by sending it out into the forest, into the loving arms of God, will we prove that we are ready to receive His saving grace." Sam's gaze fell on Jonas Robertson. The farmer's scabbed and sallow face was stony. Already he'd sacrificed significantly when he sent Charlie into the woods.

Jonas stared at his hands clasped loosely between his knees, lost in thought. After a moment, he glanced at his wife, who returned the look. Sam knew that he'd just witnessed some unspoken transaction between the two and was genuinely curious as to what it was. Perhaps God was using them to answer Sam's own desires and prayers. Perhaps it was Grace they were going to offer to Sam. Offering their eldest child in marriage to a simple Baptist pastor would certainly be a sacrifice. Sam barely made enough money to support himself, and unless Grace found work somewhere, they would be living in poverty, reliant on the charity of the parishioners. No parent wanted their child to live in a perpetual state of lacking. But to send them willingly to such a situation would meet the definition of the type of sacrifice they were all being asked to make.

He thought of the dress hanging among a few empty hangers in the small closet of the guest bedroom in his home. It was a simple thing, white with blue flowers and a little bit of lace along the short sleeves. He'd bought it in a small boutique in Birmingham over a year ago, soon after Grace had turned fourteen. At the time, he knew he was getting ahead of himself, but seeing it on the dress form in the shop's window, Sam knew with absolute certainty that it was perfect for Grace. The clerk had accepted his small story of the garment being for his niece with a polite but disinterested smile. When she'd asked Sam for the proper size, he'd faltered. Grace was still a slight thing, and while he was convinced that one day she would be his, that day wasn't anytime soon. Thinking perhaps she would hit a growth spurt, he'd fibbed and said that he wasn't sure. He fumbled over his words, his cheeks warming, as he said his niece was almost seventeen and developing . . . prominently. The clerk had understood and given Sam a dress that when held up appeared considerably larger. But, he reasoned, Grace would grow and should fit it perfectly when the time came. Now the dress hung, not quite forgotten, in the closet in the back of his house, waiting for the day that she would be his.

His daily hope that day was almost upon him sat like a glowing coal in his chest.

"Now," he said, looking out once more at the span of faces, "let us begin tonight's service. I will warn you, this is going to ask more of you than last time. But I assure you, this is what God wants. He has told me these things will bring His eyes toward us."

Sam turned and caught the attention of Thomas Caldry, who withdrew from the window. A moment later, the door clicked open and the musty scent pushed into the nave. Several of the women gasped in surprise and disgust as the young farmhand led the cow into the sanctuary, stopping at the bottom of the steps to the chancel.

Sam pulled the long kitchen knife from behind the pulpit as the uncomfortable words rose like jagged rocks in his throat. The congregation watched, mute, as he approached the cow.

They didn't remain silent. A fervor overtook them, cloaking them in a type of madness as they gave themselves fully to the ritual, buoyed by the promise of deliverance. As Sam's new prayers crashed over them, many stood and raised their arms to the heavens, shouting along with the ghastly syllables.

Hands thrust forward, eager to coat themselves in the hot blood that spilled across the floor when Sam's knife did its horrible work. Eager to feel the power in that blood.

They danced and writhed, wrapping themselves in the offal.

The air was filled with the sounds of the strange language.

And laughter.

38

Jack killed the truck's engine and slumped against the hard seat. His hands fell limp to his lap and his eyes lost focus, the steering wheel blurring. The sky slowly turned bluish gray as the sun began its painstakingly slow ascent. The night clung stubbornly to Elmer Cleary's yard, shadows stretching thin as the world slowly brightened.

The thoughts that filled Jack's mind, however, remained dark. Images flitted through his consciousness, flashes of scenes from what had just happened in the woods. Men screaming, flesh tearing, bodies spilling blood that steamed as if it had been cooked.

The figures standing in the shadows, watching it all with hideously glowing eyes.

Jack turned his eyes to the grounds around the truck. As the night retreated, it appeared to leave behind pools of itself. He could make out the darker patches of earth that had turned into the rotting mire. A few yards away, a small sapling that only days before had been firm and tall was now misshapen, its trunk twisted so that the bark had split, exposing oozing pulp. The few leaves that still clung to the skeletal limbs were blackened and withered. Small patches of a strange moss grew along several of the branches.

Farther on, near one of the dead fields, a group of men stood around a large, uneven lump. Nearby, a large fire ringed by stones licked at the last vestiges of night. Occasionally, one of the men would lift something from the pile and throw it into the flames. Jack caught sight of black wings and a drooping head in the hands of one of the men just before he tossed the dead bird into the fire. In the hazy morning light, he could make out other things in the pile, things with jutting stiff legs that ended in hooves, things like bushy tails. Another bird was removed, its eyes ragged hollow caves. Jack remembered the pitiful, malformed deer that had thrown itself against the glass and hard slats of the home, heedless of the dozens of cuts across its body, until its neck snapped and it tumbled off the porch and onto the grass.

The house stood like a malformed beast, crouching on the rotting land, all sharp angles and long facades. The window that Cleary's man had been boarding over the day Jack arrived stuck out, the pale wood like a scab. Other parts of the house's exterior shimmered in the first vestiges of sunlight, the clear sludge pouring from raw, gray sores on the wood. Black, twisted vines emerged from the dead grass and climbed inexorably along one corner of the structure, the tendrils slowly working to consume the house.

A sobering thought rang in his head like a sonorous church bell. Was all of this connected to those figures he'd encountered just hours ago? The rot creeping across the land, the malformed animals? He shook his head in disbelief, part of him still refusing to accept that what he'd seen had been real, a superstitious bedtime story come to horrible, terrible life. It was ridiculous. There had to be some other explanation. His mind reeled. He'd spent a lifetime trusting in what he could see or touch. Reality was flesh and blood, wood and stone. Men did things, men bled, and men died. But nothing about this could be killed. Not the way he understood it.

You may be able to explain the people you saw in the woods as Klan members dressed up, but how do you explain what happened to those poor bastards working the still? They died without being touched. So how could that be? The question cut through the fog, clearing away his confusion and letting in answers that were too horrible to even look upon.

The nightmares he'd seen in those trees had been real.

Movement in the thinning shadows near the house brought Jack back into the present moment and his hand shot instinctively for his pistol. He relaxed his fingers when he recognized Randall Trask, a shotgun resting in the crook of his arm. He raised a hand in a wave before returning to his post.

Inside the house, Jack found Cleary puttering in the kitchen, humming softly to himself as the smell of coffee filled the air. The farmer stood near the sink, his massive bulk hunched over it as he worked on something. Despite the early hour, the man was dressed in his ever-present light blue overalls and a white short-sleeved shirt.

"Coffee'll be done in a minute," he said. His voice was a deep, soft rumble, respectful of the early morning quiet that otherwise dominated the house.

"I'm going to need something stronger." Jack placed his hat on the kitchen table and folded himself into the chair.

"Bit early for that, ain't it?" Cleary placed a small white mug on the counter beside the sink and turned to face Jack, wiping his hands on a patterned towel. His smile melted. "You look like somebody just walked over your grave." There was a pause and his features softened. He sagged against the counter. "Something happened to the site."

Jack nodded, unable to meet the older man's gaze. In slow, sporadic sentences, Jack explained what had happened. He held nothing back. Cleary, to his credit, took it all calmly. For a moment, Jack was surprised at the lack of reaction, then recalled the story Cleary had told him the first time they'd met, sitting around that very same table. Men's bodies torn apart, found in trees with ciphers carved into their flesh, entrails on the ground forming strange symbols.

"So you saw them?" Cleary asked. He poured two mugs of coffee and handed one to Jack.

"The men? I was standing right in the middle of all of them."

Cleary's large head shook, the unkempt white hair sticking out.

"I'm talking about those figures you saw in the woods. The ones watching you."

The memory of them flared in his mind and Jack clamped down on it, pushing it away. "That could have been anyone. It could have been Dunn or a couple of his guys. It could have—"

"Jack?" Evie's voice. She hobbled into the kitchen, one arm thrown out to the nearest wall for balance. Jack stood quickly, took her other hand, and guided her to a chair. She wore a long nightgown beneath an oversized pale blue robe that swallowed her small frame. Seeing him staring at her, she gave the collar of the robe a gentle tug. "It was Mrs. Cleary's."

"It was her favorite," Elmer said as he poured a fresh cup of coffee and handed it to Evie.

"Rightfully so." Evie sipped the hot liquid. "What happened?"

Jack looked at Cleary as if for support. The old man simply watched the exchange. To Evie, Jack said, "I saw something. The men at the still were attacked and killed. I saw two dark figures in the trees watching. They vanished when I shot at them."

Evie's hand drifted across the table and she clutched Jack's fingers, giving them a reassuring squeeze. "You're okay?" she asked. Jack nodded. "Good. Then don't lie to me or hold back on telling me something just because I'm a woman and you want to protect my delicate sensibilities. What did you see, exactly?"

Jack told her everything. Cleary listened carefully to the story for a second time, his brow furrowed in concentration. When Jack was done, Evie said, "There were only two of them?"

"That I saw, yeah."

"Maybe it was Dunn. You said that he'd run off. If he's still alive, he could have—"

Jack cut her off, "No. You didn't see them. What they did . . ." He let out a long breath. "Those weren't men in masks hiding in the woods."

"So there *is* something out there," Evie said sorrowfully. "It's not just superstition."

Jack passed a hand across his face. Irritation at even having a conversation about fairy tales scratched at his brain. "We don't fully know that," he said.

Cleary grunted a mirthless laugh. "You don't even believe what you just said. I can hear it in your voice."

"Okay," Jack admitted, spitting the word out. "Okay. Whatever it was, *whoever* it was, they . . ." Christ, was he really going to say it out loud? "They did something to those men. Without touching them. They never moved. Never left the shadows, and the men, they . . ." The words died on his tongue as he thought about the man with blood pouring out of his eyes and nose, the vines that burst out of the earth and pulverized another, the shadow that swallowed a living man and spat out a decaying, dried husk of a corpse. "They never touched them," he said, softer.

"Witches," Cleary said. The word landed between them like a mutated thing stolen from a carnival freak show. It filled their minds, forcing them to look at it, to accept it.

"I . . . don't even know how to begin with that," Evie said slowly. "Witches don't exist."

"I think the people of Salem would beg to differ," Cleary said.

Evie scowled. "None of those women were witches. I'm sorry but finding a mole on a woman or some town drunk insisting that he had a dream about a girl doesn't mean they had magical powers or sold their souls to the Devil."

"How do you explain what he saw?" Cleary asked, raising a finger from his mug to indicate Jack.

Evie's lips parted, closed, parted again as she fought for some way to answer the question. She let out a long breath. "I can't." Looking at Jack, she said, "I told you the other night that superstitions run deep in this part of the country. I just never thought I'd be faced with the reality of it."

"Do we think that those things are related to the blight?" Jack asked.

Cleary stared into his mug. "I think we have to say yes to that. When my crops and land started going bad and livestock on other farms began showing sickness, I assumed it was something biological. But now? I can't accept that it's just a coincidence. Especially with what's been happening to the animals. Mutations and all."

"I saw the burn pile," Jack said. Cleary gave him a sad, weary look.

"Okaaaay," Evie said, drawing the word out. "We'll assume, for the sake of this conversation, that we're dealing with witches. Jack said there were only two of them. Right?"

Jack considered the forms he'd seen. There had been a lot happening at the time, not only with men screaming and dying in horrible ways, but the world as Jack understood it shifting and changing irrevocably as well. But the one thing he'd been certain of, was still certain of: there had only been two of the things in the woods. "Just two."

"I don't suppose any of the local legends involve witches?" Jack asked. "I've heard plenty about wendigos and ghosts and other things, haints or what have you, but nothing about witches."

"You weren't really open to the topic, if you recall," Cleary grunted.

Jack didn't reply. It was true, but eating a slice of humble pie wasn't very high on his list of priorities at the moment.

A quiet fell over the kitchen and the three sat with the knowledge that the world as they knew it had changed forever. Jack thought of the business dealings and shootings, the stabbings and beatings back in Chicago. What kind of importance did any of that hold anymore, now that reality had been redefined to include witches with the ability to tear men apart without touching them? How dangerous was Adrian Turski or Hymie Weiss compared to dark shapes with glowing eyes that commanded vines to rip a man to pieces, or for the blood inside another man to boil until it burst from his body?

"We need to find out what they want," Evie said. "If we can understand what they're after, maybe we can figure out how to stop them."

Jack barked a laugh at the sudden insanity of the conversation but swallowed it back when the other two turned serious eyes on him. "I'm sorry. It's just that those things didn't seem too interested in talking, if you catch my meaning. They showed up, turned those men into hamburger, and would have done the same to me if I hadn't opened up on them. I highly doubt we're going to find some manifesto of theirs saying what they're after. We either have to leg it out of here and save ourselves or," he added quickly, seeing the flash of shock and anger on Evie's face, "we try to kill them. I'm no expert, I'll admit that right off." He ignored the snort of derision from Cleary. "But when I was a kid I heard stories, things like you drowned witches or burned them at the stake. But those were children's stories."

"Your point?" Evie asked.

"My point is, who knows what the real truth is and what's fact or fiction? I don't know where to even begin looking for those answers. I'm willing to bet the library doesn't have books on killing witches, and if they do, can we even trust that information as accurate? I don't remember reading anything in the Bible about how to kill them. But there are other concerns to deal with. We don't know what they want. We don't know where they came from. All of that is bad enough. Bad enough to make me want to pack my bags and drive across the country and never come back. But there's something that keeps coming up in my head."

"Yeah, Jack Carmelo Chicago? What's that?" Evie asked with a wry smile.

"If that blight is part of them or came from them . . . and it's growing, eating up chunks of land . . . Hell, it's even starting to eat away at this house. What happens when it consumes the entire town? What happens when all the woods and all the fields are blackened and dead? What then?"

Nobody offered an answer, but based on the expressions on their faces, Jack didn't need them to. They all knew that whatever the answer was, it was horrible beyond all comprehension. Jack finished his coffee and set the mug down. Standing, he placed a gentle hand on Evie's shoulder. "I'm going to get my things."

"Going to drive across the country and never come back?" she asked with a slightly mocking tone.

"No. I'm coming back here and staying with you."

Cleary sat, the fingers of one hand absently tugging at his beard as he stared into the middle distance, lost in thought. He stood abruptly. "Excuse me. I need to look for something," he said and left the room, his heavy footfalls a fading soundtrack that echoed through the hall.

Evie frowned at the sudden departure. "Be careful," she said to Jack. "And don't stop at Mack's for food, okay?"

39

"Charlie?" Her brother's name came out scratchy and broken from a throat that stung from hours of shouting as Grace pressed deeper into the woods. She slapped at yet another mosquito, this one on her elbow. Swiping a hand across her forehead, she slid a sweat-matted lock of hair away. The sun ribboned through the trees, pressing warmth onto her like a heavy blanket.

Grace opened her mouth to call out again but instead let out an exhausted sigh. What was the point? She'd been out all day and was no closer to finding Charlie than she'd been the day after he went missing. She'd gotten an early start that morning, rushing through a breakfast of toast and milk. Her father had paused in his task of repairing a broken barbed wire fence when Grace hurried out of the house.

"Where do you think you're going?" he'd asked, his voice tight with exhaustion. Both he and her mother had been out late the night before attending the special worship service led by Pastor Sam. She had heard them come in and snuck into the washroom near their bedroom, listening to their muffled conversation through their closed door. She wasn't certain but thought she'd made out "sacrifice" and "save us." She didn't know what her parents had meant by those, and the words followed her into a troubled sleep.

"I'm going to look for Charlie," she'd told her father. His eyes narrowed at the declaration and for a moment, she was certain he'd forbid it and order her back into the house. He watched her coolly for several long moments before returning his focus to the fence.

Now, stomping through the dying trees, she wished they had come with her. Grace was no stranger to the woods, having practically grown up roaming these hills and valleys. But the forest was different now. The ground beneath her feet was spongy, muddy to the point that more than once she had to pull her foot out of the mire. The soil gave up its grip in those instances with a gentle sucking noise. The honeysuckle and blackberry bushes were dead or dying, their leaves blackened and dripping a thick oily substance that plinked mutedly onto the pine-needle-covered ground. Even the trees were wrong, many of them covered in what, from a distance, looked like boils—open sores that leaked a yellowish ooze.

Grace turned in a slow circle, eyes scanning the gloomy depths. Despite her lifelong familiarity with the woods, she frowned in confusion. She should be approaching what she and Charlie had always called "the Trench", her brother having bestowed the name on the depression one afternoon while playing soldier. Charlie had always fantasized about manning the trenches in France and repelling the Hun with his bayonet and a fierce shout. But the landscape before her looked like some foreign land, and nothing was familiar. A worrying feeling wormed its way into her thoughts.

What if I'm lost?

Okay, she told herself with a deep breath. *Not a problem. Perhaps I've just not gone quite far enough.* Beyond the Trench lay a small creek that fed into the Shadako River. She knew for certain she'd not reached that because there would be no mistaking it, no matter how badly the trees and ground had changed, so she couldn't have gone very far.

Still, she couldn't shake the idea that she'd wandered into a section of the woods she'd never explored. Panic filled her chest, a soft ember that pulsed in time with her heartbeat. To keep the fire at bay, Grace concentrated on remembering her path so far.

As she retraced her steps mentally, something crashed through the thick brush off to her right, pulling a startled cry out of her parched throat. Grace froze, adrenaline coursing through her with a buzzing electricity. The thrashing continued as some animal too far away to be seen rushed along its path. Its movements were spastic, coming in erratic fits and starts as though it was caught in something and staggering while it fought to free itself. Frantic, labored breathing drifted through the otherwise silent forest and Grace took one faltering, hesitant step in its direction. If it were an animal caught in a snare or some other trap, she should do what she could to help it.

But there was something about the sound of its breath that kept her from advancing. The stumbling noises faded, leaving her once more surrounded by silence.

Well, don't just stand there, she thought. *Get moving. Daylight's wasting, as Daddy always says.* She gave the area where the animal had been a final glance, then began walking once more.

She picked her way carefully for some time, stopping only to check the position of the sun. Grace had never learned to tell time by the sun, but she knew enough to keep track of its general location. By her best estimate, and the growling of her stomach, it was very early afternoon. She swatted another mosquito and pressed on, pausing only to call Charlie's name.

Half an hour later, she stopped and once more took stock of her surroundings. Everything looked the same as it had before, except for a small patch of strange flowers growing at the base of a blackened tree. The petals were a sickly green, shot through with orange veins. She blinked sweat from her eyes and when she looked back at the patch of flowers, one of the stems had bent toward her. Grace was overwhelmed with the certainty that if she went closer, it would strain against its roots in an effort to touch her. To eat her.

Grace angled away and approached a fallen tree. Her entire body sagged heavily, her dress soaked with sweat, the fabric torn and picked all over. She eyed the log, grimacing at the slime that coated its bark. But her legs screamed for a rest, and the idea of sitting on the ground gave her visions of being pulled into it, like the patches of quicksand she'd read about in adventure books.

As the wetness soaked into her dress, Grace thought about Charlie. The absence of her brother—who, she had to admit, was as annoying as a mosquito on even his best days—was physically painful to her. Every day that she woke to the lack of boyish noise as he played or his seemingly nonstop prattling as he followed their parents around was a new part of her soul torn from her body. The worst was the fact that his toys were gone, her parents having thrown them out or put them away. She'd read a book once where a character described the absence of his lover as a hole in his chest. Grace never really understood what that meant until now. The world without Charlie was like a great wave of blackness constantly looming over her, waiting to crash down and consume her.

The only thing she could think to do to keep that wave at bay was to continue with her search. Although he was younger than her, he'd spent all of his life exploring the woods and knew his way around as well. But just like she found herself lost now, she supposed Charlie had gotten equally turned around. That had to be it. That was the explanation for what had happened to him. Anything else, any of the other rumors she'd heard people in town whispering when they didn't think anyone of consequence could hear, was impossible to consider.

Her thoughts drifted to her encounter the previous day with Pastor Sam. Usually he was in a bright mood, happy to see her. She knew why, of course. She wasn't blind to the fact that he was attracted to her. But he was so much older—almost as old as her father—and he was the pastor, for God's sake. She didn't think they were supposed to think about women like that. But the way his eyes lingered on her body and the trancelike state he occasionally entered when watching her was unsettling, to say the least. It was a miracle her father hadn't said anything to the man.

Still, when she got out of the woods this afternoon, she should ride her bicycle over to the parsonage and see if he could help organize a search party to assist her efforts. *If he's not too busy,* she thought. So much was going on with the town as of late and she knew Pastor Sam was doing a lot to try and help. Not the least of which were the new sermons her parents had been attending. They'd tried to get her to go but she'd refused, insisting that someone should always be home in case Charlie showed up.

Or in case one of the town's deputies arrived with bad news.

God, what had they done to deserve these horrible afflictions? Twin waves of grief and anger crashed over her, forcing a bubbling sob to the surface. Of course the people in the town were sinners, that was natural. All humans were born with Original Sin. And of course there was a healthy amount of sinful activity that went on behind closed doors. Sam himself had occasionally spoken of such things during his sermons. Gambling, drinking, fighting were all regular vices within the community. And with the passing of the 18th Amendment, everyone knew that illegal alcohol had become a part of many people's lives.

But was all of that enough to justify everything happening? The crops going bad? The livestock getting sick and dying? The forests turning into a macabre wasteland? The memory of the potluck party only days ago came to her. She thought about the food suddenly appearing rotten, covered in worms, maggots, and roaches; the way people had reacted, not just to the food but to one another; her father slapping at himself, screaming that something was inside his skin; how Eugenia Murphy and Martha Dell had fought, and how if not for the others nearby, Eugenia would have stabbed Mrs. Dell with a butter knife.

The enormity of the things that were afflicting Jericho Springs and its people was a tidal wave crashing over and threatening to drown Grace. Her heartbeat raced and her skin grew warm and flushed as she considered the overwhelming horror of it all. To combat her rising panic, Grace clasped her hands together and bowed her head. She prayed, mumbling the words quickly. After several minutes of repeating the passages, the prayers had at least one of their intended effects, and her body relaxed.

Grace's eyes flew open when somewhere behind her, a branch snapped. She spun about, eyeing the thick, decaying brush warily. Her heart beat erratically, and her legs tensed, readying her to run.

Leaves shook in a rasping, skeletal whisper and Grace's fears came into focus as the wide, gray and white head of a bobcat pushed through the small branches. Grace stood quickly, instinctively, and took three quick steps back before she realized what she was doing and forced herself to stop. Running from a wildcat was the worst thing you could do. It was one of the rules her father had drummed into her.

If you run, they'll see you as prey, sure as the sun rises in the morning. They'll give chase. And you're not going to outrun a cat.

The animal stepped out from the bush and into the small clearing, and Grace clamped her teeth down on a scream. The bobcat wasn't big, only slightly larger than some house cats she'd seen. But there was something horribly wrong with its body.

The creature opened its mouth and a series of thin, writhing, wormlike tentacles slid out, shifting erratically as if testing the air. Between them she could see flashes of bone-white teeth. The creature's fur was wet, matted in several places. It stepped closer, angling to her left as if trying to flank her. Weeping sores marred its sides.

A fifth limb, small and deformed, flopped uselessly from where it grew near the cat's rump. But it was something on the animal's shoulder, just above its left front leg, that made Grace feel as if she had tumbled through a warped version of the Looking Glass.

Embedded in the fur was a second cat's face. This wasn't a pattern of color, she realized with mounting horror. It was an actual face growing out of the shoulder of the creature. The mouth was closed, blending into the rippling muscles beneath the fur, but she could clearly see the black of its nose and above that, two pale yellow eyes that stared at her hatefully.

Those eyes are seeing me. They're actually seeing me.

The bobcat growled, the sound dual-toned. There was a deep, rumbling growl but layered atop it was a higher-pitched, chittering sound that brought to mind images of skittering bugs and winged night-flying insects. Just as quickly as her mind registered the sound, the cat leapt forward and its front paw—the one not on the limb with the face on it, thank God—swiped at her. Grace yelped, spun, and ran. The cat gave another sickening trill and raced after her.

Small vines and weeds snapped and crunched beneath her feet. The sound of the cat's pursuit was a ghostly whisper. Fresh noise drew her attention and sent her veering to the left just as the bobcat skidded out of a new group of bushes. *Were there two of them?* she wondered as her feet pounded along the new direction. That didn't make sense, bobcats were solitary predators. So how did it get ahead of her so damned fast?

There was no time to mull over the question as the animal leapt forward, this time from behind a small clutch of saplings to her left. It screamed, the worm appendages quivering with the undulating double tenor of its voice. Grace screeched and turned sharply to the right, looking back at the creature.

She never saw the log half-buried in leaves and moss. Pain slammed into her shins and she crashed to the ground. A fiery ache rippled across her palms as the skin scraped away. Grace was aware of those things but only faintly. She twisted around and scrambled backward, waiting for the bobcat to appear over the log.

Before Grace could push herself to her feet, dozens of vines shot out from the brush and wrapped around her arms and legs. Her fear was so immense that she couldn't form words, only inarticulate snarls and gasps of anger and frustration at the strange bonds as she struggled against their ironlike grip.

The sound of the bobcat leaping atop the log diverted her attention from the vines. Both faces watched her, four eyes calmly reflecting a hungry focus. With a slow, lazy movement, it climbed down and approached her. Its steps were unhurried, and she understood that it was savoring the moment before the kill. Halfway to her, it froze and raised its head, listening. Grace heard the noises at the same time—other unseen creatures in the dimness of the forest. They rushed through the bushes and bleated out horrible, deformed mewling and other cries of hunger. Of need.

They, too, were anticipating the kill and eager for their turn at the leftovers.

The bobcat lowered its head, shifting focus back to her, and approached. It sniffed at her shoe, and Grace tried desperately to kick at it but her bonds were too tight. The bobcat brought its face to her exposed calf and the writhing appendages brushed across her pale skin, tickling and sending ripples of revulsion through her. The cat climbed onto her chest.

An earsplitting blast ripped the air and the cat's side exploded in a spray of blood. The animal tumbled bonelessly across the forest floor. The other creatures she'd heard had all gone silent.

Grace stared at the dead bobcat until movement brought her back around and she saw her parents approaching. At the sight of them, Grace gasped. Both looked waxen, as if they'd fallen ill. Her mother, in particular, seemed even thinner than she normally did. Her father's clothes hung on him like bedsheets on a drying line. Both had dark smudges beneath their eyes. Grace couldn't be certain, but she thought the veins on the backs of their hands were darker, almost black. Her father held his shotgun, smoke drifting out of the barrel in gentle curls. Grace's mother rushed forward, pulling at the vines with hands that, although strong from years of farm work, looked dry and brittle. The vines snapped and broke away, and as she worked, Grace's mother called over her shoulder, "You shouldn't have done that. Killing one of God's sacred creatures isn't the way to gain favor."

"Shut up," her father snapped as he hurried past and prodded the carcass with the shotgun. Satisfied it was dead, he turned back to his family. "Our daughter is more important than that damned thing." The words filled Grace with a sense of relief so profound, she was shocked. She'd not realized how badly she'd needed to hear that her family still considered her important in the wake of losing so much of their livelihood as well as Charlie. For days they'd treated her with quiet indifference, keeping her at a distance.

Tears streaked her cheeks as Grace gripped her mother's hand, then wrapped her in a fierce hug. Her father's warm body pressed in and she grabbed him as well, burying her face in his checkered shirt as she cried huge, racking sobs of fear and relief. Through the sniffling and tears, she babbled apologies for having wandered so far from home.

Her mother said, "I don't know if I can pay the price."

Her father's response rumbled in Grace's ear, still pressed against his chest, "We have to. Otherwise we'll all die. You heard what he said."

Grace stepped back, confused. The faces of her parents were tight with worry, with stress, and no little amount of anger. She started to apologize again, to thank them for finding her and saving her, but her father just pointed and said, "Go on." He turned slightly, indicating that she should walk ahead. "Let's get home."

Grace looked at her mother, uncertain what to say, but the woman simply stared at the ground. Grace slipped between her parents and started walking in the direction from which they'd appeared. When she didn't hear their footsteps, she turned to check on them.

Grace registered a quick blur of motion and the entire world flashed white. Her head rocked back as the butt of the shotgun slammed her forehead. Her legs turned to water and she crumpled to the ground.

Grace lay on the soft stinking soil, the world around her spinning and shifting like a kaleidoscope of colors and sounds. She tried to blink everything back into place, to fit the puzzle back together, but every time she managed two pieces, they fell apart once more.

"Here!" her father shouted. His voice careening through the trees, bouncing around and amplifying. "We've brought her, Lord! We give her to You, painfully but willingly. Send Your servants to collect her so You can take her into Your loving embrace. So that me and my wife, our farm, and our lives may be spared." He completed the cry with a jumble of strange, inarticulate words. Her mother took up the words and together they repeated them, chanting, their voices rising in an awful plea.

The snapping of twigs nearby cut off the flow of strange words that had begun to hurt Grace's head. More cracking signaled the arrival of something just beyond Grace's vision. At her feet, her parents clutched one another, their wide, panic-stricken eyes focused on something behind their daughter. Moving as one, they took several faltering steps back, never once looking away from what approached.

A dark shape entered Grace's periphery, hovering just at the edge of blurred vision. She blinked and twisted her head in that direction and the shape split. Two black, twisted figures moved closer, their feet shuffling over the putrid soil. Arms longer than any human's Grace had ever seen dangled by their sides, ending in hands with curled, knobby fingers tipped with long, wicked claws.

One of the figures turned its head—thin, limp, dirty hair swaying—and coughed a horrible language at her mother and father. Grace tried to say something to her parents, to beg them to take her home. She'd be good from now on and wouldn't go wandering into the woods anymore. But her voice evaporated, her throat a dusty coal chute.

Her view of her mother and father was blotted out as the second figure leaned over Grace. The face was a terrible black void, but she thought she could see vague features: a sharp nose, sagging skin, cracked lips peeling back to reveal an endless mouth. Fetid breath washed over her face, rippling across Grace's smooth skin. A piercing pressure formed in the center of her forehead and she understood that the thing now crouched over her had pressed one of those diseased claws into her.

The last thing Grace Robertson heard before the blackness took her was a voice like rotted coffin hinges creaking open to reveal the desiccated remains.

"Sister."

40

The tires of Jack's truck crunched over the thick stalks of strange weeds that sprouted from the cracked road. The plants smacked against the vehicle's grill with a series of sharp thumps before passing underneath with strange whispers. There were more now than the day before, and as the vines became entangled in the spokes of the wheels, Jack struggled to steer.

Not many people moved through the town. The few Jack did see walked with plodding slowness, their shoulders hunched and heads down as they trudged along the sidewalks. Their feet flattened the strange weeds and grasses that sprouted between the raised slats, only to have the vegetation slowly spring back moments later. Jack accelerated through an intersection, sliding past the library. The corner building had tendrils of black mold growing on its facade. A few doors down, blisters spotted the wood above the large picture window of Blackley's Fine Tailors. Several of the bulbous milky sores had ruptured and a viscous fluid streamed across the glass, partially obscuring the lettering of the business name.

Jack angled the truck against the curb in front of the hotel and hurried inside, hardly noticing the sour tint in the air. Within the small lobby, he moved quickly past the front desk and had almost reached the stairs when the clerk called to him. Jack ignored the man; he had far more pressing matters, but there was something in the clerk's tone that brought him around.

Dark patches surrounded the employee's eyes and his cheeks were sunken. The man's skin was slick with glistening sweat, the sickly color of old cheese. "Message for you, sir." With a hand that resembled dry sticks draped with thin fabric, he slid a yellow envelope across the counter. His fingers remained pressed against it, seemingly afraid it would go scurrying away if given even a half a chance. "Came yesterday but since I didn't see you . . ." He slid the envelope another half inch forward.

Jack shot a hard look at the clerk, who seemed to take his meaning after a moment and retreated a couple of steps. Jack crossed the room and slapped the envelope up. "Thanks," he muttered and moved quickly back to the stairs to avoid the man's watery gaze.

In his room, Jack tore open the envelope and scanned the telegram. The first reading of it drove all the air from his lungs. The second sent him scrambling for the bed, his eyes locked on the black block letters.

BAD NEWS. NORMA, DETTI GONE. A.T. SUSPECTED. REMAIN IN PLACE. AWAIT WORD.-C

Jack read the message three more times, but the words lost all meaning after the second pass. The room around him swayed precariously, as if balanced on a string. He crumpled the message in one fist as he gripped the bedding with the other, his head hanging low. Heat filled his chest and spread to his face, yet tears didn't come. *A.T. SUSPECTED.* Adrian Turski. *That Polish son of a bitch is trying to find me.* How he figured out it had been Jack who put the axe to Jacob and the McCarthys was a mystery.

He could be on his way here. The thought steadied the room and cut through the swirling cloud that filled his mind. He stepped to the window and shifted the thin drapes with one finger to look at the street below.

Beyond the slow encroachment of vines and weeds, Jack saw nothing unusual along the avenue. He studied the windows of the buildings, hoping to catch movement or any sign of another crew holed up and watching him. After several long minutes, Jack stepped back and packed his bag. He moved automatically, grabbing things and stuffing them into the suitcase without care for their condition. His mind systematically processed questions and his options. What had they learned? Norma knew nothing, only that he wasn't going to be in town for several days. There was nothing she could have told them. Not that that would have stopped them, the fucking animals. Norma had been a bitch, but whatever Turski did was undeserved.

And Tony. Jack paused in packing and forced down the lump in his throat. Jack had known him ever since Bobby had started working for the Outfit. The older Italian had been like a father to him, even more so after Bobby's death.

Jack slammed the suitcase shut and latched it. There was no way Tony would have talked. *That old son of a bitch was tougher than roofing nails.* Jack couldn't imagine anything Turski could do that would loosen Detti's tongue. And Jack could imagine quite a lot. He gave the room a final glance, saw that he'd missed nothing, and thumped his way back to the lobby. The clerk looked up from his paper. "Need something?"

"You got a phone?"

The employee's skeletal head bobbed. "Just the one." He indicated an alcove around the corner from the desk. Jack crammed himself into the small space and plucked the receiver from the wall. After a few moments of instructions to the operator, the tinny ringing filtered through the earpiece.

"Yeah?" Capone snapped in Jack's ear.

"It's me."

There was silence for a few seconds, and Jack had begun to worry that the connection was broken when Al's long exhalation came through like a burst of static. When the boss spoke again, his voice was softer, but only a little, "You got the message."

"What happened?"

"We're not one hundred percent on that yet, but we think Turski and some of his guys went around asking . . . questions. I'm sorry about Norma."

Jack chewed on his anger. "And Tony?"

"Seems they asked harder questions."

"Did he have answers?"

Across the distance, Jack could feel Al's bristling at the question of the resolve of one of his top guys. "We don't know," he answered. "But they asked really, really hard. Asked his wife too."

"I'm on the next train," Jack said.

Before he could pull the receiver from his ear, Al's voice burst out, "The fuck you are! You're going to stay right there and let us handle this. We're going to find that rat bastard Polack and spend an entire weekend with him. You come up here and you'll only fuck things up even more. I mean it. Do. Not. Come. I need you to stay down there and finish the southern operation. Things have gotten complicated up here over the last week and we need that supply."

"What about Norma?"

"We're going to take care of her, don't worry. You get things situated down there and next week you come up for the funeral. I've got a guy handling things here."

"But—"

"Next week," Capone growled. "I see you before that and you'll be sharing that room with Turski." The connection died as Al hung up. Jack stared at the phone's mouthpiece jutting from it. He slowly replaced the receiver.

Jack threw his suitcase into the bed of the truck. It landed with a heavy *thud*, but Jack didn't hear it. His focus was centered on the telegram and the call with Al. How could Capone reasonably expect him to stay here when Turski was running around up there? That Al was looking for Adrian Turski wasn't in question. Killing Tony Detti was a huge blow and one that wouldn't go without a response. But what if Turski *did* get answers from Tony? Jack hated himself for even considering it, but it was an option he had to consider. If Tony revealed where Jack had gone, it was only a matter of time before Turski or a team showed up to eliminate him.

Fuck it, he decided. If Turski *was* coming down here, assuming he wasn't already in town, he'd take a day or two to get some guys together and make arrangements. Jack would just beat him to it. Al wouldn't like it, but once Turski was dead, he wouldn't be able to say much. He'd be pissed *he* didn't get to bash that son of a whore's brains in, but that didn't matter. What mattered was revenge.

Jack threw the truck into gear and backed quickly into the street. As he accelerated forward, trying to remember the way back to Birmingham and the train station, another thought came to him. *Evie.*

She was waiting for him at Cleary's. After the conversation that morning, was he really prepared to leave her alone to deal with those things he'd seen in the woods? *Cleary can handle it,* he thought. *The man's got tons of men with guns.* Jack remembered the reaction his own gunshots had on the black forms, scattering them and breaking whatever influence they'd had over the men. If he'd been able to do that by himself with just his pistol, she'd be perfectly safe with dozens of guns surrounding her.

But the thought of leaving her without even a goodbye wasn't right. She'd been attacked because of Jack, beaten severely by Dunn. And it was Jack who had insisted that she uproot her life and stay at Cleary's farm. No, he couldn't just leave without at least letting her know. She deserved an explanation. He'd make it quick, though. Tell her that he'd been called back and had to make the next train. He could even tell her about Tony. She'd understand his need to go back and make things right.

The truck's engine growled and the vehicle shot down the road.

41

Evie sat on the wide porch of Elmer Cleary's farmhouse, and with the toe of her left foot, she rocked the chair in a slow, steady rhythm. The motion was comforting, and she knew there was a good chance of falling asleep. Within arm's reach sat a steaming mug of coffee on an empty apple crate. It was her second cup since the conversation with Jack about what he'd seen in the woods the previous night, and it was proving no more effective than the first cup had been. Her eyes drooped, sleep rising over her thoughts like a black wave. Evie inhaled deeply and shook her head as she blinked several times and the wave of sleep broke apart, receding back to the far edges of her thoughts. She focused her attention on the happenings beyond the porch.

The morning had warmed considerably since Jack departed, and after managing to eat, Evie moved outside to watch the activity of the men around the farm. There hadn't been much so far, to Evie's disappointment. Now that she was able to get out of the bedroom beyond slow, painful shuffles to the bathroom, she was looking forward to seeing how a farm operated. But the advancing blight had overwhelmed Cleary's cornfields and moved on to sections of the yard and, most strangely, some of the smaller barns and outbuildings on the property, leaving many of the workers with nothing to do.

She looked out over what had been the large cornfield. The dirt was blackened as if by a fire, but she knew it was actually the foul-smelling mud that most of the land was succumbing to. The rows were littered with short, ragged stumps—all that remained of the corn after Cleary had ordered all the plants cut and burned.

A pair of men, faces dirty and in bad need of a shave, emerged from the large barn. They pulled their work gloves from their hands and reached up to lower the bandanas tied around their noses and mouths. Behind them, the barn's wood walls oozed from the spots that covered them like a strange pox. Evie stared at the weeping sores —that was the only thing she could think to call them—and reached for her coffee with her good hand. The other remained in her lap, still heavily bandaged so the broken fingers could heal, the pain a distant constant throbbing. She swallowed the hot liquid, letting it burn against the feeling of uneasiness that had risen in her at the sight of the malignancy of the wood. The men crossed the yard, giving her a perfunctory nod as they passed her. She returned the gesture, her eyelids fluttering with weariness.

Both Cleary and Jack had mentioned the condition of the woods, their descriptions so outlandish that Evie had assumed they were exaggerating. But witnessing it first hand, how the vegetation had blackened and the dirt turned to muck . . . it was overwhelming. Even more so was the fact that Jack had encountered the dark figures in the woods, had seen what they were capable of doing to men. The idea was sour in her mind.

Witches.

How was this possible? This was the modern age. It was 1925. Mankind had moved beyond superstitious fear of the dark and things that went bump in the night. There had been a war where tools and weapons unlike anything mankind had ever seen had been employed. Man had conquered the air with the invention of airplanes. So how could it be that a couple of witches were somehow real? And what else was out there waiting to be discovered? Waiting to sink teeth into the unsuspecting?

Evie closed her eyes and turned her face to the velvety warmth of the sun. It wrapped her in a comforting embrace. Jack would be back soon, she hoped. She felt as if she'd not seen his face in days. How could that be, though, when he'd been here only hours ago? Was it hours? She frowned. She honestly didn't know how long it'd been. The haze around her thoughts thickened. Jack would be back soon. That's what mattered.

Evie's breath slowed, each inhalation stretching deeper and deeper as her head slowly drooped, her eyes fluttered, then closed. The rocking of her chair slackened to a stop.

It was a sound that brought her head up, her eyelids peeling open with the thick slowness of worms moving across the hot ground. The porch was empty. Had it always been empty? Evie blinked and tried to remember if someone had passed by a moment ago. Jack, maybe. But her memory slid off the thought like oil on water. Beyond her spot on the porch, the light was strange— flat and yellow like aged paper. A breeze stirred the trees but didn't touch her skin. Far off, someone coughed. Or maybe laughed. She couldn't tell. It echoed strangely, as if inside a tunnel. Evie stood, her legs uncertain beneath her, and turned toward the back of the house.

A noise in the barn interrupted her thoughts. She straightened and focused on the dark slit of the partially open door. The sound came again, that wet coughing. She couldn't be sure, but thought she heard a voice amid it—pained, almost pleading, but thick and clotted, as though the speaker's mouth were full. Evie went to the nearest stairs and descended onto the grass, careful to avoid the soft patches of blackened earth. The sounds kept coming, low and wet, drifting through the crack in the wood. Then, just as her fingers curled around the edge of the door, they cut off—snuffed out by a quick, slapping splash, like a sodden rag dropped onto stone. Her chest pounding, Evie pushed the door open. Sunlight flooded the barn and illuminated a nightmare.

Henry Dunn crouched over the prone body of a man Evie didn't recognize. Not that she could have identified him if she'd wanted to. The man's face was a shredded ruin of blood and flesh. One eyeball hung out of its socket and lay on the man's forehead at the hairline, staring at her. Dunn's own face was buried in the dead man's throat, the Klansman's jaw working in short pulses as he bit and chewed.

Evie's throat constricted, cutting off a cry of surprise and disgust. Dunn lifted his blood-smeared face. His eyes shined like silver coins even in the sunlight, and long strands of thick blood stretched from his lips and chin before snapping and falling quietly atop the dead man's chest. Dunn regarded her, absently chewing the last piece he'd torn out of the man's throat. Audibly, he swallowed the hunk of flesh and pulled himself to his full height. His wide body was streaked with blood, his clothes soaked with it.

"Miss me?" he purred. The question broke Evie's paralysis like a popped balloon and she shrieked, turned, and ran as fast as her damaged ankle would allow.

The shelter of the house loomed to her left, but something told Evie that going there was a bad choice; she'd be trapped inside with Dunn. Her best bet was to put distance between them, to get to the forest where she could lose him among the trees. Besides, Jack would be there. Hadn't he gone to the woods? Looking for something, hadn't it been? She couldn't remember, her mind a dust storm of broken and half-formed thoughts.

Evie hurried between the cars and trucks of workers, slid around the tree trunk with the axe embedded in its scarred surface, and approached the edge of the field. Her ankle was a chorus of painful complaints, but she ignored it and focused on quickly approaching the tree line.

Behind her, Dunn slipped out of the barn with a shuddering, ragged breath like a bull's snort. Evie risked a look over one shoulder and saw him, covered in blood, mouth slightly agape, silver eyes watching her. In that brief look, she saw scraps of meat hanging from his teeth and knew that if she didn't hurry, it would be her throat next passing across his wormy tongue.

"Where you going, kitten?" he hissed after her. Evie focused on the ground immediately before her as she crossed into the field. The sounds of Dunn's footsteps, flat and squelching, followed her.

The ground of the field pulled at Evie's shoes, each step sinking several inches into the mire. Her progress slowed, and Evie fought against the soil as if she had suddenly found herself waist-deep in sand. The wounds along her body shouted their displeasure, painful waves radiating out and mingling with the dull aches of her burning leg muscles. Her breath came in tense bursts.

"Don't run," Dunn called. "I only want to eat your heart. I want to chew your tongue right out of your mouth. It'll be so sweet going down. Come here, bitch. Come here and let me taste you."

Evie reached the tree line and once more dared a look back, expecting to see nothing but Dunn's hand, his fingers outstretched, filling her vision as he reached for her. Instead, he stood at the edge of the field, hands by his sides, grinning, and called her name. His voice cut through the air like a scythe.

Other men hovered just behind him, and Carl Stott stood at the front. The sandy-haired man licked his lips and winked at her from where he stood near Dunn's elbow.

Dunn and Evie's eyes met, and she could feel the Klansman's burning, swirling hunger. His hatred and need filled the air between them with a hot wind.

"Fuck you," she growled.

Evie turned and plunged into the woods.

The forest swallowed her. It accepted her hungrily, closing around her like the jaws of a starving beast. Evie ran blindly, the land-scape a vast tableau of blacks, moldy greens, and shimmering viscous liquid. Over her own panicked breathing, she could hear the snarling laughter of Henry Dunn and Carl Stott as they charged across the field in pursuit.

Around her, the thick shadows were separated by small spears of light that angled through the higher branches. She heard movement behind her, the sounds of monstrous men crashing into and through the brush. Despite the thick sucking ground pulling at her feet, Evie doubled her efforts.

The cold, foul air inside the trees left a scummy dampness on her skin. She ran, dodging mold-moistened trees and slapping away low branches.

"Where you going, little bird?" Dunn's mocking voice floated from somewhere behind her. "Come see me, let me take care of you."

Evie ducked around a large, dead hickory tree, her shoulder brushing across its slimy bark with a slithering noise. She stumbled, arms pinwheeling, and lost the battle with gravity. Her arms plowed furrows through the dirt as she landed, the impact knocking the breath from her. She lay there, gasping for several long seconds while the sounds of maddened pursuit drew ever closer. She caught a flash of white between trees, the pale, blood-smeared face of Dunn as he ran, his lips wide in a wolfish grin.

She gathered herself and pushed deeper. As she stumbled down a short embankment, new sounds drifted out of the dark expanse on either side of her. Her feet scuffed to a halt and she stood gasping for breath as a hissing, whispering drone filled the air. It had a rhythm to it like an ancient, sacred chanting. Evie searched the surrounding gloom but saw nobody.

At the edge of her vision shadows moved, detaching from the trees with a liquid motion. A scream punched its way out of her throat. It landed flat, as if it had been expelled against a brick wall. More shadowy forms, all hideous angles and skittering movements, slipped through the woods, moving closer. They approached from either side and soon Evie could make out the faint lines of faces, of too-wide mouths, black tongues snaking out from between jagged teeth to lap at the air, tasting her fear.

"There you are." Dunn's oily voice brought her around in a jerk. He stood at the top of the short rise, clawed fingers curled at his sides. The blood on his face and clothing was black in the low light and she thought it moved, shifting like gas on water as he leered down at her. "Don't worry, little thing," he cooed. "Those out there won't hurt you. Not until I'm done with you. We're going to finish what we started, you and I." He took a long step down the embankment. "When I'm done with you, you pathetic little cunt, there won't be much left for them. But they'll enjoy the scraps. I'll be sure to leave a little meat on your bones for them to chew. How's that sound? Hmmm?" The skin of Dunn's fat cheeks and sagging neck jiggled grotesquely as he took another large step. Carl Stott emerged over the crest of the hill and stood several feet behind Dunn. Stott raised a hand to his mouth and chewed on his fingers. Blood ran, streaming in fat lines along his palms and wrist as he bit and bit and bit. Soft chuckles puffed out of his cheeks as he chewed.

"Hey," Dunn said, and Evie broke her focus from Stott to see that Henry stood only a foot away. A rotting, spoiled-meat stench rolled out and as soon as her eyes found him, he grinned. "Better run, little rabbit."

Evie ran. Dunn's laughter followed her as did the wet, bone-popping sounds of Stott eating his own fingers. That soundtrack filled her world, underscored by the droning hiss of the shadowy things that pressed closer, hemming Evie into a tight corridor of trees and dead brush like eager children watching a parade.

At the top of the next hill, she gasped in relieved surprise. Below, alongside a small rocky stream, sat an aged wooden cabin. Soft amber light glowed behind the single dirt-caked window and through small cracks in the wooden slats, offering the promise of safety. Fighting the urge to look back, Evie plunged down the hill.

The water in the stream was frigid. She pushed her way through the calf-deep current to reach the dwelling, grunting with the effort. Its porch sagged, weatherworn boards drooping wearily. A door, stained from years of use and the elements, hung partially open. The warm light filled the crack, throwing a single shaft across the uneven porch. Evie pulled herself over the rocky embankment and climbed the short steps. Her sodden dress dragged across the wood, a weak sense of resistance as if trying to keep her from entering.

On the other side of the water, Dunn walked calmly, his silver eyes shining like stars. Behind him trailed a wide, undulating shadow like a massive cape. Feral, inhuman faces bobbed within the shadow like a pack of dogs eagerly awaiting their dropped scraps.

Evie stepped inside and slammed the door closed. She searched feverishly for a lock but saw none. There were no pieces of furniture to slide and serve as a barricade either. She drifted back, hands clasped in front of her breasts as she watched the door, waiting for it to crash open.

Fingers, pale and streaked with blood, wrapped around its edge like worms out of a nightmare. They flexed as hands pushed the door open with agonizing slowness, the wood hissing and screeching across the floor. She backed up, eyes darting around the dirt-smeared ground searching for anything she could use as a weapon. There was nothing but soil, leaves, and small twigs so old that even touching them would probably snap them.

Jack! Where are you? Why haven't you come? Hot tears trailed down her cheeks as she prayed for the strong man from Chicago to intervene. Surely he'd have found out she was missing by now. Surely he had gotten back to the farm and learned that Dunn was still alive and had chased her into the forest.

So why wasn't he here? Where was he?

Dunn's lecherous grin filled the space between the door and the jamb. "There you are, little rabbit," he cooed. Shadowy forms flitted on the other side of the window, filling it and dimming the light within the home.

Dunn stepped fully into the room. On the porch, Stott continued to suck and gnaw at the bloody stumps of his fingers as the shadowy creatures twisted and flowed around him.

Evie's knees buckled and she crumpled to the floor, her dress fanning out around her. Dunn mirrored her, leaning forward and crawling on all fours toward her. Evie pushed herself back, heedless of the splinters that punctured her palms. Dunn's bloody smile and predatory eyes were the only things she knew. Her own screams were muffled punctuations to his words.

"Evie," he whispered. One hand raised from the floor, the palm covered in dirt, hooked fingers flexing as they grasped for her. "Evie, come here. Be mine. Let me wake you up as I eat you. Wake up as I drink your blood, wake up as I swallow your tongue, and wake up as I chew your eyes out of your skull. I—"

Evie blinked. Something wasn't right. The world appeared as if through warped glass, and Dunn's eyes glowed like twin moons.

"Wake up," he said again, voice splintering into a hundred whispers. "Wake up!" The world exploded into a blinding flare of light. Pain surged through her cheek, and her head rocked to one side. She grunted and tasted blood. "Evie!" Hands were on her now, firm and pulling. She gasped in fear, tried to rip herself free but the fingers held firm. "Evie, goddamnit, stop fighting me! Wake up!"

A loud voice that wasn't Dunn's cut through the cotton batting that filled her mind. Evie blinked, her heart thrumming in her throat, and stared through impossible darkness at a man's face. Jack, his eyes filled with fear and worry, his features lit by a single flame that immediately winked out. He hissed a curse and scraped another match. The acrid smell of sulfur brought her fully back to reality.

"Are you all right?" he asked. "Are you with me now? You were sleepwalking."

Evie's head twitched as she took in her surroundings. They weren't in a cabin. There was no dirty window, no unknown source of comforting light. She sat on a hard, cold surface, her fingers half buried in a patina of foul-smelling dirt. Overhead, things like stiff wires hung from a rocky ceiling like decaying hairs from a gray skull. *Those are roots*, she thought, and chuffed a disbelieving laugh.

"Why are we in a cave?"

Jack let out a long breath. "Christ, woman. There you are. You ran in here. Don't you remember?"

"I . . ." Evie trailed off. What had she been doing? She faintly recalled the sense of being chased, of dark things and blood, of rabbits and water, but even those things slipped into the inky black of nothingness as she tried to grab onto them. "I don't know," she said. Once again the tears came, only this time they came from frustration. "I can't remember."

"I got back in time to see you running across the field. I yelled at you but you just kept going. You were sleepwalking. Doc Powell said you might do that. I'm going to skin Cleary's guys alive for not keeping a better eye on you."

"I'm sorry," she said, and fell against him. Her body shook with quiet sobs and she gripped his shirt as tightly as her broken fingers would allow. In the cold silence of the cave, she became fully aware of the burning pains of her wounds.

Jack let her cry for a while and when the moment passed, he helped her to stand. The chamber was bigger than she'd expected, spreading out about ten feet across. Overhead, the ceiling pressed close and she thought she could touch it if she stretched.

The cave stunk with a mixture of foul earth, the thin smell of minerals and rocks, and a metallic scent of water. Evie's throat closed up as she gagged, her stomach giving a queasy, nauseated roll. She brought a hand to cover her mouth and nose. The water, a small stream, flowed off to her right, slipping out of sight in the blackness behind her. It exited the cave through a small hole. Sunlight filled the front of the cave, providing a pool of illumination that stretched only a few feet before losing the battle to the dark. The sound of the water reverberated off the walls, amplifying and adding to the sensory assault.

"I crawled through that?" she asked.

"Yeah," Jack answered with a gentle laugh. "Good thing you're small. I scraped the hell out of my back and sides getting in here after you. How's your ankle? Can you walk?"

Evie tested it, hissed in pain. "Hurts like hell, but I'll manage. I may need you to help me." He held out a hand and she grabbed it. As she took her first step, moving slowly to ensure her legs that still felt like jam would hold her, her foot scraped against something in the dirt. Her first thought was that it was just a rock—the cave floor was covered with them, after all—but the *clink* stopped her.

"Wait a minute," she said. Evie knelt and brushed aside the thick, loose dirt with her good hand. It looked like a massive snake coiled atop the cool earth, watching them with its lifeless, black eyes. But as she knelt closer and Jack brought the flame near, she saw that it wasn't a snake at all.

"What the hell?" she whispered.

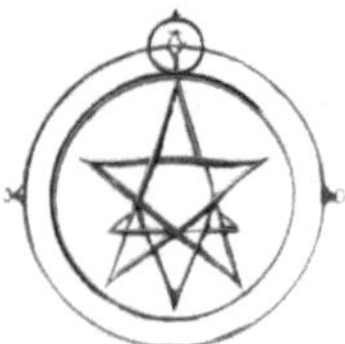

42

God's beauty was undeniable. Sam angled around the blackened trunk of a large oak. The majestic hardwood's bark oozed a thick, oily sludge that glistened in the sunlight. Sam's fingers trailed off the tree, then thin tendrils of the slime extended between his fingertips and the trunk until they snapped and fell away.

He smiled, the edges of it bitter with self-reproach. How blind he had been. How foolish. He let the memory of the dream play through his mind, filling him with renewed joy. In the dream he stood knee deep in the Shadako. The banks of the river were lined with members of the congregation, young and old alike, as they watched the events within the gently swirling water. Overhead, the sun blazed in a wide, cloudless sky, a testament to God's loving gaze as He witnessed yet another addition to his growing flock.

The only mars on the day were the mold and ever-present rot infecting the trees and grass. The stench that wafted from the dying and decaying land invaded the air, sending the smell drifting over the congregation.

Beside Sam, Elowise Durnam stood, the green water to her chest, soaking the white cotton robe and plastering it against her body like a second skin. Her pale, thin chest was visible beneath the wet cloth, but Sam's attention was squarely on her face and the open sores that plagued her skin, leaking a slow stream of clear fluid. Their appearance on this child was a shock to him, to the community as a whole, because no other person had been afflicted with them. To that point, only the plant life and, strangely, buildings had suffered the horrible abscesses. Elowise sniffled, her wide brown eyes focused on the pastor.

Sam placed his hands on the body of the child, supporting her as he readied to dunk her in the cleansing waters of the river and of God's love. He prayed for her soul, speaking loud and clear so everyone gathered could hear the strange language that now came naturally to his tongue. Midway through the prayer, Sam pushed Elowise under the swirling water. He held her for a long two count, then quickly brought her up, sputtering, her eyes closed tight. She exhaled, spraying water, then opened her eyes.

Sam's breath caught at the same time he heard the gasps from those on the bank. The girl turned to regard him, curious. Her face, now perfectly smooth porcelain skin, glowed in the sunshine. The sores were gone. There wasn't so much as a pink splotch to remind anyone that there ever had been numerous abscesses. Sam looked to the congregants and a barking laugh burst from him.

Beyond the people standing shoulder to shoulder on the muddy riverbank, the forest was alive with movement. Instead of a multitude of animals swarming through the trees, Sam watched as the blackened bark, the moldy leaves, the oozing sap all flecked off and landed on the ground. As far as he could see, on both sides of the river, the blight's effects dried up and fell away, revealing bright, vibrant growth. The grass uncoiled from its shriveled clumps, rising green. The slender form of a deer stepped from behind a thicket, its eyes golden, its antlers glowing like polished bone as it approached the river, heedless of the people gathered nearby.

As more and more of the brush and trees were revealed, Sam's eyes squinted, not in study but in response to the brightness of the flourishing life within the forest. The world was being reborn. Sam pushed through the water, guiding Elowise to where her parents waited, tears flowing along their cheeks. When he reached the bank, he wove through the congregation and fell to his knees. The fresh smell of new grass and flowers washed over him like a cleansing river.

The chanting started, low and wordless humming at first. Quickly it gathered shape, the melody coalescing into phrases, the language of the new prayers.

It spoke of rebirth.

Of renewal.

Of ascension.

Now, walking through the trees, Sam smiled as he stepped through wilted brush furred with mold and over fallen logs crawling with strange albino beetles. An odor of wet, rotting vegetation mingled with the cloying scent of decaying flesh filled the air to the point that he could practically feel it pressing against his skin as he moved. Instead of recoiling, his body thrummed with the thrill of understanding. How could he have been so blind? How could he have ever misunderstood, have doubted? With the dream, the Lord peeled away the shades from Sam's eyes and he saw, unburdened, the true glory of God's plan. This wasn't a punishment. This wasn't a slow death brought about by the sins of Jericho Springs.

It was a rebirth. The blackness, the mold, the rot wasn't death. It was a cocoon. A chrysalis from which the new world would be born.

He paused as the sound of something with significant mass crashed through branches overhead. Sam's eyes tracked up into the canopy and caught the movement, saw the misshapen form of the bird as it careened off a large branch, limp wings flopping uselessly. The creature landed on the ground with a soft *thump*, its body sinking into the moist soil by a few inches, and lay still, one dead eye staring beyond this world. Sam beamed at it, at once saddened by its passing and mildly disturbed by the grotesqueness of its form, yet happy that it was beyond and in the arms of the Father. It was a pity the bird died, but some things weren't able to handle the process of transformation, of cleansing that was necessary to push this world beyond the ruin it had come to and into the new, purified one that was still to be.

Eden. A renewed planet filled with beauty and hope, love and happiness. It was all part of God's plan, His *new* plan. Sam continued on, pausing here and there to regard a plant in the midst of transformation. He couldn't see the renewed forms, not yet, at least. Every plant, every tree, every blade of grass, and every living creature, his flock included, was entering a state of pupation. Some, like the vegetation in the forests, entered more quickly than others. But they would all enter. How long they would stay in that state was unknown to him. God hadn't deemed him fit for such revelations yet. But Sam certainly could tell that the members of his congregation were nearing their pupal stage. The Host that they'd consumed prepared their bodies and minds for it.

It saddened him that he hadn't partaken of the Host, but he had been assured that his time would come. It was difficult, being chosen as God's emissary, to be the one to lead the flock through troubled waters. He thought back to that day in the church when Clyde Hensley had questioned him and Sam's response: *I only pray that I'm worthy.* That worthiness was something Sam had strived to achieve every single day. Deep inside, he believed he had answered the call and his reward was on its way. He had to stay behind, for just a little while, and help guide the others through their change. To reassure them that when they emerged from this momentary chrysalis, they would be reborn in new, better, stronger, and healthier bodies. Their minds would be elevated to a higher plane of thought and their lives lengthened such that death would be a distant destination.

Sam would follow soon enough. But first he would have one last moment of bliss in this soon-to-be old and forgotten life. He hadn't been told directly but he knew deep in his heart of hearts that it was to be. He'd been open and receptive, eager and joyful in his mission for the Lord, and there was no way God would deny His servant as simple a thing as Grace Robertson.

Her name came to his lips and he breathed it out into the miasma. At the form of the syllables, his heart fluttered like a dove taking wing and a soothing, comforting warmth filled him. Grace's parents were well on their way to their change; they had been the first to partake of the Host, and with such fervor too. Grace would need Sam's protection and guidance into her transformation.

Sam moved through the woods and thought of the others in town, those who hadn't attended his services or partaken of the Holy Sacrament. His heart ached for them, for their ignorance or selfishness. Despite their absence from the new services and rituals—whether from refusal or reluctance, he neither knew nor cared—he still loved them and yearned to help them. That there would be some who refused completely was to be expected and Sam understood that not everyone could make the transition to Eden. There would likely even be some who tried to stop the change, to push back against God and His servants in their journey. But doing so would be as effective as pushing against the waves of the ocean.

Sam paused and studied his surroundings. The forest was silent, the black and malformed trees as still as stones. He could see quite a distance before the light was diffused and the land fell into soft shadows. He considered how far he'd walked. He'd left the parsonage midmorning after a lazy few hours spent tidying up and working on preparations for the next sermon. A small meal of bacon, day-old biscuits, and some coffee had made a sufficient late breakfast and given him the energy to walk into the forest beyond his own home and church—both of which were well on their way into their transformations, with vines having sprouted out of the blackened earth to climb and embrace the structures like loving, protective arms, even while the very wood of the buildings formed the strange lesions that leaked their even stranger fluid. He was, of course, aware of the reports of men and children vanishing completely or being found dead and mutilated, but he didn't fear such things. As God's representative and the leader of the new church, Sam's heart was pure, whereas those who had fallen under less fortunate circumstances had been shown the error of their ways. What was it that the heathens liked to decry when faced with the absoluteness of the unerring will of God?

Natural selection. That was it. Well, God was nature, and He had selected those people. Selected them as not worthy to proceed into Eden.

Another thrill rippled through Sam at the thought of Eden. He was eager to see it, to start his own transformation and shed this unworthy body. But he knew that was his own hubris—one of the anchors that dragged man down and kept him from ascending to newer, better heights and states.

Sam let out a long, contented sigh and began walking once more, one of the new prayers coming to mind. He gave it voice, keeping his words low and soft so as not to disturb the sleeping landscape. The strange words still pained him to say. Even now, after so many recitations, he could taste the blood that seeped from his gums at the formation of the language, but the pain was lessened and easily ignored.

He had just finished one of the prayers, one of the longer ones that spoke of the Lord taking the hands of His followers and walking with them into the new world, when a painful knot ballooned in his stomach. Sam staggered to a halt and blinked in pained confusion. The knot was tight and fierce deep in his abdomen, and it radiated throbbing tendrils into his stomach and lower into his intestines. The shoots of agony brought with them a roiling nausea that, despite his best efforts, sent his paltry breakfast up and past his tongue. Sam placed his hands on his knees and vomited onto the fetid ground.

When the spasms passed, he brushed the back of a hand across his watery eyes and blinked to clear his vision. He took a deep, steadying breath but instantly coughed as he drew in the foul air. The breeze left an oily slick on his tongue. Its sharp pungency brought a fresh round of tears to his eyes.

Sam coughed and hacked, spat a wad of gritty phlegm to one side, and was about to stand and move away, get clear of the area. He assumed he'd walked near a dead animal, which could only be the reason for such a harsh foulness, when his eyes caught sight of something strange a few feet in front of him. Drawing himself fully upright and holding a hand over his mouth and nose, Sam slowly approached what had drawn his attention.

On the ground, a thick, uneven runner of black rotting matter crept along the ground. As Sam watched, it inched closer. As it neared a plant not yet transformed, smaller stalks of glistening black sprouted from the main trunk and enveloped the bush. At their touch, the pitiful plant seemed to cry out in pain, an imperceptible hiss of agony that died as it wilted and blackened. The stalks moved quickly, covering the plant entirely with furry mold and seeping rot.

Horrified, Sam took two faltering steps back. All around him, the ground fell not into a state of transformation, of shedding its old form, but rather into one of pure death. The very ground beneath his feet pressed down easily, as if it were decaying.

Corruption, he thought. The word brought to mind images of a decaying horse and its leering skull-faced rider cloaked in teeming blight, sending putrefaction across the world.

This wasn't the work of God. This was something else. This was the antithesis of God's plan. Something was rebelling against the holy transformation, seeking to kill the land and everything in it before God's protective embrace could cover it.

Sam stared in the direction from which the unholy spoilage came. His eyes could easily pick out its path, winding and spreading through the trees. It was somewhere ahead, the thing that threatened all of God's work.

Of Sam's work.

Ignoring the spongy softness of the dead ground, he pressed forward, following the river of infection. Every step brought to sight new horrors as he crossed a dead and corrupted landscape. Nothing lived here now, and nothing ever would. The land where this blight had touched was forever dead. Salted ground.

Minutes later, he came to the edge of a wide field full of the blackened and broken, jagged edges of cornstalks. The dirt of the field looked like a swamp. Beyond it stood a large, white farmhouse flanked by a series of barns and mature hardwood trees interspersed with a few pines. The ground around the home was covered in the rot, and Sam's guts twisted at the sight of such a large presence of defilement.

"*Watch,*" a voice whispered in his head. The same voice that had spoken to him during his dreams, that had led him along this new path toward salvation.

God's voice. Sam held on to the sound of that voice, the presence of it in his mind, clutching at it with every fiber of his being like a man grasping for a life preserver in stormy seas.

Sam watched.

With a terrible tearing sound, the earth ripped apart. Chunks of dirt and stones flew into the air and arced to land great distances away. Massive tentacles, black and coated in oozing pustules, shot out of the jagged rifts in the dirt. Up and up they extended, until they practically blotted out the sun. The air grew cold and the breath sucked out of Sam's lungs as the tentacles of putrescence leeched life from the world. They slithered across the ground to the farmhouse, creeping along its walls. Wherever they touched, the wood cracked and softened, filling with termites, maggots, beetles, and worse crawling things. The trees of the yard succumbed to the gripping death of the tentacles and Sam clamped his hands over his ears as the world filled with their dying screams.

"*The source of the corruption is there. This home is the source of this plague that will destroy everything and everyone,*" God said. His voice a chorus of voices blended together, swirling in Sam's thoughts. "*Find it. Carve it out from where it lies buried deep. Purge the evil.*"

The world flashed a brilliant, blinding white and Sam flinched away, squeezing his eyes tightly against the flare. When he opened them again, the house stood as it had moments before, the signs of its evil defiance of God's plan subdued from what he'd just witnessed, but there nonetheless. Trees were dying, the yard pockmarked with black pools of evil. The house itself wept from dozens of open sores. A large man with white hair and a bushy white beard moved lazily along the porch, the curved form of a pipe dangling from his lips. Sam recognized him, not from his congregation but from the man's presence around town. Elmer Cleary.

Sam turned and hurried back through the woods. His walk became a trot, then a run. Before long he was sprinting as hard as he could, dodging branches and leaping bushes as he raced back to the church. When he finally stepped from the woods and into the clearing where his home and the church stood, he was covered in sweat, his clothes plastered to him much like Elowise's had been in his dream. The church stood before him, its clapboard sides covered in slowly creeping vines. *Even the house of God must undergo an evolution.* A strange light was glowing between the runners, as if some powerful lantern were alight within the building, its brilliance too intense to be contained.

Sam smiled. Tonight, he would preach again.

And this time they would *all* understand.

43

The congregation filed into the church as the afternoon faded into early evening, the sky darkening like a bruise forming on an overripe peach. Inside the First Baptist Church, lanterns and candles flickered, sentinels against the encroaching night. Sam took a sip of water from a glass hidden behind the pulpit. His hands shook, sending ripples through the water as he returned the glass to its resting place. The tremors weren't from nervousness but rather barely contained excitement. His entire body hummed, energy flowing from one extremity to another. How could he not be enthusiastic? His eyes were finally open and clear, and he was going to help remove the final obstacle standing in the way of God's divine plan.

The people gathered in the nave, at least a hundred by his estimate and probably more, sat quietly waiting for the ceremony to begin. A collection of smells rose from them, the muskiness of sweat, the green sour of damp rot, and something else, something deeper that Sam couldn't quite put a finger on. The skin of those seated before him glistened in the candlelight with a waxen sheen as if damp with fever. Hollow eyes fixed on him with dark, dilated pupils. Many of the people sat transfixed, their jaws hanging slack, the corners of their mouths slicked with drool. He wasn't certain but he thought he could smell their putrid breath. Some mouthed prayers, the sibilant sounds like a distant steam whistling from some faraway pipe.

"My friends." He gripped the sides of the pulpit in an effort to keep from leaping off the chancel and running along the aisles that separated the pews. "We have come a long way since the first days of the blight, haven't we?" A few heads bobbed in agreement, but most remained locked. "I want to tell you of a dream I had just last night. This was no ordinary dream, but rather a vision that our Lord needed me to witness. You see, I had been wrong about something. I had passed that misunderstanding on to you. This"—he swept a hand out, indicating the land beyond the walls of the church—"is not a slow creeping death. I know this because last night, friends, the Lord gave me a vision."

As he relayed the events of the dream, of the signs of rot falling away, those seated in the pews remained motionless, their faces unchanging. It was as if he'd simply recited his weekly grocery list to them. And yet something shifted—a faint hum beneath the silence, a shared stillness that vibrated with understanding, of knowing.

Sam pressed on. "It's *not* a rotting death. It's *not* a punishment for our sins. No! It's a *blessing!* We are to be reborn, just as the caterpillar must die to become something better, something more beautiful. These pains we've experienced, the decay we've seen affecting our forests and fields, the very buildings we inhabit, are no less than the essential stages of divine transformation. What has been called rot is not death, but rather rebirth. The forest knows. The soil knows. God knows. And now, you know."

Sam paused, retrieved the glass of water and sipped. His throat scratched as it swallowed the liquid. The congregation remained quiet, but that energy proliferated, buzzing just over their heads, washing back and forth across every single man, woman, and child. He took a second sip. The scratchiness in his throat subsided and he continued.

"Now," he started, stepping from the pulpit and moving slowly across the chancel, his hands behind his back contemplatively. "Just because we now understand the true nature of this transformation, that does not mean that all is well within our town. In fact, I know there is a spot where something darker grows. A cancer in the body of Christ, festering in secret, feeding on holy flesh. God showed me this place earlier today when I was taking a walk through His beautiful forest. It is a horrible place. A place where His light does not reach, where something old festers beneath floorboards, where death pretends to be holy. That place is the Cleary farm. The rot grows there, taking root and working to poison our Lord's divine path. It spreads slowly, surely, outward across our land, into our town. If left unchecked, it will most certainly destroy all of Jericho Springs and those you love before we can complete this period of transition." He stopped pacing and turned to face the people, his arms held wide. "And if we do not cut it out, if we do not destroy it totally, it will kill everything and deny us our Eden."

The congregation watched him, their attention as strong as steel bands connecting their minds to his. A few fluttering sounds of laughter drifted up, faded, and were replaced by the sorrowful hitching of breath as tears flowed. Sam's eyes caught flurries of movement here or there as a congregant twitched or writhed spastically in their seat. The energy from earlier morphed, transforming from one of rapturous elation to something darker, more concentrated.

He returned to the pulpit, slid the glass of water aside, and retrieved the dark box that contained the Host. He held it hidden behind the pulpit for a moment, his eyes tracing the strange symbols etched in the black wood. Something inside moved, eager, impatient. Sam raised the box and held it for all to see. The moment it was in view, their focus snapped to it. Every face, every eye within the church stared at the box with a singular need. The thing inside twitched again as if responding to their desire.

"Tonight we will take communion and become closer to the pure souls that God wants us to become. We will step further along the path that He has chosen for us. You will become His army here on Earth. Please, come forth and receive your blessing."

The lines had begun to form before he was finished speaking, the people sliding out of their pews with practiced ease and forming a single line down the center aisle of the church. As always, Jonas and Anna Robertson were at the head of the line. Each person reached into the box and withdrew their personal Host, holding it up over their tongues where the black thing quivered eagerly before they dropped it into their mouths.

As each person swallowed, their eyes closed rapturously, their lips curled back in a joyful smile. Many wept, unashamed of the tears that spilled down their cheeks. Several mumbled the new prayers, others jerked and writhed after consuming the Host, as if overcome with the power of the thing.

Eugenia Murphy swallowed, her seamed face crinkling more deeply as she smiled. Red lines appeared at the corners of her lips, the smile stretching wider than should have been possible. Her lips pulled back revealing glistening gums and teeth like obsidian glass. Behind her, Thomas Kreech, the manager of Jericho Springs First Bank and Trust, spasmed like a struck dog. His neck strained, the tendons hard against his pale skin. The veins in his throat looked black, as if he'd been injected with ink.

The line progressed, each person eagerly, gleefully accepting the Host. Welcoming it. They bowed their heads and spoke the prayers in that painful tongue, ignoring the bleeding it caused in their mouths. The spectacle of it all sent a thrill of joy through Sam, and he beamed at them even when eyes that had once been blue, brown, or green now glowed a deep silver. Even when a tongue that was too long lashed out from between lips to lap at tears or to lap away a trickle of blood.

Sam saw all of this and his chest expanded with a swelling of pride so powerful he thought he would burst into a cloud of sparkling embers, like the fireworks he'd watched at the last Summer Festival.

When the last of the Host had been consumed and the box returned to its place within the pulpit, Sam pretended not to notice the few eyes that followed the box with a hungry glare. He then stood at the front of the chancel and once more spoke to the congregation.

"As God's army, as His flaming sword, it falls upon you to ensure His righteous plans come to fruition. The rot at the Cleary farm must be found. It must be cut out. It must be cleansed." A tittering of eagerness drifted back from those seated. "Anyone who protects the rot is a part of it. They are guilty by association. You must find it all and let no part of the rot remain." He raised his eyebrows, giving a knowing, intentional expression. Raising his hands, he bellowed, "Go now, and be the fire in God's blood! Be the knife in His hand! Be His flaming sword! Let not a single shadow remain upon His promise to us!"

Not a single person spoke. They rose and filed out of the church in silence. The only sound marking their exodus was the creaking of the wooden pews and the feathery rustling of their clothing. Sam descended the steps and followed the last of the congregation out into the cool late May night. He stood at the top of the steps watching as they drifted like an ink stain on the ground, moving across the grass and into the trees. As the last of them slipped between the trunks and out of sight, Sam returned to the chancel and knelt before the cross affixed to the rear wall of the church. His eyes were wide, his heart full of love, joy, and pride. The chrysalis was cracking open.

Soon, they'd all be free.

44

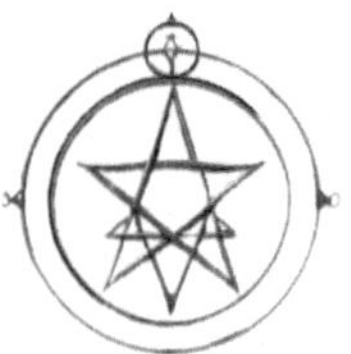

"And this was in there?" Clearly asked, his eyes fixed on the scattering of chains and rocks that covered his dining table. Several candles and a lantern filled the room with light, something Jack found comforting. By the time he had gotten Evie out of the woods and crossed the decaying cornfield, the sun was all but a distant memory over the horizon. He'd helped her into the house, his skin crawling with the overwhelming feeling of things watching him from the darkness.

Even though he'd carried them back, Jack was still surprised at what they'd found in the cave. The chain was heavy, rough, black iron. Each loop the size of his palm. They were affixed to a solid two-foot rod, at the head of which was a wide arrowhead forming a kind of spear. The sharp, angled spearhead was wider than both his hands placed side by side. Its flat, black metal was pitted and grooved with markings that, once the dirt was brushed away, formed a series of symbols arranged in a spiral pattern. The designs had immediately brought to mind the horrible ciphers that had been carved into the flesh of Morelli and the Bryant woman, and Jack had thrown down the iron spear in disgust.

That's when Evie noticed the bones. Buried in the dirt where they'd uncovered the chain and spear were fragments of bones. There hadn't been enough for a full skeleton, but Jack had counted a femur, most of a pelvis, and half a human skull.

"It was," Evie answered Elmer. She flexed the fingers of her good hand around the warm mug of coffee. "Look at the symbols."

The farmer picked up one of the rocks and turned it over. The stone looked like a pebble in his massive hand. He studied the etching on its surface and made a low humming sound. "There were symbols like this all over, you said?"

"Yeah. After Evie found the bones, we noticed them. They were carved into the walls of the cave. They were all over the place. It looked like the front page of *The Times*. That one"—Jack pointed to the rock Cleary held—"we found just outside the cave, near the opening. I think it had been part of the wall."

"They all look like this?" Cleary held up the symbol.

"Mostly. They weren't the same, of course, but all were those lines and curves in different configurations."

"Do you know what they are?" Evie asked, hopeful.

Cleary shook his head. "Indian, I'm guessing. Old too. Haven't been any Indians around for a long time. Well over a hundred years, I reckon."

"They look like the ones we saw," Jack said. Cleary raised his eyebrows and glanced over. "On Morelli and the Bryant woman."

"Nadine Bryant?" Evie asked. "She's dead?"

"Her and William," Cleary confirmed in a tone that suggested he didn't want to upset Evie with the news. "We found 'em both the other day."

"What was left of them," Jack said. "How do we know these symbols aren't the same as what was carved on them? How do we know that those things didn't draw them?"

Cleary's beard shifted as he pursed his lips in thought. "I didn't see your guy's body, but the ones on Nadine and on the trees and bodies of the other men who had been killed all looked different. Felt different, is what I mean. There's something about these that . . ."—he sighed and shrugged, placing the rock back atop the table—"feels different."

"So are you saying that those things out there are Indian? Or something conjured by the Indians to kill the white man?" Jack asked. He felt ridiculous suggesting it.

"Ain't no Indians around here no more," Cleary said. "There's some reservations in the state, sure, but nothing in those woods."

"Wait a minute," Evie said thoughtfully. She picked up the rock and placed it before her. "These things were all around that cave and on that big spear thing . . ." she trailed off, her eyes losing focus as she drifted on her own thoughts.

"What about them?" Jack asked. The question came out short and clipped. He was losing patience quickly. Between the events at the still, the news from Capone, and having to chase Evie across hell's country, he was beyond exhausted, his nerves frayed like an old blanket. Luckily, Evie didn't seem to notice his irritation.

"What if these symbols"—she raised a finger to indicate the lines carved into the rock—"were put there to keep them locked up? Some sort of protection or binding? And that chain physically restrained them?"

"Who would have done that?" Jack asked. "Somebody in town? Who would have kept those things out there? And if that's true, how did they get out? It doesn't make sense."

"The Indians," Evie said. "Or the people from Providence. That cave isn't too far from the old ruins."

"What are you suggesting?" Jack asked, fighting to keep his words calm. His fingers twitched and he fetched a cigarette.

Evie turned her hazel green eyes to him. They were placid now, a far cry from the frantic energy they'd held when he'd snapped her out of her sleep state. But beneath that calm, he detected an excitement. *She's enjoying this. Like reading a mystery novel and trying to work out who did it before the end.*

"I'm suggesting that this isn't the first time those things have caused problems. I'm saying that at some point, what if someone—Indians, the settlers of Providence, I don't know—figured out how to trap them? Chained them up and buried them in that cave, then carved all the symbols as a way to protect against them getting out."

Jack regarded the chain, the iron spear at the end. Something about it bothered him, yet he couldn't figure out—

It hit him, slamming into his thoughts like a baseball bat connecting with a curveball. "Jesus, Mary, and Joseph," he muttered around his cigarette. He picked up a section of the chain. Its rough surface scratched against his skin as he ran his fingers along the rings. "There's not enough for two." The chain was heavy, and the links clinked together as he lifted, holding it up to Evie and Cleary as if in offering.

"What are you saying?" Evie asked.

"Only one of them was buried there."

Silence filled the kitchen as they processed the statement.

Cleary coughed, clearing his throat. "I need to show y'all something." He thumped out of the kitchen and down the hall.

When he was gone, Evie said, "But you said there were two of them."

"There were," Jack confirmed. As he answered, another thought pricked at the edges of his mind, demanding attention. He pushed it aside as Cleary's heavy footprints returned.

Elmer entered the kitchen carrying an impossibly large book. It was the single biggest book Jack had ever seen in his life, and when the farmer placed it down, it shook the entire table and reverberated through the floor. "Family Bible," he said.

"Jesus." Jack whistled. "Is your entire family a bunch of giants?"

The old man ignored the jab and opened the book. The musty odor of old paper drifted from it. His large fingers flipped aging, yellowing pages filled with tight script. Occasionally, Jack noticed things written in the margins, fading pencil marks from generations gone by. "There," Cleary said, finding the page he wanted. He jabbed at it with a calloused finger.

"Exodus?" Evie asked.

Jack tried to focus on the small black lettering on the page as Cleary spoke, "This Bible has been in my family for hundreds of years. Usually passed down from father to son, but sometimes an uncle or cousin would keep it, holding it for a time before sending it on down the line." He looked at Jack. "I don't know how they do things up north, but down here, families write things in their Bibles. Birth and death dates, marriage dates, things like that."

Jack thought about his mother's small Bible. "Yeah, Ma used to do the same. Mostly in the back."

"What's so important about Exodus?" Evie asked, then added, "I didn't go to Sunday school."

Cleary gave her a scolding look and pointed. "Chapter twenty-two, verse eighteen."

Evie followed his finger down the page and read aloud, "Thou shalt not suffer a witch to live." Glancing up, she added, "Fitting."

"I was always fascinated by this book when I was a kid." Cleary went on, "I loved reading the Bible, had my own copy even, and this one being so large, I was like a moth to a flame. But it was this"—he shifted his finger across the page to indicate a series of faint handwritten notes in the margin— "that I couldn't get enough of. Every time I was allowed to look through this book, I always stopped and read this note."

In the margin, in handwriting so narrow and sharp it was nearly illegible, were three sentences.

The three came before sin, born in the dark between stars.
Sealed with iron and prayer.
God help us if they are ever made whole again.

"Who wrote this?" Evie asked.

"No idea. Nobody could ever tell me, so it had to be old, even back then. Someone from Providence maybe. My family's been in this area since the region was founded."

"It says there were three," Jack reiterated. "But I've only seen two."

Cleary turned heavy, sad eyes to him. "Which means there's a third one buried out there somewhere."

"Oh, this just got so much worse," Evie moaned and put her head in her hands.

"Okay," Jack said, taking a seat. The possibility of a third witch sent a quivering sense of dread through him and he couldn't be certain his legs would continue to support him. "Let's back up a minute. We're saying these things are so old that they were a problem for the people in Providence? That was when?"

"Settlement was made in 1697," Cleary said. "No idea when it broke up. Jericho Springs was founded in 1713."

"Christ. Okay, so that makes them a few hundred years old, if you can believe that. They were trapped, one buried in that cave. Which makes sense considering the bones we found. But aren't you supposed to burn a witch? And what's with the chains?"

"I'd say that it was used to secure her to the ground," Cleary said, picking up the spear. "Wrap the chains around her, bury this in the dirt or the trunk of a tree to hold her in place, then light her on fire." The arrowhead made a heavy *thunk* as it was placed back on the table. Elmer pulled out a chair and lowered into it, the wood creaking as he settled.

"Jesus." Evie made a disgusted face.

Jack lit another cigarette. "All right. So she's wrapped in chains and burned to death. Then someone carved all those symbols in the rocks to keep"—he waved his hands exaggeratedly—"her spirit trapped. So how is she out there walking around now? She couldn't have come back to life, right? Fire kills witches. Everyone knows that."

"Look who believes in the supernatural now." Evie smiled.

Jack shot her a dark look. "I'm just saying, if she was really killed by fire—and that's a guess on our part because she could have just been bound with these chains and left to starve to death—then how did she come back? How did she get out of the cave? And why did it take her over two hundred years to do it?"

"I'd say those bones we found suggest that she died," Evie said. "Or at least her physical body did." She stood and refilled her mug.

"So how is she and that other one out there walking around? How did she get out of that cave with all the symbols there to keep her locked up? It makes no—"

"Where did you say the cave was?" Elmer interrupted. Jack told him, trying his best to describe the location. Cleary's shoulders sagged as he absorbed the information. "Shit," he growled and thumped a fist on the table. The iron chain clinked softly. "I think I know how it happened. I had a crew in that area a couple of months ago. The Klan had been finding our operations, so for a couple of weeks we'd been pushing deeper into the hills. Two of my guys, Jimmy Blackwell and Freddie Salter, come to me one day saying that they found a stream down in an area some of the guys call Potter's Hollow. Jimmy said he was certain there was a larger spring somewhere in the area, so he wanted to take some sticks of dynamite out there—"

Evie whistled, soft and low. "You have that kind of stuff?"

Cleary nodded. "We keep some of it stored in hay under the barn out there." He jabbed a finger in the direction of the yard. "So I'm betting that ol' Jimmy . . . he never was the sharpest tool in the shed, but I don't know how he could have known what was in that damned hill . . . Anyway, I'm betting he blew that hole you two found."

"Where is he?" Jack asked.

Cleary shook his head. "Never saw him again. They were the first crew to go missing. The attacks started up pretty fierce and regularly after that."

"Didn't you go searching for them?" Evie asked. "Surely the men who did saw the cave."

"We looked for 'em, sure. Didn't find any trace of Jimmy or Freddie or the two negroes who was with them. Found the still completely intact, though. Which was strange, considering at the time we assumed it was the Klan or revenue men."

"And you stopped looking for them?" Jack asked. He thought about the times one of Al's men went missing. It didn't happen often, and if the sap didn't show up a few days later hungover like the devil with a hangdog look on his face, then he wasn't going to be found. Unless the people who did him wanted what was left of him found.

"Had to," Cleary said matter-of-factly. "Don't get me wrong, I don't like losing guys. But it's a part of this business. I'm sure you understand. Sometimes guys run off. They get scared of the law or the Klan and just light out. But considering this was around the time that Dunn showed up, we eventually just assumed that Henry and his boys had found them. Probably heard the blasting and walked right up on them." His eyes flicked over to Evie and he left the rest unsaid. "And in addition to Dunn's attention, we had our hands full with your fella Morelli and the new deal."

That answers one question, Jack thought. If the blasting blew the hole in the cave wall and broke the protective barrier, that would explain how the witch got out. But it left how she came back to life and escaped the chains still unanswered.

Christ, Bobby would ring my bell if he knew I was thinking and talking about witches like they were real, Jack thought. But the memory of those two dark shapes with the glowing eyes watching as men were torn apart without being touched resurfaced, and he knew that even Bobby would understand.

"So what do we do now?" Evie asked. She held up a hand and raised a finger for each item she listed off. "We know there's at least two of these things free. We know that, at least according to those notes in your Bible, there were three. God, I hope that's all. I don't know if I can handle it if there are more than that." She looked at the two fingers and let her hand drop. "Oh, and we know that apparently horrible things happen if they're made whole, not that we really know what that means. We don't know how they came back to life, and I'm saying that under the assumption that they can actually die. Or rather that their physical bodies can."

Jack rubbed his cheek. The stubble there was rough against his palm, reminding him it had been quite a while since he last shaved. "I don't know how important it is for us to know what they want. Not specifically, at least. I guess we can assume that turning the land into a rotting swamp is on their agenda."

"Isn't that enough?" asked Evie. The words came out in an incredulous bark of a laugh.

"It is," Jack agreed. "Beyond that, I don't care what they want. What we need to know now is how to stop them. Can we kill them with bullets? I don't know too many things that can take multiple slugs and keep whistling."

"Did your shooting at them the other night have any effect?" Cleary asked. "You find any blood trails or anything afterwards?"

Jack's face grew warm. "No," he grumbled.

"So let's assume that bullets don't hurt them," Evie said. "For now," she added quickly, seeing Jack's sharp look. "The way I see it, there are two outstanding questions that we have to find answers to. The first is, assuming there's a third witch: where is she, and is she alive or waiting for some ritual to bring her back? The second is: if the chains are strong enough after all this time to hold them so we can burn them, how do we get close enough to trap them?"

The men stared at the chains on the table in silence. The thought Jack had dismissed earlier resurfaced. "That's not enough chain for a single witch," he said quietly, almost reverently. Cleary's eyes gave a look that said he had the same thought. "I need to go get the other chain," Jack reasoned. As he stood to leave, Evie's fingers grasped his sleeve.

"What are you doing?"

"I think I know where the second witch's chains are. If I'm right, we'll work out a way to keep them contained, or at least slow them down long enough to get the chains on them."

"I'll come with you," she said, letting go of his arm and starting to push out of the chair.

Jack put a hand on her shoulder, stopping her progress. "Stay here. I won't be long, and I'll feel better if you're here and safe. You've had enough adventure for one day. You need to rest and not reinjure that ankle." She started to protest but Jack cut her off, "I will be right back, I promise."

Cleary followed him down the hall. They paused at the door. "You're not going to do anything stupid, are you?" the farmer asked.

Jack, his hat in his hands, said, "No. As long as I don't get stuck in that damned well, that is." Glancing back down the hall, he added, "Try to keep her in the house if you can. I don't need to be worrying about her running off again."

Cleary chuckled. "If only it was that easy. But don't worry, I'll sit on her if I have to."

45

A hazy ring of light surrounded the moon that hung mostly full behind a veil of thin clouds. Jack parked the truck in the fat shadow thrown by William Bryant's house. For a few minutes, he remained in the stifling warmth of the truck's cab, his eyes shifting between the still, quiet house and the dark expanse of the field where the old well was.

He thought about the evident destruction of the property: the torn screen on the back door, the kitchen in disarray.

He recalled the blood, so much blood. And the pile of cooling meat next to the well that he was certain had been William. The twisted and broken body of Nadine, her flesh carved with strange symbols. Of all the moments of violence that Jack had witnessed or even acted in, the extent of the wounds on those two bodies was something he'd never experienced. Images of the ripped flesh popped within his mind like bulb flashes, bringing crystal clear details of what he'd seen.

Nadine had suffered. The cuts in her skin, the scalp hanging like fabric partially torn from a dress, and the unnatural bends and twists of her limbs where the bones had broken so severely, had all been proof of her final agonizing moments.

But William's body had been worse. His flesh lay like a deflated and discarded suit among the wide pool of coagulating blood and red lumps of organs atop the fetid grass. An involuntary shiver writhed its way down Jack's spine as the idea that the man's skin and muscles really did seem like a sort of clothing someone had removed and let fall in a careless heap.

What in God's name had been done to them?

Jack chided himself for having thought the bodies in the house and field had been the work of Henry Dunn and the others in the Klan. So much had changed in only a few days. His fingers drifted into his pocket and found Bobby's old trolley token. He pulled it out and studied it, turning it over and over, forcing himself to concentrate on its patterns, the etched words and lines. His racing thoughts slowed, slowed, then cleared away like ducks scattering from a pond.

He placed one hand on the door handle of the truck and twisted in the seat to survey the front yard and road. Everything was quiet. The few houses opposite the Bryants' farm were dark silhouettes against the darker trees behind them; no lights burned beyond any windows. Jack frowned at that, but forced himself to focus on the immediate situation. Pulling a long-handled flashlight from the passenger seat, he closed the truck door quietly and crossed to the gate and the field beyond. His boots whispered through the thick grass as he walked up the gentle slope. He picked out the original path that led from the well to the house and walked parallel to it. He couldn't explain why, but the thought of walking along that same track brought a crawling sensation to his skin. Jack's nose wrinkled as he climbed the hill, the stench from the decaying land heavy like a fog.

The hole stared up at him like a depthless black eye. Jack resisted the morbid urge to splash his light over the nearby bloody shreds that had been William Bryant. Deep fetid fumes rose from the well and Jack covered his mouth and nose with a handkerchief to blunt the stench. He played the light over the ropes that emerged from the void and remained knotted around the post buried in the dirt. He recalled Cleary saying that if they pulled on one, they'd be rewarded with the body of a cow. Several tugs on the ropes near their anchor points told him they were secure enough, so he clicked off the flashlight and slipped it through the hammer loop of his overalls.

Lowering himself into the hole was like dipping into a vat of ice water. The rope was rough against his palms and he prayed he wouldn't lose his grip. He cursed himself for forgetting to bring a pair of work gloves. Only God knew how deep the shaft went, and the frightful image of his hands slipping on the rope just before his body fell the rest of the way to land in a broken, agonized heap next to that poor dead cow flared in his mind. His entire body tensed with the urge to stay above ground and as his head dipped below the lip, Jack threw one last glance at the sky and its disarrayed scattering of stars. They watched with cold indifference. *Fall to your death. We will still be here.*

Slowly, hand under hand, Jack moved down the black throat of the earth. His breath, short jerky gasps, echoed around him. Not wanting to stop and pull the flashlight, he raised a foot and reached out with a cautious toe. The leather of his boot scraped against rough stone.

After several minutes, his feet touched down with a damp squelch. His body sank a few inches until the mud was over his ankles, but thankfully, solid ground was beneath the layer of slime. Clicking on the flashlight, he squinted in the sudden flare of light as the beam rebounded off the walls of the well.

The shaft he stood in was at least four feet across. A watery sludge covered the ground, rippling lazily as he adjusted his stance. The feeling of the loose sediment seeping into his boots was like worms crawling over his skin. The foul odor was stronger here at the bottom, bringing back memories of standing in the cave with Evie only hours ago.

When his eyes adjusted, Jack swept the light around the space. A few feet away, half covered in the black muck, was the bloated corpse of a calf. Maggots, brilliant white in his flashlight beam, writhed across the brown fur. Jack's gorge rose and he coughed and sputtered as he turned from the dead animal, determined not to vomit down here. *Focus,* he commanded himself. He brought the light to bear on the stone walls of the well.

Jack's lips turned down in a grimace as he saw symbols like those he'd seen at the cave carved into every stone. Jack played the light over the dozens of strange glyphs, trying to imagine the person or people carving them. The beam slashed across one spot where the rocks had broken and fallen away, revealing an opening that gaped like a missing tooth.

That's how she got out. Somehow, the wall was broken and she got out. He glanced at the dead cow, the picture forming in his head. It had fallen down here and as it struggled to get out, it knocked the stones away. But that still didn't explain how whatever remained of the witch climbed out. *Never mind that,* he thought. *Find the chains.* Jack crossed the space to the broken rocks. He inspected the hole, prodded a finger into the soft dirt but found no evidence of chains. *No, they wouldn't be buried in the wall. They'd be . . .* He looked at the black layer of watery sediment into which his feet vanished. The thought of getting on his knees and reaching a hand down into the odorous soil sent a shiver of revulsion through him. Instead, he moved across the well, shuffling his feet as he went. When he reached the opposite wall he turned, moved an inch or two to the side, and repeated the process.

He was dangerously close to the rotting corpse of the calf when his left toe brushed against something hard that moved with the impact. Jack spent another few seconds inching his foot under it, feeling the thing drape across his boot. He had to throw an arm out and lean against the closest wall for balance, the stones wet and colder than anything he'd ever touched, as he brought his foot out of the sludge.

A loop of mud-caked iron chain hung across his foot, and he grabbed it and pulled it the rest of the way. When the wide, pointed flat of the arrowhead emerged, dripping black water and swinging gently like a pendulum, he let out a relieved breath. Draping the chain across his shoulders like an awful scarf, Jack wiped his hands on his shirt as best he could before gripping the rope.

The ascent toward the distant circle of night sky was the hardest thing Jack had ever done. He hated to admit it, but even without the weight of the chains around him, it would have been a struggle. He was able to find purchase here and there and planting his feet against the uneven rocks, he made slow but steady progress.

Despite the stench that permeated the ground, Jack sucked in cleaner air the moment his head cleared the blackened grassy lip of the hole. His muscles burned with the effort of the climb and for a heart-lurching moment, he thought they would betray him and he would lose his grip, only to plummet dozens of feet, breaking either his legs or his back. If that happened, he would spend what remained of his miserable life inches from the rotting cow, watching as the maggots devoured their nesting ground and waiting for them to make the short journey to him.

His muscles didn't give out and Jack pulled himself the rest of the way out of the well. He rolled away, ignoring the slimy feel of the dead grass against his body. When he was a good distance from the hole, he lay on his back sucking in deep breaths. His exhalations blossomed above him in misty plumes.

Jack allowed himself a few minutes to rest before climbing to his feet. The iron chains clanked as he crossed the field and he smiled bitterly. *It's like I'm Marley, come back to warn Ebeneezer.* He started to drop the chains into the bed of the truck, then his eyes drifted back to the road.

His breath caught in his throat.

On the opposite side of the road were dozens of people. They all shuffled in the same direction, like iron filings drawn toward a magnet buried deep in the earth. The night was silent, as if even the wind was afraid to pass through the boughs high overhead. There was only the soft scuffle of feet, a smattering of inarticulate grunts as heads strained forward, and another, stranger sound: a rhythmic *click-click* like distant, ragged applause. It took Jack a moment to recognize the gentle clacking of teeth as several of the people gnashed their jaws with mindless repetition.

Most carried crude weapons: axes, kitchen knives, sickles, their blades twitching through the air as their wielders spasmed. More than once a knife nicked a neighbor's sleeve or shoulder, the victim seeming not to notice.

Almost as disturbing as the jerking swipes of weapons and the clacking of teeth was their gait. Halting, jerky, as if their muscles were locked in an argument with the bones inside them. Some limped. Some lurched. One old man staggered sideways like a marionette tangled in its strings.

Somehow, their faces were worse. Eyes bulged, mouths hung slack or twisted into rictus grins, runnels of drool spilled over lips and swung from chins. One woman's jaw hung loose and crooked, swinging with each step until it smacked wetly against her collarbone. She didn't seem to notice. Or care. Many of the faces seemingly caught mid-smile, their expressions filled with a grotesque joy, as if what they felt was holy.

Some of them look small, he thought. Clothes hung in strange ways: pants puddled around ankles, sleeves dangling like wilted flags. But Jack realized it wasn't just size. It was the shapes beneath the clothes that were wrong. Spines bent at unnatural angles, necks stretched painfully, fingers curled like stiff claws.

Over the years, Jack had seen mobs in every imaginable configuration. He'd witnessed the awful power of the angry, the desperate, and the righteous. What lumbered before him was something else entirely. Something wrong. These people moved as though not of their own free will but by some other, darker momentum.

Jack swallowed hard as they passed, the smell of rot and sweat brushing against him like a hot, wet breath. He followed the angle of their movement and saw they were heading in the general direction of Cleary's farm. Cold worry seeped into him. He didn't know who these people were, but there was something *off* about them. And if they were heading toward the farm and Evie, he needed to get there first.

He dropped the chains into the bed of the truck. They landed with a crash that ripped through the quiet night. Jack winced and started to pull open the door when a hissing *screech* stopped him.

Three of the strange people stood motionless as the rest of the crowd slipped into the forest. Jack held his breath as he waited to see what the trio would do. His fingers curled around his pistol, his thumb resting on the grooved surface of the hammer. The people, two men and a girl who looked no older than sixteen, remained where they'd stopped. Their heads quivered atop necks stretched forward, tendons straining beneath skin. Moving as one coordinated group, they turned in jerky movements to face him.

"Son of a bitch," he mumbled at the sight of their faces.

Their eyes shined silver in the dark, bringing back the memory of the same glowing orbs that had stared balefully at him through the trees as men died in horrible ways around him. The three people focused on him, their bodies giving quick twitches, the air filling with a soft clicking as they bit the air in anticipation of sinking their teeth into his skin. With a screeching howl like steam escaping a burst pipe, they raced for him, their bodies twitching in pained, jerking movements.

leary placed the tray across Evie's lap, a bowl of soup and a glass of iced tea rattling nervously on its surface. He observed the tray, happy with his efforts until he noticed something missing. He mumbled a curse and shuffled away quickly, returning moments later with a spoon. "This would be helpful."

"This looks amazing," Evie said, leaning forward and taking a deep breath.

"Old family recipe. There's more on the stove, so just holler if you want a second helping." He pointed at her foot. "Don't need you trying to carry hot soup on a bum leg."

"Will you join me?" she asked, glancing at the bedside chair.

Cleary hesitated. "I should get outside, make sure the boys aren't lollygagging. Just in case . . ." he trailed off, unsure how to finish the thought without bringing back the memories of what had been done to Evie.

"Just in case Henry Dunn tries to come back and finish what he started?" she asked. "I don't think even he would be that stupid." She paused. "Is that why there's a man with a shotgun standing outside the room?"

"I'm not taking any chances. Jack asked me to make sure there was someone posted outside your room when he wasn't able to be here himself."

"How would they even know I was here?"

He shrugged. "Everyone knows you and Jack are an item. Same as they know Jack's been helping me. I may not have made it past the fourth grade, but even I can do that math. It's unlikely, but we're taking no chances with your safety. If the Klan decided to try sneaking in here, I have fifteen of my guys in and around the house, all armed to fend off the Hun."

Taking up the spoon, Evie looked pointedly at the chair. "Sit, Mr. Cleary. I think fifteen men is more than sufficient to keep us safe for a few more minutes so I can eat."

"No, thank you." Cleary frowned. "I can't eat this late. If I do, I'll be up half the damned night with indigestion." Evie stirred her soup lazily while blowing on it. Elmer took another step toward the door. "Just holler at Jesse there when you're done or if you need anything else."

Just as he reached the door, Evie asked, "What time is it?"

Cleary twisted his left wrist and glanced at his old Timex. "Little after ten." Seeming to read her thoughts, he said, "He'll be fine. I expect he'll be back here any minute now."

"You have any idea where he ran off to?"

Cleary thought about the well and the lump of ground meat and hair next to it. "He didn't say. Probably didn't want you to be able to coerce it out of me and have you go running off after him."

Evie's cheeks colored at the light scolding. "I wouldn't have done that."

"Damn right you wouldn't have," Cleary said, giving her a conspiratorial smile. "I told Jack I'd sit on you if that's what it took. And believe it or not, I'm heavier than I look."

He closed the door behind him to find two of the men he'd assigned to stand watch on the front porch, Vernon Ray and Wade Fischer, loitering in the hall, their faces lined with concern.

"You need to come see this," Vernon said. Behind him, Fischer's eyes were wide and his tongue flicked over his lips in a nervous tic.

Cleary's face hardened. "What is it?"

The younger man glanced over his shoulder at his partner. "I don't know how to explain it. It's people."

"The Klan?"

"Not sure," Fischer answered. "But there's a lot of 'em."

Cleary glanced at Jesse. "Stay here."

Three men stood in the front room of the house, peering out the windows and mumbling to one another. They turned and stepped back from the glass as Cleary approached. "You're supposed to be outside," he rumbled, then threw open the door and stepped onto the screened porch. "What am I looking at? I—"

Beyond the porch, the tree-filled expanse of the yard was bathed in a pale light from a nearly full moon. Cleary's eyes scanned the crooked angles of the barns, the vehicles parked haphazardly on the grass, and the horrible, misshapen forms of trees. He settled on the shadowed border of the cornfield. A surprised curse withered and died on his tongue.

At least two dozen people stood scattered across the property at odd, uneven intervals. They faced the house in absolute stillness, like mannequins in the dark. Cleary couldn't make out their faces, but the one thing he could see turned his legs to water. Eyes. More than a dozen pairs glowed faintly with a cold, unnatural sheen.

"What's wrong with them?" asked Vernon, his voice barely above a whisper. At first, Cleary thought he was talking about their eyes as well, but after a moment, he understood what the man meant. None of the people stood naturally. They were caught in twisted poses, as though frozen mid-movement. Arms jutted like broken tree limbs, fingers hooked into claws, knees bent wrong, spines bulged or curved as though someone had pulled them taut and let go. It looked like the aftermath of a dance choreographed by a lunatic.

Then he noticed the weapons.

Knives. Cleavers. Hatchets. A few full-sized axes, their blades twitching in unsteady hands and catching dull flashes of moonlight.

"Jesus," Vernon breathed.

"I don't think He's here right now," Cleary growled and stepped to the edge of the porch. His voice rang out, loud and authoritative, "You're on private property. I'm within my rights to have you all shot. I don't want to do that, so I suggest you go back to your homes now."

Nothing.

Now that his shock had subsided and his eyes had adjusted to the moonlight, Cleary recognized a few of the faces. Some by name, but most he just recognized from town. However, recognition brought no relief. The people remained motionless, their expressions vacant or frozen mid-smile, their lips pulled back in grotesque contorted grins. The night breeze ruffled the hair on a few heads, sending tufts flapping lazily. One woman's mouth sagged open, jaw unhinged and swinging with the breeze like a loose door.

The wind stirred once more, and something slithered across the ground. Curling runners of mist extended from the blackness of the forest, thin and slow at first, thickening as they crept forward blanketing the grass. The mist pooled and billowed, obscuring legs, swallowing the figures. Still, they didn't move.

As if reacting to some silent alarm, the mob surged. The blurred shapes in the mist didn't run. They lurched. Limbs spasmed, bodies twitched forward in jerking, unnatural strides as if some invisible hand pulled them violently forward. Cleary's breath caught as a memory of a marionette show he'd seen as a boy at the state fair rose in his mind. Only these movements were wrong, both in the way they sounded and in the awful, dragging weight behind them. A low, guttural moaning drifted through the fog. The kind of pained cry that bubbles out of a broken throat.

Along the porch the men shifted nervously, fingers flexing over and over against the stocks of their shotguns. Cleary drifted back a few steps, his stony gaze fixed on the dense mist. Sharp voices barked questions and commands from the right of the porch as the farm's threshing boss, Albert Distel, approached with several others from his crew in tow.

"What is it?" Distel asked Cleary, but the old man's throat was frozen and he could only stare into the mist as the jerking shapes advanced. Next to him, a heavy *thump* and a rattle broke Elmer from the fugue state. Vernon stood, arms limp by his sides, mouth slightly agape, his shotgun resting across one toe where he'd dropped it.

Before Cleary could reach out and shake the man, Vernon shouted, "Ernie, where the hell you been? Christ, we looked all over for you!" He paused, head cocked slightly as he listened, but all Cleary could hear was the pained groans of the approaching people. "Come look at what?" Vernon asked and staggered down the stairs. His first step sent the shotgun spinning lazily until it bumped against Cleary's own booted foot. He picked it up as Vernon reached the bottom of the stairs and pushed past Distel and the others who watched him go with stunned curiosity. In the blink of an eye, Vernon vanished into the mist.

A moment later, his screams burst out of the fog. The sound was terrified, agonized shrieking that rose higher and higher until it cut off abruptly, as if someone had snuffed a candle. In the void of the screams, a palpable sense of fear swept out from the other men on the porch. The air was electrified, buzzing with tension as the men glanced nervously at each other.

With an earthy tearing, gnarled roots erupted out of the dirt and ensnared a man. They covered his body with lightning speed and constricted, the sound like thick ropes scratching across one another. The man's howls of pain were inhuman and blood seeped from between the thick, hard bands of the roots. Another man, this one near the end of the porch, screamed and slapped at his body as if he were besieged by a swarm of biting insects. He turned and ran blindly, hands flapping in the air in an attempt to ward off the invisible attackers.

On the ground a younger Black man collapsed, his face a rictus of pain. Blood welled in his mouth, slicking his teeth as he writhed, hands pushing at something unseen on his chest. With a loud *snap*, the man's rib cage collapsed.

"Shoot the sons of bitches!" Distel screamed, and the night exploded in a cacophony of shotgun blasts. Long fingers of flame leapt from barrels and strobed the mist. Men scattered, searching for targets. The fog swallowed all of them.

His vision reduced to only a few feet, Cleary held back from firing the weapon he'd picked up. Instead, he dashed down the stairs, searching wildly for his men. He needed to get them into the house, get them behind some kind of barricade so they could better defend against these people and whatever the hell was happening. At the bottom of the stairs he cast about, searching for people but seeing only the occasional tongue of flame from a muzzle flash. He turned to the left and started moving, searching the fog for anyone he recognized. His foot connected with something solid that rolled slightly as he connected with it. Stumbling, Cleary dropped his shotgun and threw out his hands, grunting in pain as they hit the rock-strewn ground.

As he worked to stand, the fog shifted, revealing what had tripped him. The human leg had been torn off right at the knee and ended in a heavy black boot. Between the striations of blood, its exposed skin was the color of long curdled milk. Fragments of prayer bubbled out of Cleary's mouth as he staggered away, his feet dragging through wet and trampled grass. He had to check on—

All thought rushed out of his mind like a gamebird flushed from the high weeds as a wet, tearing sound cut through the din of screams and gunfire. One of the people from the mist, a middle-aged woman with slightly graying hair and a soft yellow dress, squatted over Albert Distel, one foot on either side of the man's hips. In one hand she held a long-bladed kitchen knife, and her other hand was thrust into Distel's gore-smeared abdomen. With soft grunts of effort, she pulled fistfuls of blood-covered meat out of the man. Distel was missing a limb. The pants of his right leg deflated at the knee like an old ball left in the sun for too long. Every so often, Albert's body would convulse, rustling in the grass with a thin scraping. His face, spattered with inky black blood, stared at his former employer wide-eyed as if to ask, "What the hell happened?"

Cleary swallowed hard against the rising sickness as he took a step to one side, giving the woman full clearance.

Yellow Dress paused, her gaunt, bloodstained face twitching as her shining eyes found Cleary. She relaxed her hand and let the glob of Distel's insides slop to the ground. Her knife now raised and pointing at Cleary. "Source . . . of . . . the rot," she said. The words seemed forced out, as if she'd forgotten how to speak. Her neck strained, tendons taut as she struggled to cough the words. "You're . . . to . . . blame." She gave the air a vicious slash with the knife and stepped over Distel's body. Cleary staggered away, propelled by not just fear of the weapon but also the smell that surrounded the woman. It wasn't the hot, metallic scent of Distel's insides but rather an earthen stench full of the sour tang of rotting vegetables and the cloying sweet of mold.

Cleary turned to run back to the stairs, shocked at how far they were. *Not going to make it,* he thought as he lumbered toward the porch. With each step, he expected to feel the icy sting of the knife plunging into his back, the blade scraping against bone as it sought softer tissue deeper within. *I'm going to die in the yard, having my guts torn out by the woman who owns the fabric store on Mulberry Street,* he thought dimly.

"Get down!" Randall Trask screamed. He burst out of the fog, a shotgun tucked against his shoulder. Cleary dove, an ungraceful lunge forward that would have left him several feet short of third base had he been on the diamond. Trask's shotgun boomed. The woman flew back like a doll tossed by a tornado, a horrible red hole in her chest.

Trask lowered the shotgun and broke the breech, ejecting the two shells he'd fired simultaneously. At the same time, he fished into his breast pocket and pulled out two more shells. He kept his eyes on the thick fog that swirled around them and the shifting dark shapes within it. "Get out of here," he barked over the gunfire and screams. "Get in the house," Trask commanded as he slipped the first shell into the barrel and started pushing in the second.

Another of Cleary's men—his panicked mind scrambling for the name *Willie Reese*—approached the woman. "Christ, that's—" The curved blade of a sickle flashed out of the mist and raked across his face. The blade punctured Reese's right eye—Cleary saw it go in, followed by a spurt of yellowish fluid-before continuing down and tearing the man's cheek open.

Reese stumbled to one side, shotgun slipping from limp fingers. His remaining eye spun in its socket, finding Cleary still sitting in the mud. Reese's mouth worked, the teeth and jawbone shifting in the open hole. Trask placed a firm hand on Cleary's chest. "Get in the fucking house!"

The command grounded the dazed farmer. "Get the others. Get inside. I have to check on Evie." Elmer rushed up the steps of the porch. From inside came the treble of glass breaking and the confused shouts of men mingled with the labored, coughing cries from those assaulting the house.

"The . . . source!"

"Find it . . . cut it . . . out!"

"Kill . . . rot!"

"Salvation! Purification!"

Just before he slammed the door closed, Cleary threw one last look into the mist. It was thinning now, trees and the prone forms of dead people becoming visible. Farther back, just at the edge of the fog, two dark shapes stood close to one another. Despite the severe angles of their shoulders and twists of their spines, the beings stood upright. Spidery arms extended, clawed fingers twitching as they watched the attack.

Cleary slammed the door and leaned heavily against it. In the front room, two men stood shoulder to shoulder, their weapons darting back and forth as they reacted to every sound. Elmer pointed out the front door. "Trask and some of our guys are still out there. Don't shoot them. Anyone else, you put everything you have into them. You understand me?" The two men shifted to monitor the door. The old man continued down the hallway.

"They're coming in from everywhere," Wade Fischer shouted as Cleary burst into the kitchen. Remembering he dropped his shotgun outside, he crossed the floor and pulled a butcher knife from a drawer.

"How many?"

"Hell if I know. Sounds like a hundred or so. Jesus! What's wrong with them?"

Cleary ground his teeth and ignored the question. He moved back into the hallway and turned toward Evie's room when another large form collided with him, sending him hard into the wall. Pain raged through his right shoulder as the tines of a meat fork sank deep into him. The metal prongs scraped against bone and Cleary's screams rose with the bright blossoms of pain.

Blindly he stabbed and slashed with the knife in his left hand, feeling it sink into the flabby side of the figure. The man convulsed with each impact, grunting with pain. With a violent tear, he stepped back and pulled his fork out of Cleary's arm. His lips curled back in a hateful sneer. "Kill the rot," he growled and raised the fork again. Before he could bring the weapon down, Fischer stepped up, placed his shotgun barrel against his head, and pulled the trigger. The man's skull erupted in a geyser of blood, brains, and bone.

Cleary pulled in a deep, shuddering breath and shook his head to clear the ringing from the blast. Wade, eyes wide with panic, reloaded his weapon. "Go help the others," Elmer said, pointing down the hall. "I'm going to get Evie somewhere safe." Fischer hesitated, fear warring against his loyalty to the boss. "Go!" Cleary said in a final tone. His man vanished down the dark hallway, shouting for the others.

Cleary, his shoulder on fire and his right arm hanging useless, hurried down the hall to Evie's room. A twisted lump in the dark at the far end held his attention, and for a stabbing moment of panic, he thought it was Evie herself until he was able to make out the features of Jesse Walker, the man assigned to guard her door. Elmer stepped over the dead man and threw open the door to the bedroom.

It took him a long, breathless moment to understand what he was seeing. The bed was empty, the sheets thrown back. "Evie?" He darted a look in the closet, then at the far side of the bed.

Evie Marrow was gone. The window was closed, which meant that at some point she'd fled the room. Cleary spat a curse and gripping the blood-soaked knife, hurried back into the hallway.

Two men stood in the corridor, eyes shining in the dim light. They stepped over the headless body of their companion and raised their weapons—an axe and a boning knife. Cleary looked around, the only means of escape for him was back into the room from which he'd just exited.

I'm not running anymore, he thought. He held the knife tightly before him. *Please, God, take care of Evie.*

"Purification!" the men roared. Cleary answered with his own bellow, putting every ounce of his fear and anger and pain into it.

The men charged.

47

Evie set the tray on the floor and leaned against the headboard. Sweat beaded her forehead, drops crawling down her temples from the effort. Despite some of her wounds healing, eating the soup had proved more difficult than she'd been ready for. The soup, which was little more than water that a chicken may have once dipped a toe into, wasn't all bad and had warmed her considerably. But sucking it down past broken and scabbed lips, loose teeth, and the nasty cuts inside her mouth hadn't been easy.

She wished Jack were here. It frustrated her that he left without even mentioning where he was going, which clearly meant he was doing something dangerous. Her fingers twisted the blankets, the folds digging into her. What if he ran into those things he'd seen in the woods? The witches. Images of Jack screaming as his body contorted, bones snapping and skin splitting filled her consciousness, and she choked back a sob. Evie gave her head a firm shake. *What's wrong with you, Evelyn Marrow? He's a capable man. He'd have to be to survive doing what he does in Chicago. Jack will be just fine.*

The real question was: how long would he stick around once the threat of the witches was over? *If we even* can *beat them,* she reminded herself. Of course they could beat them. They had to. What other choice was there? To run? To abandon Jericho Springs and the people in it to a horrible death? The thought of running away was bitter, a jagged pill she wouldn't—couldn't—swallow. No, they would find a way.

But then what? With the land ruined as it was, and assuming it could even recover, which could take years, there was no real reason for Jack to stay. He'd come for Cleary's moonshine and if that stream dried up, he would go back to Chicago. If he were to leave, what would that mean for her? She was falling for him, she knew that much, and she was rather confident he felt the same. But would he stay in Jericho Springs just for her? She was willing to bet the people who employed him would most certainly want him back.

Could she move to Chicago? The thought sent a flutter of fear mingled with excitement through her chest. She'd been in Jericho Springs most of her life and knew a lot of people here, but it had never really felt like home. Especially not since Daddy had died. Now that some measure of justice had been dealt and Carl Stott was dead, there was nothing keeping her in this town. The flower shop was doing okay, but it wasn't going to buy her a penthouse suite anytime soon. And besides, a city like Chicago was big enough for another flower shop.

She managed a smile and thought that yes, she could see herself living in Chicago. Wearing new dresses and finally getting a new pair of shoes and one of those pretty cloche hats with a bow on the back. The thought surprised her a little. Evie had never been much of a person with an eye toward fashion, but the idea of dressing up and going to eat at nice restaurants with white linen tablecloths, taking in a show at the theater, maybe even a movie, caused a wave of excitement. Evie had seen a movie once in Birmingham; her father had taken her to see *Dr. Jekyll and Mr. Hyde* on her thirteenth birthday and it had been one of the greatest things she'd ever experienced. So yes, lots more outings like that would be in her future with Jack by her side in grand old Chicago.

Would she get to meet Al Capone? Jack had told her a little, and from what she'd read in the papers about him and the gang he called the Outfit, it seemed like a once-in-a-lifetime chance to meet the man who some were already starting to call the "King of Organized Crime." This sent another tickle of excitement coursing through her. She imagined them sitting in a fancy dining room, toasting with champagne while the waiters brought out huge steaks slathered in butter and lobsters the size of cats. She would be resplendent in her new dress, a shimmering silver—

The crash of a window shattering broke her from her fantasy with a start. From the hall came the soft shuffle of her guard's boots on the floor and fainter and deeper in the house, muffled shouts and more glass breaking. Evie pushed back the sheets and swung her bare feet out of bed, touching them on the floor before hesitating again.

"Jesse?"

"Miss Marrow, stay in there. Don't come out here, okay?"

"What's going on?"

Jesse didn't answer. Evie pulled herself fully out of bed and padded to the door, leaned close, and placed an ear against the wood. The shouts were louder now. There was the blast of a shotgun, as loud as a train in the confines of the house, and she stepped back reflexively. Like a dam breaking, more shotguns went off, accompanied by the sounds of men screaming.

Strained shouts tore through the halls like lunatic battle cries from damaged throats.

"Purification!"

"Cut out the rot!"

Evie put a hand on the doorknob, her fingers tense and ready to turn it, when it shook with the impact of something slamming against it. Through the wood she could hear a man—*Oh sweet Jesus, is that Jesse?*—babbling, pleading, his voice sliding higher and higher into a scream, the sound gushing out of him like water from a busted hose. Through his cries, she could make out snatches of a prayer before the door shuddered. A crack appeared at eye level, splinters of the wood spearing toward Evie's face.

The tip of a knife winked at her from within the crack, and a stream of red trailed down the wood.

Evie stepped back, eyes fixed on the broken door and the blood. On the other side, she heard the hissing of a body sliding to the floor. From the hallway came the clashing thunder of footsteps as people moved about in the tight space.

She turned from the door, hurried across the room, and peered through a crack in the curtains. The landscape beyond was a milky haze of fog within which she could just make out the hulking shapes of trees and the barns. Evie cupped her hands on either side of her face to cut out the glare from her lamp and searched the yard.

Something flashed by close to the window and she leapt back, unable to stop the frightened gasp that flew out of her throat. The person stepped back into the frame of the window and turned their face toward the glass.

That's Hattie Dean, Evie thought. But there was something wrong with her usual kind, soft features. The woman, despite being only a few years older than Evie herself, was now gaunt and haggard. Her cheeks were sunken, the skin on her face drooping and sallow. Thin jagged streaks of what looked like broken blood vessels extended up her forehead, vanishing into a thicket of dark hair matted with dirt and sweat.

But it was Hattie's eyes that pulled another croak of fear out of Evie. They glowed silver. Evie tried to tell herself it was a reflection, a trick of the light glowing through the window pane, but she knew it wasn't.

She's changing. Just like the land. The thought was absolute, and Evie understood it as a truth, even though she wasn't sure where the thought came from. Hattie was changing, and Evie was willing to bet that so, too, was anyone else with her. On the end of that came one last terrifying idea.

I don't think they're finished changing.

Hattie's lips spread back in a rictus grin, revealing bloody teeth. Her palm, red with blood, slapped solidly against the window. Her fingers curled and with an irritating whining noise, she dragged them along the glass. When they reached the bottom, she slapped the hand back above and began the process over.

Slap, scrape.

Slap, scrape.

Evie let the curtain drop and stepped back, one hand creeping toward her mouth. *I have to get out of this room.* Either Hattie would succeed in breaking the glass, or the people in the hall would realize Evie was in here.

But where to go? Where would she be able to hide? Immediately, she dismissed the barns or anywhere in the fields. Based on the footsteps she'd heard through the door and the presence of the woman at the window continuing to paw at the glass, Evie was confident that she wouldn't make it far. Probably not even out of the house. No, she needed to get a weapon and hide. Somewhere she could—

It came to her. Cleary's root cellar. He'd mentioned it in passing before making the soup, how he kept onions down there. If she could find it,—she assumed it would be somewhere near the kitchen—then she could bar the door and hide. It wasn't great, but it would have to do. She went back to her bedroom door and moving to one side to avoid the splinters and the blood, placed her ear against it. This time she heard nothing except the muffled thumps and crashes of fighting deeper in the house. She had no way of knowing if the person who had killed Jesse was still out there. *Only one way to find out.* She took a deep breath and pulled the door open.

The guard lay in a crumpled heap. His throat was a gaping wound. Red painted his chest and the floor. Evie stopped short, shocked by the amount of blood and the sheer brutality of what had been done to the young man. She dared a look along the hallway, relieved to see it empty. More men screamed beyond the front door. Another shotgun fired.

Evie bit her lip against the throbbing protest of her ankle and limped as quickly as possible, ducking into the hallway that branched off to the kitchen. Along the dark corridor, she saw the even darker shapes of doorways. Moving closer, she found one open, revealing a staircase leading up to the second floor.

As she raised her foot to continue past the steps, a thought occurred to her. Whirling back, she hurried as fast as she could to the previous hall and peered around the corner. It was still empty. She held her breath and limped to Jesse's broken body. Carefully, she stepped over one of the dead man's legs, wincing at the already cooling slick of his blood beneath her bare feet.

"I'm sorry," she whispered as she moved his arm and grasped the discarded shotgun. The gun came out of the puddle of blood with a soft sucking sound. There were two barrels and two triggers offset from one another within the large curve of the trigger guard. She had no idea if it was loaded or how to even check, but the weight and solidity of it made her feel better, more secure.

Gripping the weapon clumsily, she tiptoed back to the hall and the deeper recesses of the house. Outside, the screaming had subsided. Wincing from the flares of pain from her ankle, Evie continued along the corridor until she passed the doorway that gave access to the stairs. Ahead, dim light showed what appeared to have once been a formal dining room and an old, scarred table littered with baskets, metal pails, and various tools.

"Where are you going?"

The voice, full of a playful malice, froze her mid-stride. Turning on bloodied feet, Evie stared into the dark maw of the stairwell. Nothing moved within the shadows. She fumbled with the shotgun, found it was too heavy to lift to her shoulder so she held it tight against her waist and waited, her breath coming in fast spurts.

Movement at the extreme edge of her vision pulled her attention back the way she'd come. Her eyes widened as the slender hulk of a man entered the hallway. "Oh Christ," she heard herself mutter. Evie stared at him, a dark outline against the light of the hall. He held a curved blade in one hand and the straight length of a knife in the other. In the blackness of his shape, two glowing silver eyes focused on her. Evie's own eyes watered as a pulsing wave of foul air reached her.

"You're . . . responsible . . . aren't you? The rot is here . . . can smell it . . . in you. God . . . sent . . . to cut it out." The knife now raised to point at her as the man pushed into the edge of the pool of light thrown by the dining room window. His face looked much like Hattie's had, except framed by long, stringy hair. A thin mustache sat atop his lip, filthy with dirt and blood. "Gonna . . . cut it out . . . of you," he said with a lilting giggle.

"Fuck you," she grunted and pulled the forward trigger.

It refused to move. Evie's heart lurched as she tightened her finger again and again. The trigger stayed locked. The thin man's titter turned into a deeper, more amused laugh. It filled the hall and thundered in her ears. "Shit." Evie Marrow turned and ran. The hallway, the house, the very earth shook with the man's pursuing footsteps. Evie focused on reaching, then skirting the dining table and not tripping on the body of a man slumped in the blood-splattered corner. Most of his neck had been torn away and his head hung obscenely to one side.

There was a banging and a heavy *thud* as her pursuer collided with the table, followed by more thuds as items were jarred from their resting place and crashed to the floor. Evie paid no attention to them, her focus set only on what was immediately before her. She hobbled through another doorway and into the kitchen. Her mind registered the stove, sink, counters, and cabinets, but saw nothing that looked like a root cellar.

Another doorway to her right beckoned and despite not knowing what was on the other side, Evie rushed through it. Pain flared in her hip as she collided with the rounded front of a metal washing station. The man with the thin mustache entered the kitchen, his gore-smeared face inching into the light from the dark of the hallway as if it were rising from black water.

She stepped around the washing machine and felt for another door; her hand flailed up and down, fingers twitching in the air. Her breath burst out of her as soft grunts of impatience and panic teetering on the edge of absolute terror. Behind her came the *thump* of the man's steps as he moved closer, approaching slowly, sensing that his quarry was trapped.

His soft chuckles filled the washroom at the same time that Evie's frantic fingers brushed against a handle set at waist height in the wall. A cry of triumph burst from her mouth and she twisted it and pushed, lunging forward into the darkness. The smell of wet, dank earth, musty and moldy, enveloped her just as she tumbled to the hard dirt floor.

Instantly the man was in the doorway, filling the space as he fought to press himself into the frame. One long arm came in, the curved blade swiping the air only inches in front of Evie's battered and tear-streaked face.

The searching blade dug into the dirt, carving a large furrow in the stonelike ground. The man inched closer, grunting with effort and the need to reach her, to cut open her skin. Evie scuttled backward, her feet slipping over the shotgun. Frantic, she gripped it by the barrel and swung as hard as she could in the small space. The stock connected solidly with the man's hand and his scream of pain was undercut with the sharp *crack* of bones breaking. The sickle dropped to the dirt floor.

Evie swung again. The butt of the gun landed with a meaty *thunk* against her attacker's nose, splitting it like an overripe tomato. Blood streamed down his face as he jerked back, hands flying to his broken nose. In the dim light, Evie noticed a small metal slide in the center of the shotgun's grip. Understanding what it was, she shouldered the weapon and pressed a thumb against the slide. It moved stiffly, emitting a soft *click* as it released. She leaned close and stuck the barrel through the cellar door.

This time when she pulled the trigger, her world erupted into a blinding explosion of light and noise. Fire erupted from the barrel and the left side of the man's head collapsed in on itself like a balloon. He slumped immediately, hanging half in the root cellar.

Evie shifted the angle of the gun and pulled the other trigger. The rest of the man's head vanished in a spray of blood.

Evie threw the shotgun aside and scrambled back until she collided with a wall. She rose carefully, nearly able to stand upright. Keeping one hand on the wall, she moved along it until she reached a broad set of wooden shelves lined with jars. She pushed a couple aside and peered into the larger space of the root cellar. The space was pitch-black save for the faintest trickles of light that seeped through cracks in a door ahead and to the right. The air was thick with the dank smells of earth and dust. She must have accessed the root cellar through some old access panel, or maybe some emergency escape in the event the main door had been blocked by debris after a tornado. That would explain why she was behind a set of shelves rather than in the room proper.

Moving carefully, her ankle screaming at her now, she shuffled sideways to her left, keeping the wall behind her and the shelves in front. When she reached a corner, she carefully squeezed herself around the bend and was starting forward again when the door opened and light flooded the room.

Bodies crowded into the space, thumping their way down a short flight of wooden stairs with labored breaths and soft grunts. Evie crouched, hoping that the shadows cast by the shelves and jars were enough to mask her as the people pressed deeper into the room. The grunts became words, the same ones she'd heard shouted in the halls and from the man she'd killed.

"Find . . . it."

"Dig . . . it . . . up."

"Cut . . . it . . . out."

"We . . . will be . . . saved."

The people shuffled through the room and Evie pressed hard against the earthen walls as several drifted closer to her hiding spot. Just as she thought they were going to see her, they all stopped and stood completely still. Evie's eyes darted from them to the others filling the room. Each and every one stood frozen, bodies bent and twisted in uncomfortable angles. As one unit, they then turned to face the door where new footsteps thudded on the wooden treads.

Evie's mind flared with brilliant, painful bursts of squirming, screaming noise. Images of decaying animals, eyeholes swarming with maggots, fur rippling and expanding only to burst and collapse as rot consumed the meat and bones. Scenes of entire forests withering and dying, but not just dying, being sterilized—the soil infected with corruption so no living thing would flourish there ever again. That same corruption spreading like an ink stain on a map, consuming and growing.

In the span of a heartbeat, the sounds and images were gone. A dry, brittle voice like dead spiders cut through the darkness.

"There she is."

48

Jack rounded the back corner of the house, his options flicking through his mind with shutter-like speed. The pasture lay to his left surrounded by the thin lines of the barbed wire fence. The house itself stood only a few feet to his right. While ahead, draped in shadows from the surrounding trees, was a building that he assumed was a barn or some kind of external garage.

Which one? Footsteps close behind forced a decision and he darted up the back steps of the house, plunging into the blackness of the kitchen. The smell in the home was worse than it had been when he and Cleary first discovered the bodies. Not slowing, Jack slipped through the hall, passing the mangled ruins of the farmer's wife with a quick elongated step, and entered the front sitting room. Slipping around the corner, he put his back to the wall and pulled his pistol.

Muffled voices drifted through the open kitchen door, and silently Jack cursed himself for not having shut it. No sooner had the curse crossed his mind than the sound of boots on the kitchen floor reached him.

The heavy wooden door gave a soft whine of the hinges as it swung the rest of the way open. Jack angled his head so he could just see around the edge of the doorway. Two shapes crossed the threshold and once both were in the wider space of the kitchen, they separated. One approached the opposite end of the short hall and hesitated. A young girl bent and observed the remains of Nadine Bryant with reverent curiosity.

Jack stepped out and brought his pistol up, finger squeezing the trigger twice. The girl jerked violently with the impacts, the spray of her blood a black cloud in the moonlit doorway. She toppled over and lay in a lifeless heap. Her companion grunted in surprise and anger. Instantly his odd frame filled the doorway. Jack fired again, the figure spun away at the same time and the round punched into the cabinets next to the sink.

Before he could get off another shot, the second person crossed the hall with a speed Jack didn't think possible based on how they had moved outside. His finger jerked the trigger involuntarily and the shot went low and wide, slamming into the floor with a hollow *thunk*. The figure, a young blond-haired man in his late teens, uttered a sound like a gurgle and swiped a hand at Jack. The blow connected with his outstretched arm, hitting him just at the wrist and knocking the .45 out of his grasp. The blond boy's other hand came around in a looping arc, fist aimed at his assailant's head. Jack stepped into the blow, letting his shoulder absorb the impact, and drove his own fist up into the younger attacker's throat.

The boy pinwheeled back, both hands flying to his neck. A strained gurgling coming from his mouth. His eyes were wide in shock and pain. For a split second, Jack thought he saw something else in them. Fear? The look gave Jack the impression of a trapped animal who knows it isn't long for this world.

Damn right you're not, he thought as he quickly picked up the .45 and shot the kid in the face. The boy dropped in that strange way people do when they've died instantaneously, like a puppet whose strings had been cut. He landed with his head atop the hip of the girl.

Jack stepped over the bodies and into the kitchen. As soon as he cleared the doorframe, the flooring to his right gave a soft *creak.* As he started to bring the pistol around, pain erupted on the side of his head. Blossoms of light exploded behind his eyes and he dropped to the floor, catching himself on one knee and throwing a hand out for balance. The floor creaked again and he looked up, his vision still cloudy, in time to see the shovel arcing down once more. Despite his dizziness and the blood streaming down the side of his face, Jack dropped his shoulder and rolled toward his assailant. The floor vibrated with the impact of the shovel inches away.

The attacker, a lean man with thinning black hair and buckteeth, gave an angry, gargling cry as Jack crashed into his legs. The stench of his body forced its way down Jack's nose and into his throat like a snake, then twisted. The man's knees buckled and he collapsed to the floor, the shovel slipping from his grasp. Jack pushed back and away, scrambling for distance.

The shovel lay between them, and Buckteeth lunged for it. Just as his fingers curled around the handle, Jack grasped the shovel below the head and gave it a hard yank. It pulled out of the man's clutching fingers and Jack used it to help himself stand. His head swam from the initial blow, the room pitching and yawing, and he spread his legs wide to maintain balance, as if he were on a rocking ship. Buckteeth snarled in frustration and started to pull himself off the floor. He was slow, his movements uncoordinated. He planted a foot and was pushing up when Jack slammed the shovel into the bent knee. The sound of the kneecap snapping was like a dry limb cracking as Buck-teeth's watery howl filled the kitchen. He toppled over, both hands clutching his shattered knee.

Jack blinked the blood out of his left eye. Hefting the shovel, he staggered to the man writhing on the floor. Through his pain, Buck-teeth's silver eyes glared at Jack with a burning hatred. The rest of his face bulged, distortions beneath the skin as if the bones were grow-ing, shifting.

"We . . . cut out . . . kill the rot," Buckteeth growled. "You're . . . destroying . . . everything."

"I ain't doing shit, buddy," Jack said.

The man laughed, a hearty chuckle that came from deep in his chest. "We're going to . . . kill everyone at . . . that farm. We'll . . . save this town . . . everything will be purified. You're—"

Jack slammed the blade of the shovel down, ramming it through the man's mouth and deep into his skull, ending the thought. Teeth broke away, blood splattered the shovel blade and slopped to the floor as Jack leaned on the handle, driving the tip farther. The man bucked, his back arching and slamming onto the floor while his feet kicked spastically, tattooing a dying rhythm on the wood.

Jack turned, found his gun, and went out into the cool night. He started for the vehicle but stopped, wheeled to one side, and vomited in the tall grass against the house. When he was finished, he dragged the back of his hand across his lips and hurried on shaky legs to the truck, his pistol up and ready.

The road was empty. He pulled the door open and stood, breathing heavily, staring at the trees in the direction of Cleary's farm.

We're going to kill everyone at that farm.

Jack cranked the truck and drove through the dark streets, accelerator pressed to the floor.

The cut on his scalp had stopped bleeding, but his vision was still a little shaky by the time Cleary's home came into view. Jack let out a soft puff of disbelief at the sight of the farmhouse. A body was draped over the frame of a shattered window, blood painting the wood below. The door of the porch hung by a single hinge, the screen shredded. Across the lawn lay the dark, tangled shapes of numerous men sprawled where they fell. Four that he could see.

Jack ran across the property, passing the bodies. The first three he didn't recognize; their faces masks of blood broken only by slivers of white bone shining through massive cuts. A shotgun, the breech open, was near one of the men. A scattering of red shells lay in the grass like demented Easter eggs. He leapt over the broken form of Willie Reese, the man staring with his one remaining eye at the pulpy red ruin that had been his mouth and lower jaw.

The interior of the house was silent, as if the very air mourned for what had happened. From deeper inside came the soft, ghostly bumping of a shutter swinging in the night breeze. Two men he didn't know were dead at Jack's feet, both having died from shotgun blasts to the chest. Near their outstretched arms lay knives and a meat cleaver.

Jack bent and picked up a flashlight lying discarded in the center of the room, its cylindrical body smeared with two wide swipes of drying blood. He pressed the brass button and breathed a sigh of relief when a beam speared out. Stepping quickly to the hallway that led to Evie's bedroom, he stopped, his breath trickling out of him in a weak stream.

Halfway along the corridor lay the large form of Elmer Cleary. The farmer was on his stomach, his head turned so that one cheek rested on the hardwood floor. The man's throat was gone. Three knife handles jutted from his back, the weapons pressed so hard against his bloodstained shirt they dimpled the material. A butcher knife, cruor-covered, lay inches from one outstretched hand.

Find Evie.

Another body lay outside her bedroom, a man whose name Jack couldn't remember. Holding his breath, he turned the knob and pushed his way inside, his weapon coming up and sweeping the room.

Nothing. It was empty, the bedsheets thrown back. The rest of the room showed no signs of struggle; nothing was knocked over or broken. Not a single section of wall or item in the room showed any trace of blood, which meant she'd gotten out somehow. He checked the window and found it locked. *Not that way. Deeper into the house, then.*

Wincing at every *creak* of the old flooring, Jack followed the hallway toward the dining room and kitchen. He paused briefly by the stairs. A dead man was sprawled halfway up, his severed hand resting on the tread above him like a pale spider.

Jack stepped carefully around several tools and a metal bucket lying on its side on the floor of the dining room but didn't slow as he passed another corpse, this one nearly headless, in one corner of the room. The kitchen was empty but a large, ragged hole had been blown in the thick wood of the door leading to the backyard. Spent shotgun shells littered the floor and skittered away like roaches when his foot connected with them. Jack lowered his pistol and took a deep breath. She could have gotten out by the door, before or after the hole had been torn into it. Or . . . He turned and looked past the dining table and along the hallway.

Another thought came to him as he moved quickly back along the corridor, through the front room, and around another corner. He passed more bodies. Some were Cleary's men but most were the pale, sickly-looking people he'd seen earlier. Jack stepped over them with barely a glance, making his way to a space near the back of the house where the paneled door to the root cellar hung open. The floor was littered with dirt broken by the small arcs of boot prints. He angled his flashlight into the dark space and dragged it across shelves lined with glass jars full of pickled foods, settling on a large hole in the far left corner of the dirt floor.

"Jack?" Evie's voice was soft, wavering, and threaded with terror and hope. He whirled, eyes searching along with the flashlight. The jars reflected his beam back in painful flares, but he saw nothing else. *Outside,* he thought and started for the door.

"I'm here," she said. The voice came from his left and he turned, saw a hand emerging between two jars of pickled okra.

"What are you— How did—" His mind couldn't focus long enough on a single question. He pushed the jars aside. They smashed against the floor, sending a cloud of vinegar rolling up. Evie's head filled the space created on the shelf. Her eyes normal, and thank Christ for that, peered out at him from a face smeared with dirt and blood. "Are you all right?" he asked.

She nodded, a small, mousy gesture. A lock of her dark hair fell across her face. "I'm okay. They were here."

"I know," he said quickly. "But they're gone now. Looks like Cleary's men got several of them. We need—"

"No," Evie said. This time her voice was stronger. "The witches. They were *here.* In this room." She let go of his hand and pointed. "I don't know how but they were controlling all the people and had them dig that hole. I have no idea what they were looking for."

Jack let out a long breath and approached the hole. On its opposite side, a pair of spades lay half-covered in the excavated dirt. The hole was deep—at least four feet, he guessed. He played the light over it and froze when he saw the twisted coils of black iron chains lying at the bottom.

"It was the bones of the third witch," he said. "The chains are still there. Come on, we can figure this out later. Can you get out the way you came in?"

"No. There's a dead man in the doorway and my ankle is hurting too badly."

"Can you move back a little? That's good." When she was pressed against the wall, Jack stepped to one side and gripped the shelving unit. With a single hard pull, it toppled forward. Jack stepped out of the way just as it slammed past and crashed onto the ground with the sound of jars breaking. Once more, the sharp smell of preserved liquids filled the space. Jack helped Evie across the shelves until he could pull her into his arms. She came quickly, clawing at him, her need overwhelming him. Hot tears brimmed in his own eyes at the thought of what she'd endured, at his own joy that she'd survived. For several long minutes, she just sobbed against him. Occasionally, she would lift a weak hand and slap at his chest, then her fingers would turn to iron and they would grip his shirt tightly, winding themselves in the material.

Jack held her, stroking her hair and speaking softly and calmly to her. When the crying passed, she was able to tell him what had happened. How she'd been in bed and heard the screams, the glass breaking, the gunfire. She told him about taking the shotgun from someone named Jesse and being chased through the house by the — "Jesus, they're people from town. I saw Hattie Dean with them. They were people I knew." She stared at him. "How is that possible?"

He shook his head. "Doesn't matter how."

"Get me out of here?" she asked quietly.

Jack picked her up and carried her out of the root cellar and through the house. Outside, free of the hot, cloying confines of the house, the warm smell of honeysuckle drifted past. She gasped and tucked her head against his shoulder as they passed the dead men in the front yard.

When he had her in the truck, he turned back to the house. "What are you doing?" she asked.

Jack stared at the silent home. "I need to go get the chains. We're going to need them. Besides, Cleary's in there. I can't just leave him."

Evie, small in the passenger seat of the truck, said, "I'll be okay." Something in her voice cut through Jack's concern for the old man.

"No. He's not going anywhere. I need to get you to Doc Powell. I'll come back for the chains. They left them behind, so I don't think they feel they're important. And it's not like we're going to go after them tonight."

They rode into town in silence. Jack drove carefully to minimize bouncing the truck on the uneven roadways and hurting her further. Evie's lips were a tight line as she fought through her pain, grunting only twice when the Ford jarred violently against potholes he couldn't avoid entirely. She slid one hand across the seat and he took it, amazed at how small and fragile her fingers were, like the hollow bones of birds hidden beneath parchment-thin paper. Still, he held her.

Despite the late hour, when Doc Powell saw Evie being helped out of the truck, he hurried to help, with a napkin tucked into the front of his shirt as he chewed slowly on his last bite of dinner.

They got her inside to a guest bedroom. After the doctor retrieved his bag, he cleaned and bandaged her wounds, then took a look at the cut on Jack's head. Through all of it, he listened as Jack told the story of the assault on Elmer Cleary's house. Powell gasped audibly when he learned that Cleary had died protecting Evie and defending his home.

"We have to call the police in on this," Powell said. "Staties even."

"No. No cops. Not yet. I need to get as many of Cleary's men together as I can. Get them out to the house to take care of things. There's a lot of bodies out there."

"I'll go and make sure they get it done. My Susie can watch Evie."

"No," Jack said. "You stay here and take care of her." He stepped closer, looming over the small, portly man. "You're responsible for her safety now. If even a hair falls out of her head, I'm going to take you to task for it. Hear me?"

Powell's cheeks jiggled in agreement. "Now, can you get her something for the pain?" Jack asked. Again the cheeks wobbled. The doctor pulled a bottle of clear liquid and a syringe out of his bag and administered the drug into Evie's arm.

"She'll sleep for a while with this." He packed up his bag. "I'll be in the front room."

Jack sat on the bed, holding Evie's hand.

"What are you planning?" she asked weakly, the drug already slipping its fingers around her.

"I'm going to get those chains. The ones from the cave and the ones down in that cellar. We're going to need them, and sooner than later. I'm going to see that Cleary's body is taken care of. Then I'm—"

"Stay with me. Please. We can do all that tomorrow. When the sun's up." Evie's fingers pulled at him. Jack allowed himself to be pulled down onto the bed and he lay behind Evie. She pressed her small form against him and he draped one arm gently over her. She clutched it with her good hand and held it tightly against her chest. She gave a gentle tug on his arm and for a moment, he thought she was trying to keep him next to her. He realized she was fading under the weight of the drug Powell had given and wanted him close to hear her speak. He leaned forward. She angled her head and whispered to him, "Don't leave me again, Jack Carm—" The drug pulled her all the way down.

He watched her sleeping face, amazed at the beauty despite, or maybe even because of, the wounds and bruises. He'd known a lot of strong women in his life, but never someone as tough as Evelyn Marrow. He craned forward, kissed her softly on the cheek just in front of her ear, and lay his head back on his arm.

He was asleep in seconds.

49

They stood, silent and still as death, and watched as the swarm entered the clearing. The creatures, pathetic in form, wretched in spirit, scuttled in short uneven bursts on limbs that were still forming. The click-clack *of teeth and tattered breathing was the only sound. Even the insects and night beasts had enough sense to flee or bury themselves.*

The swarm filled the clearing, spreading out like a writhing stain across the moonlight-dappled rotting grass. When all gathered—well over a hundred strong despite the losses only hours ago—they froze, silver eyes trained on the large rock at the edge of the space.

The ancient ones watched the gathering. Their minds were a swirling chaos of hate for the miserable things before them, a burning and a painful abhorrence of those that still lived, going about their worthless existence. And beneath all that, a feeling of emptiness ran like a molten river. The hole in their coven was an abscess, agonizing in its existence.

But not for much longer. The seed had been planted in the worm. Soon it would grow, emerge from the pitiful shell, and they would be whole. The coven complete. And when that happened, those still living would experience a wrathful terror beyond their comprehension.

The two studied the gathered, the thralls, and knew with dark malice the blood these malformed creatures would spill in the name of death and corruption. Already, even at this stage of transformation, they had proved their usefulness by killing those who sought to keep Sister's remains hidden.

But they still had more to do, the final metamorphosis yet to endure.

As if sensing that sentiment, one of the worthless things scuttled forward, jerking and lumbering as it pushed its way to where the two ancients stood. Its long, bony fingers clutched a carved box, its wood as black as the ancient ones themselves.

As the thing drew closer, its legs folded, lowering it to the stinking ground. Its head, milky white and already starting to show signs of elongation—the mouth just too wide, the nose flattening—lowered in supplication. It raised the box high, holding it out as if in offering to the black spirits that stood before it.

Moving as one, the ancient things reached across their decaying torsos, talons carving deep. Dead flesh peeled like fruit skin, revealing black meat that writhed with unnatural vitality. Each held up the hunk of putrid meat, black gore dripping. They deposited the flesh into the open box, dragging an elongated finger across the lid and pulling it closed.

The wretched thrall garbled a supplicating word of gratitude and shuffled back several feet before standing. A galvanizing feeling of anticipation swept over the clearing as the swarm watched their brother return with the Host. Their bodies stiffened, their eyes blazing with a need that went beyond mere hunger, beyond a desperate longing, to something primal.

Opening the box, the thrall approached the closest of its kind, an elderly female with thin wisps of white hair still clinging to her piebald head. Her face twitched, a rasping clicking spilling from her throat. She reached into and pulled the Host from the box. At its appearance, the rest of the swarm stared at it, rapt and eager. The Host danced and jiggled like a worm plucked fresh from the soil as the woman held it over her widening mouth. She dropped the piece in, her jaws snapped shut and she chewed, black gore spilling past her closed lips and down her cheeks. Her eyes squeezed shut in rapturous joy. When her throat bobbed as the thing was swallowed, the woman gazed up into the black sky and let out a shuddering cry of pure ecstasy. Just beneath her collarbone, the skin rippled as if something crawled; something wriggling fast beneath her skin, like a worm making a nest.

The thrall holding the box moved to the next person, and the process was repeated. As each took their turn with the fetid Host, the ancient ones sensed the oncoming changes, the further destruction of old forms and the excruciating formation of the new. In the blackness of the night, they smiled in wicked anticipation.

Soon, the swarm would be ready. Soon, Sister would rise.

And the world would scream.

50

Grace had always lived under the certainty that hell was a real place. Ever since she was old enough to understand the things her parents said to her, she'd been told that hell was real and was exactly where she would end up if she strayed from the path. Pastor Solomon, the clergyman who had preceded Pastor Sam, spent every Sunday extolling the fiery realities of what he called "the Pit." During one particularly enthusiastic sermon, he'd laid out the types of suffering souls and the demons who would gleefully torment said souls. In every sermon, Solomon had described hell as a hot, dry, barren place, full of choking dust and insufferable heat.

Grace knew with absolute certainty that the old pastor had been wrong. Hell wasn't hot and dry, full of winged devils jabbing at you with wicked blades.

No. Hell was wet. Hell was a murky, muddy swamp where things crawled and slithered over the parts of you submerged beneath the brackish sludge. Hell was diseased trees and dead grass, rotting and oozing moss, the stench of a million corpses, bloated and rotting. That was hell, and Grace was in it.

She flinched as something unseen slid past her calf. The putrid water rippled, the tiny islands of moss shifting with the disturbance.

Grace gripped the rusted bars of the cell and pulled, struggling to lift herself out of the morass that filled the bottom third of the cell. Her arms shook with the effort and she drew her legs up, bringing her knees clear of the water, but within seconds her strength failed her and she slipped back. Her feet sank into the mud and she tried not to think about the things down there crawling over her toes.

Grace awoke to find herself in the cell, water up to her chest, and struggling to remember how she'd gotten there. She could remember looking for Charlie, could recall her parents finding her and saving her from the bobcat, but after that, everything was a blur. The cell consisted of a barred metal door set into three walls of stones packed tightly together and extending only a couple of feet above the marsh. The trees and landscape were a tableau of death and decay. Black trunks sprouted dead and oozing limbs. Large patches of moss hung from the trees, dripping a yellow ooze that plinked into the water swirling with strange colors atop the swamp. Any grasses or weeds that extended above the waterline were equally rotted and drooping. She'd screamed for a while, the words going nowhere, her voice swallowed hungrily by the swamp.

Not for the first time, she wondered where she was, and like all the previous attempts, came up with no answers. Despite spending a lot of her life playing and exploring in the woods, Grace had never encountered a swamp or the remains of buildings. Perhaps she was in the old settlement of Providence? That was the only thing that made sense. Charlie had often talked about finding it, insisting that there would be buried treasure somewhere amid the remains of the town, but since she'd never been, she couldn't say. Whatever this place might be, she was clearly being held in what had once been a jail. The trees grew close together overhead, filtering the sunlight and casting the land in a perpetual early twilight. Across from the remnants of the jail, dark shapes of other ancient buildings bulged out of the muddy ground. Some appeared to still maintain walls and roofs, while others collapsed long ago under the weight of time.

The woods echoed with the sudden cry of a bird, a sharp rising call that Grace had never heard before. It sounded three more times, distant and hollow. She clutched the bars and shivered. She was cold, yes, but there was something terrible about that bird's song. It sounded like the creature knew it didn't belong in this world. It was a sound of fear, of desperation, a terrified need for the solace of others of its kind.

Grace rested her head against the bars and cried. When the tears dried, she sloshed to the rear corner of the cell and sank down, grimacing at the feeling of the thick water sliding along her body, of the sensation of her rump settling into the mud. Leaning her head against the slick, moss-covered rocks, Grace forced her thoughts beyond this place, this literal hell on earth. Surprised, she found them settling on Pastor Sam. What was he doing at that moment? Most likely he was preparing for another of his more frequent new worship sessions—the ones her parents had begun attending weeks ago. Before they withdrew from neighbors and friends. Before they changed. She hated to admit it, but sitting here in a cell in the middle of a swamp, she had to face the hard truth: her parents and others had begun to change. And not just in their personalities, but physically. She'd noticed the way her parents had started to stoop, their bodies bending to one side or the other; their skin had turned milky and waxen; their cheeks sinking in and eyes darkening, as if a poison was consuming them from inside.

Was it an illness sweeping through the congregation? If so, what about Sam? When she'd encountered him the other day he'd seemed tired, exhausted, and a little pale, but otherwise he appeared as tall and stout as he'd always been. So why wasn't he affected?

A deep, guttural growling broke the questions apart and snapped Grace's attention back to the present. From the other side of the wall came the sounds of something large moving slowly through the swamp. The thing's breathing was heavy and labored as it sniffed about, searching. *It's looking for me,* she thought.

Grace sat completely still, afraid to even breathe lest the creature hear her. Was it a bear? No, couldn't be. She didn't think there were bears in Alabama. The breathing downshifted into a bubbling moaning within which she could hear the animal's hunger. Grace shrank back, pressing her back against the stones as the creature moved along the wall. *Oh Jesus, it's just on the other side of me. It's right there.* Her eyes tracked along, following the animal's movements as it turned the corner and crept closer to the edge of the cell door.

A piercing, hissing shriek exploded out of the swampy forest, bouncing among the trees. Grace squeezed her eyes closed and tried to concentrate on stopping the tremors that reverberated throughout her body. As the scream died away, the creature on the other side of the wall gave a long, coughing grunt. Water slapped against the cell wall as it moved quickly away.

She kept her eyes closed, listening to the fading cacophony of the thing's movement until she couldn't hear it any longer. She drew in a long, slow, shuddering breath, which came out in a hot rush when she opened her eyes.

A few feet away stood a man in filthy clothes, his dark hair muddy and matted, posture bent forward, hands dangling by his knees. A large hump crested between his shoulder blades, forcing his stained shirt into a perverse parody of a mountain. His bearded face was streaked with dried blood.

That's Andrew Merritt. So the others in the new congregation have *changed.*

Another equally filthy man sloshed around the low stone wall and stood next to his companion. This second man, bald with a scar along his jawline, was Clarence Pearson, who owned the gas station on the south end of town. Normally reasonably well-groomed, both men now looked as if they'd spent months living in the swamp.

Clarence grunted something to Andrew that Grace couldn't make out. The bearded man waded toward the cell. He reached up and his hand came down with a rusted key that he slipped into the lock. A wet, sinking feeling slid through Grace as she realized the literal key to her freedom had been just out of reach the entire time. Then Andrew was swinging the door open, its hinges screaming at the motion. A bony, gnarled hand reached in. Fingers like rail spikes gripped her by the hair. Fire raced across her scalp as the man pulled, forcing her out of the water. Grace shouted, her hands slapping ineffectually at his as she was pulled free of the cage.

Andrew held her upright, his fingers twisting her hair as if the strands had been caught in a winding gear. His eyes ran along her face, studying her. Grace's stomach lurched as the man's breath washed across her—an oily stench of rotting food and another smell that brought to mind her grandfather's outhouse on a hot August day. His beard was matted with mud and twigs, but Grace also caught glimpses of movement within the curly hairs as small bugs crawled about. The hair on his head had been pulled out in patches, the scabbed places proving to be the origins of the blood that lined his face and neck.

Andrew guided Grace and with Clarence following, walked her through the ruins and deeper into the swamp. She struggled to keep up, her feet snagging on unseen stones or roots beneath the stinking water. Andrew never released his grip on her hair, content to drag her if she couldn't remain upright.

They passed buildings that had most likely been homes and were in better shape than the jail she'd recently occupied. Grace barely noticed them, however, as she continued to flail at the burning pain in her head. Finally, Andrew released her and she collapsed, her hands sinking to the wrists in the muck. She raised her fingers to gingerly touch her scalp. It was hard to tell, but she thought there wasn't any hair missing.

"Go," Clarence grunted from behind her. Grace glanced back and saw that he was pointing. When she saw where he wanted her to go, Grace leapt back, splashing in the water.

"No," she gasped. "God, please." She scrabbled back through the muddy swamp until her back collided with Clarence's legs.

The building was, or had been at one time, a church. It still maintained most of its walls, the wood structures extending up from a rough stone foundation. The land around it was dry, the water coming to an end about fifteen yards short of the church itself, as if the swamp was afraid of getting any closer.

The church rose out of the muddy ground like a leprous corpse.

Its wooden facade was covered in large open sores that oozed yellow liquid. Blind insects, worms, and the small white shapes of maggots crawled at the edges of the discharge and around the cracks in the wood. Symbols of strange angles and curves hung from broken slats of wood, and Grace realized with dawning horror that they were formed out of entrails. More viscera was scattered about the ground, draped over the glassless window sills, piled haphazardly next to the large arched open doorway.

Two figures mounted onto poles flanked the door to the church, affixed in a crude parody of the crucifixion. Their mouths hung open, their chins coated in a slick of black slime. Empty eye sockets stared out at the landscape as if searching for some meaning to assign to their fates. The abdomen of each corpse was hollowed out and there were other things packed inside—the rotting bodies of small animals all piled together.

A rough hand shoved her and she pinwheeled as she fought to remain upright. The hand pushed again and again, driving her to the yawning mouth of the door. Grace's feet squished on the viscera that covered the small porch and she pressed back, recoiling from both the feeling of the organs beneath her toes and the smell that drifted from within the church. Andrew and Clarence stood close behind, an unbreachable wall blocking her retreat. "Go," Andrew ordered and gave her another violent shove.

Grace entered the church.

The inside of the ancient building was lit by a few candles positioned on small ledges or on piles of broken and rotting furniture. The walls, Grace had no way of knowing what color they'd been at one time, were covered in symbols painted in blood. More symbols, these crudely fashioned from the torn bodies of rabbits and foxes, hung throughout the space. Her feet crossed a floor covered in dirt squirming with countless worms and centipedes. The things wriggled over and around her feet, searching. With a lurch, Grace bent and gagged.

She dragged a hand across her mouth and looked over at the altar. When she understood what she was seeing, Grace screamed.

She continued screaming, her throat shredding, and the world around her dimmed as her mind rushed to shut down. Hands gripped her by the arms, powerful and unyielding, propelling her along the aisle and toward the altar. Toward the perversion made of human bodies, their bones shattered and twisted, flesh ripped and broken. Blood-streaked faces stared out, mouths gaping in silent screams.

The men lifted her and placed her on the altar. Grace's screams pitched higher as the knobby bones of a spine pressed against her own back. She kicked and thrashed in an attempt to dislodge herself but one of the men repositioned to hold her legs.

As he gained a grip on her ankles, the air in the room changed, swelled, the pressure of it threatening to burst Grace's ears. She continued to fight her captors, but found her attention drawn to a corner where the shadows thrown by the paltry light gathered the thickest. Something moved within those shadows, darker shapes within the inky black.

Like smoke seeping through a crack, the darkness filled the shadowy alcove. It plumed and shifted, settling into the shapes of two people. The figures approached the altar and Grace's mind wheeled, spinning and threatening to snap under the reality in which she found herself.

The abominations stood over her, skin blackened and blistered from burns. Lightning-shaped cracks zagged across their bodies, showing the deep red of their own muscles. Silver eyes stirred in the burned horrors of their faces as they studied her. Grace struggled but the two men held firm, not allowing her even a fraction of an inch. Her screams had withered to pitiful whimpers as she watched one of the creatures place a bundle of rotting burlap cloth on her stomach.

The church filled with a rhythmic hissing, the whispering sound falling into the cadence of chanting. The words were nothing Grace had ever heard before—guttural syllables and growling pronunciations that were painful to hear, each one stabbing into her mind like a branding iron.

One of the witches raised a hand, then elongated fingers hooked over Grace's flesh. One claw extended and lowered until it touched the smooth skin of her upper thigh. It jerked and traced a cold line of pain across her leg. Grace whimpered at the sudden flare of agony. But when the witch plucked something from the burlap bundle, holding the pale, jagged fragment of bone up as if to inspect it, Grace's whimpers shifted into a higher gear. When the witch positioned the bone against the cut in the girl's leg, hesitating as if to savor the moment, Grace mumbled, "No," over and over.

When the bone was pushed into her flesh, Grace screeched, and blackness swallowed her mind.

She became aware of her surroundings and stumbled over her own feet. She collided with the rough bark of a pine tree and remained there, breathing heavily, her hair in wet clumps across her face. She stood alone in the woods. The swampy hell she'd been in—or thought she'd been in, she honestly couldn't tell at the moment if that had been real—was nowhere to be seen.

Her dress hung in torn strips, barely covering her nakedness. Remembering the cuts, the flash of black claws against her skin, Grace extended trembling fingers to the first spot high on her thigh. Instead of an open bleeding wound, she found a raised angry welt. The skin was tender and red, but no more so than a bad insect bite. There were several more of these marks along her body—across her other leg, her arms, her abdomen, and breasts.

Grace drew the remains of her dress closed, covering herself as best she could, then began walking. She didn't know where she was going, only that her only option was to continue moving. Eventually, the trees thinned and through them, she could see the expanse of grass leading to a wooden building painted white.

At the sight of the church, images of bloody symbols and an altar made of violated human bodies flashed through her mind as bright as a lightning bolt in a midnight storm. Grace staggered back, turning from the sight of the building. Her feet carried her a few more yards deeper into the woods before rational thought forced its way through her fear.

That church belonged to Pastor Sam. Grace looked at the structure through the swaying tree branches and breathed a sigh that was followed by a bubbling sob. The church was whole, clean, and unspoiled. Grace staggered through the brush, her tears burning across her cheeks as she entered the open meadow.

On the small steps to the porch of the parsonage, Grace's legs started to give out, but she extended a hand and gripped the small wooden railing. Her other hand slapped at the door, her head bowed in exhaustion.

She barely noticed when the entrance swung inward. She didn't hear Pastor Sam's voice saying her name, didn't see the shocked, confused look on his face. Legs that had been quivering with exhaustion to that point finally gave out, and Grace fell into the arms of Pastor Sam McCauley.

51

"Think there's much left?" Doc Powell asked as he placed his mug of coffee on the porch railing.

"The house was still standing when I found Evie."

Powell shook his head, the midmorning sun reflecting in a wavering square on his bald head. "Not what I meant. I'm talking about Cleary's guys. His operation."

Jack stared at the black liquid in his own mug, a chipped sky blue ceramic thing that looked like it had been old when the Civil War ended. He considered the question, thought about the bodies he'd seen around the property.

"I honestly don't know." He sighed. "I have no idea how many of his guys were there last night, and to be honest, I didn't bother checking all the corpses because I was a bit too focused on her." He angled his head toward the house, where Evie still slept. "But there were a lot of bodies."

Powell shook his head in disbelief. "And you're saying people from town did this? It just don't seem right."

"There's a lot of what's going on that isn't right," Jack responded and sipped his coffee. "But the people I saw last night, the ones that attacked me ..." He let the sentence trail off. A cool drift of wind passed across his face, brief and soothing. Birds chirped their early summer songs in the boughs of the trees that dotted Powell's property. The sun bathed everything in warm, comforting light. It was a strange sensation, the fact that the world could just continue along normally after something so horrible happened. As though life was able to compartmentalize the violence and shut it away, lock it in the back of a closet, and leave it to be forgotten.

It was a sensation that, despite his familiarity with it, was still disorienting. Even after all this time, all the violence: the threats, the beatings, the hits, even those moments in that basement with the McCarthys and Jacob Turski. After each act was done, as the blood thickened as it cooled, Jack would pass hundreds of people going about their business: men in suits walking hurriedly on their way from one business meeting to another, women in dark skirts and fashionable hats pushing carriages or clutching their pocketbooks protectively as they passed along the shop fronts. When he was younger and just getting started in the world of violence, Jack had gawked at them, unable to believe that nothing in their world had changed when only a few blocks away someone was screaming over a broken knee, or putting ice to a busted lip, or men lay in a lake of blood, their bodies hacked into pieces. The people on the streets knew nothing about it, their worlds completely unaffected. Their biggest worry was not getting a promotion or burning the roast for dinner.

"Tell me about them," the doctor prompted, popping the bubble of remembrance that had surrounded Jack.

"I thought I did already."

"Tell me again," Powell said with a gentle smile.

So Jack did.

When he finished, Powell leaned back in his wicker chair and stared at his lap. Jack let the moment linger, not sure what to say. Honestly, what else could be said? People were changing, physically, and had attacked the home of Elmer Cleary, killing him and most of his men. Which brought Jack back to Powell's initial question: with

Cleary dead, along with most of his men, what would happen to the operation? And how would he explain that to Al?

"Jack?" Evie's voice drifted through the screen door. He placed his coffee on the railing next to the doctor's and hurried inside, taking care not to let the door slam behind him.

She stood in the doorway to the bedroom they'd shared, her hair lumpy and matted from sleep. Her face, still bruised and swollen in areas, looked like she'd not slept in over a week. She turned her tired eyes to him as he crossed the living room, reaching for her.

"I'm here," he said, slipping a hand around her waist and taking her good hand in his other. "Do you need anything?"

She shook her head. "No, I'm okay. I just woke up and you weren't there. I got . . ."

"I was on the porch with the doc. Do you want to go out there, get some air?"

Evie gave a snort. "God no. Looking like this? I can't risk him falling for me too." She chuckled weakly at her own joke. "Take me back to bed." Jack carefully escorted her to the room and helped her sit on the edge of the mattress.

When he was settled next to her, she twisted slightly to face him better. The exhaustion was still in her eyes, but it had diminished slightly, replaced with a steely resolve. "What do we do now?" she asked.

"'We'?" Jack asked. "*We* are doing nothing. You are going to stay here and get some rest and—"

Evie cut him off by gripping his hand and giving it a hard squeeze. The iron in her grip choked off the flow of words. "If you think after what I've been through, with Dunn and last night, that I'm going to play the role of gentle, helpless female and stay here while you go off and fight—"

"No," Jack interrupted. "It's nothing like that. Do you honestly think I'd call you a gentle, helpless female? No thanks, lady, I like my nose and balls where they are." Evie's lips twitched in a half smile. "But you *are* still hurt." He looked pointedly at her bandaged hand.

She stared at him for a long moment and he could see her

warring against herself over the desire to argue, to insist that she could do whatever was needed, go wherever she needed to go. But he remembered as well as she did the struggles she had moving through the woods just before they found the cave. She was getting better, but if things started to happen, she would be a liability.

"Fine," she said, the word a sharp jab. "What are you doing?"

"The first thing I have to do is get back to the farm and see what's left. Who's left, I mean. I need to—" Jack blinked, inwardly surprised at the tightness in his throat as he considered the rest of the sentence. "I have to take care of Cleary."

Evie stilled, her face a cracked, porcelain mask. "So you have to see how the operation is going to continue, is that it?"

"What? No. Well, yes, partially. I do have people I report to—people who aren't down here, don't know, and sure as hell won't understand what's actually going on. If I call Chicago and say that the operation is done for and it's because of ancient witches, they're going to send a team down here. And it's not going to be to help kill those old bitches. It's going to be to put two in the back of my head on their way out to set up a new still. So yeah, I do have to check on who's left and determine how operations can move forward. But that's not the important thing. I have to find out who's left so I can take them with me to go kill those things."

"You're going to go after the witches?"

"Eventually. But I'm talking about those bastards who attacked the farm and nearly killed you. Those things under their control."

Evie was quiet for a long moment. "I'll go with you. To the farm. I want to, at the very least, see Mr. Cleary taken care of." Before he could protest, she said, "I'm not going to be talked out of this. I'm going with you, either sitting in the truck next to you or in one that I steal. Understood?" Jack swallowed back his concern and irritation at her stubbornness. It had been a long time since he'd been around a woman who still had fight in her. Who hadn't just given up and crawled inside a needle.

"All right," he said. "But you're coming back here afterwards. No arguments."

She held up her good hand in mock surrender. "Promise. Now help me get dressed. And don't let me catch you staring at my ass for too long, Jack Carmelo Chicago. We don't have time for that kind of hanky-panky."

"No promises," he said, then chuckled as she playfully slapped at his arm.

When Evie was dressed, an act that took a bit longer than it should have due to her injuries and the fact that the two of them took a break for a long kiss, Jack helped her out to the porch, where the doctor was still in his chair staring out across the yard.

"Blight's moving in," Powell said. A patch of grass, which that morning had been fine, was now black and oily. The doctor stood, offering his chair. When Evie waved him off, he approached her and gently touched the wounds on her face, inspecting them. "You're healing well, all things considered."

"We're going to ride out to the farm," Jack said.

The doctor turned from Evie. "Let me get my hat."

Powell followed them out to Cleary's property, where they found several men moving about under the shouted direction of Randall Trask. He stood on the bottom stair of the porch, one of his suspenders over his shoulder, the other dangling next to his thigh like a dead snake, his hair jutting at wild angles as he pointed at a cluster of three men struggling to carry a body. He threw the new arrivals a dark look and returned his attention to the men.

"Hurry up!"

"It's fucking heavy!" one of the men shouted back.

"My foot in your ass is going to be heavier!" Trask countered as Jack approached.

"You okay?" Jack asked.

"Getting by," Cleary's right-hand man answered, not taking his eyes off the trio as they moved around the corner of the barn. When they were out of sight, Trask finally looked at Jack. "What are you doing here?" His eyes drifted to Evie, who was just getting out of the truck. "And you should be in bed."

"Mr. Trask," she said as she limped past the front of the truck, "it is not too early in the day for me to slap the stupid off you if you talk to me like that again."

Trask's eyes widened and for a moment, Jack thought the man was going to continue the argument. But he simply grunted and looked back out over the blighted ground. "We've gathered all the bodies of those sons of bitches who attacked us. They're in a pile other side of the barn."

"What are you going to do with them?" Powell asked, then jabbed his glasses higher on his nose.

"Burn 'em. Something's wrong with them. Fire's the only way to cleanse them. Besides, after what they did, they don't deserve burial."

"I'd like to take a look at them first, if you don't mind," Powell said. Trask's jaw worked for a moment as he considered the request. He jerked his head in the direction of the barn. The doctor hurried off, pulling a handkerchief from a back pocket as he went.

"Y'all want something to drink?" Trask asked, watching the doctor stump across the yard, swerving to avoid the patches of rotting earth. Without waiting for an answer, he turned and disappeared into the house.

Jack helped Evie up the stairs and together they went inside. She hesitated in the front room, her eyes fixed on the dark patches of the hallway floor where Cleary and the man assigned to guard her had died.

Jack put a gentle hand on her lower back. "Come on." They continued to the kitchen where they found Trask standing against the sink, a glass in his hand.

"All we got is water," he said. "I ain't made coffee yet, so if you want that, it'll be a while."

"Water's fine," Evie said as she sat at the small table. Jack filled a glass and placed it in front of her.

"How many are left?" he asked Trask.

Randall raised his glass to drink, then spoke, "There were about fifteen of us here last night. There's six left of that. I got five here now. I sent Bucky Gentry to fetch the others. Well,"—he shrugged—"the white ones anyway." He set his glass down. "The coloreds won't do shit, not unless we pay them."

"But their people were attacked, too," Evie said. "Maybe not last night, but at the still sites."

Trask grunted. "None of those attacks were by those deformed sons of bitches out there in that burn pile. And no disrespect, Miss Marrow, but I've worked with those people a lot more than you have. They're superstitious to a fault. It was only because we were paying them so well that they even stayed on working the stills. This"—he pointed in the direction of the barn—"falls outside their circle of 'giving a shit.'" He returned his attention to Jack. "So, assuming Bucky doesn't get distracted by a bottle, he should be able to get about twenty more guys."

"What then?" Jack asked.

Trask stared at him for a long moment. "Well, we ain't gonna fire up the stills just yet, if that's what you're asking."

"It's not."

"Good. I figured once they get here this afternoon, we're going to go find these people . . . things . . . whatever you want to call them, and fill them full of buckshot."

"You know where to even start looking?" Jack asked.

"Recognized a lot of them last night. I figured we'd split up into teams and start visiting houses, kicking in doors."

"And what? Shoot them right there?" Evie asked. There was a note of disgust in her voice that surprised Jack. After all she'd been through, as close to death as she'd come, part of her was disgusted at the thought of retribution.

"Yes," Trask said flatly. "Unless you'd rather we brought them back here so you could watch."

Evie shifted her attention to Jack. "What about the witches?"

Trask glanced at Jack. "You're on board with that now, huh? Funny how times change." Back to Evie he asked, "What about them?"

"We have the chains the witches were bound and buried in. Why not go directly for them? End this once and for all? We don't know what they're going to do with those bones. Well, I suppose we do. Or at least I think I have an idea. I gave it a lot of thought last night and this morning. I think they're going to use them to bring the third witch back to life. There's no telling what will happen once that's done."

God help us if they are ever made whole again. The quote from Cleary's Bible floated in Jack's mind like a dead fish.

"They're going to get what's coming to them," Trask spat. "Don't you worry. But those people killed my guys. They killed Cleary. They almost killed you, in case you forgot."

"I remember," Evie said. "I don't think I'll ever be able to forget. But what I'm trying to say is that these people are still people. They're human. They're our friends and neighbors. I don't think they were acting on their own. I think they were forced, under a spell."

Trask scoffed. "They seemed pretty eager to me."

"They're also transforming," Jack said. "You had to have noticed. Their eyes? There's other things wrong with them too. Growths and the like."

Evie let out a long breath. "That's my point. I think the witches are doing that to them. I think that if we kill the witches, use the chains on them and burn them, that will break the spell and all those people will be freed."

"No," Trask snapped. "Those people killed Cleary." He pointed at Jack and Evie. "You want to go after the witches, you go right ahead. Me and the rest are going after the ones that did the killing." He stomped toward the door. "You can come with us if you want. But we're leaving as soon as Bucky gets back with the others." Then he was gone, heavy footsteps retreating down the hall. The slamming of the screen door punctuated his departure from the house.

Evie slumped back in her chair. "He's going to slaughter those people."

"Payback is hard to ignore," Jack said. "I'm surprised that you're not on board with the idea."

"If they're truly beyond redemption, sure. But I can't help but think that they're just puppets in all this." She met Jack's eyes. "Are you going with them?"

"I am. After that spot of trouble I had with those three last night, I'm not fully convinced they're acting under the command of those creatures. As far as I could see, the witches weren't anywhere near when those three attacked me. And I won't lie to you. After Cleary, I want to even the scales a little myself. So I'm going to go with them to see. If it looks like these people are helpless, being controlled, I'll do everything I can to stop Trask from hurting them. But considering how they've changed. The deformities . . ." He shook his head.

"What?"

"They're probably better off dead."

52

The drive across town to the first house, a small single-story home with a wide front porch on Denfield Street, took longer than Jack could have imagined. The convoy of trucks struggled to find a clear path through town. Large sections of roads, especially Heart Avenue, the main thoroughfare that bisected the town, had finally succumbed to the encroaching overgrowth that burst from beneath the tar. One of the trucks was lost when its front tires sank into a wide patch of softened earth hidden by a thicket of oozing, black grass. Trask had screamed every curse word in the book as the men struggled to free the vehicle. Eventually, they had to abandon it, and the remaining truck, now laden with more bodies, detoured with agonizing slowness. The sun was sliding behind the hills by the time they parked in front of a row of houses.

"Whose house is this?" Jack asked as they got out of the truck and picked their way around a pool of foul-smelling ground.

"Eddie Cosgrove," Trask said, his eyes locked on the shadowy facade of the house. Stone columns flanked the three steps to the porch. A pitched roof threw the small deck into complete darkness. He pointed at the dark shapes of two houses on the right, each separated by a wide swath of lawn. "Dick and Lucille Grimes. That last one is Peter Junkins."

"And you know he was with them? Those others too?"

"Cosgrove? Yeah. Saw him with my own eyes. Took a shot at the bastard but missed."

The stench of rotting vegetation rolled along the street and a few of the men cursed. Trask glanced over. "You four come with us. We'll start with Cosgrove." He pointed at the others. "Stay out here. Keep an eye out in case any of their friends show up, or if we get into a scrape and need reinforcements." The three men looked irritated at the assignment but nodded, hands flexing on shotguns and rifles.

"Let's go," Trask said and started across the yard.

Their footsteps thumped like hollow drumbeats as the group mounted the porch. Jack pulled his .45 and stood back while Trask tested the doorknob. It turned and he shoved the door inward before stepping back quickly. The other men raised their weapons, bracing themselves in case Eddie Cosgrove came exploding out of the darkness, eyes shining and teeth bared.

After a few seconds of nothing, Trask slipped inside. Jack stepped into the gloom of the front room and winced at the reek of rot mingled with the faint tang of body odor. The house held a disquieting silence. The rasp of matches being lit broke the quiet. Small bursts of light popped, then caught and became steady flames as men ignited oil lamps.

The living room was sparse, clearly a space used by a single man. A radio stood against one wall, a thick chair with torn blue fabric exposing yellowed stuffing next to it. A single table flanked the chair, supporting an ashtray overflowing with crushed white butts.

"There," Trask said, pointing at the black mouth of an open doorway.

Bucky Gentry, a short man with a freckled face that made him look no older than twelve, raised his lamp. "Hallway." In the wavering ochre glow from several lanterns, the walls of the corridor shimmered.

"Be careful of the walls," one of the others said, eyeing the patina of sludge. The stuff seeped from baseball-sized sores all along the wood. Jack passed carefully, disturbed by the manifestation of sores on inorganic material. Had he not witnessed it in other places around town, he'd be dumbstruck. Instead, he forced his attention on the rooms that branched off the hall, giving each one a lingering look to ensure nobody hid in ambush.

The corridor ended at another door and this time the men in front didn't hesitate. The door swung open quickly and the group surged forward, eager to find their quarry and put paid to the account that they'd come to collect. But the bedroom was empty. A closet door stood in the corner. Near it was a scratched and chipped four-drawer dresser missing several handles. The small bed sat along one wall, the covers smooth and undisturbed. One of the men got down on his knees and peered beneath the bed, only to climb back up, shaking his head.

"He's not here," Jack said. "Come on. The others may be—"

"Holy shit!" The exclamation was a shaky gasp that drew the attention of everyone in the room. Bucky stared into the closet, his lantern held high. Trask pushed others aside and peered over the man's shoulder.

"Jack," he said with harsh finality.

The closet held only a couple of shirts and a single pair of pants, the items dangling from a thin rod on even thinner metal hangers. But it was the floor of the closet that held the main attraction.

Eddie Cosgrove lay naked in the darkness of his bedroom closet, his back facing the open door. The man's legs were drawn up in a fetal position. His wide back was the color of spoiled milk and streaked through with jagged, black veins. Lumps—*Those aren't lumps, those are bones!*—pressed against his flesh, tenting the skin in disturbing angles. To Jack, it looked as if the man's spine had expanded, the vertebrae enlarging like the spikes of that dinosaur he'd learned about as a child. He couldn't think of the creature's name.

As he stared, something shifted beneath the skin with a wet squelching sound.

"What the fuck is wrong with him?" Bucky asked.

"Eddie," Trask said. He pitched his voice so as to break through the man's slumber, but there was a fearful, wavering note to it. Still, the large man didn't stir. Trask reached forward with the barrel of his shotgun and poked the pasty skin beneath one shoulder. The skin dimpled and remained indented when the barrel was removed.

"Someone turn him over," Trask said, backing away. Nobody moved.

"Fuck's sake," Jack growled and bent to tug one flabby arm. The skin was thick and cold, yielding like a bag of pudding. Eddie Cosgrove flopped onto his back like a sack of rice. His bloated gut extended like a diseased balloon. A chorus of disgusted grunts rose behind Jack as those gathered took in the man's face. His lips were gone, the ragged flaps exposing Cosgrove's teeth in a demented grin. Black blood caked his chin and cheeks and dribbled from his nose. Sores dotted his skin.

"Look at his hand," Trask said. It took Jack a moment to understand what Randall wanted him to see. The fingers of Eddie Cosgrove's left hand were fused together, their tips black where they met in a point.

"Still think there's hope for them?" Trask grunted.

Jack shook his head. "I never really thought there was. But Evie .. ." he trailed off, his gaze wandering along Eddie's body to his face. His eyes, shining silver despite the lantern light, were wide and staring at the ceiling. "Is he dead?" Jack asked.

"He's breathing," Trask said. "Chest is moving." He leaned forward, placed the barrel of the shotgun against Eddie's temple. "Wake up, asshole!" Seconds ticked by and Eddie gave no indication that he'd heard the command. "Fuck it. This is for Elmer, you fat cocksucker," Trask grunted and pulled the trigger. The gunshot was so loud it consumed the world and for several moments after, Jack's ears rang. Eddie's head exploded, black blood and a pale oatmeal-like substance slopping against the wall.

Trask spat on the corpse, muttered something Jack couldn't make out through the ringing of his ears, and turned to leave. Jack pitched one final glance at the body and took a moment to wonder if the others, those like Eddie, had felt it when he died. Were they aware one of their own had just been murdered? He shook off the thought and followed Trask and the others outside.

The three men who had been left as reinforcements stood a few feet away on the grass, their faces sculpted into nervous expressions.

"What is it?" Jack asked.

"Guess y'all found him," one of the men said.

"We did. You boys go check Peter Junkins. We'll take care of Dick and Lucille."

Like Cosgrove's, the Grimes family's front door was unlocked, and the group slipped quickly and quietly inside. Bucky's lantern sent crazy shadows leaping from the furniture in the main room. Jack winced at the bitter smell of the home and stared into the dark corners where the light didn't reach.

Trask led the way through the house until they reached the bedroom. The door was partially open, the room beyond shrouded in darkness. Jack took the lantern and motioned for Bucky to hang back. Jack gripped his .45, gave Randall a nod, and followed him inside.

The bedroom was empty, save for a couple of shabby dressers and a bed crammed into a corner, sheets rumpled and thrown aside as if the couple had been roused by a late-night emergency. Trask swept the room with his shotgun, poking the barrel behind the door and into small spaces between furniture and the walls. Jack stood at the foot of the bed, knelt, and peered beneath. Nothing more than a few balls of dust and a pair of women's shoes stared back at him.

Trask stood close to the closet, his shotgun held at the ready. He threw a questioning look at Jack. Cosgrove had been sleeping in his closet, he remembered. There was no reason to believe Dick Grimes and his wife weren't doing the same.

As Trask's fingers tightened on the handle, the old familiar twinge at the back of Jack's mind flashed through him. For a heart-stopping moment, he fought the urge to warn Randall, to tell him not to open the door. There was something horribly wrong here. But just as the warning was forming on his tongue, Trask opened the closet. The faint light from the lantern illuminated two large, dark shapes.

Jack stared in frozen horror at the things inside. They wore the shape of humans, but only just. The limbs were too compact, curled in on themselves, the bones bent in painful contortions. Their torsos were sunken and twisted, as if something had collapsed the rib cage. Neither wore any clothing, their skin no longer pale but blotched with patches of bristle and a filmy gray crust like a mottled fungus.

"What in the name of God?" one of the others, a bald man clutching an ancient six-shot pistol, whispered just as the two bodies erupted into movement. Jack barely had a second to register a flurry of naked, slick, tangled limbs before one crashed into the man, sending him flying backward and his pistol sliding across the room. Lucille's feet slammed into Baldy's chest with a wet *smack*, and clawed hands curled over his shoulders. A flattened face pressed into his throat, its jaw unhinged like a snake's, and with a crunching burst of gore, tore his neck open. Lucille's silver-tinted eyes flashed with rapturous glee. The man's scream cut off in a choking gurgle as they tumbled backward, the thing still attached, still feeding. Baldy's scream brought Bucky running.

Dick surged forward on all fours, but not with any animal grace. His elbows and knees bent too far, his limbs jutting at terrible angles. He scuttled like a broken marionette and lunged, claws slashing upward. One hand, no longer a hand but a mass of fused digits like a single blade, hooked into Bucky's thigh and ripped free a massive chunk of flesh. He cried out and his lamp crashed to the floor, plunging the room into darkness.

"Jack!" Trask shouted. The room flared in bright light and a violent, deafening *BOOM* as the shotgun fired. Lucille shrieked, a nightmarish two-toned wail, as she lurched to one side. She recovered, snarled at Trask, and leapt. Jack raised the pistol and squeezed off three fast rounds. The first two slammed into Lucille and knocked her off her path. The third smashed into the wall beyond. She recovered but staggered on her feet. Blood seeped out of her malformed mouth. Her silver eyes shifted from Jack to Trask and back, the muscles beneath the strange mold-covered skin rippling as she readied for another attack.

He and Trask fired at the same time. Jack's rounds caught her high in the chest, blowing sprays of blood from her back, while Randall's shotgun round removed the top half of her head. Lucille flew back, crashing into the bed and knocking it askew. Jack's finger tensed on the trigger of his pistol as the small, muscular frame gave a final spasm before falling still.

Trask stepped to the body, his face screwed into an expression of confusion and stress. Screams and guttural snarling brought Jack around to view the rest of the room. Of the five men who had entered the house, only three remained standing. Baldy lay in a pool of gore, his face a ruined mask of blood and exposed teeth. Bucky was on his knees, his ass in the air, head resting on the floor. The space beneath him was filled with the wet loops of his own intestines.

The last of the men in the group was backed into a corner, screaming for God to save him as Dick slashed with claws that cut deep into his flesh and slung blood across the walls. The victim's voice rose higher and higher, propelled by pain and the terror of his own mortality. Jack crossed the room in two large steps and placed the barrel of the .45 against the side of the creature's head and pulled the trigger. What had been Dick Grimes crashed against the wall a second after his brains splattered on the blood-streaked wood. Trask's man in the corner continued to howl, what remained of his hands held up defensively. He was covered in blood and through several of the gashes, long stretches of white bone peered out.

"Shut up," Jack snapped at the man, who managed to clamp down on his shrieks. He fell into a huddled heap in the corner, whimpering hysterically.

"What in the fuck was that?" Trask asked. Jack stared at the transformed creature that had been a person only hours before. "They were so goddamned fast." Trask continued, coming to stand next to Jack. "I've never seen anything move that fast before."

Jack couldn't bring himself to answer. The reality of what he'd just experienced warped his thoughts, bending them into nonsensical feelings. He took a shuddering breath and started for the door. "Come on."

Jack threw open the door to the home of Peter Junkins and staggered as his foot slipped in a thick puddle of blood. He caught himself by throwing out a hand and grasping the smooth, curved bulk of a radio. As he collected his balance, he took in the carnage before him.

The bodies of the three men sent to deal with Junkins littered the floor and furniture of the house. Like images exposed by the strobes of lightning, Jack registered heads severed from bodies and arms and legs scattered, tossed away like cordwood. Blood covered everything, the blanket of red disturbed only by the remains of bodies and the oddly shaped forms of organs ripped from abdomens or chests.

Footsteps behind him signaled the arrival of others from outside. Gasps and strangled curses joined the stench of death. Jack heard the sound of one of the men retching, the vomit's wet splatter on the floor adding to the horror.

"Jack?" Trask whispered. His voice wavered, bordering on hysterical fear. Jack looked to where Trask's eyes were focused. A cold, hollowness blossomed in his guts. Like the Grimes home, a dark hall branched off the main room. From the shadowy depths of the space, three sets of silver eyes stared out at the men gathered near the door.

Jack risked a glance back at what remained of the three men Trask had sent earlier. "We can't beat this," he said and was distantly shocked at how calm and steady his own voice was.

"W-what?"

Jack held out a hand, patted the air behind him in a "Get back" gesture. "Get out. Everyone. Trask, keep that shotgun up and ready." In the hall, the eyes bobbed as the creatures watched the retreating men.

"We have to end them," Trask said with determined anger as he moved toward the porch. "They killed Cleary."

Jack grabbed Trask by the forearm. "If we stay here, we're going to end up just like those guys. We have to regroup and think of a better way. If this is what we're up against now, if this is what they've all become, there won't be any of us left by the time we finish. Come on." He increased his pressure on Randall's arm, and after only a second's hesitation, Trask relented and stepped back.

Jack walked onto the porch and pulled the door closed. As it settled into the jamb, the creatures screeched and rushed across the room. The heavy wood rattled in its frame as they slammed into it, but only for a few moments before the sounds of the things on the other side retreated. Jack stared at the door, expecting to see the handle turning, but nothing happened. He backed down the stairs onto the grass, pistol shifting from window to window, fully expecting the glass to explode outward as monstrous bodies leapt out.

When the attack didn't come and silence settled back over the home, he gestured in the direction of the trucks while continuing to watch the dark-shrouded house. "Load up," he said to the men. "Let's get back to the farm."

When they arrived at Cleary's place, Jack could see the men left as guards standing on the porch. Their faces tightened as they quickly did the math on how many men had returned. The entire drive over, Jack had struggled with accepting the fact that the people he'd watched last night standing together in the woods had, in a matter of a few hours, transformed into feral, stunted creatures whose violence was staggering.

Suddenly he was spun around, Trask's fist screwed up in his shirt. The man's stubble-covered face loomed an inch away from Jack's. "We ain't fucking running. We're going back and killing those things."

Jack gripped the other man's hand and shoved it away. "If you want to die, you go right ahead. There's three in that house for you to start with." His eyes drifted over Trask's shoulder to the other men. Two of them were helping the man who had been clawed by Dick Grimes toward the front door where Doc Powell waited, silhouetted by yellow light. Jack didn't see Evie, but had a feeling she was somewhere just behind the doctor, hovering nervously, awaiting news. The other men, most of the ones who had been posted on the road, stood in a loose knot near one of the trucks, watching the exchange. Jack pitched his voice toward them. "That goes for the rest of you. You didn't see what those things can do."

"You're just a coward," snarled Trask. He opened his mouth to say something more but the thought was cut off as a .45 pressed against his lips.

"You want to say that again?" Jack asked, his voice as cold and even as a frozen pond. "I'm not sure I heard you properly." He pressed the pistol harder against Trask's mouth, the flesh turning white from the pressure. Randall gave soft moans behind his closed jaw. "I didn't think so," Jack said and removed the weapon. "I'm not saying we're done," he told Trask. "I don't walk away from fights. But I am smart enough to know when one approach isn't working and it's time to consider another. If we continue going into the homes of the ones we know about, it's going to be an exercise in futility. By your own admission, that's not even half of them. To translate for your hillbilly brain, that means we'd have better luck walking straight into a meat grinder. We can't kill them all like this. Not fast enough. Not before they rip us all apart. You saw how fast they were, how strong they were."

Trask spat a dark wad of blood onto the dirt, touched a finger to his lip where Jack's pistol had split the skin. "So what do you propose, Mister Chicago?"

"We take the witches. They may be more powerful, but there's only two of them." *If we're lucky,* he thought. *If they've not used those bones to raise the third one.* "If we can stop them, they won't be able to make more of those things. Because I don't believe for a second that they're done with the people of this town. They're not going to stop until every last one of us is either dead or turned into one of those creatures."

Trask barked an incredulous laugh. "More powerful? I'm betting we've not even seen a tenth of what those bitches can do. How do you know that's not its own kind of meat grinder?"

Evie's slender form stepped into the doorway of the house after Powell and the other men moved inside. Jack watched her from the corner of his eye. "I don't. But it's a start. We take the witches, maybe we weaken those creatures somehow. At the very least, we know there won't be more of them. We kill the witches, and we'll have our revenge for Elmer and the others."

"And if we don't?"

Jack's mouth formed a hard, thin line. "We'll go down swinging."

53

Sam screwed the palms of his hands into his eyes and yawned. Blinking the kitchen back into focus, he willed the percolator to finish its laborious process. Within the dirty glass knob on the top, a flurry of brown liquid danced, and he forced himself to wait a bit longer before pouring a cup.

He didn't honestly need it, he had to admit. His body was tired, absolutely. But his mind was buzzing with excitement and anticipation. Sam realized he'd not been this eager since he was a child waiting on the long hours of Christmas Eve to crawl by. The only other time he could think of was the night before his first sermon as an official pastor of a church.

The sermon tonight would be just as important. No, it would be the single most important sermon in his entire life, according to God —the whispered voice waking Sam in the middle of the night, infusing him with a sense of eager preparation that refused to allow him to return to sleep.

This ceremony would mark the end of the process of transformation. It would be the rebirth of not just the town but the faithful, the devoted. All who had accepted God's guidance would step into a new day filled with peace and beauty. And those who hadn't, who had shunned the invitations for worship, who had not partaken of the Host? Well, they would have a final chance tonight. Even with all the flyers he'd handed out and plastered in shop windows, all the neighbors he'd stopped on the street and held up at a cash register to steal just a moment of their time so he could invite them, stressing how important it was for their souls and for the soul of Jericho Springs that they attend . . . most of them had simply stared back in that vacant way that so many people had assumed as of late. Sam's heart ached at that thought, but he couldn't blame them. Not really. They'd lost so much. Most would not have enough to start over. His insistence that God would provide, that the new Eden would be bountiful and they and their families would thrive by reaching successes only dreamt of before, fell on deaf ears.

If only they would attend the final ceremony. If only they would accept the new prayers. If only they would take communion with the Host. If they did, they would be delivered.

The Ceremony of Deliverance would be their saving grace. Afterward, the town's pupation would cease and those whose belief was strong enough, whose hearts were pure, would emerge renewed and cleansed. It didn't matter what denomination they were, they were all God's children and together they would all bask in the glory.

Forever and ever, Amen.

Although he knew it was selfish and therefore sinful, he couldn't help but feel eager for his own transformation. Now that the Host had been disseminated among the flock, Sam wondered when he would be instructed to consume his own holy wafer and shed his corrupt suit of flesh. The same way the others in the congregation had their old, sinful, and prideful humanity burned away so that they could emerge cleansed and divine.

Perhaps it would come tonight during the Ceremony of Deliverance. It only made sense. He had been devout, ready and willing. He had followed God's words to the letter and seen his flock swell as more and more accepted the truth of what once was believed to be simply a blight upon the land.

So yes, it would be tonight, at the same moment that the scales fell from the eyes of the town, allowing the true beauty to be witnessed. Truth be told, beyond the prayers and a final communion, he wasn't exactly sure what to expect for the upcoming ceremony. Perhaps God Himself would appear with a flaming sword to cleave the air and split open the blackened husks of the earth, letting new life spill forth. And in doing so, spare Sam the stages of transformation that those like Jonas and Anna Robertson were enduring and endow him with his new, renewed self instantly.

It was going to be beautiful.

He reminded himself that he needed to find the ornate box. It wasn't in his bedroom, where he usually kept it, which meant he most likely had left it in the office within the chapel.

The percolator finished its job and Sam poured the steaming black liquid into his old, stained porcelain mug. As he raised it to his lips, the soft scuffle of footsteps brought him around. He lowered the mug, coffee untouched, as Grace appeared in the doorway. She wore a pair of his light blue and white striped pajamas. They were all he had to offer, and the material hung on her frame. She'd rolled up the pants cuffs to not trip over them and Sam's eyes went instinctively to her feet —the short, perfect toes, the curved arches. Catching himself, he jerked his gaze higher, past the impressions of her nipples through the patterned fabric to the girl's tired face. Her eyes were puffy from crying and the stress of being in the woods for so long. Her hair looked like a rat's nest and he made a note to run to Rangle's for a brush.

She was the most beautiful thing he'd ever seen. And Christ had seen fit to deliver her to him, bringing an answer to his most personal of prayers. Once the ceremony was complete, her parents would have no use for such earthly things as concern over who their daughter married. Their focus would be on propagating Eden with new life and bringing those who had refused the new path across the threshold into salvation to wash the feet of God's messengers.

"Did I wake you?" he asked, then sipped his coffee. It burned his lip but he didn't notice. His entire focus was on the angel standing in his kitchen doorway.

"No," Grace said. A strand of hair drifted across one cheek. She tucked it behind her ear absentmindedly and Sam's breath caught. The girl stepped into the kitchen. Her eyes flicked to the far corner where a washtub sat hidden behind sheer modesty curtains, before she continued to the small dining table like a cat slinking into a room, attempting to go unnoticed. She sat in one of the two straight-backed wood chairs and hunched forward, her hands in her lap, fingers picking nervously at one another.

"I couldn't sleep," she said. Her voice was thick, heavy with fatigue. Sam thought about the moment he'd opened the door to find her, shivering, filthy, nearly hysterical. Before he'd even registered who stood on his stoop, Grace had fallen into his arms, her exhaustion having gotten the better of her.

After carrying her inside, his heart racing at the feel of her warm body against his chest, he had lain her on his small sofa in the front room. The dress she'd been wearing was little more than rags, the undergarments torn and beyond repair as well. Sam was more than a little ashamed to think about the reaction his body had at the sight of so much of her exposed skin—the gentle curves of her breasts, the smooth valleys of her thighs. He knew it was wrong to look at her that way; she was still just a girl. But hadn't God delivered her into his care for a reason? He'd covered her with a quilt, a gift from Martha Bell the previous fall, then set about cleaning the dirt from her face with a warm, wet cloth.

She'd slept for a couple of hours, rousing as he prepared a simple supper of vegetable soup. Over dinner, and wearing his pajamas in lieu of her own ruined clothes, she'd related how she came to his door. When she'd spoken of a desecrated church and nightmare creatures, Sam patted her hand and reassured her that such things weren't real, that she most likely suffered a delusion from dehydration. It had been a warm few days, after all. Grace had looked at him, deep skepticism lining her face, but she never pressed the issue. After supper Sam had promised to send for her parents but Grace, strangely, refused and asked if she could stay the night and return home when the sun was up. Trying not to sound too eager, Sam had agreed and made up the small guest room.

He chuckled and pointed at the percolator. "Well, would you like some of my superb coffee? It's my secret recipe, you know."

"Sure." She looked at the other mug—Sam only owned two—sitting in the drying rack next to the sink. He hurried to pour the coffee and set the cup on the table, then slid the other chair out and perched on it, crossing his legs and forcing a relaxed air.

"Bad dreams?" he asked and immediately regretted it. His neck grew warm in embarrassment as he saw the pained expression on her face. He silently cursed himself for causing her even the slightest degree of discomfort.

A silence stretched between them. Finally, Grace said, "Did you have another sermon? Last night, I mean."

"No. I spent last night preparing for *tonight's* sermon. Well, other than caring for the pleasant surprise of my guest, that is." He gave a smile, hoping it conveyed how welcome she was in his home.

"What do you talk about during the services? My parents haven't told me anything. They barely speak to me anymore." She paused, her eyes going glassy as she focused on some memory. Her voice was small and sad, barely a whisper, when she continued. "I've not seen much of them these last few days."

"Your parents are very well," Sam said. "They're helping me a great deal, actually. The sermons themselves have been focused on helping people prepare for the coming salvation. Readying their bodies and souls for the passing of the darkness."

"You mean the blight?"

"Yes. But you see, God has shown me that it's not a blight to consume and destroy. Rather, it's a transformation. The land has to go through this stage to emerge stronger, healthier, more pure. Kind of like when farmers burn some of their fields so that the soil is better prepared for the next growing season."

Grace nodded, but Sam thought he saw a glimmer of doubt in her eyes. "Tell you what," he began, leaning forward. He slid a hand across the table and let his fingers graze the back of her hand.

"Tonight on the stage over on Heart Avenue, I will be leading a special ceremony. I'm calling it the Ceremony of Deliverance and will mark the beginning of our new, revitalized world. It will be glorious. All of my congregation will be there, and, I sincerely hope, the rest of the town. I will offer them communion with our special Host, the very one that God provided for this rebirth. If they take communion, they will shed their impure bodies and souls and emerge new and clean in Eden. At the end of the service, all of us will witness the birth of the new land. We'll put these dark times behind us."

"How can you know that?"

"God has told me. His preparation of not only the land is almost complete, and I, as His shepherd, will lead us all into the light of renewal." He smiled. "It would mean everything to me if you were to attend. You'll sit by my side. You won't have to do anything other than bear witness. Your parents will be there. They've been instrumental in gathering the flock and preparing everyone for life in Eden. I would love to have you there, standing with me as we face the dawning of a new day." He paused and added, "There's a dress you could wear, it's in your closet. I think it would fit you perfectly." Deep down he held his breath, waiting for her to ask why a dress that just happened to be her size just happened to be hanging in the closet of the guest room.

Grace stared into her coffee for a while, one finger tracing a circle around the rim of the cup. "Okay."

Sam's chest swelled with love. He straightened and gave the tabletop a light rap with his knuckles. "Okay, then." He glanced through the window over the sink. Outside, the land was as black as a coal mine. "It's still early. Or late, depending on your perspective. Why don't you try to get some sleep?"

"What about you?" Grace asked as she stood and drifted to the doorway. "You've been up all night as well."

"I couldn't sleep even if I wanted to. I have so much to do. I want everything to be perfect tonight. Don't worry about me, I'll be just fine. I have plenty of my special coffee"—he winked—"and my love for—" He almost said "you" but caught himself. "—this town to fill my sails. I can sleep tomorrow, when we've all entered the new world. When salvation is finally upon us."

Grace's lips curled in a soft, sad smile. She turned to go and Sam did his best not to watch her derriere shifting beneath the pajama pants as she went.

He failed. And in the dim light of the kitchen, he thanked God for the gift of her.

54

Grace lay on the small bed in the spare bedroom of the parsonage and stared at the ceiling. In the wake of the dream, her thoughts swirled like smoke disturbed by a strong wind. Like the others she'd had since emerging from the woods, this one was rapidly fleeing into the abyss of her memory. She was able to hold on to a few fading images: flame shrouded buildings in a small town deep in the forest; people screaming, their faces streaked with blood as blackened shapes darted; strange, uneven totems made out of rocks carved with symbols, knocked asunder by the shoes of white men who laughed as they kicked.

She didn't understand any of it. None of the images had any connection to anything or anyone she knew in the real world, yet the lingering sense that all of those things had happened, that they were real in some way, stuck with her like sap on her fingers.

At first, she'd considered telling Sam about them, then quickly dismissed the thought. The pastor had enough to deal with, especially the preparations for his final ceremony. Even this morning, after waking with the screams echoing in her mind, she'd reconsidered calling out to him. But something stilled her tongue.

After she'd gone to bed, Sam had remained in the kitchen for a long time as he prepared for the Ceremony of Deliverance. She could hear him puttering about, talking to himself, often in a language she didn't understand and that made her slightly nauseous to hear. Once, she wasn't sure what time it was but based on the feeling in her stomach, it seemed to be creeping up on lunchtime, she'd heard his footsteps in the hall. He had stopped just outside her door and she lay there, holding her breath and imagining him bending one ear to the wood, listening. Grace had remained, stiff and still, on the bed until she heard the despondent, plodding thumps of his retreat. She didn't know why that was her reaction; Pastor Sam had never harmed her nor indicated that he would ever hurt her.

But even despite his excitement earlier in the morning, his jubilation at the success of the service he'd led in the woods, and his expectations of what he'd been calling the "final ceremony," there was something wrong about him. It wasn't anything Grace could point to and say, "There, that right there is bad." It was something that remained hidden, slithering beneath Sam's features and demeanor like a water snake twisting under the surface of a lake.

Grace frowned. She wasn't sure why the word "slithering" had come to mind, but there was no other way to describe the feelings she got when she looked into the pastor's eyes, fever bright with hidden knowledge and plans. She'd seen him excited and lost in the moment during some of his more passionate sermons. But even in those instances, there'd never been anything like what she saw now. Was the same thing happening to her parents? Had they accepted this new path of worship and devoted themselves to it completely? Was that why she'd not seen them in days?

Once more, she thought back to that moment in the woods when her parents had shown up out of nowhere and her father had shot the wildcat. It hadn't been a normal bobcat, Grace remembered that much. It had changed, becoming something worse, just like so many other animals and so many areas of land around the town. Even the buildings were showing strange signs of rot— oozing sores appearing on the old wood of homes and other structures.

But in the moments after killing the bobcat, the look in her parents' eyes had been the same as what Grace saw in Sam's. *Not quite, though*, she corrected herself. With Sam, it was the look of someone who knew the secret ending to a story and was excited to see others reach it on their own. With her parents, however, the look was that of those lost in the story and afraid of the outcome. Or was it not the outcome they were afraid of, but rather the fear of *not* reaching the end? That felt more like it.

And where was Charlie in all of this? Grace's chest tightened with the thought of her brother. She pictured his face, chubby cheeks framed by the mop of blond hair as he laughed and teased her about something or other. She raised a hand and with the tip of her middle finger wiped away the tear that spilled from her eye and ran down her cheek. The thought of Charlie being lost in the woods after so long was too much to bear.

He's dead, and you know it. The thought came out of nowhere. Slithered out of the darkest cracks of her mind. She hated the thought, hated it with the fury of all the fires in the hottest part of hell. But she also knew that it was the correct thought. Charlie was a good boy but he was young, and while he did spend a lot of time playing out in the woods, he wasn't prepared to survive for long on his own. He didn't know how to fish or hunt because those were things their father had promised to start teaching him when he turned seven, much to Charlie's chagrin. So how could she expect him to find food?

The memory of the bobcat returned and her chest tightened at the idea of Charlie stumbling across such a creature. That was too awful to consider, and she squeezed her eyes against it. There was something worse, she knew, something far more awful for an innocent boy to have encountered in the woods far from home.

She thought of the dark things with glowing eyes emerging from the shadowy corner of the church, then began to cry.

Eventually, the tears slowed and Grace forced herself to sit up. Her body still ached from her time in the woods and she let her fingertips trace over the small raised areas of angry pink flesh that dotted her legs. With a soft hiss, she pulled back her hand as the pain radiated out from one mound. She told Sam that she thought they were spider bites from when she had passed out in the forest. In the moment, she'd barely registered the lie. The thought of telling him about the church, the altar made of human bodies cobbled together like a stone fence, the fragments of bones those black hateful things had put into her, was too much.

Grace let out a long breath and stood from the bed. She couldn't just lie there any longer, at least not until Sam returned and insisted that she attend the ceremony with him. She needed to eat, and she needed to get clean. The last thing she wanted was for the wounds to become infected. She went into the kitchen, peered through the window over the sink, and spotted a well in the yard marked by a small ring of stones. A survey of the surrounding area told her that nobody was outside who would see her going to fetch water wearing the pastor's pajamas.

She returned a few minutes later with a full bucket that she emptied into a large pot on the stove. She got the fire stoked and returned to the well thrice, adding the water to the pot each time. When the water was hot enough, she transferred it with a pitcher into the tub that occupied the rear corner of the kitchen. After pulling the modesty curtains closed, Grace undressed and slipped into the warm water, moving slowly to acclimate to the heat.

As the warmth of the bath began to relax her muscles, she thought about what she should do next. The idea of staying with Sam wasn't appealing, despite his affection for her. Whatever was affecting his mood, that thing just beneath the surface, left her with an oily slick of unease at the thought of staying. She didn't think she could go back home either. If her parents were lost to the new religion, then being in the same house as them wasn't an option. But at the moment, she had nowhere else to go.

I could just leave, she thought. *Dry off and go home, pack a bag, then leave town.* The idea sparked a feeling of excitement, a tiny flash in a much darker room. Where would she go? How would she manage on her own? She was only fifteen, but she was sure to get a job as a seamstress or perhaps working in a factory somewhere. Birmingham, maybe even Atlanta. The idea of a city as huge as Atlanta brought a nervous smile to her lips, and she let it tumble around in her mind as she bathed.

The destination wasn't certain, but as Grace passed the soap across her smooth skin, taking care around the painful bumps that dotted her body, she came to accept that staying in Jericho Springs wasn't an option any longer. Things were bad and only getting worse. The blight was everywhere and now more and more people were missing. She couldn't say exactly what it was, but something about this ceremony that Sam was so eager for filled her with a sense of impending doom, as if the town were a mouse and there was a massive, invisible train barreling down on the pitiful creature.

So, yes, she made her decision. She would finish her bath, change, go home, and pack a bag, which wouldn't take long as she didn't own much beyond a few dresses and a couple of books. She would leave the pastor's pajamas folded on her bed; her parents could worry about returning them. Then, she would start walking south toward Birmingham. She wasn't quite ready for a city like Atlanta. Best to get her feet wet with Birmingham first.

Grace let go of the soap, letting it slip under the water and settle somewhere beneath one of her legs. She put her head back against the hard curve of the tub and sighed. For the first time in a long time, she was filled with a sense of contentment. She had a plan and everything would be all right.

Without meaning to, Grace drifted into sleep.

She opened her eyes to find herself sitting on a rock overlooking a wide, grassy expanse ringed by thick, choking woods far in the distance. Near the trees she saw small homes, but not the structures she was accustomed to. These were primitive, constructed from branches and mud. Thin columns of smoke drifted up from a few of them and Grace shivered as a chill wind swept across the rock and into the field. The grass swayed, undulating like worshippers in the throes of a sermon.

Her eyes swept across the field and picked out another oddity: a ring of stones within which stood dozens of people. They were dirty and ragged, wearing what appeared to be animal furs. Were these Indians? No, she decided, they couldn't be. Indians wore deerskin and had feathers, didn't they? That's what she'd always been taught anyway.

At the head of the crowd stood a tall, imposing figure— Grace felt confident it was a man—shouting and gesturing wildly as if preaching. She giggled to herself, wondering if this was Sam or a dream version of him leading one of his new worship services.

As she watched the man shouting strange words and his rapt congregation, she noticed a change in the air. It hadn't gotten colder, although it was certainly uncomfortably cold, but this was a feeling of pressure. Was a storm coming? A glance to the sky showed a wide blue expanse and no hint of storm clouds.

A scream erupted from the small congregation. The crowd had parted, people lining either side of the ring of stones. In their midst were several figures on their knees in a loose gathering, arms raised in supplication. Grace couldn't be certain but from where she sat, she thought she saw well over twenty people kneeling. Another person, smaller and slender despite the many furs that dangled and swayed as they moved— Grace was certain it was a woman—stepped out from the head of one of the groups and approached one of the kneeling supplicants. The arm of the woman came up and Grace caught the brief, shining glint of something as it swept forward and across. A faint cloud of red mist sprayed from the kneeling person's throat and they toppled backward, their feet bent unnaturally beneath them. The woman with the weapon moved quickly, slipping behind each person kneeling and dragging the blade across each throat.

When the final body had fallen, the grass around them slowly turning dark from blood, the woman turned and shouted something to the man standing over all of them. With a howl, the two groups rushed forward and tore at the bodies, ripping them apart, fingers digging into flesh and pulling away sopping handfuls of gore-streaked meat. They smeared the blood and viscera across their faces and bodies and chanted in their strange language.

I think I'd very much like to wake up now, Grace told herself and pushed back along the rock she sat upon. The pressure in the air was continuing to increase and movement within the field pulled her attention from the slaughter within the stones. The air shimmered, a swirling, wavering spot about ten feet off the ground and much closer to where she sat than where the people reveled in their blood orgy.

A black line, jagged like a bolt of lightning, appeared with short, jerky expansions in the air. When it stopped, a black sludge seeped out of it. The blackness billowed like smoke but appeared more substantial, more oily. It poured out like some nightmare blood from the wound on a demon.

The people in the circle screamed as they noticed the sludge expanding out into the field. They cheered and hugged one another, then broke from the circle of stones and rushed toward the horrible blackness. Grace wanted to scream at them to stop, wanted to warn them away but couldn't find the words. *Not that they would hear me anyway,* she thought. Something about the stuff that seeped out of that crack filled her with the sense that it was death come to the world. It was rot and decay, corruption and perverseness coming to take everything away.

The people stopped, gathering in a cluster several yards from the crack and watched as the sludge spread, slowly taking form.

The scream died in Grace's throat as the smoke coalesced into three black figures with shining silver eyes. Where they stood, the land died; the grass turning black and oozing, the soil becoming marshlike and fetid. Tendrils of rot and decay raced out from the three figures. Some reached the gathered people before they even realized what was happening. The screams that erupted as their bodies were broken and ripped apart by unseen forces were drowned out by the laughter from the three black figures. Laughter as they caused and soaked up the pain and suffering of everything and everyone.

Grace finally found her voice and added her screams to the chorus. One of the silver-eyed figures cocked a head and twisted to stare at her from across the expanse. Horrible fingers crawled across

Grace's mind, probing and violating. A deep, scratching voice slithered in her ears.

"*Sister.*"

Grace woke in a fit, her arms and legs flailing and sending waves of water sloshing over the sides and across the kitchen floor. The bath cold now, she shivered as she climbed out of the tub, ignoring the water pooling on the floor. She dried herself quickly, then wrapped the towel around her chest and hurried to the bedroom where she redressed in the pajamas Sam had loaned her. Her cheeks colored as she realized she lacked undergarments. She would have to be quick on her walk home. She could only imagine the whispers that would spread through town if she were seen wearing a grown man's pajamas and no undergarments in public. Standing in front of the small framed mirror on the wall over the dresser, she ran her fingers through her hair. Sam had told her he'd pick up a new hairbrush, but that had only been this morning.

Unbidden, Grace's mind started to replay the dream but she closed her eyes against it, forcing it back. She didn't want to consider it right now. She wanted to get dressed, go home, pack a bag, and get out of town. Something about that dream lingered as a certainty of what was to come. She believed she'd seen the train that was on a collision course with her town—the mouse.

Her throat tightened and she swallowed, the movement painful and difficult. Grace coughed and pounded a fist on her chest. She tried swallowing again but found she couldn't. It was as if something were lodged in her throat. Her spittle dribbled past her lips and fell to the floor between her bare feet. Leaning close to the mirror, she opened her mouth, searching for the obstruction.

An eye stared back at her from just beyond her uvula. Grace's own eyes went wide, her breath bursting from her nose in short, frenzied puffs as she yawned into the glass and stared at the eye that sat on the back of her tongue, nestled in the thickness of her soft palate.

The eye rolled, as if turning to observe from a better angle.

Grace screamed but only a breathy whimper drifted out. A heaviness filled her, weighing down her muscles as if they'd been filled with lead. Her arms fell slack by her sides, and she stood motionless in front of the mirror for a long time. She remained completely still, her mouth propped wide, drool sliding over her lips and down her chin. Her chest moved slowly and evenly with her breath. Her eyes, no longer wide in horror, stared unseeing into the depths of the mirror.

Voices whispered in her head, colliding with one another, tumbling and twisting around, filling her.

The small home fell into silence as time slowly ticked by. The minutes turned to an hour, then an hour more.

All at once, Grace's body slumped and she staggered back a few steps from the mirror. She gasped in a deep breath as if she'd been underwater for minutes, and blinked her burning eyes. She screwed her fists into them, rubbing at the painful scratchiness.

Not wanting to look into the mirror again, Grace turned from the dresser and approached the small closet within which hung a white dress patterned with small blue flowers. It was the only garment in the closet, hanging there among a few empty wire hangers. Its presence struck her as odd, that Sam would have a dress for her already in his closet when he had no idea she was coming. Grace herself had no idea she would be at his house until she was slapping at the wood of his kitchen door.

She slipped the dress on, fingers working the small buttons. It hung on her; the fabric sagging at the chest and hips, obviously made for someone just a little larger than her slender frame. Still, it fit for the most part and she worked the buttons, sliding the thin ivory discs through the threaded eyelets with lazy focus. Gone from her mind were any thoughts of going home and packing a bag, of Birmingham and work in a factory or as a seamstress. Gone were any thoughts of Charlie, of her parents, of any of her friends. There was only one thing left, repeating in her mind like a chant shouted as a chorus among a circle of stones.

The ceremony awaited.

She was Sister.

55

"You're sure we're safe here?" Evie asked as she peered out at the forest bordering the ruined cornfield.

"Trask has guys posted all the way out to the main road," Jack said. He crossed the kitchen and placed a hand on her shoulder. There were four men that he could see facing the field, standing several yards apart, shotguns close at hand as they stood watch. "Those guys have the field covered and enough open space that they won't get ambushed. We have more guys spaced all around the property, but I don't think they're needed." He hoped the lie sounded natural. In truth, if the things that had once been Evie's neighbors decided to return to the farm or were directed to come back, he didn't believe that the men Trask had managed to scrape together would prove much of a defense.

Evie's gaze lingered on the guards at the edge of the field for a moment longer, then she turned and shuffled to the table and sat with a tired sigh. "Do you think they need any help?" she asked after a moment.

In the grass, a small knot of men stood around a brick pit. White smoke rose from a metal grate where several beef patties lay sizzling against the flames. The men watched the cooking meat with the sober expressions of people engaged in the most delicate and volatile exercise.

"I think they know what they're doing. Grilling hamburgers isn't my forte." He turned and smiled at her. "Now if you'd like a good tomato sauce, I'm your guy. Or, better yet, we need to get you up to Chicago, have some of my people cook for you. Those burgers would taste like shoe leather in comparison."

Evie raised a skeptical eyebrow. "Considering your high opinion on the food at Mack's, I have to seriously question that statement." Jack glanced at her, saw the corners of her mouth twitching in suppressed laughter. In that moment, seeing Evie laughing despite her injuries, seeing her breaking past the fear and uncertainty in order to poke fun at him, he knew without a shadow of a doubt that if he survived whatever was coming, he was going to spend the rest of his life with Evelyn Marrow.

"Let's go make sure they don't set the place on fire," he said.

They stepped into the yard and found Trask at an old, warped table. His shotgun was propped against the scarred planks and he sat looking out across the cornfield while smoking. Jack helped Evie into a chair, then went back to the kitchen for plates and silverware. When he returned, a steaming platter of dark brown patties sat in the center of the table. Trask reached for a patty. "I'll have the guys come in shifts to get some," he said.

When the meal was done, Trask went inside and returned with dark brown bottles of beer. "Coffee's brewing, but Cleary had some beers that he'd stashed in the icebox." He popped their tops and passed them around, then returned to his seat. Crossing his legs, he took a long swig and stifled a belch. "So now what?" he asked.

Jack leaned back in his own chair, letting his fingers slowly turn the bottle as he thought. "Just as I said this morning. We're going to go after the witches. I figure that if we kill them—"

"You don't think that will turn everyone back, do you?" Evie asked.

"No," Jack said. "I think what's been done to them has been done and won't be reversed. But I'm thinking—I'm *hoping*—that if we kill the witches, that will affect these people in some way. Weaken them a little maybe. But at the very least, killing the witches will stop more of those things from being made."

"So," Evie began, "the question is: where do we find the witches? Do either of you have any idea of where they would be?"

Those gathered at the small table fell quiet. Overhead, the skeletal fingers of the blackened, barren tree swayed in a warm breeze, sending shifting shadows dancing across the scarred tabletop. The sound of branches rubbing against one another made Jack think of wind chimes made of bones. He sipped his beer while considering the question.

Several minutes passed and Trask gave an irritated grunt. "I ain't got no idea. They could be anywhere. Hell, they could still be in the root cellar for all I know."

"They're not," Evie answered in a tight voice.

"It would make sense that they'd want to be somewhere secluded," Jack proposed. "Somewhere close enough to town that whatever influence they have on those creatures is still effective, yet not so close that just anyone could stumble on them."

"Not that that person would live long enough to warn anyone else," Trask said. Jack raised his eyebrows in agreement.

"Where were the first attacks?" asked Evie.

"Not far from the cave you found," Trask answered. "The crew that blasted it open went missing. A few days later, crews started getting hit. Didn't seem to be a pattern and we didn't know about that cave. Just figured that crew ran off or got themselves picked up by the Prohis."

Evie looked at Jack. "You don't think we missed something, do you? At the cave?"

Jack pursed his lips. "I don't think so, no. If the witches had been in that cave when we were there, we'd be dead."

"Maybe they weren't home when we came knocking," she

suggested. "Maybe they were away, I don't know, creating more of those creatures."

Jack thought about it. She had a point, and the cave did make the most sense. It was isolated but not so far out of town that people couldn't get to it, giving the witches proximity to things. And he couldn't deny that something had been *off* about the place. But he would have expected a hideout, a "base of operations" as Al liked to call it, to have been . . . His brain searched for the word and could only come up with "bigger." Not bigger in size. Right now there were only two of them, after all. But bigger in evil. Bigger in corruption. If the witches were slowly destroying the land, twisting and killing the people, didn't it make sense that the place where they slept—if such a thing was even possible with creatures like that—would be a literal hell on earth?

It came to him.

"Morelli," he mumbled.

"I'm sorry?" Evie asked.

Jack didn't answer for a moment, his eyes focused on the beer bottle as if waiting for it to reveal all the answers. "My guy, Morelli. Came down here to set up the initial deal with Cleary but went missing. It's one of the reasons I was sent."

"I'm not following you," said Evie.

"I found him. What was left of him anyway. He was in an old house that Cleary later told me was part of the Providence settlement. A lot of the house was still intact, and he'd said that several generations of people stayed in that old town even after Jericho Springs was founded. So some of the houses and buildings were still there, but others were just ruins or completely gone. That house and the woods around it were some of the worst things I'd ever seen. Everything felt . . . wrong. It's . . . ." He sighed in frustration. "I don't know how to describe it. I ain't a poet. But if Providence is where the witches originally were, and nobody has lived there in years . . ." He let the rest go unsaid, just held his hands up in a "There you go" gesture.

The others mulled it over. Evie said, "It makes sense. They wouldn't want to set up here in town where just anyone could find them. But like you said, they'd want to be close enough that their spells, or what have you, still worked."

As they spoke, Jack became more certain of the idea. He could practically feel the concepts clicking into place like pieces of a jigsaw puzzle. He thought back to the ruins where he had found Morelli's body and tried to remember what else he'd seen, what other structures. But all he could picture was the house itself and Morelli's mutilated corpse hanging, symbols carved into his flesh.

"Let's assume Providence is the place," he said. "What I need to know now is the layout. Has anyone been there? I need to know what we're walking into. I'm not going to have us wandering the woods looking for witches in random buildings. We need to know what's still there, then we can determine what would be the most likely place to find them."

"That's easy," said Trask. "They'll be at the church."

Jack frowned. "How do you know that?"

"Witches are evil. Sold their souls to the Devil and all that shit, right? Don't make sense for something like that to make its bed in a schoolhouse, does it? They'd want to desecrate holy ground. So, the church. If there's much of it left, that is."

Jack glanced at Evie, who nodded her agreement. "Good," he said. "Let's get out there."

Jack expected and received an argument with Evie. As he went inside to collect Morelli's Thompson and the chains, she followed him, insisting that she accompany him. "I can't just sit here again while you go out risking your life."

Putting the heavy machine gun on the bed, Jack said, "And I can't do what I need to do if I'm having to worry about you. I can't be distracted right now." *It's bad enough that you'll be here unprotected from those other creatures,* he thought but didn't say. No reason to terrify her. "Plus,"—he pointed at her ankle—"if the ground out there is worse than it was when I found Morelli, or we have to move fast, how well do you think you'd do?"

Evie set her jaw, tilting her head up defiantly. "I can manage."

"I'm sure you can. But someone needs to stay here and keep an eye on Doc Powell."

"Are you serious?" Evie's cheeks reddened and she narrowed her eyes. "You're nuts if you think I'm staying here with just the doctor for protection."

"Then go to his house," Jack suggested. He hefted the Thompson and picked up the drum magazine. "That's in town and less isolated. You're better off there, surrounded by people, than you would be out here on the farm."

For a long time, he was certain she would continue the argument. Evelyn Marrow was no one to just roll over. But she was also one smart cookie and understood reasoning. She let out a frustrated sigh and wagged a finger in his face. "You'd better not get yourself killed out there, Jack Carmelo Chicago. If I'm going to play the role of dutiful ..." —her eyes shifted in her uncertainty of what to say next—"whatever, waiting for you to come home to me, then goddamnit, you'd better hold up your end of the bargain. Or so help me, whatever those witches out there do to you will look like a quilting circle when I'm done with you."

"I believe that," Jack said, eyebrows raising appreciatively. He dropped the machine gun and magazine back onto the bed and pulled Evie close. Bending his head to hers, he kissed her, gently at first, then quickly growing into a deeper, more passionate caress. His fingers dug into her upper arms and she gripped his waist tightly, her own fingers like nails. Jack's pants tightened as he grew excited in the moment and he quickly stepped back, his breath coming in deep, steady pants. "I'm sorry," he said. "I should—"

Evie took a step closer, once more pressing her body against his. "I know what you should," she said. "If you're walking into what we both think you are, then that can wait a few minutes more. Do you understand me?"

Jack did.

Half an hour later, he stepped out of the house, the Thompson held loosely by his side, the heavy chains draped over one shoulder. He handed the Thompson to a man sitting in the back of one of the trucks and dumped the chains into the bed of his own truck before climbing into the cab next to Trask, who gave a knowing smile.

"Don't," Jack said, his eyes fixed on the small figure standing in the shadows of the porch, one hand gripping a support post. Evie gave a small wave as Trask threw the truck into gear. As they rumbled across the property toward the main road, Jack found himself praying for the first time in years. Praying that she would be safe and that he could find his way back to her. His fingers found the trolley token and he turned it over and over as he thought about returning to Evie.

The woods where they began their trek toward the ruins of the settlement of Providence were little more than a dead swamp. The ground was soft, and every step sank into the mire several inches. The muddy ground released each foot with some resistance and a loud squelch. By the time the group of men had made it half a mile in, they were drenched in sweat and calling for a rest every twenty minutes. The late afternoon sun filtered through the dead and dying trees, wide shafts of light angling to spear the corpse-like earth. Jack swallowed a sip of water, recapped his canteen, and cursed their progress. He'd hoped to have reached the ruins by now. At this rate, according to a couple of the men who had a rough idea of the location of Providence, they wouldn't reach what remained of the town until just before dusk. Jack didn't know much about witches, but the idea that they were probably more powerful in the dark felt right to him. Evil things liked the dark, thrived in it. At least according to the stories.

"Let's get going," he commanded. The weary men around him moaned their displeasure; the three men carrying the heavy iron chains groaning the loudest before they hauled themselves off whatever log or moss-covered rock they'd chosen. "We don't stop again until we get there," Jack said loudly.

After what felt like two more hours of walking, the air took on a new stench. It was as if they'd crossed some invisible border, as the decaying vegetative smell grew into a deeper, more cloying reek. The men around him all grunted in disgust. Jack knew that smell.

The smell of dead men, of spilled blood and offal.

The terrain grew softer, dark water seeping up from saturated soil when their boots pressed into the ground. Around them the trees were slick with yellowing ooze, and the blackened leaves of the undergrowth dripped with some awful moisture.

Jack noticed the bloated corpse of some animal floating half-submerged in murky, algae-coated water several yards away. The creature's stiff legs stuck out like obscene flagpoles mounted in the distended landscape of a stomach. Thankfully, the animal's head remained beneath the water.

"There," the man guiding them said and spat a mouthful of tobacco juice onto a clump of oozing weeds. He pointed one dirty, crooked finger. Off to the left, and closer than Jack would have expected, were the broken ruins of an old house. The sight of it sent a spear of nervousness through him and despite holding the massive Thompson, he slipped a hand back and reassuringly touched the .45 tucked in his waistband.

Within minutes, more signs of ruins became visible. Most were old stone walls, only the top foot or so above the waterline. Jack's feet snagged on unseen roots and stones, and he stumbled through the water as the group entered what remained of the settlement of Providence. Jack reached a wide gap between trees, something he thought had once been a road or some main thoroughfare, and with the Thompson held ready to fire, he turned and surveyed the area. He counted eight buildings, most identified only by the rock foundations, but a few still had walls and roofs, although they were rotting and sagging significantly.

Dead black vines crawled along the broken and ruined facades. And where the vines weren't, the oozing sores could be seen, sending their constant trickle of unholy sludge cascading down into the mire.

"Jesus, Mary, and Joseph," Trask gasped.

Jack turned quickly, staggering as yet another root connected with his foot. He regained his balance and blinked in disbelief. How had he not seen those?

Throughout the swamp, corpses of men were mounted onto the broken shafts of dead trees. Jack counted at least twenty. One of the other men pointed out more on the other side of the clearing. The bodies were in various states of decay. Some seemed to have been killed by a horrible wound to the throat, leaving a ragged hole. Others slumped on their perches; each dead face staring at the ruin that had once been their stomach but was now a hollow cavity. Some heads lolled, deformed, and it took Jack a moment to understand that their skulls had been crushed.

The skin of each one was patterned with horrible symbols, crude angles and curves, intersecting lines all slashed callously into the bodies. Jack was certain it had been done when the men were alive.

"They're ours," Trask said. The words were pinched, forced out through an uncooperative throat. "They're all our guys. The ones that went missing. That we never found."

"You're sure?" Jack asked. It was a stupid question; the identification of the dead men meant nothing to the current mission, but it felt like the right thing to say.

Trask nodded dumbly. "Yeah. All of them."

"You notice the symbols?" Jack asked and pointed. The light being faint here, they were hard to spot, but he could pick out a few of them hanging from trees. They were constructed from the broken and reassembled bodies of dead animals, and they swayed lazily in a breeze he couldn't feel. Maggots crawled over the dead flesh of foxes, rabbits, and what Jack assumed was a deer or two. The animals had been torn apart and reconnected to form the cryptic totems.

"I'm going to be sick," one man cried. A moment later, the sounds of his gagging and the wet splashes of his vomit broke through the nightmare state.

Jack blinked his daze away and grabbed Trask by the shoulder. "We have to find the church." To the guy who had been guiding them, he said, "Get moving." The hunch-shouldered man threw an uncertain look back at Jack, spat again, but began walking.

It didn't take long to find the church. Jack stood in the calf-deep muck and stared at the putrid building. What remained of its wooden walls shimmered from the cascading ooze and writhed in places where maggots and other insects crawled. More of the symbols hung from different broken pieces of clapboard. A sour burn rose in Jack's throat as he saw that instead of broken woodland creatures, these were fashioned out of bloody ropes of intestines.

Two more corpses mounted onto poles flanked the open doorway, their heads bent back so their dead faces could stare at the heavens they would never reach. Their chests were blackened from blood, and within their hollowed abdomens lay the decaying bodies of small animals. Through the doorway, the interior of the church pulsed with flickering firelight.

"You think they're inside?" he asked Trask.

His tight, tense reply, "I fucking hope so. Let's get this over with."

Jack flexed his fingers around the grips of the Thompson and sloshed through the last several feet of water before the dry land surrounding the church. He focused on the open door and the shadowy interior, ignoring the piles of entrails scattered across the porch. He passed over the threshold, sweeping his weapon left to right.

More disgusted curses rose from the men as they mounted the porch and stepped into the nave. Symbols painted in blood covered the walls alongside more of the horrible emblems made from broken animals. The paltry light came from a small number of candles positioned on ledges along the walls or on piles of broken and rotting, mold-covered furniture.

"Spread out," Jack said. "They have to be here somewhere." He moved deeper into the sanctuary, his eyes focused on the shadowy corners beyond the altar.

"Holy Christ!" The shout brought Jack around, the Thompson rising and finger tensing on the trigger. Instead of a threat, he saw one of the men staggering toward the door, his eyes wide in pure terror. Looking back, Jack saw what had caused his retreat and the pure awfulness of it drove him back several uneasy steps.

He'd been so focused on the rear of the sanctuary that he'd not even noticed the altar. For several long seconds he tried to make sense out of it, tried to understand how many bodies he was seeing. He counted at least three faces among the confusion of torn flesh and broken bones, visages locked into expressions of agony beyond imagining. Jack grimaced and turned away. He stopped, something nagging at the corner of his mind. Turning back toward the altar, he forced himself to look closer. Despite the shattered bones pushing the features into an uneven plane, one of the faces near the warped and dirt-caked planks of the chancel was familiar.

"Son of a bitch," Jack whispered at the sight of Henry Dunn's mug glaring at him in a brilliant expression of pure horror. He had no idea if the remains of the toad-like man's body were mixed into the blasphemous tableau—the rest of the altar being a confusion of body parts, pulped flesh, blood, and the small writhing shapes of maggots. The son of a bitch had met a fitting end, even if it wasn't at the end of Jack's gun.

The skin around Henry's fat boiled egg of an eye bulged grotesquely. A thick black centipede slithered out, its multitude of legs propelling it away and over the decaying ridge of the man's nose.

The voices of the other men as they noticed the befouled altar mingled in a soup of fear and disgust, drifted toward the door and the swamp beyond when the horror of their surroundings wormed its way into each of them.

Jack cursed. He needed to get these men focused or they were all dead. "Find them!" he shouted. The command punctured the air and broke the men from their focus on the blasphemous display. They fanned out, poking rifle barrels into corners, into piles of rotting pews. Some went outside and circled the church.

Jack, careful to keep his eyes averted from the insanity that was the altar, mounted the chancel and moved along the outer wall. A single broken window on his right gave a glimpse of the dead ground. Jack noted one of the men moving slowly in parallel with himself; the man's shaggy blond head swiveling as he searched. Jack continued on, following the rear wall of the church to the opposite corner. There, the wall jogged out, giving the impression of a room beyond. Jack studied it but saw no door. He reached a tentative hand toward it, fingers feeling for a hidden entrance. The wood was sticky and spongy, and a shudder of revulsion gripped him as he pressed against it. As he'd expected, the section of wall swung inward, revealing a small, pitch-black space.

"Lantern!" he called out. Moments later, one of the men hurried over and passed the wire handle to Jack. He held up the light source, peering beneath it into the area. The room was small, about five feet wide by three feet deep, just big enough to allow the storage of a few items or to give the cleric a moment's reprieve. The walls were lumpy, seemingly waterlogged, but Jack couldn't see the seams of wood panels as he would have expected.

"What the fuck is on the walls?" the man behind him asked.

Jack, satisfied that the room was clear, held the light closer. His stomach rolled as his mind identified the strange coating lining all the walls.

Human skin.

This time he didn't stop himself from vomiting.

Jack staggered out to the openness of the chancel. He dropped the Thompson and bent forward, hands on his knees as he retched. His throat burned and his chest constricted as his body spasmed.

A scream from outside forced him upright. He snatched up the Thompson and pounded down the aisle as the others inside the church threw concerned, questioning looks at the doorway. Jack reached the porch, desiccated organs skittering away as his feet slid to a halt.

On the ground near the stairs, one of the men was on his knees. Standing over him, its jaws working as it chewed a bleeding chunk of the man's throat, was one of the corpses that had flanked the door. It swallowed the meat and the chewed flesh dropped into the hollow cavity with a wet *plop*. The creature smiled at Jack, then bent forward to tear another gaping wound in the man whose screams became wet gurgles.

Movement from the darkness of the trees beyond the church forced Jack's attention away. Beneath him the ground swayed like a ship on rough seas as the shambling forms of the other corpses crept toward the church, drawn to the men inside like moths to a flame.

But what turned Jack's guts to water were the other shadowy

forms that flitted among the slower reanimated corpses. The lanky, twisted shapes that moved with a chittering, clicking noise that filled the air like a lunatic chorus.

As the first mottled figures with bristling, unnatural outlines broke from the cover of the trees, Jack raised the Thompson and squeezed the trigger. The weapon roared, drowning out his terrified screams as the creatures advanced, baleful hunger in their eyes.

56

"**Y**ou're lucky the stage is still there."

In the dying sunlight, Theodore Buck eyed the large wooden structure. It was a wide stage with waist-high guardrails running around most of it. A short flight of steps led to the street from the front center. Tall posts on the four corners supported a framework of wood rails from which hung colorful bunting and streamers, all advance decorations for the canceled festival. A pair of torches, now lit, jutted from the front posts, their flames throwing a comfortable glow across the first few rows of those gathered, their faces curious.

"Yes," Sam said, "we're truly blessed." He glanced at the crumpled paper in Theodore's fist. "I'm glad you're attending."

The other man saw what Sam was looking at and shuffled uncomfortably. "Oh, uh, yeah. Preacher Michaels doesn't want us to but . . ." He glanced at the nearby building and the strange, wet sores dotting its surface, then down at the black, foul-smelling weeds growing through the hard dirt of the street.

"I understand," Sam said and placed a hand on the smaller man's shoulder. He gave a reassuring squeeze. "I thank you for your bravery and trust me when I say that tonight will be the night all of us will experience true salvation. All our worries will be stripped away and a true Eden will flourish. You'll see."

"How can you know? Even Preacher Michaels is starting to say that we're being punished for allowing the bootlegging to happen."

Sam looked at the rotting buildings, the mold and dripping moisture that was covering more and more every day. "Men and their liquor are a match made in sin. On that, Preacher Michaels is correct. But this"—he waved a hand to indicate their surroundings—"isn't a punishment. It's a chrysalis."

"A what?" Theodore's face screwed up in confusion. "A krist-liss?"

Sam chuckled. "Chrysalis," he repeated, speaking the word slower. "It's what happens when a caterpillar goes into a cocoon. What you see as blight is actually our cocoon. And what happens when that caterpillar emerges?" He raised his eyebrows expectantly, waiting for the other man to make the connection.

Theodore's face was placid for a moment, then brightened. "A butterfly!"

"That's right." Sam beamed. "And our town and everyone in it who trusts and believes in the Lord will emerge as beautiful butterflies. Not as actual butterflies, mind you, but rather new and better people, free of despair, worry, and suffering. Now, you go find a place among those out there, and we'll begin shortly." Theodore's head bobbed enthusiastically and he hurried off, Sam's flier still clutched in one hand.

Sam peered around the edge of the stage and took in the crowd. It had begun with just a few small groups of twos and threes as people noticed the placement of the pulpit and the installation of torches earlier in the afternoon. Now that the sun was setting, the torches had been lit and he noticed quite a few lanterns clutched in hands as the crowd grew and word spread about the upcoming ceremony. Sam was glad to see them. Ever since he left the house and Grace, it had been a concern that so many in the town who had kept their distance from his new services would abstain from such an important ceremony. But the days of posting fliers and speaking to anyone in town who would stop and listen seemed to have paid off. Whether or not they were believers in God's plan for salvation, or they were just there for spectacle and under a sense of skepticism, would soon be revealed.

But still, they had come. He took in the faces, all various shades of curiosity, and guessed close to forty people were there. Not nearly as many as he'd hoped, but perhaps as the ceremony began, more would be drawn in by his words and the prayers.

More disconcerting was the absence of members of his own congregation; those folks who had accepted the new path and Host, including Jonas and Anna Robertson. He'd been counting on their attendance. While he was happy to sermonize to new faces, there was something to be said about speaking to people whom you knew closely, who attended your services every week. If those in the town who had avoided the new sermons, or frankly didn't even know about them, saw a gathering before the stage of people who understood what was going on, the outsiders were more likely to drift closer. If they saw people they knew, friends and neighbors, involved in a public ceremony, they might be less inclined to stay away. There were even more new people slowly making their way along the street now.

But where was his congregation?

His gaze drifted from the crowd and passed along the darkened, silent buildings. He watched the windows and shadowy doorways for signs of movement but saw none.

"Sam?" Grace stood nearby.

She wore the dress he'd bought and Sam's heart leapt in his chest at the sight of her. "You came," he said and reached for her.

She pulled back. Then, realizing what she'd done, allowed him to wrap his arms around her. Under his embrace, she was tiny, fragile. Sam released her and held her at arm's length. "Are you feeling better? You look breathtaking."

A nervous smile touched her lips and she lowered her gaze. "Thank you for the dress. I've never had anything so nice before."

"You should have only the best of things," he said. "Especially for tonight, when we have such an important moment to witness. Are you ready? I was about to take the stage and begin. We have a wonderful crowd, don't you think? Not quite as many as I'd hoped, of course. I suppose there will always be those who are skeptics and intentionally turn from the light of truth. But we will demonstrate to those out there that the blight ends tonight and together we will all step into Eden."

Something changed in Grace's expression, a heaviness overtaking her features. She turned her face to his and he gasped at the depth of sadness mirrored in her eyes. "It's not what you think it is," she said in a soft, mournful voice.

"What?" He gave a confused smile.

"This," she said, looking to the stage and the crowd beyond. "All of the things you've been preaching. It's not what you've been led to believe. It's been done before, and the result was blood and ruin."

"I don't—"

Grace took a step closer, her small, cold hands finding his own and squeezing. "I've had a vision. I saw the truth. The messengers you've been speaking with? They're not angels. They're witches, or something like them. Ancient and the blackest evil. They've been poisoning your mind with lies. I—"

"Grace," Sam interrupted, "maybe it was too soon for you to be out. I think you might need a bit more rest before you're recovered sufficiently. That is my fault. I was so excited to share this moment with you, to have you stand with me while I guide the people into this new dawn, that I overlooked how exhausted you were. I apologize. Please, go home and get some rest. I'll be there after everything is done here and we can talk."

"But something awful—"

Sam didn't wait to hear what she had to say. He turned and climbed the stairs to the stage and made his way to the pulpit. The murmuring of the crowd intensified as he came into view, but quieted as he reached his place and held his hands up.

"Friends," he said, casting his voice out, "I want to thank you for coming. Tonight is not a night for us to fret or worry about the troubles of the recent weeks. Tonight is not a night for lamenting those lost. Tonight is a night to celebrate! To rejoice in the promise that the

Lord has made to us, that He has made clear to me only recently, that these things we're experiencing are *not* some devilish curse or punishment." There was a rolling wave of murmurs at that. "He came to me to tell me of a new way, a long forgotten set of prayers and ceremonies that spoke directly to His loving heart. These prayers have prepared us, those in my flock, for the coming of a new Eden. Tonight we will witness the tearing away of the darkness that has consumed our town and rejoice in the rebirth of clean, beautiful, renewed life!"

A smattering of applause rippled up but mostly the faces remained impassive, if not outright skeptical. Sam nodded enthusiastically, as if the entire crowd had erupted in cheers. "Tonight I will lead us all in the final set of prayers. These will cleanse our minds and souls and allow the Lord's power to burn away the chrysalis of change."

"A butterfly!" Theodore Buck shouted from somewhere in the group. Several people laughed at the outburst, but Sam pointed in the direction of the voice.

"Young Brother Buck is correct, my friends! Jericho Springs will be renewed, washed in the blood of Christ, and a new Eden will emerge. Tonight we celebrate our deliverance!" He closed his eyes and focused on the prayers. The words, ugly on the surface, clawed and scraped their way out of his throat. The people let out a collective gasp as the words slammed into them. The prayers, the passion of the truth of salvation, retribution, and the deliverance into purity filled Sam with energy as he strode across the stage, back and forth like a caged animal while he spoke the strange language. With each utterance, the faces of those before him softened, turning from uncertainty to placid understanding.

As he continued, the last of the light drained from the land. Overhead, the sky was a black, unblinking eye; a void into which anything could fall and be lost forever. The air, despite the earlier warmth, grew colder, and through the shouted prayers, Sam heard a couple of people cry out in surprise. But only a couple. The rest of the crowd stood undisturbed, their faces slack, their eyes locked on him. He ceased his pacing, positioned himself front and center of the stage, and bellowed the prayer, starting it over as soon as it had ended. His ears popped as the pressure in the air increased. Despite the blood that filled his mouth from pronouncing the awful syllables, Sam grinned, sending scarlet streams spilling past his lips.

"Behold! They come to take us into a new life!" He didn't turn to look but could feel the sudden manifestation of angels behind him like a cold block of ice. "Fear not! They are God's own messengers! They—" The words were cut off as a hand shoved Sam roughly to one side. Biting pain screamed through his knees when they collided with the stage floor. He looked over his shoulder to see Grace, her pale face turned to the crowd.

"Go home!" she yelled. "You are being lied to! These are not angels! They are witches! We've all been lied to and now we are damned to hell! They are here to devour us all! This has been their doing!"

Sam glanced at the rear corners of the stage where the dark figures stood. Silver eyes shined, unblinking, watching the girl shout and plead. He caught the twitch of movement from one, the flick of a finger perhaps, then pulled himself to his feet. At the edge of the stage, Grace doubled over as a coughing fit overwhelmed her. Huge racking spasms coursed through her and she held one hand to her chest, the other out at an angle for balance. Sam approached her. He needed to get her somewhere safe. She was clearly delusional from whatever she'd endured during her time in the woods and needed more rest.

He placed one hand on her back, felt the convulsions of her coughing but turned his face to the crowd. "Worry not! This is all God's plan! We will see the rebirth of our town and bathe in the glory of—"

Grace vomited. The stream splattered onto the ground in front of the stage. Sam recoiled in horror. There were things crawling in the black liquid as it pooled on the dirt. The crowd pressed back, bodies knocking into one another in their haste to escape the surge of bile and the writhing, multi-limbed things that squirmed within.

When the convulsion passed, Grace remained bent forward,

hands on her thighs. Strings of black spittle dripped from her lips, swaying as she sucked in deep breaths. Sam forced himself to take a step closer. His shaking hands rose, reaching tentatively for her. Grace turned her head to look up at him. Her mouth and cheeks were smeared with a thin, viscous layer of the black liquid, but her eyes were soft, brimming with sorrow.

The dark figures—the angels—left their corner, bent and twisted limbs moving unnaturally. As they crept closer, a cold wave of nauseating fear swept through Sam. Sweat broke out all over his body and his throat closed as their shining eyes fixed on him. Sam gaped at the things—ebony shapes like holes cut in the fabric of reality through which could be seen the velvety blackness of a cold and infinite hell. A chorus of low, mocking laughter filled his mind and he knew with absolute certainty that it came from the two dark figures.

Grace's back arched, her face thrust toward the sky, mouth straining open in a silent scream. The flesh of her cheeks rippled and bulged, and Sam waited for another round of the unholy vomitus.

What came was so much worse.

Fingers, pallid gray and tipped with curved black claws, rose out of Grace's open mouth. They wriggled like worms made sluggish from a deep cold, before bending and grasping the girl's lower jaw. A sound like tearing cloth filled Sam's ears as a fissure opened in Grace's cheek. A jagged tear split the skin all the way to the ear, and blood streamed down her face in a solid sheet. The fingers pushed harder, forcing the chin lower and lower, until Grace's mouth hung at an impossibly wide angle. She staggered, her body lurching to one side and turning to face Sam. Despite the extreme angle of her head, her eyes wide and pleading and full of unimaginable terror found Sam's. Soft wet choking sounds drifted around the hand that now fully held her mandible and continued to force it lower.

Something in Grace's slender, blood-covered throat bobbed as if she were swallowing a large pill. The skin opened, rupturing along some invisible vertical seam. Grace's entire body jerked in short, stiff spasms, her arms thrown out from her sides, fingers writhing as she clawed at the empty air.

The flesh of her neck expanding, first tentatively, then falling back as the thing inside forced its way out. Sam's legs gave out and he collapsed to his knees as a face, black beneath the blood and gore that covered it, emerged through the slit. As it broke into the world, a rounded bony point rose from Grace's stomach. The dress that Sam had bought billowed like a tent, rippling with each twitch beneath it. *That's a knee,* his mind realized. *That's a knee inside her stomach.*

The world filled with the sound of tearing meat. The dress was saturated as Grace's stomach tore open. Blood and viscera streamed onto the stage, slopping wetly where they landed between the girl's bare feet. The bony, rounded impression of a knee was replaced by that of a long-toed foot. The terrible claws that tipped each digit sliced into the sodden fabric and pressed downward, shredding the dress.

Grace Robertson's body convulsed as the thing inside her continued to push and pull, rip and tear itself free. Sam was numbly aware of thin clumps of hair matted to a bloodstained scalp as the creature's head fully emerged. The eyes opened and silver orbs glared down at him. Lips curled back in a contemptuous sneer, revealing jagged black teeth.

Grace's head flopped fully back and bobbed against her shoulder blades like a cork on rough waters. Her body slipped to the stage like a discarded robe. There was a heavy, dull *thunk* when her skull connected with the boards, followed by a wet *slosh* as the rest of her collapsed. Sam stared at the broken, torn folds of skin and noticed that one hand lay palm up with fingers outstretched, as if in her last moment, Grace was reaching for him. With great effort, he pulled his eyes from the remains and focused on the thing that towered over him.

The creature—*No, that's a witch just like the others, just like Grace said!*—stood dripping blood as it glared at him. The witch's chest heaved as she took her first breaths in this new world. More cold laughter echoed from the two dark shapes watching the horrific rebirth. And at that moment, Sam understood. Realization crashed down like a detonated building. His soul withered against the burning horror of reality. He'd not been hearing the voice of God. He'd not been chosen to lead his people and this town through the plague. He'd been used, lied to, and manipulated into preparing the town and its people for the arrival of the final witch. The three reunited were now a coven, and everything Sam knew about the world was going to die. Grace had been right. They are not angels. They are unholy abominations.

They are witches.

Oh, dear God, what have I done?

Sam's head filled with a cacophony of tormented screams, the buzzing of flies, and through it all, a contented chuckling. He slapped his hands to his ears in an attempt to mute the noise, but it remained, crashing around inside his mind like a panicked bird trapped in a cage.

Through the din, images bloomed like blossoming flowers, opening to him before dying and wilting away. He saw an infinite blackness, a void filled with tormented, alien creatures. Things with tentacles and without true shape, beasts with countless eyes, worms with screaming faces all along their segmented bodies, untold horrors cast into a cold purgatory and left to feed on their own hatred.

He saw the witches passing through a tear in the blackness, stepping onto a grassy plain where people dressed in blood-drenched furs fell to their knees in worship. He saw the land consumed by decay, its people driven further into madness and transformed into twisted, broken, inhuman versions of themselves, made only to serve the three witches as they continued to corrupt the land and everyone in it.

The white-hot rage of the vile creatures swept over him like the wind, witnessing their power weakened as the mutated people rotted from the inside out and died. As the witches were destroyed by a conquering army that brought strange magic and rituals with them, binding the inhuman creatures and burying them deep within the land, sending them once more into darkness.

More images came. Images that spoke to the black hunger to

create a world in which those abominations from the dark void would thrive. There was a desire, a singular focus to unleash all that blackness into the world in the name of "reclamation." He didn't understand why, but knew with absolute certainty that the witches and those creatures in that unknowable nihility were somehow of *this* world, the one into which Sam was born.

The world that had been meaningless until Grace Robertson had come into being.

The newly born witch turned her eyes from him and the screams and sights within his mind cut off like a candle snuffed out. She uttered something, the words like the hissing of snakes underscored by a pained mewling. Similar sounds answered as the other creatures crossed the stage.

The three witches gathered close to one another. Heads bent forward and touched. The original two stepped back, positioning themselves to either side of the newest arrival. Together the trio turned to face the street and the people still gathered there. At the sight of the black things at the edge of the stage, the paralysis that had held the crowd through the ritual snapped, and terror slammed into them like a tidal wave. People screamed and clawed at one another in their haste to turn and flee.

Three claw-tipped hands rose in unison. The ground in front of the stage erupted as writhing roots and vines blackened with rot burst forth and whipped toward the fleeing crowd. People were ensnared, the roots constricting around bodies and squeezing until the flesh burst like overripe tomatoes. Others were pulled apart like a fly under the callous fingers of a mean-spirited child.

Bodies and broken limbs littered the ground as people raced about, confused and terrified. Women pulled or carried small children. Men shoved one another aside as they bolted in all directions.

On either side of the street, doors crashed open and windows blew out, sending glittering shards of glass spilling onto the road as new bodies emerged. Sam recognized them all, but his brain associated a new word with the creatures.

Thralls.

The people who had once been his congregation, fervent believers in his new message and the ancient rituals that promised redemption and salvation, now raced into the fray. Their bodies had transformed into mottled gray and yellow abominations. Spiny growths jutted from their limbs and backs. Mouths yawned hungrily with overlarge jagged teeth, and black-tipped clawed hands slashed at the people who had once been friends, neighbors, lovers, or kin.

The thralls poured into the chaos and a new round of terrified shrieks filled the air as people fell to the tearing claws and rending teeth. To Sam's left came a brief flare of light as a lantern crashed to the ground. The flame spread across the dirt, following the widening pool of kerosene until it found a new source of fuel: the dress of an older woman. Fire chewed hungrily up the cloth and within the blink of an eye, the woman was engulfed. Her arms beat helplessly at the wreath of flames that covered her head. She lurched wildly about before being knocked away by the bleeding and torn body of a child as it was thrown violently by the creature that had once been Jonas Robertson.

Sam stared helplessly as the flaming woman and the body of the child crashed through a plank door and disappeared from sight. He pulled himself to his feet and stood swaying. He needed to go help that woman. He needed to get her out of there. She shouldn't be in there with an open flame. That was the storage shed where the fireworks were housed for if or when the Summer Festival was rescheduled. Henry Anderson hadn't removed them and if she didn't get out of there, they could all go up.

The shed exploded in a brilliant flare of phosphorus light. Rapid crackling like gunshots filled the air as the fireworks ignited. Bright arms of sparks arched into the night sky, the embers falling down like glowing snowflakes onto the dead and dying. Once fallen, small wisps of smoke curled upward from thick pools of blood scattered along the dirt road.

Through all the pops and smaller explosions of fireworks came a screaming whistle. A sparkling ball of light trailing smoke shot from the ruins of the shed and Sam followed its level track down the street that connected to Heart Avenue, where it went through a window and dipped out of sight. For the span of a heartbeat, Sam was relieved that the small rocket hadn't hit anyone.

Then he understood what building it had entered.

A giant fist of heat slammed into him, throwing him back across the stage and onto the hard earth as the oil and kerosene tanks inside Oscar Tanner's warehouse exploded.

57

Jack swept the Thompson across the swampy landscape. The weapon bucked in his hands and he fought to keep it level as he poured round after round into the charging creatures and shambling undead. Bullets slammed into trees and the muddy ground, kicking up spikes of dirt-flecked water. Many, however, found their marks and slapped into dead tissue. Limbs already thinned by decomposition or bloated by too much time in the swamp blew apart. Chunks of flesh flew as bullets exited the bodies of the things that had hung like scarecrows.

Several of the walking nightmares fell and continued writhing in an attempt to reach their target, still powered by whatever evil spell compelled them but unable to gain ground due to their grievous wounds. Others collapsed in a true lifeless heap and did not move.

The other creatures, the ones that had at one time been human beings until they consumed the black and squirming Host the pastor had fed them, ignored their wounds and rushed forward with mindless need. A few fell when bullets or shotgun blasts removed their heads or tore massive holes in their chests. But Jack was learning quickly that if the wound was to a limb or a noncentral part of the torso, these things were only mildly inconvenienced in their pursuit.

"We can't keep this up!" Trask shouted. He and four others had formed a loose box and were blasting in each direction as the scarecrows closed in. "We ain't got much ammo left!"

As if to prove the point, the bolt on Jack's weapon fell on an empty chamber as the last of the rounds in the drum magazine blasted into the drooping, half-eaten face of a one-eyed Black man. The corpse continued two more lumbering steps, pitched forward, and didn't move again. Jack scanned the area around the church. Of the twenty men who had made the trek through the dying woods, he could only see Trask's group and a scattering of five more men remaining, each one standing by himself, firing into the swarming bodies. Several bodies, or pieces of them, littered the muddy ground by the stairs and floated in the murky water like flotsam.

He could only count six corpses of the people-turned-monsters. The howling screeches of the ones still circling and searching for a way past the wall of hot lead echoed through the swamp. Jack threw a glance over his shoulder into the church. Could they retreat and make a stand inside? There was enough furniture that they could barricade the doors. They could use the few windows as firing ports.

But to what end? Would the creatures do as those inside the home of Peter Junkins had done and stop attacking once their quarry wasn't in sight? A scream to Jack's left brought him back to the immediate threat. The man's voice died as the spiny creature clamped its unnatural mouth onto the bootlegger's face. Powerful jaws slammed shut and pulled back in a spray of blood and gristle. The gory cavern of the man's head flopped as his body fell into the muck. The creature turned its silver eyes to Jack as it chewed.

Fuck this. Jack slung the Thompson across his back and drew his pistol. "Trask! Get your men up here!" Not waiting to see if his order was received, Jack turned and screamed at the other men to do the same. The four surviving men moved in slow, laborious steps as they fired and reloaded, fired and reloaded. The intensity of their shooting served as an effective deterrent to the faster creatures who darted from tree to tree, shrieking in fury at being denied warm flesh.

Jack took careful aim and placed his shots purposefully, aware of the limited range of his pistol compared to the powerful machine gun. Trask's group pounded up the stairs before turning to give covering fire for the others. One of the four men on the ground tripped on something beneath the water and fell with a *splash*. He thrashed, screaming in terror as he fought to regain his footing and find his rifle, but two of the hideous things were on him in an instant. Their claws ripped apart his body and spilled his blood into the black water.

The other three men sprinted as hard as they could for the relative safety of the church. They reached the bottom stair and Trask and the others gripped them and hauled them up. When they were all inside, Jack shouted to close it up. Two men pulled on the massive, rotting wood doors and managed to swing them together. Jack wasted no time and began hauling broken pews to stack as a barricade.

"Okay," Trask panted when the work was done. "What now?"

Jack pointed to the few lanterns that had been left throughout the church. "Those still have oil, right?"

Trask looked at the closest lantern. "You have to be kidding me," he groaned.

"You got another plan?" Jack asked.

The other man chewed on his lip, thinking. Finally, he shook his head. "Nope."

"Great." Jack turned to the rest of the men. "Two of you start breaking out the windows back there. You three, blow out all these candles. We don't need these fumes going up before we're ready. The rest of you stay here and make sure this barricade holds a bit longer." He gestured to Trask and together they collected lanterns. They unscrewed the caps to the oil wells and poured the kerosene over the remaining piles of pews, making sure to splash plenty on the walls and floor. The pungent stench of the church grew worse with the sharp, bitter smell of kerosene.

Bone-rattling blows shook the old doors, causing the barricaded pews to shift. "This ain't gonna hold long," one of the men shouted as he backed several feet away, the heavy iron chains looped over his shoulders clacking together.

"It doesn't have to," said Jack. "Everyone get to the windows. Make sure none of those things have snuck around back."

Men poked heads through the openings. "Looks clear back here," one said. "I see a few of those scarecrows still wandering around, but they're a ways off."

"Good," Jack said. "Everyone climb out. I'm going to wait until they break through, then light this fucking place up."

"Will you have enough time to get out?" Trask asked.

"I'll be fine. Give me one of those pump guns, though. I may need to knock them back before I can throw the match." He accepted a shotgun and checked its load. "Go on. I'll be right behind you. When this place goes up, we'll blast them through the windows until they're all burning."

The men scrambled through the windows. Trask went last, hesitating as he straddled the sill. "You sure you don't want me to stay and watch your back?"

Jack shook his head. "Don't worry, I'll be right behind you."

Alone, Jack faced the barricaded doors. They rattled violently as if a hurricane was blowing on the other side. The broken frames of the benches toppled away, and the pile slid across the floor as the snarling, shrieking monsters made headway.

Jack reached into a pocket, pulled out the matchbook. His fingers closed over the cardboard and immediately he knew he was in trouble. The fabric of the pocket was damp, but the flimsy matchbook was completely soaked. His fingers worked back the cover and he ran a thumb across the phosphorus heads. The movement left a small smudge of green on the pad of his thumb. He glanced at the candles around the church, their wicks blackened and unlit. Small tails of smoke rose from a couple.

Good plan, you dolt.

"Fuck," he growled and threw the book down just as the doors slammed open. The faces and arms of the mutated people filled the space. Their silver eyes settled on Jack and the church thundered with their rage. He worked the pump on the shotgun and took a few steps back until his heels connected with the chancel. He widened his stance, shouldered the shotgun, and took aim as the last of the barricade flew apart and the creatures spilled inside.

The shotgun boomed and bodies flew back as the things fought one another to crawl past the last of the barricade. Jack worked the pump methodically, keeping count of the rounds he had remaining. More blasts filled the church as Trask and two others stood at the windows, firing into the surging mass of flesh.

As he twisted back to resume firing, Jack flinched as one of the creatures darted forward. Its powerful clawed hand sliced the air inches in front of Jack's chest. In his attempt to dodge, his feet became entangled with one another and he toppled over, landing hard on his side on the edge of the chancel. Pain flared in his ribs and for a moment, the breath was taken out of the world. The shotgun toppled away and Jack's fingers spasmed in an attempt to maintain control of it. The trigger kicked back in his efforts and the weapon coughed flame, the recoil of the blast knocking the gun from his hand.

The creature that had lunged for him corrected its course and bent toward Jack, jaws opening impossibly wide as horrible teeth, oozing a viscous saliva, gleamed in the dull light. The side of the monster's face exploded in a burst of red mist and it tumbled away. At the same time, an enormous wave of blistering heat blew past Jack. His skin sizzled and against the screaming pain in his ribs, he twisted, pulling one hand over his head protectively.

When he didn't die, he scrambled back onto the platform of the chancel and watched, stunned, as the entire church was engulfed in flames. The creatures that had streamed inside were immediately overwhelmed by the fire. They flailed about, slamming into one another, colliding with piles of flaming furniture and collapsing in shuddering, convulsing heaps upon the burning floor.

Arms, sudden and powerful, wrapped around Jack's chest and he was hauled to his feet. A swell of blackness passed over his vision as the damage to his side protested the movement. "We have to get the fuck out of here," Trask's voice growled in his ear.

Jack climbed through the window, black oily smoke billowing out, obscuring the men and ground beyond. Hands reached out and grabbed him, helped him down, and led him away. They moved several yards from the church to a point where the air was clear of smoke and paused, panting, as they watched the structure burn.

"What—" A coughing fit ended the thought and sent shards of pain shooting through his side. *Fucking rib's broken,* he concluded irritably.

Trask answered, "When you fell, the shotgun went off and hit one of the empty lanterns on the floor. The sparks ignited the kerosene. Fucking dumb luck, that."

A chuckle of pure astonishment bubbled up past Jack's lips, but brought with it fresh grinding agony from his ribs and he bit down on any further amusement. "Were they all inside?" he asked. "What about the scarecrows?" Another panicked thought came. "The chains?"

"We got 'em. They're safe. Most of those scarecrow things were inside," one of the others said. "A few hauled ass when the place went up. Ran off into the woods that way." He pointed. "There's still some of those scarecrows. But they move slower, so if we don't stick around, we should be able to—"

The man's words cut off when a massive explosion rumbled in the distance. Jack wasn't certain but thought the ground beneath his feet vibrated slightly from the shock wave. "The hell was that?" he asked. Nobody answered. All the men stared into the trees in the direction of the sound.

"Whatever it was, it was huge," Trask said. "Someone get hold of a bomb?"

"That was from town," another man said anxiously. "Something in town blew up."

"We don't have anything in town that . . ." Trask responded harshly, then let the thought fade as his eyes glazed over, his mind pulling up something for him to consider. "Oh God."

"What?" asked Jack.

"The oil and kerosene tanks. In that distribution warehouse off Heart Avenue. That's the only thing that would have caused an explosion like that." He ran a hand through his sweat-soaked hair. "Unless someone did manage to get a bomb."

"The Klan?" asked one of the men.

"No," Jack said. "We fucked up, coming here."

"What do you mean?" Trask asked as the others followed.

Jack sloshed into the swampy water and grimaced as the bobbing parts of men bumped against him. He turned his head and said over his shoulder, "While we're out here wasting time and getting killed, the witches are attacking Jericho Springs."

58

Eli looked at the squat building and curled his lip. "You think *this* place is going to have decent food?"

Adrian shrugged. "I doubt it. Looks more like they serve botulism. But we need to eat and this will kill some time, make sure we get there when it's dark. Besides, my ass is numb." He got out of the Chrysler and crunched his way across the gravel lot. The diner was small with clapboard siding covered in sloppy red paint. Large white letters in a shaky scrawl to the left of the door proclaimed it to be *The Wooden Nickel*.

It was bigger inside than its exterior boasted. A massive counter dominated the left side of the floor plan. The rest of the space held a couple of old tables, only one of which had customers. A series of booths near the rear of the place completed the dining area. Adrian led the others across a marred black-and-white checkered tile floor to the far corner. He, Frank, and Eli settled into a booth beneath a large painting of a train racing across open countryside. The other men crammed into the other booths, dour looks plastered on their faces. Adrian's stomach gave another insistent rumble at the smell of frying meat mingled with the thick aroma of coffee.

A waitress emerged from a swinging door that led to the kitchen, the sounds of cookware slamming together announcing her arrival before muting as the door swung shut. The woman, a girl, really, Adrian thought, pulled up short when she saw the group that had seated themselves. She stared at the well-dressed men with unabashed surprise. Adrian caught her attention and raised an eyebrow expectantly. After another moment, she blinked out of her shock and gathered menus.

Turning back to the table, Adrian's eyes settled on the small form of Frank's camera perched on the tabletop next to the man's elbow. The sight of the camera and the knowledge of all the horrors it contained sitting in plain sight of upstanding citizens brought a chuckle bubbling past his lips.

"The fuck's so funny?" Eli asked.

"Nothing," Adrian said as the waitress placed mugs in front of them and set about filling them with coffee. "Get that fucking thing off the table," he said, glaring pointedly at the camera. "You forget where it's been? Because I haven't." Frank, his eyes vacant, slowly placed the camera next to him on the seat.

"Anything good to eat here?" Adrian asked the waitress.

Her eyes flicked between Adrian, Eli, and Frank, who sat chewing on a toothpick, his fingers dancing along the rim of his mug. "Gosh, we ain't seen guys like you in a . . . well, ever. Y'all up from Birmingham?"

"We are," Adrian said with a slick smile, putting a slight purr into his words. "Got some business around here."

The girl, a pretty thing with sandy hair held up in a bun secured by three pencils, gave a gentle, airy chuckle. "What kind of business around here would a bunch of well-dressed gentlemen like your-selves have?"

"You were saying, about what was good here?" Adrian asked.

The waitress blinked. "Oh. Sorry. We have everything from burgers to breakfast all day. You like hash? Willy back there makes a good one."

"Three of them."

"I don't like hash," Frank said quietly. The waitress glanced at him, as if he were a snake that had suddenly coiled and was eyeing her.

"I'll eat yours," Adrian said. "Three," he repeated to the waitress, who slid over to the second booth to take orders. That finished, she hurried away, stealing glances over her shoulder as she vanished into the kitchen. Adrian turned to Frank. "You got her scared." Frank simply shrugged.

"Are we gonna do this today or what?" Eli demanded, his voice low but as hard and pointed as a penny nail.

"We are," Adrian said. "But I'm not doing a damned thing on an empty stomach. Look," he said, leaning forward after Eli's exasperated sigh, "I know the McCarthys were your countrymen and you'd run with them some in the past, but Jacob was my fucking nephew. I'm going to see Carmelo's heart ripped out of his chest for what he did. But we can't go off half-cocked. This isn't Chicago. We don't know the area. We have to get to this shitkicker town first and if it's as tiny as it sounds, we'll stick out like a couple of niggers in the wrong swimming pool." Adrian bit down on his anger. The need to put a knife in Jack Carmelo's eye was like a rat gnawing at his brain.

"We're going to eat. And roll into town at night."

"Then what? How do we find him?" The men paused the conversation as the waitress delivered three large oval plates piled high with steaming eggs, bacon, potatoes, and what to Adrian's nose smelled to be in the neighborhood of corned beef.

When she'd retreated, Adrian continued. "What we're going to do is find a place to hole up outside of town. From there we can start to look around, ask around a little, but quietly. An Italian from Chicago in a tiny hillbilly town is going to be the topic of conversation. We'll hear if people know where he is. Then it's a matter of getting him back to our place and . . . Taking. Our. Time."

When the meal was finished and paid for, the men climbed back into their cars and rumbled into the fading light. The sky was a tableau of deep purples edged by soft pinks as the sun gave up the ghost for the day, and with every mile that brought them closer to Carmelo, the rat chewing at Adrian's mind grew even more frenzied.

The road twisted and turned through a myriad of shadowy forests, and as they neared the town, the sweet smell of early summer grasses and pastures gave way to a sharper, more pungent scent. "The fuck is that?" Adrian asked, his head angled toward the open window.

"Smells like smoke," Frank said quietly from the back seat.

"Yeah," Eli agreed, his own face in the opening of his door. "But there's something else. Smells dead. Animal or something."

"Look at that," Frank said, leaning over the seat and staring at the horizon.

In the headlights, the road stretched for several hundred yards before disappearing into shadows. The forest, a massive wall of black, stretched to the sky—a pulsing glow above the rounded and jagged tree tops.

"Something's on fire," Eli said assuredly.

The rat in Adrian's brain gave an uncertain twitch. What if something had happened and Jack was already dead, some victim of an accident? He quashed the worry with a shake of his head. "Let's go. If something's happened, we'll be able to slip in completely unnoticed." He started the car and drove on. Fifteen minutes later, the trees that lined the pitted road ended and the town of Jericho Springs opened before them.

"Son of a bitch," Adrian muttered.

The town was on fire. Thick sheets of flame licked at the sky several blocks away, filling the air with heavy curtains of smoke. Through the haze, a few untouched buildings could be seen stretching along the street, but there were no people. Nobody fleeing the inferno or rushing to form a water brigade.

"What in the hell?" Eli asked as the distant sounds of gunfire cut through the night.

Adrian stared for a long moment, taking in the scene, listening to the far-off pops of shooting. A smile split his face. "We're in luck, boys," he said, barely able to contain his happiness.

"How so?" Frank asked.

Adrian pointed to the fire. "I think we got here just in time for a good old-fashioned hillbilly gang war. Those gunshots? I'd bet dollars to doughnuts that it's a couple of rival bootlegger gangs shooting each other up. That, or it's those bumpkins in the Klan fighting with some shiners. These idiots will be so focused on killing each other, they won't notice a few extra people carrying guns. I'm also willing to bet that Carmelo is in the middle of it all. We'll just park a few blocks away and mix in. You guys don't mind shooting a few extra rednecks, do you?"

The silence that came from the other men spoke volumes. Adrian laughed softly, put the Chrysler in gear, and slowly drove into the thick smoke.

<h1 style="text-align:center">59</h1>

Evie screamed at the massive *BOOM* that sent the windows in the front sitting room of Doc Powell's house rattling in their frames. The glass on two of them cracked into spiderwebs. Doc Powell hurried in, a kitchen towel in his hands.

"What in God's name was that?" he asked.

"It came from downtown," she said. Her eyes fixed on the reddish glow pulsing over the dark forms of trees. A massive column of black smoke cut through the light, rising into the dark sky.

"I have to go," Powell said. "People may be hurt." He vanished into another room, returning quickly with his black medical bag. As he threw open the front door, he said, "Stay here. There's no telling what's going on."

"I can help," Evie insisted, pushing up to her feet.

"No," Powell snapped. "Stay here. I'm sure Jack will be along shortly." Then he was gone, slamming the door behind him.

Evie watched the shadowy form of the man hurry across the yard and down the tree- and house-lined street. At the end of the block, he turned left on Blackwell Lane and was gone. She waited another agonizing minute just to ensure he didn't double back, having forgotten something important. When she was satisfied he wouldn't return, she pushed up from her chair and hurried out of the house. Already the air was tinted with the sharp tang of fire. The column of smoke had grown, extending into the sky like a horrible snake. A few other people had drifted out of their homes and stood in yards in twos and threes, looking at the glimmering firelight and pointing.

Evie stood on the porch and thought about the best route to take. Before she could make a decision, the faint chorus of screams rose in the distance.

She gritted her teeth against the pain in her leg and ran, choosing to take the shortest direction and follow Powell. Blackwell Lane intersected Heart Avenue, so she would be in the center of downtown in a couple of minutes. When she reached Heart, she stumbled to a halt, the moisture in her mouth vanishing. The carnage was overwhelming. At the end of the street, the stage that had been built for the Summer Festival and town anniversary was awash in flames. Bodies lay scattered, many on fire. The buildings to the right of the stage were engulfed in an awful inferno. Evie backpedaled against the ferocious heat that flowed against her, searing her skin.

Screams drew her back to the scene unfolding in the middle of the firelight-bathed avenue. The street was a carnival of confused, frantic activity. Several people attempted to quash the flames, hurrying out of nearby businesses with buckets filled with water to slop the liquid at the stage. Others ran, chased by dark, hunched figures who moved with a skittering, loping gait. A man was slammed to the sidewalk as one of said figures leapt onto him, clawing viciously at his back. He screamed and writhed under the assault.

"What?" That was all Evie could manage. The attacker wasn't human. The thing was covered with sickening yellow and gray patches of mold. Terrible bony growths extended from its body at obscene angles. Its face was wide, the features stretched in a mockery of a human expression. A too-large mouth stretched to its ears, jagged teeth bared in an expression of pure ecstasy as it hacked and dug at the man with fingers tipped with wicked talons. The claws slashed into the shrieking man's back, throwing blood high into the air.

All around, the streets were filled with dozens of the creatures.

They leapt from victim to victim, tearing and biting, mutilating people as they shouted for mercy or screamed in unimaginable pain. *Are those the things Jack and Trask fought?*

Worse than the brutality of the attacks were the three dark shapes outlined by the flaming ruins of the stage as they moved through the middle of Heart Avenue. *God in heaven. They brought the third one back.* How was this possible?

The witches observed the chaos with cold detachment. Occasionally, one would gesture and a nearby patch of ground would erupt with rotting vines that writhed and slashed at anyone and anything that came near.

Evie watched, frozen, as the witches strode along the street, oblivious to the bodies that littered their path. The creatures attacking the people ignored the witches, and so the three continued until they reached an intersection. Casually they turned and continued on, gesturing as they walked, either sending vines and rot crawling up buildings or ensnaring a hapless person trying to put distance between themselves and the carnage.

With the witches out of sight, Evie forced herself to focus. What could she do to help? The fire was beyond control. It was obvious even at this point that if the entire town didn't burn, most of it would be ashen rubble by the morning. She didn't see Doc Powell anywhere, so helping him tend to survivors wasn't an option.

A scream, close and sharp, drew her attention. A young girl, probably eight years old, ran down the sidewalk, her red hair streaming behind her as one of the creatures gave chase. It was clearly taking its time, slowing its gait in order to prolong the joy of the pursuit. Every few steps it would reach out and swipe at the girl, its claws snagging on the flowing pleats of her skirt.

The thing's hideous mouth stretched in a toothy smile.

Evie pushed out from the building and started across the street to intervene. At the same time, the girl darted down a side avenue. The creature paused at the corner, watching its quarry gain distance. It leapt forward, covering half the range in a single motion. Evie ran as fast as her bad leg would allow, pushing the drumming pain to the back of her mind.

Ahead, the girl stumbled and fell, and the thing pounced. It landed over the girl, muscular legs straddling her as she shuffled backward. She screamed as it angled one clawed foot and pressed it on her leg, pinning her down.

Evie, still half a block away, searched for anything she could use as a weapon against such a monster. Her eyes fell on the side door to Rangle's. An idea came to her and she plunged into the store, searching for what she needed. She found it in a row with rakes and shovels, then stumbled back out into the street. A claw hammer clutched in a tight fist.

The creature was taking its time with the young girl. Blood streamed from a horrible gash on one thigh, soaking into the warped wooden slats, and she squirmed in agony as it stabbed a claw into the wound.

Evie raised the hammer as she reached the pair. She swung, putting everything she had into the blow. The hooks on the back of the hammer's head sank into the thing's skull with a meaty *thud*. Immediately, the creature stiffened, arms jutting spastically. It spun, ripping the hammer from Evie's grasp.

With black fluid streaming along its neck and down the wiry muscles of its lumpy chest, the monster glared balefully at Evie with silver shining eyes. Reaching back with one massive hand, it tried to wrench the hammer free, but couldn't grasp it. It blinked stupidly and took an uneven step toward her. Before Evie could react, its claw slashed out and fire screamed across her arm and side. She flew into the street, where she landed awkwardly, her already injured leg sending up a fresh pulse of agony.

The creature wavered as more black blood poured out of the wound in its skull. It took a single tottering step onto the road and collapsed with a meaty *thud*. Evie pushed herself partway up, arms shaking, and stared at it, waiting for the unholy thing to move. The young girl pulled herself to her feet, both hands gripping the wound on her leg. She looked from the monster to Evie and back.

"Are you—" Evie began, but the girl turned and hobbled away, blood streaming down her leg, leaving a trail on the concrete.

Evie stood, having to move slowly as waves of dizziness passed over her. Her side was a hot mass of blood and through the ruined tatters of her dress, she saw two deep cuts along her side. For a few seconds, she stood frozen, torn between the decision to return to Rangle's and dress her wounds or chase after the girl, who needed medical attention as well.

The appearance of two more creatures at the end of the street ended the debate. Evie ran, grimacing and grunting against the searing pains that racked her body. The monsters gave a hissing scream and scurried after her, the slaps of their grotesque limbs and guttural breathing filling the whole of Evie's world.

She limped past businesses, her mind noting and dismissing them as potential hiding places. She thought of her shop. If she could get there and up to her apartment, she would be safe. But only until the flames chewed their way through the rest of the town.

"Here!" The voice cut through her panic and Evie searched the street ahead. Seeing no one, she continued running. "Over here! Lady!" Across the street, the face of a teenage boy peered through the partially open door of Springline Dry Goods. He leaned out, gesturing wildly. Evie didn't look back, just ran in his direction. Behind her the creatures screamed their frustration.

The boy threw the door open wider and Evie crashed through, tripping over her feet in her haste and tumbling to the floor. Just as she heard the bolt being thrown, the things on the other side crashed against the door. The space filled with the thunder of their attempts to get in, the heavy blows mingled with the sharper sounds of claws rending wood.

Hands were on her immediately and she was pulled to her feet. "Here," someone—a woman—said. "Get her to that chair so we can look at her."

"What about those things?" the boy asked. He guided Evie to a short wooden chair positioned at the end of one of the long rows of shelves filled with bags of flour and canned goods. The sweet smell of tobacco filled the space along with a dusty, grassy undertone.

"If they get past that door, we'll get into the basement," the woman answered and bent into Evie's view. She was an older woman but pretty, with gray hair pulled back in a bun. "I'm going to look at your wounds." Evie managed a nod and the woman inspected her side.

"What happened?" Evie asked. The words were soft, brittle, and she realized her throat was dry. She tried to muster saliva, something to bring relief.

"A nightmare," the older woman answered. "What came out of that girl . . ." She shook her head. Instead of finishing, she turned to the young man. "We need to move her downstairs. I need to clean and stitch this. Watch her while I get some bandages." She shuffled off, her feet scuffling quickly across the floor as she slipped between the aisles.

"I don't think that door will hold much longer," the boy said, throwing the shaking wood a fearful look.

The woman returned, her hands holding a box that Evie assumed contained bandages and ointments. "Then I suggest we go now." Once more, hands slipped around Evie and she was lifted and guided between the rows of shelves and a wall featuring bolts of fabric set into cubby holes. Near the rear corner of the floor was a door with a small brass plate affixed to its face. Black block lettering read *STAFF ONLY*. The woman pulled open the door and Evie was helped into the dimly lit confines of a musty stairwell.

Right when the door to the hall was closed, from across the store came the sound of splintering wood as the creatures broke down the main entrance. Their hissing cries filled the shop front, punctuated with the thuds of their feet on the wooden floor. Evie let the people guide her down into the basement, as a new round of pounding rattled the door to the stairs.

60

The town had been transformed into a literal hell on earth. Jack leapt from the truck, one hand gripping the open door, and stared down the length of Buckner Road to Heart Avenue. On every street, buildings were engulfed in flames, massive columns of inky black smoke streaming into the sky. Bodies lay scattered, broken, and desecrated, the ground stained by wide, irregular pools of dark crimson. Windows were shattered, streets and sidewalks glittering with the shards as they reflected the firelight. Some windows had bodies hanging limply over their frames, blood streaming down the brick walls and collecting in the gutters. Screams filled the air, competing with the snarling and popping of the fire.

"What the hell is happening?" Trask gasped. Jack could only shake his head, his mouth unable to form words as his eyes flicked from body to body. Two blocks ahead, the wooden stage that had been erected for the festival was a collapsed mass, the boards fully engulfed. The air was a searing, hot blanket that stung Jack's exposed skin.

"I have to find Evie," he said and started away. Trask's hand gripped his arm, spinning him back.

"We need to find those evil bitches and end this. Evie's at Powell's, right? That's over on Dearborn, blocks away from all this. They would've had time to get out." He hefted the loop of an iron chain out of the bed of the truck. "If we don't stop them now . . ."

Jack twisted his arm free of the other man's grasp and pointed down the street. "Evie is out there. We can't—" Before he could finish, a group of people burst from around the corner, eyes wide with terror as they ran toward the trucks. Jack's pistol was in his hand before he realized he'd moved. The other men raised their own weapons, but the people never slowed or showed any indication that they'd even noticed the new arrivals.

A second later, Jack understood why.

Three spiny, twisted creatures burst around the corner, silver eyes glowing with preternatural delight in the firelit darkness. Their wide mouths gaped in parodies of grins as they raced closer.

Nobody spoke. Every man understood at the same time what had to be done, and the narrow street reverberated with the deafening roar of gunfire. Rounds smashed into the monsters, throwing them back, spinning them around. Their bodies burst in dozens of places, throwing black blood out like confetti at a parade. Flesh flew and Jack watched over the sights of his pistol as the face of one of the things blew apart, teeth flying.

When the bodies lay still and the gunfire faded, Jack reloaded and glanced at Trask. "Okay, we need to split up. You, me, and a few others will go after the witches. Take the lanterns, we'll need them to burn those bitches. The rest of you will need to focus on killing those prickly bastards. Once we're done, we'll join back up and help clear out the rest of them." Trask counted out the men he wanted in each detail and the groups split up to accomplish their tasks.

Jack and his men moved through town, darting across the open spaces, keeping as far from the blaze as possible as they searched. Every new street was awash in fresh horrors. Bodies lay everywhere like destroyed and discarded toys. Buildings or homes that weren't covered in flames, crawled with wriggling vines blackened and oozing with putrescence. The runners slithered into structures through windows and doors, punching through the thin barriers like they were eggshells. Jack flinched and changed direction as the brick walls of Jericho Springs First Bank and Trust cracked under the constricting pressure of the roots, shards of red clay spinning out into the street. The ceiling collapsed with a rending groan as the massive shoots fought to pull the structure into the ground.

Gunfire erupted from the men as the mutated creatures darted through the choking smoke, flittering shadows that appeared quickly between structures. Occasionally, and with blinding speed, one would materialize, cutting through the group, slashing or biting at the men. Jack lost three of his crew that way and almost lost more when one of the men, a boy barely out of his teens, spun and shot at the retreating shadow of a beast as it vanished into the smoke. The older man had been lucky; the boy's bullet only clipped the top of his hat.

After that, Jack mandated that nobody fire their weapon unless the target was clearly visible and not moving. He had no illusions that such an opportunity would present itself, but he was also painfully aware of their dwindling supply of ammunition.

The group crossed Hawthorn Avenue and Jack saw the witches for the first time. They stood in a line in the center of the street two blocks away. At first, Jack thought they were survivors or a cluster of the spiny nightmares, but on second glance, he realized that was wrong. The three witches moved slowly and calmly through a tornado of chaos. All about them raced the twisted former humans who had consumed the diseased Host, hunting and killing indiscriminately.

Jack's body tensed, his muscles trembling against the phantom sensation of vines encircling him, tightening and crushing. Before he knew he'd moved, he'd taken a quick step back, thumping against the body of one of the other men. The contact broke the memory of his near death in the woods only a few nights ago, and Jack blinked to regain his focus.

One person—through the smoke Jack couldn't tell if it was a man or woman—lifted off the ground as if by invisible hands. The victim's arms and legs kicked and swayed for a few moments before their entire body was torn apart in a massive spray of blood. The sections of the corpse hurled callously to the dirt, and the evil trio continued on.

They're not touching the ground, Jack thought as he stared after them. The witches hovered a few inches off the street, their movement forward a smooth, level progression. He started toward them, the heavy chain looped over his shoulder and across his body clanking softly as he went. The other men followed close behind.

"What's the plan?" Trask panted as he moved alongside Jack, who slowed, that question cutting through the fog in his mind. In his haste to close the distance, Jack had not considered tactics, and he inwardly cursed his arrogance. "What's ahead? Where does this road go?"

"There's a barber shop on the corner and across from that is the post office. This street dead ends into Martin."

"What's on the other side of Martin?"

"Trees. Used to be a cotton field, but Irvine Martin, a guy who used to own a lot of property here, died and his kids didn't want to—"

"Save the fucking history lesson," Jack said. "We need a place to set up so we can ambush them."

Trask scanned the street ahead, his lips moving in a silent whisper as he worked through the options. "Yeah. There's an alley that runs next to the barber shop. We could set up there."

"What about the post office?"

"No alley."

"Is there a back entrance?"

"Hell if I know. But there'd have to be, right? For the delivery of mail and shit?"

Jack nodded. "That'll have to do. You take two of the chains and circle around. See if you can get into the post office. I'm going to take a couple of guys and"—he pointed to his left—"move down that street until we get to the alley. We need to move quickly; they're not going to have much by way of obstacles soon. One of us will create a distraction while the other group slaps the chains on them. You guys move first. If you can get the chains on two of them, that should weaken them enough that we can take care of the last one quickly. Once they're bound, we'll light the bitches on fire."

Trask barked commands at some of the men and the smaller group angled away, slipping into the smoke. Jack waved for the remaining men to follow him.

The alley next to the barber shop was a short, narrow corridor made even smaller by the maze of vines. The black things stretched out of the broken ground, leaving practically no path through which to walk. The bent forms of trash cans peered from between some of the stalks like pitiful rodents caught between a constrictor's looping body. Roots angled into the brick walls as if they had punched through the solid clay.

Carefully, Jack entered the alley, his men following close behind, panting and coughing from the smoke that burned their throats and lungs. As they slid around or stepped over the torturous vegetation, the roots shuddered and flinched, seemingly sleeping but disturbed by the contact of living flesh. The men moved to the far end and positioned themselves as best they could among the vertical, slimy growths. In the tightness of the space, Jack couldn't tell which was worse: the stench of the vines and the goo they wept or the smell of the town burning. He peered into the street where the screaming was winding down like a phonograph in need of a recharging crank of its handle.

The group of witches was halfway to him, their tall, hideous forms cutting through the haze. Behind them in the distance, wild tongues of flames lapped at the sky, giving the creatures a hellish backdrop. The twisted things that served the nightmarish wraiths were still present but, he noted with a feeling of relief, there were fewer than before. It was as if the witches, seeing that their quarry was nearly wiped out, had sent their minions off in search of fresh kills.

Across the street, the post office was a collapsed ruin covered in black tendrils of rot. The sidewalk was littered with broken glass and shards of bricks. A partial wall of brick, part of the front corner of the building, was the only thing still standing. The rest of the structure was a confusion of splintered wood and twisted metal.

Trask's face appeared over the jagged edge of the partial wall, his eyes wide in fear. He gave his head a quick jerk by way of greeting as Jack spotted him. Jack told the men behind him what he wanted and they positioned themselves as best they could, using the black roots and vines as cover.

Jack thumbed the hammer back on his .45 and waited for the witches to come into view.

61

"Wait," Jack said softly. The word didn't reach those around him. He was saying it more for himself anyway. The men wouldn't do anything until he fired first. The three witches were close now, just twenty yards away. They floated steadily onward, the ground beneath their gnarled and taloned feet turning black and soft as they passed over it. Tendrils of rot raced out in ragged lines ahead of them, breaking the road apart. From the cracks, fetid water bubbled out. Jack risked a glance to the left at Martin Street and the thick trees beyond it. Already the outgrowths of decay were reaching the first trees, the mold climbing the trunks of evergreens quickly, eagerly devouring the life within.

Jack angled his head, catching Trask's attention. The man's eyes shifted to the trio of witches, their skin blackened as if charred, and back to Jack, who raised his eyebrows questioningly, asking, "Are you ready?" Trask licked his lips and gave a quick nod. Jack returned his attention to the witches.

When the coven drifted to within ten yards of him, Jack stepped out of the alley and raised his pistol. Two of the men who had been crouched opposite him followed suit, their own weapons coming up. Jack's finger tightened on the trigger as the heads of the witches swiveled, moving as one unit, focusing their silvery glowing eyes on him.

Jack was so focused on his target that he didn't notice the two large black cars racing down Martin Street toward him. The drivers slammed on their brakes, the cars fishtailing to a screeching halt. Just as Jack's finger squeezed his trigger, the doors of the cars swung open and several men poured out. The roar of Jack's pistol drowned out the shouts of the new arrivals. His shot went wide, slamming into the vines that covered the feed store across the street. At the same time, the world filled with the deafening roar of other weapons.

Jack adjusted his aim and squeezed two more shots. One went wide but the second hit a witch in the shoulder, the creature twitching from the impact. A second later, he realized the gunfire wasn't coming from Trask's group. A sharp cry and a grunt came from one of the men next to him. Jack glanced over to see the man collapsing to his knees. Everything below his nose was a ragged, red mess. Something passed to either side of Jack's head, hot and whizzing as it sliced through the air.

Adrian Turski and Eli Kinnerk stood in the broken and cracked street in front of a large black car. They held Thompsons at their waists and angled them back and forth as large tongues of flame leapt from the barrels. Seven other men were positioned nearby, firing shotguns or pistols. The air was filled with the angry hornet buzz of rounds and Jack threw himself back into the alley as bullets tore fiery hot pain across his left arm and right thigh.

The other man who had stepped out with Jack turned and got off one more blast from his shotgun before dozens of rounds slammed into his body, jerking him in a horrible dying dance. His last shot blew open the chest of one of the men standing next to Turski and sent him flying.

Jack scrambled back, retreated deeper into the alley. He pressed against the wall of thick vines, silently willing them to shift and shield him, but they held fast like iron bars. For a split second, his mind reeled at the sudden appearance of Adrian Turski. *How in the hell—*

Then it hit him. Al's telegram about Tony and Norma. Norma hadn't known where he was going. But Tony . . . Jack's gut clenched. *Jesus, Tony.* They must have worked him over until he gave it up. Al's words came back to him: *Seems they asked harder questions.* Rage surged up, hot and sour. Whatever they'd done to Tony, it hadn't been quick.

There was no time to dwell. Jack shoved the thoughts aside, leaned out, and fired a quick shot around the corner. One of Turski's men screamed and dropped against a car, blood spraying from his thigh. His screams died a heartbeat later as a bullet smashed through his cheek and out the back of his head.

A voice cut through the gunfire as Turski shouted something at Jack. Most of the message was drowned out by the blasts of shotguns and automatic fire, but Jack did catch ". . . payback!"

Jack's response died on his tongue as the street in front of him filled with the darting black shadows of the mutated creatures, the witches' servants, racing through the haze and into the cluster of gangsters. The sound of gunfire shifted, slowed, then died altogether as men were cut down. Around the cars, bodies fell as the spiny forms slammed into them. Nightmare jaws bit, mutilating throats, ripping apart faces, or tearing open stomachs to feast on the steaming guts. The surviving gangsters shifted their focus and began shooting at the monstrosities.

Two of Turski's men dropped their weapons when their bodies spasmed. Blood streamed in gushing waves from every orifice of one of the men, coughing and sputtering as he died. The other's eyes bulged, his lower jaw rocking back and forth as he tried to give voice to the torment he endured. His head caved in, the skull giving way like a walnut. Blood and brains seeped through his torn scalp and he fell in a useless heap atop his companion.

Turski, Eli, and a man who, oddly, had a camera draped around his neck and a cigarette casually hanging from the corner of his mouth, turned their weapons on the three witches in the center of the street. The trio was directly in line with Jack now, and the Thompson rounds slammed into all three of the hellish creatures.

Their bodies jerked as the bullets hit. Black gore splashed out and dotted the mucked ruin that had once been the street.

Movement from the post office drew Jack's attention. Trask and one other man darted around the edge of the broken wall and raced out onto the street, ignoring the bullets that poured into the area. Jack fired his pistol at Turski and Eli, hoping to draw their fire long enough to allow Trask and the other man to wrap their chains around the witches. The whole plan would go to shit if either man caught a bullet before they could complete their task.

Standing only a couple of feet from Turski, Eli sprayed hot lead over the street, raking the three witches. One made a gesture in the air, a scrawling trace of symbols carved with a hooked talon. Eli ejected the magazine from his submachine gun and slammed in another. He raised the Thompson to his shoulder but before he completed the movement, stopped. For a split second, he did nothing, only stood frozen in the act of raising his weapon. Bullets plinked off the hood of the car and rattled the leaves of trees behind him, yet Eli never moved.

Until he pulled in a deep breath and let out a high, shrill scream. His Thompson fell from his hands and he slapped at his body, fingers grasping and pulling at his clothing. Jack could see the man's mouth moving, words being shouted, but over the gunfire couldn't make out a single syllable.

Eli's body seized, his muscles locking. His head angled up, his lips pulled back in an agonized grimace. His fingers hooked into frozen claws and he balanced on his toes. Dark lines pushed along his neck and forearms, spreading along his face. *Those are veins,* Jack thought in stupefied wonder. *His veins are close to bursting.* Beneath Eli's shirt, the Irishman's chest rippled, lumps forming and sliding as if something moved just beneath the dermis. Spittle flew from the man's teeth, arcing high. A scream burst through his paralyzed throat. An instant later, his skin tore open. Wide cracks split all over Eli's body, blood saturating his clothes and spilling along his arms, down into his pants, and pooling on the pavement.

The blood changed, growing darker. What began as trickling

soon carved its way into channels, the channels swelling into a constant, unrelenting flow. *That's not blood,* Jack thought when he saw the wriggling legs of things within the streams. Insects, multitudes of them, came erupting out of Eli Kinnerk's body through the dozens of cuts in his skin. As they fell to the street, they landed with a *sizzle* that Jack could hear over the roar of guns and the screams of the terrified and dying. Small curls of smoke rose where their bodies landed and putrefied.

Eli went down like a shot animal, knees giving out first before the rest of him followed. His cheek landed on the street with a meaty *smack*. He remained that way: knees and cheek on the ground, ass in the air. The streams of insects slowed as the man expired. The final thing to crawl out was a long, thick, centipede-looking creature. It squirmed its way out of Eli's right eye and melted as soon as it touched the blood-soaked ground.

The head of the man with the camera snapped back when a bullet in the eye took him. His cigarette tumbled out and bounced off the hood of a nearby car in a shower of sparks as he fell. Turski stopped shooting and turned to look at his comrades, a look of stunned disbelief painting the massive face. Jack grinned and sent a round toward the large Polack. Blood flew from Turski's shoulder, spinning the man around and causing him to lose his grip on the Thompson.

He bent to retrieve it, but reversed course as another of Jack's bullets smashed into the round drum magazine, sending the submachine gun skittering away. Turski threw a hateful glance at Jack, then ran for the thick trees and fields beyond. After his second step, a bloody swath appeared across his back, the fabric of his shirt ripping and flapping. Turski stumbled and held up his hands, staring at them with wide-eyed horror. More slashes appeared in his flesh, and Turski diverted his gaze from his arms to his chest and stomach.

Through the splits in his flesh, dark strings emerged, pulling out of the man like strands of yarn unspooling from a larger ball. More strands tore free as his veins were ripped out of him by an unseen force, unfurling like ribbons. Adrian staggered in a lazy circle, eventually turning to face the witches. His eyes were saucers, huge with blind disbelief and pain. His skin rippled as larger shapes thrust their way through the cuts, sliding between the openings of flesh like fat tongues slipping between lips.

All of Adrian Turski's organs climbed out of his body like perverse slugs, only to slop to the ground where they lay in a growing pile. Turski jerked once, twice, his shoulders hunching forward as something emerged from his back, bright red and pink tips peering over his shoulders like strange wings.

Lungs. Those are his lungs.

Adrian's eyes vanished. Instead of falling free and joining the rest of his internal parts on the ground, they fell into his skull. A horrible sucking noise pierced the roar of the gunfight, and Jack saw something that to his dying day he would never forget.

Adrian Turski's skin sucked in on itself. The flesh pulled inward through the cuts as though someone was on the other side drawing it in like bedsheets through a hole. His body jittered with the force. The skin tore away, leaving the sickening slick muscles exposed to the world. Adrian stood like an inverted, grotesque flower of raw meat and exposed bone, twitching and steaming in the firelit street.

Adrian took one final, clumsy step. His head angled around as if searching for something specific. His jaw opened, the teeth horribly exposed, leering. No sound came out, his tongue having already detached and fallen free. Beyond the gleaming uneven teeth was just a bloody ruin.

Jack's finger tightened on the trigger one last time, ready to end the immeasurable suffering of the man. He thought of Norma and Tony Detti and let his trigger finger relax. Adrian remained upright for only a breath longer before slapping wetly to the dirt. The remaining men quickly retreated around the cars and vanished down the street.

In the absence of gunfire, Trask and his man leapt into action. They came up behind the witches and looped out their chains. The two creatures stiffened the instant the iron links touched them. There was a faint sizzling sound and black smoke drifted from the skin where the iron contacted it. Jack stood, paralyzed with focus as Trask hurriedly wrapped the iron chain around one creature. The third witch, the one closest to Jack, screeched in rage and turned toward the men. She lashed out, her clawed hand slamming into the face of Trask's companion, who dropped his chain and staggered back, hands flying to his cheek as blood poured from some unseen laceration.

The witch he'd been trying to restrain stepped clear of the bond and turned to her attacker. She uttered a garbled mass of syllables. The man's face bubbled as boils and abscesses erupted from his skin. They expanded and burst, spilling bloody pus along his body. More and more lesions and sores emerged, crowding against one another, growing atop each other until there was nothing recognizable about the man. He wavered on his feet, a solid, bubbling mass of pestilence. He collapsed, his body bursting apart as it hit the ground, spreading diseased slime across the earth.

Trask, meanwhile, had managed to wrap his chain completely around one witch. He held on to the shaft that connected the arrowhead and pulled, drawing the chain tight. His face was a pale mask of strained effort and stark terror.

"Let go!" Jack screamed. Thankfully, Trask heard the command and he released the arrowhead. It swung down and bounced against the witch's leg. She struggled, twisting back and forth as her charred skin sizzled and smoked. Jack reached out to one of his men for a lantern, screaming for Trask to get out of the way. The other two witches shifted their attention to the man who had restrained their sister, just as Jack's hand closed on the wire handle of the lantern.

The bound witch growled something, the language more a series of grunts and wet barks, and the chain wrapped around her fell to the ground like a dead snake. Trask stared in complete disbelief at the black loops of metal for a long moment before remembering the more immediate threat. He staggered back and managed to take two steps before stiffening as the now freed witch raised a hooked hand and gestured.

Wide red lines appeared on Trask's face as strips of his flesh peeled away, exposing the muscle and bone beneath. The skin under one of his sockets tore free and the eye itself ruptured with an audible *pop*, like a small balloon bursting. Ocular fluids streamed out of the ruined orifice, mingling with the blood that covered his face and neck. Blood soaked into his clothes as the flesh beneath his shirt and pants was stripped away. Trask's choking screams of agony filled the world as the unholy trio stood over him, watching as he was slowly skinned alive.

Jack stared at the chain. How had that not worked? How had she managed to shed it as easily as slipping off a robe? Christ, was there any way to actually beat these things? How in the hell had people managed to trap them all those years ago? He focused on the flat points of the arrowheads. He understood. The chains weren't supposed to be wrapped around the witches. The arrowheads and their shafts weren't for anchoring into the ground or a tree.

They were for driving through flesh.

He had to impale the witches with the chains.

Jack unwrapped the loops of iron from his shoulder. Hefting the spearpoint, he moved into the street.

62

Sam walked through hell. The world around him was a searing inferno; tongues of flames lapped greedily at a night sky that pulsed with the orange glow of a demonic forge. The ground under his feet was a rotting black mass of mold and stinking decay. Bodies, none whole, lay everywhere. Dead eyes stared at him with the same soul-rending question: how could God have allowed this?

Sam's chest burned under the terrible weight of that question. Worse than the feeling of betrayal was the knowledge that he had perpetrated the farce, had led so many of the people of Jericho Springs to their ruin and death.

Grace's sad eyes flashed in his mind.

It had all been lies. All the whispers, the visions he'd had. All the promises of salvation and redemption and of a new Eden were lies. Hundreds of people were dead because of the falsehoods that Sam had repeated. Dozens more were changed, morphed into inhuman creatures who killed their former neighbors and friends gleefully. And at the heart of it all were the witches. Sam understood now, the images that had exploded in his mind as he sat on the stage looking up into the nightmare visage of the third witch were the truth.

They weren't of this earth. They came from some black abyss, some pit beyond knowing. They'd been drawn here by the darkness in men's hearts, powered by hideous rituals and cursed prayers. They'd come with one single purpose: to corrupt and destroy the land, the people, everything.

Sam's foot connected with the fleshy remains of a lower jaw and sent it tumbling away. So many were dead. And where the town wasn't being consumed by flames, it was rotting. Buildings were covered by rough, black vines slick with vile effluvium that shimmered as it reflected the distant flames. The vines twitched occasionally as they reinforced their grip. Sam had already grown numb to the sudden pops and cracks as the buildings collapsed beneath the crushing weight of the vegetation.

He drifted, pushed along by the heat on his back as the fire chewed its way through the town. Faintly he was aware that he was crying, but the stifling warmth dried his tears as soon as they slipped past his eyelids. His aimless path brought him to an intersection. Without thinking, he chose a direction and continued on. More bodies were scattered across the ground, and Sam's numb gaze fell on a shape against the wall of Mackey Dental. The bodies of a woman protectively clutching a small child peered from between rotting runners of vines. The woman's throat was a wet red ruin beneath a missing jaw. A small voice in the back of his mind wondered if it was the same one he'd passed moments earlier. The child, however, was only recognizable as such by one leg that dangled untouched by the violence that had reduced the rest of the body to bloody rags.

The sight of the woman, the mother protecting her offspring in their last horrific moments, brought the image of Grace to Sam's mind, filling him with clawing, screaming despair. Grace would have been a wonderful parent. She would have loved their child with the soft, unending care that bonded a mother to her children. Sam stood in the dirty, smoke-filled street and stared at the two corpses, then screamed his unfathomable sorrow at the loss of the one thing he'd wanted more than anything else in the world. He screamed until his already stinging throat grew a fiery ache and his shouts faded into a series of coughs that doubled him over.

Everything was gone. The world meant nothing anymore. From several blocks away came the sound of gunfire and he flinched at the suddenness of it. *More death,* he thought. *More things scraping to stay alive in a world that is doomed for the Pit.*

And all of it was his fault. That knowledge, that certainty, was the knife in his ribs whose wicked point tickled at his heart. He was aware that it was a selfish thing to feel that degree of self-pity, but there it was. All of this was because of him. Of course he'd not brought the witches back himself; he had no idea how they'd arrived to this plane of existence. But the corruption of the people, the feeding of the Host—*Oh God, the writhing Host!*—and the ceremonies that he was sure had fed power to the fiends, those *had* been his doing. It didn't matter that he'd been an unwitting pawn. It didn't matter that his mind had been infected with lies. It was his duty, his responsibility, to serve the people who looked to him for guidance and comfort. It was his obligation to protect them and lead them to God's loving grace.

And he'd failed. He'd led them, but to their ruin and damnation. He'd led them into the mouth of hell and sent them to eternal torment. All those poor souls, all that innocence, gone. Grace Robertson had been the purest light of them all, an unblemished soul full of love and promise. Her light had not only been snuffed out but muddied first. The knife at his heart dug deeper, found the tender flesh, and twisted, sending ribbons of tormented agony throughout his body.

Sam collapsed to his knees, his hands slapping the soft ground. Around his fingers, black brackish water seeped out of the dirt. His head hung, and once more he wailed in an attempt to purge himself of the hopelessness that consumed him.

Some time later, Sam forced himself to his feet and continued on. The gunfire had died down but still, he drifted in that direction. If there had been men there, perhaps some were still alive. It was a long shot, he knew, considering how fast and violent the thralls were. But maybe he would find a tiny spark of luck in this endless blackness.

His foot brushed against something, the contact sending a flash of pain through his toe at the same time that he turned a corner and saw the ebony figures at the end of the street.

Sam was unable to believe his own eyes for a moment. A few dozen yards away, the tormented figures of the witches stood in the center of the road. Beyond them were two black cars surrounded by several bodies lying in bloodied heaps on the street. Sam glanced down at the item he'd inadvertently kicked. It was a metal rod, two or three feet long, slightly bent from where it had broken free of whatever thing it had been a part of.

Once more, his eyes drifted to the end of the block and settled on the tallest of the three blackened figures. The witch that had killed Grace, tearing her apart from the inside as the infernal thing clawed its way out, stood to the left of the others, her attention focused on something Sam couldn't see.

Without thinking, he picked up the iron bar. It was heavier than he'd expected, but the weight of it felt good in his hands. It was a real, tangible thing; a true weapon that, with a little luck, if God hadn't completely turned His eyes away from Jericho Springs, could help avenge Grace.

Sam's upper lip curled up in a hateful sneer. He started toward the witch, his walk sliding into a trot, then a full sprint as he held the iron bar forward like a spear. His entire world shrank until the only thing he could see was the tall, dark, angled shape of the thing that had stolen his love.

The nightmare creature sensed him at the last second and turned to face the new threat that came at her from out of the smoky haze. With a grunt of effort and rage, Sam thrust the pole forward. There was a moment of resistance before the iron bar slid into the witch's body with the ease of a toothpick sliding into a cake to test for doneness. A soft bubble of shock slipped from the pit that was the witch's mouth as the rod impaled her chest.

The rest of the world came back into focus and Sam, shocked by what he'd just done, took his hands off the rod and stepped back. The black, burnt features of the witch's face snarled. Her silver eyes bore into him and he gave his own gasp of surprise at the hatred they contained.

Powerful bands of steel wrapped around his forearms and pulled. The movement was so fast and unexpected that for a second, Sam didn't resist. The witch's hands crushed his arms so hard that he was certain the bones were going to snap and splinter.

His mind registered what was happening and sent a screaming message to his feet to reverse course at the same time that a sharp pressure localized on his upper chest. The pressure grew and grew, coalescing into white-hot agony. The sensation of something popping rippled through him and the blaze of pain expanded to a full inferno. All the air in the world vanished, and Sam's mouth opened and closed in a frantic attempt to draw in even the smallest breath.

The witch grew closer. Sam looked to where the iron rod now pressed into his own body. His torso jerked and the bar slipped another inch deeper into him. The witch was even closer now, and he understood what was happening to him.

The witch pulled him along the length of the iron rod, drawing him closer. Her stench, the smell of decaying flesh mixed with rotting vegetation and death beyond knowing, filled his nose, his mouth. The silver eyes became as large as moons and her mouth as black and yawning as a nightmare sun, jagged with horrible teeth.

The pain when she bit out his throat wasn't a sharp, fiery blast but rather a dull, crushing pressure followed by the sensation of water sluicing off him, as if he'd just stepped out of a bath. The witch leaned back and Sam saw the jiggling pieces of his throat clasped between her teeth. She grinned at him around the mouthful of bleeding flesh and began to chew.

The world at the edges of his vision grew fuzzy, then darker. That blackness crept in, closing down until all he saw was the blood-coated smiling face of the witch as she chewed and swallowed his own throat.

That, and the tall man creeping up behind her, a metal pole that ended in a wide sharp point held in one hand.

<h1 style="text-align:center">63</h1>

The pastor's eyes focused on Jack and the dying man opened his mouth as if to speak. Instead of a prayer, a fat line of blood trickled out, running past his lips and down his chin. Jack raised the heavy spearpoint. As he brought it down, Sam's head lolled to one side, his eyes glassy and vacant.

Jack slammed the rod's pointed arrowhead into the creature's back, driving it forward with everything he had. The pain in his side screamed at the motion and impact, and a dark wave of nausea momentarily slipped over his vision. There was a jerk as the iron passed into and through the body of the witch. She screeched with inhuman pain, the sound filling the world. For a split second, Jack was stunned, surprised the attack had worked at all. He shook himself back into focus and angling around the creature, grabbed at the bar protruding from her chest. His hand slipped over the spearpoint and a razor-thin line of pain shot across his palm. He gripped the exposed few inches of the pole and pulled, drawing the heavy loops of chain through. With each link that slid into and through her body, the witch convulsed. Her arms swung wildly, but Jack was too close and her movement was restricted by both the pastor's iron bar and his corpse, which still hung from it.

Working quickly, Jack pulled the length of chain through and brought it all around her body. Without hesitation, he shoved the spear into her again, aiming for a spot in her lower back just to the right of her spine. Again, the abysmal creature shrieked, the sound deafening. Jack stepped quickly to one side and with fingers slipping in the black gore that coated the chain, he worked to pull it through once more. He wrapped her legs, shoving the spear tip through one of her thin, muscular thighs. With every impalement and wrap of the iron band, the witch shuddered, her movements growing weaker as the restraint did its job.

He wrapped the last few feet of the chain around her legs, looping it back over itself to form a loose knot. He stood and kicked her in the hip. With no way to balance herself and the added weight of the pastor's corpse, the witch slammed to the ground and writhed in small twitches.

Jack rushed back to the alley and grabbed the lantern. With shaking fingers, he unscrewed the cap of the kerosene reservoir and with the other hand dug into his pocket for the fresh matchbook he'd taken from Trask's vehicle. Shouts on the other side of the street drew his attention. The remainder of Trask's group stood in a circle, surrounding another of the three witches. The creature, having been distracted by the attack on her sister from both the pastor and Jack, howled in rage as the chain was driven through her body.

Several feet away, the third witch gestured and uttered a wet bark. Two of the men fell to the ground, eyes bleeding and hands clawing at their faces. Their nails dug deep, bloody furrows in their skin as their throats swelled like the neck of a bullfrog. The skin ruptured, spilling hot blood and a gout of squirming insects.

At his feet, the bound witch's struggles against the iron chain had stopped and she lay in the soft dirt, her mouth open and eyes rolling wildly. Jack threw the cap aside and turned the lantern over, shaking the kerosene free. The stinging smell of fuel filled his nostrils as the liquid splashed over the creature's cracked, black skin. With trembling fingers, he grasped at a match, then slashed it across the strike pad of the pack.

The street between him and the men finishing the binding of the other witch was empty. The third sister had slipped away. Jack noticed a shifting shadow down the street as she moved around a corner. His match caught and he dropped it, stepping away as the kerosene-soaked body ignited. Heat bloomed up, and the screams that burst out of her infernal throat slammed into him, causing him to stagger crazily to one side. Recovering his balance, Jack grabbed another lantern from the mouth of the alley and the remaining chain. While the men were finishing dousing the second witch, he sprinted past the burning abomination, in pursuit of the last one.

A new cacophony of howling erupted as the men lit the body of the second witch. The air filled with a chorus of agonized and enraged wails along with the smell of burning meat. Then Jack was down the side street and racing through the growing haze, searching.

In the growing smoke, the streets practically vanished, becoming little more than blurry, hazy stretches of dirt as the fires spread from building to building, greedily consuming block after block. Jack's chest burned as he struggled to breathe in the cloying fog. He ran several blocks, vaguely aware of businesses as he passed their dark and silent windows. After crossing the street in front of his hotel, he slowed to a walk. The chain was heavy and he readjusted it in an attempt to bring some relief to his strained muscles.

An eerie quiet filled Jericho Springs. The screams that had been everywhere only a short time ago were all but gone, reduced to faint, distant punctuations. The noise of the fire devouring the town was a low hum that he barely registered. Flecks of gray ash drifted through the air, floating to the ground like snow.

Jack passed carved footprints in the thickening blanket of ash and he blinked rapidly as specks of cinders landed on his face. He squinted, peering into the thickening smog as he moved on. Occasionally, a shape would appear farther down a street—a flickering shadow as someone raced for safety, the sounds of their panicked breathing echoing between buildings. Often those were immediately followed by thinner, faster shapes of the creatures who served the witches giving chase. More than once, Jack heard the pursuit end in a sharp, piercing cry that abruptly cut off.

"Where are you, bitch?" he mumbled. He continued past Mack's and paused once more at an intersection. To his left, down Horton Street, barely visible through the smoke, was Ida's Baked Goods. A tall, black form darted into an alley directly across from the bakery and Jack smiled. "Gotcha."

He moved toward Horton. The avenue vanished in a thick swirling curtain of smoke shot through with orange light from the distant flames. *She's somewhere ahead, using the smoke as cover*, he thought. His footsteps were flat, dead clicks in the haze. Jack slowed his pace, his eyes straining to pick shapes out of the landscape ahead. A searing pain tore through his back, sending him stumbling forward, the chain slipping from his hands. His legs tangled with each other and Jack went down. For a moment, he lay with his cheek against the ash-covered road and gasped for breath. His entire back was awash with fiery agony and his skin tickled with a thick warmth as blood poured out of the wounds. With effort, he rolled onto his side and struggled to get an elbow beneath him as he searched for his attacker.

The witch stood ten feet away, her sharply angled body hunched in the gloom. She studied him with her silver eyes. Blood, his blood, dripped from the tips of the claws on one hand, quietly pattering onto the ashen ground. The hatred that pulsed out of her pressed into him like the crushing weight of rocks. Images flooded into his head: unwanted pictures of bodies broken and torn apart, splintered bone stabbing through ragged flesh. Around the images of destruction wove sounds of tormented screams and the dry chittering of insects.

Jack coughed, the spasm sending a splintering scream of raw pain from his wounds throughout his body. The witch took a step closer. One of her hands, the one not covered in Jack's blood, drifted up, fingers twitching. Invisible bands wrapped around his chest and squeezed, pushing all the air from his lungs. Deep inside, something ground painfully, and Jack's face lifted in a silent, agonized grimace.

The witch's hand remained as it was for a long moment. Then she brought it down and the torment ended. Air flooded into his lungs and Jack sucked it in greedily despite the lingering pain from whatever had scraped inside him. The creature remained where she was, misshapen head cocked, eyes boring into him as if savoring the moment. Jack searched for the chain, saw it against the gutter, too far away to reach. The lantern lay on its side several feet away, resting against the angle of the curb. He reached for it, gritting his teeth at the stinging pain the movement caused.

The witch shot forward and slammed a powerful foot on his left wrist. Sickening pain rolled through him as the bones of his forearm ground together. Jack stared up at the looming figure. Once more, her claws danced in the air, small slicing movements that promised a long, torment-filled death. For the transgression of murdering her sisters, she was going to tear Jack apart herself. She wanted him to suffer and to feel every piece of him being ripped away, to feel the life flowing out of his body as she reduced him to a bloody ruin.

Jack's vision dimmed. His limbs suffused with a deep, bone-rattling cold that surged like an underground river beneath the all-encompassing agony that burned through his muscles.

Through the fading light in his eyes, Jack watched as the witch leaned close.

And grinned.

64

Evie stood in the small, cramped basement of Springline Dry Goods and stared at the wood beams of the ceiling. Tiny fingers of light drifted through the small spaces between the overhead flooring slats, each shaft filled with lazily drifting motes of dust. The entire ceiling shuddered as the horrifying creatures flooded into the store, filling it with their stink and thunderous hissing cries.

She tried not to think of the last time she was in a small cellar while the house was invaded by things intent on killing her. Of course that had been different, they were mostly people then. They'd not undergone whatever nightmarish transition had turned them into the spine-covered things they now were.

These are folks I knew—neighbors, customers. The reality of that thought was surreal. She still couldn't believe it. Despite having seen the people when they'd attacked Cleary's farm and Jack's recounting of fighting them, it seemed impossible to believe that someone as nice and reserved as Floyd Washgrove, the barber, was now a . . . monster. But there was no denying it. Floyd and so many others became monsters. All traces of humanity had been washed away, replaced by mottled skin, sharp claws, and gnashing, hungry teeth.

"The door will hold," the woman said. Evie jumped at the sound of her voice, whispered though it was, but distinct over the din of the destruction of the store above. Evie hoped the woman was right. The bar that had been placed horizontally across the door was thin and didn't strike Evie as sturdy enough to withstand a crazed, thrashing assault.

"Is there anything we can use as a weapon down here?" Evie asked the teenage boy. The youth stood near a stack of old apple crates, a shotgun held across his body. The gun looked comically large in his hands and his wide-eyed, terrified stare didn't fill Evie with confidence. "Hey!" Evie hissed. "Is there another weapon down here?" The boy started to answer but a massive crash overhead, followed by the twinkling sound of plates breaking, cut off any response.

The woman picked her way through the cluttered piles of furniture and old barrels filled with moth-eaten fabric to the foot of the steps. She clasped a handkerchief in one tight fist held against her breastbone. Her other hand drifted out and lightly touched the railing. Evie's body hummed with the need to pull the woman back into the shadowy maze of the basement. To distract herself, she began pawing through the piles of junk, searching along the walls and in corners for anything that could be used to defend herself.

In a far corner she found another barrel. Cobweb-coated tools poked out of its open top. She pushed aside a rusted garden hoe and a pitted and cracked shovel before finding an axe. Evie clutched it and turned back to the rest of the cellar as the pounding on the door at the top of the short flight of stairs increased.

"Oh no," the boy muttered. Where light had filtered between the overhead slats, smoke now wafted. It drifted through the small cracks and blossomed out, forming a layer of thick haze just above their heads.

"We have to find another way out of here," Evie said.

"What?" The woman turned from her post at the foot of the stairs. Her face was a knitted ball of confusion. "What do you mean? We can't go out there. Those things are out there."

Evie pointed at the smoke. "The whole town is burning. It's reached us now. The store is on fire. Those things will be the least of our worries in a few minutes. Is there another way out?"

"There's an old coal chute." The boy pointed into the dark recess. "I don't know if it's clear."

"Show me," Evie said. The boy wove through the stacks of old inventory. Both he and Evie spun around when the door at the top of the stairs bucked violently, the wood splitting with a sharp *crack*. The things on the other side came tumbling into the stairwell as the door split open. Smoke and the dark forms of bodies filled the tight space at the top of the steps.

The woman screamed and tried to turn to run but a shape leapt through the smoke-filled doorway, bounced off the wall, and threw itself down the stairs toward her. It landed on her back and drove her to the dirt floor with a sickening *crunch*. The woman gave a small, strangled cry, followed by the wet sounds of her body being torn apart.

Her son shouted for her and took two quick steps before remembering he held a gun. He shouldered it and fired. The blast deafened Evie, but it also removed the head and most of the shoulders of the thing that was in the process of eviscerating the poor woman. The creature flew back and collided with the edge of the stairs. The boy had only just looked up from the sights of the shotgun when more of the twisted mutations slammed into him.

Evie backed away, slipping into the shadows and hoping she hadn't been spotted. On the other side of the basement, the things hissed and screeched and snapped at one another as they fought over the bloodied remains of the boy and his mother.

Turning a corner, Evie swept her bandaged hand back and forth in an attempt to navigate. She wasn't exactly sure what a coal chute looked like but hoped she'd know it when she came across it.

The sounds of crates collapsing behind her brought a soft cry of surprise from her throat and she risked a glance back. Four pairs of silver eyes bobbed in the gloom. An icy ball of dread formed in her guts, threatening to turn her legs into jelly. Evie gritted her teeth against the pain that continued to thump through her body and focused on finding the coal chute.

It was an old, soot-stained wooden funnel mounted into the brick wall. A pitch-black gap at the top narrowed to, she assumed, the exterior door. The thought of trying to climb the angled chute and cram herself into the narrow opening was almost enough to cause Evie to collapse where she stood and wait for the inevitable end.

The section of the basement wall covered in deep shadows held a narrow, horizontal pane of glass so coated in grime that it barely allowed any light through. Evie hurried to the bottom of the chute as the sounds of bodies thrashing through the piles of junk filled the cellar. The creatures were quickly drawing closer; their thin, tortured shapes were outlined in the murky light.

Evie slapped the axe at the window, an uncoordinated and weak motion since she could only use one arm. Glass shattered and yellow light, along with some curling wisps of smoke, filled the space. Three more hits cleared most of the shards from the small frame. Evie hopped, hands stretching for the sill but she couldn't get more than a fingertip's grip on the edge before slipping back to the floor. "Goddamnit!" she yelled and turned to find something to stand on.

Propped against the bent and curved frame of a child's black tricycle sat a wooden drawer with ornate metal handles attached near the edges of the front. With her undamaged hand, Evie moved it to the bottom of the window. It wobbled precariously as she stepped on it, then she slapped a hand on the bottom of the window's opening to steady herself.

The drawer provided enough height that she was able to reach the sill. Determined not to be caught without a weapon again, Evie tossed the axe through and pushed herself up, working her head and shoulders into the opening. Her arms shook, her mending fingers screamed with blazing agony, and her muscles threatened to give out. Screaming through the effort and pain, she pushed and pulled herself into the window.

A fiery trail of pain shot across her legs. It was so sudden and immense that it stole her breath and she could only gasp silently, her mouth opening and closing like a fish left on a dock. She continued to worm forward through the window to her waist, when more pain slashed across her legs, ripping the thin skin covering her shins. Evie kicked and one of her feet hit something soft and yielding. In a final desperate shove, she thrust the rest of her body out of the window and onto the lawn beyond.

Smoke poured from the basement, black and oily. She could see the shifting forms of the creatures through the miasma as they fought to reach the window. The sharp *crack* of the dresser drawer snapping, collapsing under the weight of the monsters, brought a wicked smile to her face. Evie crab-walked back from the store until she was several feet away. Only then did she risk a look at her legs.

The skin was crisscrossed with deep, jagged cuts that poured blood. Everything from her knees down felt like it was on fire, and she squeezed her watering eyes against the rolling waves of agony. She needed to get the wounds cleaned and bandaged, sooner rather than later. Standing was a shaky act that sent her head swimming and black poppies blooming in her vision. When the moment passed, she grabbed the axe and started across the grass toward the empty street.

Evie moved in a shuffling run, the axe held in front of her. As she crossed the road, she searched for the next street or business, anything to help get her bearings. Two blocks later, she came to the corner of Horton Street. She swiped a hand across her face, palming sweat from her eyes and clearing a small clump of hair that had plastered to her forehead as she thought about the businesses up ahead. She knew the bakery was there, but that wouldn't do. However, the Velvet Mirror was on Horton, and though only a beauty salon, Evie was sure she could find something inside to help stop the bleeding, if only temporarily. That would have to work until she could find Jack and get back to Doctor Powell's house.

Or out of town altogether, she thought grimly.

Evie shuffled toward Horton and could see the sign for the Velvet Mirror that hung above the door, when the sounds of a man screaming in pain cut through the air. She froze, fingers tight around the axe as she searched the smoke-filled street. If it was someone being attacked by one of the creatures, she didn't know if she'd have enough strength to save them.

Moving slowly and keeping close to the storefronts, Evie crept along the sidewalk, painfully aware of the sounds of her footsteps despite the volume of the man's pained cries. After a few moments, she saw a tall, dark figure hunched over the smaller form of a person in the middle of the road. The man on the ground writhed in pain as the thing above him brought clawed hands down and across his chest. The smoke shifted, a soft wind momentarily clearing her vision, and Evie's body locked in panic as her mind registered what she was seeing.

Jack lay in a widening pool of blood. His chest was soaked with it, his face a red mask. The black form of a witch crouched over him, her taloned feet on either side of his hips. She hissed down at him in her strange language as she swiped again, bringing a fresh round of screams. The witch extended a finger and pressed the long, terrible claw into one of the wounds in Jack's chest. He jerked as if he'd been electrocuted, his back arching and feet spasming with pain.

Evie growled, a deep rumbling in her chest, then stepped into the street, bringing the axe up to knock the creature off Jack when her foot scraped painfully against something. Seeing what it was, Evie swapped her axe for it, then rushed toward the witch.

She screamed as she plunged the black iron spear into the witch's neck. The flat blade slipped in as easily as a knife through warm butter, punching out the other side with a gentle *thump*. The witch froze, one clawed hand raised for another swipe at Jack's ravaged and bloodied body. She abandoned the attack and clawed at her neck, fingers slipping over the iron blade as a viscous inky fluid streamed out and down her body.

Jack bucked his hips and the witch tumbled onto the ground, continuing to paw at the iron rod. Black blood poured from her mouth and her throat emitted a strangled gurgling.

"Help me up," Jack gasped. When he was on his feet, Evie slipped an arm around his waist to hold him steady. He swayed for a moment, then nodded. "I'm okay."

"The hell you are," she said. "You look like hamburger."

He chuckled. Seeming to remember something, he looked around. "You see a lantern anywhere?" Evie left him long enough to retrieve the oil lamp and shake it. The reservoir was three-quarters full of liquid. Jack pointed at the witch who continued to convulse. "Pour it on her."

"What?"

"The kerosene. Douse the bitch and I'll light her." He pulled a matchbook from his pocket and held it up between two fingers.

Evie twisted the cap free, flung it aside, and poured the acrid contents over the black form of the witch. When she was done, she stepped back and took the matches from Jack. "I've got this." Evie plucked one free, approached the snarling, gurgling figure, and stared down at her. The last remaining sister's silver eyes glared up, her blackened skin glistening with the kerosene.

"Do it," Jack mumbled.

Evie lit the match and tossed it, stepping back quickly as the body went up in a blaze. She returned to Jack's side and held on to him, steadying him once more, as the ancient horror shrieked in hellish pain, her body thrashing against the consuming fire.

His eyes locked on the writhing sheet of flames, Jack asked, "How did you find me?"

Evie smiled. "I'm pretty good at finding things that need to be found."

They fell into silence, both watching as the charred corpse gave its final twitches and fell still. "What now?" Evie asked.

"I need a doctor," Jack said. "So do you." He lifted his eyes to the buildings across the street, a crown of flames atop their roofs. More long tongues of fire extended through broken windows and lapped at the sides of the buildings.

Evie voiced what he was thinking. "By now, if Powell is even still alive, his house and office are both gone. Can you walk?"

Jack winced as he took a tentative step. "It looks worse than it is.

She wanted me to suffer, wanted it to last." Seeing the deep gashes across Evie's legs, he asked, "What the hell?"

"It looks worse than it is," she said. "Come on. Let's find a car and get out of here."

"Where?"

She gave him a weak smile.

"Anywhere you want to go, Jack Carmelo Chicago."

65

Jack stepped onto the porch, pushing the door open with his hip. He maneuvered the two mugs of coffee through the doorway and crossed to where Evie sat in a rocking chair. She accepted hers with a whispered "Thanks," then returned her focus to the thick trees across the dead field. Jack wondered if she was reliving the sleepwalking incident where she imagined a monstrous Henry Dunn chasing her.

"You all right?" he asked.

"Yeah."

The morning sky was still a darker shade of blue in the direction of Jericho Springs. For the past two days, a hazy orange glow had pulsed in the distance as the blaze ran its course through the town. After killing the final witch, Jack and Evie had barely made it out of downtown, driving recklessly through streets made into flaming tunnels. Jack had started to point the truck in the direction of Birmingham, but as they neared the main highway with the sounds of sirens rapidly approaching in the distance, another thought had come to him and he'd wrenched the steering wheel down a side road.

"What are you doing?" Evie had practically shouted in her fear state. "We have to get out of here!"

"We are," Jack had said. Ash fell like rain, giving him only a few feet of visibility as he steered along the narrow street. "But we can't leave them."

"What?"

"The bones. The witches. I can't leave until I know they're really dead."

"We just stabbed them with iron and burned them. Plus, the town is a bonfire," Evie shot back, incredulous. "I think they're fucking done for."

"No," Jack said. "That fire won't get hot enough." He tightened his jaw and gave her a quick glance. "Trust me."

"So where are we going?"

"Cleary's."

"That's still in town," she protested.

"It's out enough. Besides, I'm betting that pretty soon the roads will be blocked, if not by trees then by the cops. Once that's done, we won't be able to get back in to find the bones. Cleary's is far enough out that we won't cook." He hadn't been sure. He'd only hoped the fire would starve before it reached the farm.

As it turned out, he was correct. They'd made it to Cleary's house to find it still standing out of sheer stubbornness. Where the exterior walls weren't suffering from the strange open sores, they were pockmarked by bullet holes. Some walls bore wild black smears from lantern oil or falling torches and most of the windows were broken. The patch of plywood, charred and splintered, still covered the place where Trask had said a deer attempted to leap into the house.

The fire never came close to the farm and for the last two days, the couple lingered in the house, recovering and trying not to dwell on the horrible events that had occurred there. Evie refused to go into the kitchen, saying that it was too close to the root cellar. They spent most of their time in the bedroom where she had stayed. When the bullet holes, blood splashes on the walls, and atmosphere within the house grew too much to bear, they would retreat to the porch to watch the slowly drifting ash.

Evie looked at the field. "Is it just me or does that patch of land over there look healthy?"

At the edge of the plot, just past the wooden rails of the fence, a small fist-sized raft of bright green grass was visible in the middle of the marshy ground, like a small island in a dead sea. Jack stared at it, rapt, as if it were the first signs of life he'd seen in months.

"And that tree, just there." Evie pointed. "It's not covered with slime or those horrible vines." She turned to Jack. "It looks like the blight is going away."

Jack's attention drifted to the brightening sky. He pulled in a deep breath. The air still held the oily stink of the fire and a deeper yet fainter smell of charred meat, but it was greatly reduced from what it had been. "Fire's out by now," he said. "You okay to go this morning?"

"Do you think the cops are all gone? I mean, will we be able to get into town?"

"Maybe. We'll just tell them we're going to check on your apartment, see if we can salvage anything."

Evie's face darkened. "We already know there's nothing left."

"They don't know that," he said. "Finish your coffee and I'll go find a sack."

What remained of Jericho Springs was not much more than a black smear on the land. The charred remnants of buildings were like bones of some alien thing. The fire was out but smoke still curled up from the ruins like ghosts. The streets were empty of life, no police or fire brigades lingering about. Most of the bodies still lay where they'd fallen, blackened lumps of unrecognizable remains. "They just left them all?" Evie asked, shocked.

"Their focus would have been on putting the fire out," Jack said. "They'll start collecting the bodies today. Probably within the next hour or so, once the sun comes up a bit more. We need to be gone before that."

Thirty minutes later, the Model T was chugging its way back toward the farm. The bed of the truck held a large burlap sack and three disfigured iron chains rattling with every rough patch of road.

"I hope we got them all," Evie said, snapping him out of the moment. She turned her face to him, her eyes full of worry. "I won't lie, I honestly don't know if we got all of them. What if we didn't? What if someone found them first and, I don't know, took some?"

Jack didn't respond. She was right, after all. There was no way to know if they had all the bones. The most they could do was hope and deal with what they had collected.

After a moment, Evie said, "I'm sorry. I'm just frightened about them coming back." She risked a glance over her shoulder at the bag. "What are we even going to do with those?"

"I have an idea," Jack said, his face hard. Evie looked at him questioningly and he continued. "I'm going to drop you off at Cleary's, then I'm driving out to Elden Mills."

"Why in the hell are you going all the way out there?"

"They have a textile factory. Trask told me about it when we were looking at them for new grains."

"You're going to get a new bag to put them in?" Evie asked, jokingly.

"I'm going to get a couple of cans of hydrofluoric acid. We're going to dissolve those things in that big washtub of Cleary's. May take a full day, but there won't be anything left. Those bitches won't come back from that." In the cramped truck cab, he could feel Evie's worry, could predict the next thing she would say.

"You say that like you've done this before."

Jack kept his eyes on the road. "Not exactly this, but close enough." Beside him, Evie was perfectly still, as if she were afraid of saying or doing the wrong thing and ending up in the washtub alongside the bones.

A few minutes later, she said, "I'm going with you." Jack didn't argue. There was no point. Besides, he didn't want to leave her alone. They'd not seen any since the confusion during the fight with the witches, but he was pretty sure there were more of those mutated people still out there. He doubted very much that they had all died when the witches had.

The sun was low in the sky by the time they returned to Cleary's farm from Elden Mills. Both Jack and Evie were exhausted, their movements slow as they climbed out of the truck. Jack brought the containers of acid into the house, thick-walled canisters with long curved spouts capped by screw-on lids, setting them in the bathroom next to the washtub. Evie followed with the sack, which bounced against her leg, the bones inside clacking like a lazy rattlesnake. She started to open it and dump the bones into the stained white tub, but Jack held out a hand.

"Don't. I don't want them out." She looked at him for a moment, her eyebrows furrowed in confusion. Jack didn't want to have to say out loud that he was worried about what might happen if either of them saw the exposed bones. That he was afraid, suddenly and overwhelmingly terrified, that he would snatch one up and slice himself open, or worse, Evie.

She dropped the bag heavily into the tub. It landed with a rattling *thud*. Jack motioned for her to leave. Out in the hall, he said, "You can't be in there when I do this."

"I'm not afraid," she protested, but he quickly held up a hand.

"That's not it. The acid's dangerous. Touch it, it'll eat through. Breathe it in, it'll burn you up."

Her eyes widened. "What the hell are you going to do? How are you going to protect yourself?"

"I'm going to get a pair of thick leather gloves out of the barn, and I'll tie a rag soaked in whiskey or vinegar around my nose and mouth. If there's a rain slicker around, I'll wear that too. It's not perfect, but it'll do."

He found the gloves in the barn. There was no rain gear or oilcloth to be found, so Jack made do by pulling a thick wool blanket off the bed and cutting a hole in the center for his head. He soaked a kitchen towel in whiskey and tied it around his face. The only thing he didn't have was something to protect his eyes. Tony Detti had told him once about a guy who used acid on a body and some of it splashed into his eyes. "Poor fucker practically clawed his eyes out from the pain," Tony had chuckled before shoving another forkful of lasagna into his mouth.

"Stay out here," he told Evie as he approached the bathroom door.

"No matter what, don't come in." The worried look in her eyes almost made him scrap the plan entirely. But they had to do this. They had to make sure the bones were destroyed. He lifted the towel, kissed her quickly, went into the bathroom, and closed the door.

He opened the lone window for ventilation and turned to the tub. The familiar pull tickled at the edges of his thoughts. Taking a deep breath and holding it, Jack unscrewed the cap of the first canister and tipped it over the bag. The clear liquid spilled out, its fumes filling the small room. Jack's eyes instantly watered and he closed them tight, using the sound of liquid splashing against the burlap as a guide. A quiet hissing rose as the acid started to chew away at the bag and its contents. Jack emptied the first canister, set it down, and grasped blindly for the second. He twisted the cap off and upended the can. His lungs burned. Behind his closed lids, lights danced as his need for air turned urgent. The second canister still held some liquid but he could take it no longer. He dropped the can into the tub and bolted for the door, his gloved hands slipping on the knob in a moment of heightened panic.

Out in the hall, he slumped against the closed bathroom door and pulled in huge lungfuls of air. Each breath was tinged with the taste of booze. Evie approached, a wet rag in one hand. Jack waved her off until he'd removed the makeshift poncho and then the gloves. As soon as he tossed them away, Evie hurried forward and ran the cool, damp cloth over his skin.

"Is it done?" she asked.

"Both canisters. It'll take a while, but it'll get the job done. Help me outside."

Jack sat heavily in one of the rocking chairs on the porch, then Evie went inside to bring him a glass of water. They sat there, neither speaking, for a long time. The sun dipped fully behind the trees and after a moment, Jack began to notice the lazy flickers of light dancing through the air as the fireflies began their nocturnal mating ritual.

The next afternoon, he risked a look in the tub. The acid filled the bottom, its surface covered with bubbles. The burlap sack was completely gone and beneath the suds, Jack saw only a few irregular white smudges. Satisfied, he went outside to tell Evie that they could leave later in the day, or better yet, first thing in the morning.

"Where are we going?" she asked. "Chicago?"

"I thought we could go to Birmingham," Jack said. "I can call Al from there, see what he'd like me to do next."

"I can only imagine he'll want you back."

Jack smiled. "Probably. But I have an idea that I'm going to pitch to him. There's no reason for me to be back in Chicago. I think I can do him some good in a city like Birmingham."

Evie laughed. "I knew you'd want to stay . . . the food, the overalls . . . I think you love them more than me."

Jack stood up, took her hand, and pulled her out of her chair. Holding her tightly against him, he said, "Why don't you step into my office for a moment and I'll show you how I feel about you."

Evie beamed. "Lead the way, Jack Carmelo Chicago."

The next morning, Jack risked another look in the tub. The bubbles were gone, and the smell of the acid had been reduced to a mild irritant, thanks to the small window. At the bottom of the tub, the remains of the bones were nothing more than a thin layer of pale sludge. He stared at the remnants for a long time. It was so strange to think of what they were, what they had been, and the horrors they had borne. All those years, all the deaths, the torment, the anguish, now reduced to a smear of sediment. Just enough to fill a coffee mug.

"Good riddance," he mumbled.

Outside, he found Evie standing near the truck and talking to a group of eight men. Each wore denim overalls and wide-brimmed hats that shaded their features. Every one carried a shotgun or hunting rifle held by their sides. As Jack stepped onto the porch, the man closest to Evie looked up. He didn't know his name but recognized him as one of Cleary's guys.

"Mr. Carmelo," he said. Jack flicked a hand in greeting but said nothing. The man continued. "Miss Marrow said you guys were heading out of town. That right?"

Jack's pistol was a heavy, reassuring weight in his front pocket. He calculated how fast he could pull it before the other men fired first.

"That's right," he said with a tone of caution. "There a problem with that?"

"No, sir," the man answered. "We was hoping you'd stick around. We've been hunting those things, those creatures that served those demons." Jack thought about the townspeople-turned-monstrosities with huge teeth, spines, and sharp claws. "We've killed quite a few already." The man continued. "Just thought you might be interested in helping us hunt down the last of them."

Jack descended the stairs and opened the truck door for Evie. She slid onto the seat, her eyes watching Jack warily to see how he would respond. "I can't help you," Jack told the man. "I have business else-where and need to get on the road." The faces of the hunting party took on disappointed looks.

"Hate to hear that," the leader said. He patted the hood of the truck. "Well, best of luck to you both."

"Luck to you too." Jack closed the truck door and crossed to the driver's side. The men lingered for a moment as if either unsure what to do or in hopes that Jack would reconsider. Then the one who had spoken gave an order and the group turned and crossed the property, moving toward the dead cornfield where, amid the black and slimy ruin, three small green shoots of new growth extended out of the fetid soil.

Jack cranked the truck and steered it toward the main road. As they bumped and rattled past the cemetery-now with a new makeshift gravestone constructed from sections of fence post lashed together-Evie touched her fingertips to the glass of her window.

"Goodbye, Mr. Cleary."

Jack turned onto the hardpan of the main road. As the truck accelerated, his hand found Evie's. They held on tightly, watching the landscape slide by as the truck rumbled into the new morning and the city that awaited.

The End

Thank you for reading! If you enjoyed this book, please leave a short review. It doesn't have to be fancy. But, as I said at the front of this book, we authors live and die by reviews. They help me get more eyes on my work and I greatly appreciate every single one!

~

Find me on the web where you can email me, learn about new things coming soon and even get a free story for signing up for my newsletter! www.byjonathandaniel.com

ACKNOWLEDGEMENTS

I want to take a moment to thank the people without whom this book would not exist.

First and foremost, my wife Kinley. Thank you from the bottom of my soul for your support and encouragement. Thank you for your keen eye and catching all my horrible, terrible mistakes in the earliest drafts. This book is better and stronger because of you. I love you more than you'll ever know.

Thanks to the Hellhound, Buster. Your constant insistence that I stop writing and play ball made this book take longer than it should have to get written, but also helped keep me sane-ish.

Thank you to Riley Quinn for the amazing cover art, and for being an all around great guy to work with.

Massive thanks to my editor Danielle Yeager for making the pile of words I threw together into something coherent and really remarkable. I'm sorry for all the poor grammar choices I made that you had to wade through!

If you find any errors in this book, they are my fault, not hers nor those of any beta readers.

And to all my friends and family for their encouragement and support, without any of you, this book would just be another file on my laptop. Your help means the world to me. Thank you.

BONUS MATERIAL

I wanted to thank you for taking the time to read Feast of the Unclean. It means the world to me that you spent some time in Jericho Springs.

I thought it may be fun to give you a little background on the book, and talk about how I came up with the idea, including the first draft which was COMPLETELY different than the book you just read. Well, not 100% different...Jack, Evie, Dunn and Cleary were all there. The town had a different name, but otherwise....

So the idea came about back in late 2019, just before COVID hit. I had just moved back to Alabama. For the past several years my wife and I had been living in Seattle. We moved back due to her job and were staying with her parents for several months while we got our feet under us and looked for a house. I had two books out, The Uninvited and a mystery/thriller called The Killing Tide. I was ready to get back to my horror roots after writing 'Tide' and had always liked the idea of werewolves. Still do, truth be told.

Anyway, I got to thinking one day about how I had learned about my family's history with moonshining, and the question popped in my head, "What if moonshiners set their stills up deep in the woods and ran afoul of a pack of werewolves?"

Pretty cool, right?

I decided to take it a step further. Considering when moonshining was really popular, my brainstorming led me to Chicago and Al Capone. I found Jack Carmelo, and fell in love with the idea of a morally reprehensible main character. I had a mental picture of Jack standing in a room covered in blood, an ax in his hands after the wholesale slaughter of a bunch of rival gang members. That naturally led me to figure a way to get Jack to the small Alabama town.

So now I had a story.

Pretty cool, right?

So I spent the next couple of months holed up in an isolated cubby at a small local library, writing the book. Actually, I wrote the opening scene sitting in the Starbucks of a Target while my wife shopped. This was about a month before COVID.

I wrote the entire draft, and was really, really happy with it. I had intense scenes where the werewolves slaughtered men working stills, a surviving boy transforming in front of Jack (who then got an ax and quickly put the poor kid out of his misery). I had scenes at the abandoned house deep in the woods where the werewolves were squatting, scenes with werewolves sneaking into town and killing people, swarming over the Cleary farm. I even had a climax where Jack is being chased through the woods by not only Dunn and the Klan but the werewolves. The final stand was in a small house that had been attacked by the werewolves early in the story. Jack, Dunn and the other Klan guys found themselves forced to work together to fend off a swarm of snarling, bloodthirsty beasts.

It was awesome.

The whole thing ended with Jack, scratched during that final fight, and Evie driving to Seattle where they started a flower shop. Problem is, Capone didn't give Jack permission to just leave the Outfit. So the last chapter was Jack working the desk, closing up for the night when two trench coat wearing goons stroll in, reminiscent of the Dean O'Banion killing. They tell Jack that they're not interested in escorting him back to Capone and reach for their weapons.

Jack, knowing what he is now, grins at them and feels the change boiling up.

That was it. That was the original idea and ending.

Pretty cool, right?

So why did it change into the book you just read? Easy. After finishing the first draft, I put the book on ice (as I always do) to get some mental distance before editing/cleaning it up. At some point I stumbled across a graphic novel entitled, "Moonshine" (coincidentally, that was the title of my book at the time). I looked a little more into it and found out that it was not only very successful but also about a mobster from Chicago sent to a small southern town to establish a moonshine pipeline only to cross paths with...surprise, surprise....werewolves.

Color me crushed.

I was seriously devastated. I had been so excited about this idea and, at the time, had so few others that I found myself lost. So what did I do? I thought and debated with myself for weeks. I'm not naive enough to think that all my ideas are perfectly original...I can't remember where I read it but someone once said that there were no more original ideas, that every story was some variation of the same few core concepts. I can accept that - now - and further believe that while that may be true, the idea that any writer can still bring something fresh and original to those core concepts.

Except at the time, I couldn't find a fresh spin on it. Putting it in a town in Alabama (the comics were based, I believe, in Kentucky or one of the Carolinas) wasn't enough. So I shelved the idea and the book, figuring that at some point, I'd find a viable angle.

I moved on, and wrote other things, one of which was Blood Night.

While writing Blood Night, it hit me. Why try to force the werewolf story when I could just change the antagonist? It didn't have to be werewolves that Jack has to contend with.

Why not witches?

So, I started exploring that idea. I knew I didn't want to do the "standard" witch thing, as much as I love those stories. I wanted something deeply dark and disturbing (if you'll forgive the alliteration). Through my fleshing out of the idea, I stumbled on the idea that these were beings from a dark plane of existence, a black void filled with only the most nightmarish of evils. They were summoned to our world by a nomadic tribe of people called the Shadokar (not a real thing, at least as far as I know) that settled in the area back when Pangea was a thing. The Shadokar wanted power and, under the influence of the witches, conducted terrible rituals that increased that power. Ultimately the Shadokar imploded under their own evils and the witches faded into the wilderness. They were brought back by the horrors that the white settlers imposed on the Native Americans. But, as mentioned in the story, the Native Americans came to the rescue and banished the witches until that fateful day that Freddie Salter and Jimmy Blackwell blew up that cave looking for the natural spring.

So that's it...that's how the book you hold came into being. Most of the story stayed from the original draft....Jack still came to town, met Evie, all of that. I did have a sidekick for Jack at one point, a guy named Clemente Ferri who was a wisecracking little shit and who had a sub-plot involving heroin, but honestly it overcomplicated the plot, so he had to go.

And that's it. I hope you enjoyed my rambling explanation of how this book came to be. I had so much fun writing this, figuring out how to grow and change the story to accommodate the threat of the witches, and-not to sound my own horn-I think I did alright.

Again, thank you so, so much for reading. And, while I know I've said this a few times already elsewhere, let me once more say that if you could find a moment to leave a review, it would mean the world to me.

ABOUT THE AUTHOR

Jonathan Daniel lives in Birmingham, Alabama with his wife and hyper Boston Terrier, Buster (the Hellhound). When not writing about nightmarish things, he enjoys cooking, reading, brewing beer and trying to watch every horror movie made in the 80's.

You can learn more about him and his other works as well as contact him at his website: www.byjonathandaniel.com

ALSO BY JONATHAN DANIEL

The Uninvited: An unrelenting creature horror novel (Author's Updated Edition)

There's nowhere to run. Nowhere to hide. They're coming. And they're hungry.

Still struggling with the tragic death of his wife, Owen Decker is determined to battle the debilitating fear that continues to haunt him. Traveling to a tropical island to fully face the crippling terror he harbors appears to be his only option. However, Owen is unaware of the unforgiving evil awaiting him.

On the island, Owen awakes to a horror unlike any he's ever witnessed before. Survival seems impossible as the mutilated and the dead surround him. Teaming up with the only two other survivors of the massacre, the three search for an escape.

But something ravenous and incomprehensible refuses to let them off the island alive.

There's nowhere left to hide.

With time running out and the sinister beings close behind, will Owen's chance at a new beginning be the end he feared all along?

ALSO BY JONATHAN DANIEL

Blood Night: **A Brutal 1980s Small-Town Slasher Horror**

No reason. No remorse.

It's June, 1987, and with the single flip of a coin, Death has come to the quiet town of Elden Mills.

No one is safe; a flicker of movement or a sudden noise is all it takes to draw his attention. Lurking in the shadows behind a pale mask, he is driven by the need to fill the streets with blood and screams.

If he sees you, you're dead.

Morgan Bell fled Elden Mills and everyone who cared about her after a life-shattering assault. Now, after years of self-alienation, she returns to her hometown to pick up the pieces of her former existence. But Morgan's hopes of starting over are ripped away during a deadly encounter with the madman.

In her darkest moment, Morgan must confront both the painful memories of her own attack and the cold, unfeeling brutality behind the mask.

Will she find healing in the shadows, or add her voice to the chorus of screams?

ALSO BY JONATHAN DANIEL

The Killing Tide

In the silence, doomsday whispers; in guilt, screams echo – who will survive the Killing Tide?

Colin Dowey can't forgive himself. Plagued with survivor's guilt for freezing up during a lethal workplace shooting, the bank teller pours his heavy heart into elaborate roleplaying games as the ultimate detective. But he lands one last chance to ease his conscience in real life when a deposit box's cryptic contents attract the attention of a psychotic assassin.

Desperate to stop the homicidal lunatic from gleefully torturing his loved ones, Colin takes the encoded info to the smartest pair of redneck preppers he knows. But when the wise-cracking brothers break the cypher, he's shocked to discover an obsessed billionaire with a gun aimed at the whole world's head.

Can he overcome his post-traumatic fears before his first live-action adventure triggers a deadly game over?

The Killing Tide is a fast-paced standalone thriller. If you like captivating protagonists, ethically driven villains, and hilarious sidekicks, then you'll love Jonathan Daniel's high-octane race for survival.